The Confetti Kid!

To Paul and Tina,

With Warmest Wishes,

[illegible]

Mary Lane

April, 1999

ALSO BY ROBERT LANE

A Solitary Dance

The Confetti Kid!

a novel
by

Robert Lane

Serrell & Simons
Wisconsin

THIS IS A LOTUS BOOK
Serrell & Simons, Publishers
P.O. Box 64
Winnebago, WI 54985

This is a work of fiction.
All characters and events portrayed
as well as the Peace River Mental Health Institute,
are products of the author's imagination
or are used fictitiously.

Library of Congress Catalog Card Number: 96-67684

BOOK DESIGN BY MARY LANE
PRINTED IN THE UNITED STATES OF AMERICA
FIRST PRINTING: JANUARY 1997
SECOND PRINTING: MARCH 1997

ISBN 0-943104-97-1

in gratitude

I WISH TO EXPRESS MY DEEP APPRECIATION TO MY friend, Paul Donhauser, who provided the drawings and much good counsel; to my aunt, Mara Lane, and friend, Merle Wolford, who pointed me toward the spiritual path; to Ralph Baker, who shared his friendship and medical expertise; and to Sara Blackburn, who contributed her considerable editing skills to the final version of the manuscript.

I need also to acknowledge the special support of Kathryn Whitford, Tom Montag, Dick Domrath, and Chuck Aronson, along with many other friends, some of whom are former students. All have read various versions of the manuscript and have offered their insights, suggestions and encouragement over the years. A heartfelt thank you to each.

And, as always, my boundless gratitude to my soulmate and wife, Mary, who has been editor, word processor, consultant, and therapist as the need arose during the years of writing this story.

a note about this story

ALTHOUGH THIS IS A WORK OF FICTION, I HAVE relied upon my experiences and imagination to build a story that could very well be true. It is an attempt to cast some light into the deep shadows of mental illness and its treatment.

In another sense, this account is true: Hundreds of thousands of people courageously struggle with serious mental problems that disrupt their lives day in and day out.

This story is for them.

My hope is that those fortunate enough not to be so afflicted will extend their tolerance and compassion to those who are. . . .

I

It is one
of the most beautiful
compensations of this life
that one cannot help another
without helping himself.

RALPH WALDO EMERSON

1

THE OLDER I GET, THE MORE I'M CONVINCED: OUR LIVES don't just collide like atoms and then spew off in another direction. They're linked. We're all linked. People show up in our lives for a purpose, as often as not to teach us something, direct us to a new path.

Except this time I couldn't even imagine a purpose. This patient was so deeply disturbed that he seemed forever lost.

Leaning against the door jamb of the small hospital room, my hands in my pockets, I watched as the psychiatric technician, a wiry fellow named Chet, put both arms around the young man and lifted him to a standing position. Chet raised one of the patient's arms, then the other, and slipped a shirt on him. It was like dressing a department store mannequin. He couldn't—wouldn't—talk, so he'd been admitted as "John Doe."

I noted the same dazed expression he'd worn for weeks, the sallow skin, the gauntness of his frame. His arms stayed horizontal after Chet released them, a hallmark of the genuine catatonic. Occasionally Chet, who was silver-haired and in his late fifties, spoke to him in a nice grandfatherly tone, but the patient never gave a flicker of understanding.

I marveled at Chet's patience. Only parents and psych techs know how to button someone else's shirt without being awkward. When he finished, Chet gently lowered the patient's arms back down to his sides and sat him on the bed. Then he knelt and began to put socks and slippers on him, humming softly to himself, absorbed by his task.

I studied the patient. His unfocused eyes stared into hyperspace, and he seemed oblivious of everything around him. Reality was a zero.

Finally, Chet stepped back and viewed his work. Satisfied, he nodded his approval and drew the patient back to his feet.

"Okay, he's all yours, Doc," he said. "I got him toileted earlier."

"Thanks, Chet."

Now it was my turn. I moved to confront the glassy eyes and tried to force a smile. Then I put one arm across the small of the fellow's back and the other hand on his forearm, surprised by how cold and clammy it felt.

"Let's put a sweater on him," I said. Chet walked over to a locker, rummaged a bit, and came up with a hideous argyle cardigan of clashing mustard yellow and purple. Sensing my mental wince, he nodded at the patient. "He won't mind."

Together we steered the chilly hands and arms into the sweater. My movements were clumsy compared to Chet's. Then I put my arm around the patient's back again and prompted him:

"Okay, let's alley-oop down to the dayroom for your review meeting."

Very slowly, he shuffled one slipper forward. When I gave a slight tug on his arm, the other slippered foot edged ahead, making a distinctive crinkly noise. Inch by inch, we moved out into the hospital corridor. Frankenstein and his keeper. The slow, tedious journey gave me plenty of time to think. How long had he been here now? Six weeks? Two months? More? My mind wound back to the first time I had seen him, the day he'd been admitted.

That particular morning I was gazing distractedly out my office window, as I often did to reset my thoughts. A fringe benefit, curious person that I am, was that the window overlooked the admissions entrance, giving me a perfect vantage point for the comings and goings of hospital life.

My second-floor office was sunny and bright most of the day, due to the large thermopane window that filled the outer wall. I had positioned my desk for the view it offered: Across the street stood a beautiful grove of Austrian pines, a splash of intense dark green set against the western sky. Except for that vista, the office was spare and functional, its cheerfulness muted by gun-metal gray steel furnishings—my chair and a cluttered desk, several bookcases, a couple of molded plastic chairs. The only exception was a sleek black leatherette recliner that looked like something from the space shuttle. The previous occupant had dabbled in psychoanalysis and somehow convinced the Purchasing Department that such an extravagance was a necessity. I inherited it when I was hired.

On the lawn beneath my window, surrounded by a border of blue and white petunias, was an imposing limestone block. The face of the buff-colored stone, in brass letters tarnished soft green, read PEACE RIVER MENTAL HEALTH INSTITUTE. Below that, smaller letters inscribed STATE OF WISCONSIN.

As I stared out the window that morning, I saw a police car pulling up to the curb in front of the building. Not so unusual—it happened several times a week. But when I looked out again a few minutes later, I realized the two police officers were having trouble coaxing their passenger from the car. They were leaning into the open back door, gesturing. Occasionally they glanced toward the building, apparently uncertain about what to do. Intrigued, I swiveled my chair around for a better view. Who could be lurking in the back seat?

Then one of the officers started walking toward the building. When he had almost reached the door, the other one called something urgent to him.

I looked back to the squad car and blinked in disbelief. Climbing out of it was a young man dressed in a bizarre costume covered with tiny, sparkling dots. He looked ready for a Halloween party, except that it was May. A colorful cape billowed in the breeze. Even his running shoes were multicolored. The whole outfit glittered in the sunlight, making him almost shimmer when he moved. He was dazzling.

Then he waved his handcuffed arms and I watched, amazed as a shower of confetti cascaded over the police officers. While the bits of color fluttered about them, the young man arched up on his toes, threw his handcuffed arms skyward in Superman's take-off position, and jumped again and again high into the air.

He was trying to fly.

Before long, though, the leaps became little hops, his arms sank lower and lower, and his shoulders drooped with fatigue. Head down, he dejectedly eyed the handcuffs. Then his whole body heaved, and from somewhere within came the sound of deep, racking sobs, so intense that I could hear them despite the sealed office window.

The poor, desperate kid. What on earth was going on with him? I saw the police officers put their hands under his arms and gently guide him toward the admissions entrance. They disappeared into the building and after a moment I returned to the reports I was dictating.

An hour or so later the phone rang. It was Sharon, the admissions clerk, telling me a new patient was on his way up. I had barely hung up when there was a knock and Larry, a heavy-set, muscular psych tech, peered around the edge of the open door. He nodded, disappeared for a moment, and returned with the dazzling young man.

"This way," he said, pointing toward the chair beside my desk. "Dr. McGarry would like to talk with you."

At first I couldn't take my eyes off the remarkable outfit, a white form-fitting long underwear suit strewn with multicolored metallic sequins—circles, hearts, crescent moons, and stars—all in bright shades of red, green, blue, violet, purple, gold, and silver. It was a work of art, the detail extraordinary. The cape, decorated the same way, hung limply behind him, and the patches of color on his running shoes had apparently been applied with colored pens. Two large letters, "CK," intertwined across his chest. The overall effect was stunning.

He hesitated at the doorway for a few moments, which gave me time to study him. He was tall, at least six feet, and his well-muscled frame, broad shoulders, and slim hips were accentuated by the form-fitting costume. But what really drew me in were his eyes. An intense, almost luminescent hazel, they seemed almost too big. Too bright. Too wary. I had the strong impression of barely suppressed terror. And yet, amid all the external chaos, I sensed a certain gentleness.

He had a sharply-hewn nose with high, prominent cheekbones, and they gave him a kind of symmetrical ruggedness, an air of character beyond his years. His tanned, windburned complexion added to the rugged, outdoors look. A mass of wavy brown hair framed his face. He was the kind of young man women look at twice.

I smiled inwardly at my initial reaction, which was a holdover from my youth in Southern California—the notion that all handsome men, along with all beautiful women, led serene, untroubled lives. Movie star lives. As a teenager I had envied such unusually good-looking people; I'd really believed they had a big edge over the rest of us.

I worried about this all through my teens, constantly

comparing myself to my friends and always coming off a poor second. Not surprisingly, this often became a self-fulfilling prophecy, and for years I had a large hole in my self-confidence until I finally realized that good looks promise nothing. In fact, I'd learned how often they can actually make life more difficult. It took a while for me to figure that out, but after I did, the self-confidence hole shrunk by quite a bit.

"C'mon now," Larry said, in a tone that demanded compliance. The young man quickly covered the distance to the chair beside my desk. He slumped into it, covering his downcast eyes with one hand. The handcuffs had been removed downstairs, but their chafed imprints remained on his wrists.

Larry handed me the admissions folder. All it contained was a brief admission note and the "Order to Treat" papers from the court. In the space for the patient's name, someone had penciled in, "The Confetti Kid." Apparently this was how he'd identified himself to the police.

"You want me to hang around, Doc?" asked Larry. He was really asking if I thought our new patient might become violent.

I looked at the young man again and smiled. "No, I don't think that'll be necessary, Larry. Thank you."

"Okay, give me a call on the ward when you're through." He started for the door.

The Confetti Kid glanced up and then quickly down again. But in that instant I had seen sheer wildness in those intense eyes. That swift appraisal disturbed me. It was akin to a cornered animal measuring a predator, readying for fight or flight. In that split second he seemed to have judged me and the situation with unnerving skill. He knew the odds would be better once Larry was gone. I wasn't about to ignore the warning I felt in the pit of my stomach.

I cleared my throat. "Larry, on second thought, perhaps you'd better stay."

Larry quietly closed the door, turned, and eased into a nearby chair.

My attention focused on the enigma seated by the side of my desk.

"I'm Dr. McGarry. Patrick McGarry. Can you tell me your name?"

Silence.

"Well, do you know where you are? What this place is?"

The Confetti Kid remained tense and still, his down-turned face covered, and I couldn't see his expression. But his energy seemed to crackle across the room. I glanced at Larry. Even with all his experience, he looked a bit uneasy, I thought. What were we dealing with in this young man?

"This is the Peace River Mental Health Institute," I said. "A psychiatric hospital. You've been brought here because people were concerned for your safety. Do you have any idea why they might think you need help?"

I waited for a while, but he didn't answer.

"Can you tell me—do you have another name? The papers here just say 'The Confetti Kid.' "

His thumb twitched slightly, but he said nothing.

I paused, then tried again. "Is there anything you'd like to ask me? Is there anyone I should notify—that you're here?"

No answer.

I sensed his enormous tension. He was like a piece of badly frayed rope with lots of broken strands and the others rapidly unraveling. I felt powerless, not knowing how to grab the ends, or how to avoid the snapping that would surely follow if that pressure wasn't released.

If I could just establish some small bond of trust. My neck muscles began to ache from the strain of concentrating, as I tried to think of something, anything, that I could say or do to penetrate the barrier of silence and reach him.

I tried again. "Look, a lot of people come here when things in their lives aren't working out too well. When pressures and stress become too much. There are all kinds of things we can do to help. But you'll have to tell me what's wrong, where it hurts—''

Slowly the young man raised his head, and his eyes met mine. For an instant I saw a raging desperation in those eyes. In the next split second, his whole face twisted into the face of a madman. Springing out of the chair, he vaulted onto my desk, scattering books and papers. His arms outstretched, The Confetti Kid hurtled forward.

I felt a surging horror once I realized that he was going to leap right over me and through the sealed window.

Somehow I ducked, and my whole body flinched at the resounding crash when he smacked into the glass. Fortunately, the thermopane held and he staggered backward, dazed for a moment. Then he clambered onto the wide marble window sill, stood, raised his arms in the takeoff position, and prepared to launch himself again.

But Larry was on him, gripping one of his wrists and giving it a quick flip. The Kid catapulted off the ledge and landed on his feet with a thud. With another deft motion, Larry flattened him to the wall, arms locked behind his back, face and chest pressed tightly against the paneling.

When I grabbed for the phone to summon help, I witnessed something I had heard about but never seen: the ''psychotic rush''—the tremendous burst of energy when a floridly psychotic person gains superhuman strength. Before we knew it, The Kid had wrested free of Larry's hold and attacked him in a vicious, brutal assault.

Dropping the phone, I jumped behind the patient, trying to bearhug him. At this new invasion, he gave a tremendous roar and I found myself flicked off his back and twisting through the air. His strength was extraordinary.

The racket brought a crowd of techs pouring in from the nearby wards. Their sheer numbers overpowered The Kid, but even then it was a few minutes before they managed to restrain his flailing arms.

Larry stood up, rubbed his swelling jaw, and grumbled, "They don't pay me enough for this."

After a few more moments of confusion, the psychiatric phalanx headed quickly for the locked ward, with The Confetti Kid buried somewhere in the middle. He struggled all the way—grunting, kicking, twisting against the collective grip of the techs. When we reached a seclusion room, he resisted with all his might, but the techs at last succeeded in separating him from his costume, and the glittering suit was exchanged for a hospital gown.

While this was going on, I looked around the seclusion room. It wasn't a Holiday Inn. Gray vinyl pads like the ones used in gyms lined the cement block walls. A heavy mesh screen covered the single window, and a well-padded, double-bolted metal door provided the only way out. Except for the thin blue-striped mattress on the floor, the room was empty.

By the time the service chief, a grim-faced Dr. Stacey, appeared, The Confetti Kid was whimpering softly. With six techs assisting—one for each limb, head, and trunk—he was spreadeagled face down on the mattress. Thus pinioned, he was powerless when the psychiatrist administered Haldol, a potent tranquilizer, into one exposed hip. Then we all quickly withdrew from the room.

His freedom regained, the young man began screaming incoherently. I could make out only a few words as he ranted through the small porthole window in the seclusion room door: ***"Cursed infidels—death to depraved miscreants!"*** That was a nice change. Most patients in this condition threw four-letter words at us.

At lunchtime I stopped back and checked on him again. Now he was crouched in the far corner, bouncing on his haunches like a crazed chimpanzee. Snarling, he attacked imaginary enemies, repeatedly hurling himself against the mat-lined walls. Time and again the force of the impact sent him sprawling backward. But with a singleness of purpose which both fascinated and appalled me, he would pick himself up, study his invisible opponent for a moment and then, teeth bared, breath coming in great gasps, he would renew the attack.

I couldn't imagine what powerful inner forces drove him to such frenzy. And yet, as terrible as it was, I couldn't help but admire his magnificent spirit.

I looked in on him again shortly before I left for the day and found a very different person. By then The Confetti Kid was crying uncontrollably. His shoulders heaved and convulsed, and choking sobs spewed out in waves of gasping breaths. I chilled at the rawness of his total anguish and despair.

A few minutes before I left that afternoon, five techs and a nurse appeared to administer his evening medication. When they opened the heavy door, the sobbing ceased abruptly and The Kid's expression turned to absolute terror. Howling at his tormentors, he darted into a corner of the room, literally clawing the walls in an attempt to get away.

Subduing him involved a lot of coordination. The techs held his thrashing limbs down while a nurse, this time, deftly plunged the hypodermic needle into his buttock. Then, on the count of three, everyone released him and quickly backed out the door. The double locks slammed home, and then the hoarse ranting resumed. He seemed to consider our efforts the ultimate humiliation.

For the staff, though, there was no other choice. Trying to reason with someone in his state of mind was out of the question. Once The Kid's delusional bubble burst in my office, these raw, primitive instincts were all that remained to govern his shattered personality.

He was a rogue human, lashing out, screaming his fury at everyone and no one. Certainly dangerous, potentially homicidal, perhaps even suicidal, he represented a graphic portrait of the darkest side of human nature.

On my way out, I stopped at the nursing station and

noticed the Watch Order in his chart. This would require a check every few minutes around the clock to be sure he was okay. Unlikely as it was that he could come to much harm in the seclusion room, no one wanted to take any chances.

We had a very, very disturbed young man on our hands. A victim of psychological meltdown, The Confetti Kid was acutely psychotic and totally unpredictable.

That was weeks ago and now "John Doe" had plunged into catatonia without ever having recovered enough to even tell us his name. He and I had finally arrived at the staffing room and I pushed the door open. I felt the eyes of the other psychiatric team members watching while I steered him to a chair, then sat down beside him. An involuntary sigh escaped me and I glanced around, hoping no one had noticed. All I saw were expressions of understanding.

2

A REFUGEE FROM THE UNIQUE CRAZINESS THAT MARKS Southern California, I'd moved from Los Angeles to Wisconsin only shortly before my dramatic introduction to The Confetti Kid. That's another story.

I'd lived practically my whole life in L.A., but we were never a good fit. What made it tough for me was that the culture there is based upon two values: money and appearances. Nothing else matters. Whether or not you have money, it's assumed that you'll always act and live as if you do. Otherwise you're not a player. By my late teens I'd wised up to the cynical exploitation of others that often goes on beneath the glitz, the hype, the deal-making. I wanted a life very different from all that.

Eventually I discovered that a very good way of gaining control over your life is getting an education. I'd always rebelled against the totalitarian demands of a lockstep system and had skirmished with my teachers for twelve long years. But when I went to college it was different. I was more motivated and, while graduate school wasn't easy, the study of the mind was fascinating. I finally earned my Ph.D., got married and for the last five years had worked as a psychotherapist on the Children's Unit of a large state hospital. By then, I felt good about what I was doing. I felt gratified about helping the kinds of kids I worked with and was enjoying the life I led.

But then it all unraveled.

First came the state budget crunch and a severe reduction of our services that the politicians called "consolidation." We had far too many seriously disturbed kids for that, of course, but we were told we'd have to treat them for shorter periods, with increasingly fewer staff. And every time someone left or retired, the position was eliminated.

There was never an opportunity to express an opinion, even though we'd embarked on TQM—Total Quality Management—a method patterned after the Japanese model of allocating more on-site power to lower organizational levels. This was supposed to produce cost-effectiveness and increased efficiency, along with higher "customer satisfaction." I'm not sure what our hospitalized "customers" thought of the TQM, but in fact, none of the promised power ever dribbled down to us. Morale was dismal. With each new directive, the treatment team sighed and complained that TQM really stood for "Time to Quit and Move on." And more and more people did.

Into all this turmoil came a more personal disaster. My wife, who was a "rapidly-advancing" computer company executive, announced almost casually at dinner one night that she was filing for divorce. Our lives together were going nowhere, she said. She felt stifled. I was moody, dreamy, a loner who lacked ambition, and—the major irritant—spent all my time and energy with the kids at the hospital. She worked long hours, too, but had tried hard to make time for us; she was tired of coming home to find messages on the answering machine that something had come up and we'd have to do whatever it was we'd planned another time. I should have married someone who was content to stay in the station, she said.

I listened, a calm expression on my face. Not registering reactions, especially emotional ones, was part of my therapist's training, and I reacted instinctively that way as my world disintegrated before my eyes. The glass of wine that had been moving toward my lips hung suspended; my arm seemed to have frozen. Actually, it was as if I had been flash-frozen. I knew my wife was talking to me, but it was like overhearing a stranger talking in a restaurant.

I remember at some point sputtering something like, "Psychologists don't get divorced, they communicate . . ."

The period that followed was tumultuous. I kept hoping it was all a bad dream, that I'd wake up and everything would be as it had been. Instead, my wife's coolness toward me deepened. She told me she'd been thinking about a divorce for a long time, and I swore I'd never had a clue. Or so it seemed. Well, perhaps there had been a few. Determined to change her mind, I made a conscious effort to get home early, spend time with her on weekends. It was too little, and far too late.

Before long, the anger broke through. And the blame. I demanded to know if there was someone else, if she'd betrayed me. She assured me there wasn't, she hadn't.

Then I wanted reasons. Specific reasons. I was accusatory, confronting, demanding. My imagination ran and reran all the possible scenarios over and over again, adding a twist here, a turn there. Revenge fantasies boiled to the surface and she could sense that I was close to going over the edge. She was frightened, and when I saw that, I exploited her fear to obtain a perverse vengeance.

Eventually she fled. When I got home one evening, I found she had left with most of the furniture and the cat.

And that was when it all closed in on me. I crashed. Fell apart. I drank too much, which set off raging tirades that went on until I passed out from exhaustion. I tilted into depression, constantly aware of an aching throb in my stomach that got so bad I thought I was getting an ulcer. All the things I'd been taught—so I could recognize other people's emotional crises and help them deal with them—were suddenly happening to me. And I didn't have the faintest idea of what to do about it.

I had been writing in my journal and now it was bulging with half-crazed diatribes. The anger would explode across the pages in savage, indecipherable bursts, only to be followed by tear-stained memories and long paragraphs of self-pity. Even though I'd gone back into therapy, everything inside me was totally chaotic. The saving grace was my work at the hospital. The kids kept my mind focused throughout the day.

It was the nights that got to me. I'd come awake from a restless sleep, thoughts roiling, my heart pounding with massive surges of adrenalin. Obsessive questions scrolled endlessly through my mind: How could she do this to me? How could I have been so wrong about someone? If she changes her mind, should I take her back? And the relentless fantasies returned: I wanted her to suffer.

Weekends were the worst: using the same dish for every meal; eating too fast and not tasting a bite; waking up to a beautiful day and not even caring because there was no one to share it with.

Finally, after three months of this craziness, the intensity of my grieving slowly began to subside. Sitting on a borrowed mattress in the nearly bare apartment one Saturday afternoon, I realized I'd turned a corner. The memories were fading, my defenses doing their job of repairing my shattered ego. I was healing.

It was time to take stock.

I decided I had lived for too many years with clogged freeways, smog-induced headaches, and the frenetic pillar-to-post Southern California lifestyle. My marriage had disintegrated. And now the job I loved was in peril, devalued in a coup executed by remote bureaucrats.

One morning I wandered aimlessly into the bathroom,

stopping at the mirror to take a hard look at my thirty-three-year-old, rapidly aging face. I'd noticed that my eyes tended to be more blue when I was in pain, more green when I was content and happy. They hadn't been green for a long time, but now I thought they would be again someday. The squint lines on the outer edges were deepening, and I realized that I looked seasoned in a way I hadn't before.

I pushed my hair back. The sandy brown, sunstreaked shock that fell across my forehead had a hint of gray. Hmmmmm. So did my beard, which had become a fixture because everyone expected clinical psychologists to have beards. The males, anyway.

"What next?" I said, addressing myself in the mirror. For a minute all the old doubts resurfaced: Will there ever be anyone for me? Am I good enough for anyone? Would one failure just translate to another?

Finally, I made a declaration, most of it actually out loud: "What you need, Patrick McGarry, is a change of scenery. A Complete Break. A Thoreau-type experiment—back to nature, rural simplicity. A slower pace. Clean, fresh air." I paused for effect. "Always the romantic idealist, aren't you?"

I nodded agreeably. And smiled. It felt right.

My parents were fairly supportive about the decision to move. They were getting on in years and had hoped I'd stay closer, but they understood my need to make a change. The toughest part would be leaving the kids I was working with. I dreaded telling them.

I responded to ads in my professional journals, generating a flood of form replies and inviting Chamber of Commerce materials, but nothing concrete. Then a national psychology convention came to town. I registered at the employment center and one of the people who interviewed me was an older fellow I especially liked. His name was Ben Farrell, and he was Chief Psychologist at a medium-sized state hospital in rural southwestern Wisconsin. The way he described the area seemed to fit perfectly with what I'd been hoping for. When he offered me a job as staff psychologist there, I grabbed it, concerned only that he might change his mind.

Then I went back to my apartment and looked Wisconsin up on the map. Being a true Californian, all I knew was that it was somewhere "back East."

There is a gentle gracefulness to the terrain of southwest Wisconsin. When I arrived that spring, the softly contoured hills were lush with vibrant new growth, from soft yellow-greens and rich kelly greens to the dark, almost black splotches of evergreens. As I crested the summits, each new vista seemed more surreal to me than the last. The switch from Southern California's toast-brown landscapes to a place of such pristine beauty was a shock. So was the air. The first couple of weeks I went around practically hyperventilating, amazed at how good it felt just to breathe in a fresh, clean atmosphere.

And the people! They waved from their tractors as I drove by, nodded warmly in stores, motioned me with smiles through four-way-stop intersections. No one snarled or measured my affluence with their eyes. I couldn't believe it. This was a much more civilized way to live.

And so would my living quarters be, I hoped. One important resolution in my fresh start was: no more apartments. I wanted a small house, preferably a log cabin deep in the woods, something with charm and warmth. But I also wanted all the comforts. I wasn't going to carry the Thoreau thing too far.

The only rental houses were in town and those quickly shattered my fantasy. I put a "Wanted to Rent" ad in the paper and resigned myself to a couple of weeks of motel living. The very next morning, a Saturday, I got a call from a retired couple who said they had a small house available on their farm. Did I want to see it? I drove right out. The nondescript white clapboard structure stood in a field, but a huge oak shaded it and across the road were dense woods. Close enough.

"It's kinda small," the elderly man said as we crossed the lawn toward the house. A short, stout woman was hard at work in the patch of dark brown earth that lay between the farmhouse and the little house I'd come to look at. I could see tiny green shoots emerging in neat, straight rows. At the far end, the new growth was more haphazard. Later I would watch it become a mass of flowers.

". . . we built it for the herdsman," the man was saying, "but I sold off the cows a few years back—had forty-five head. Got to be too hard on me, but I still get up at five a.m. I miss milking the girls, you know?"

As we neared the woman, she straightened and walked briskly over to us, wiping her hands on her apron.

"Name's Shafer," the old man said. "This here's Mrs. Shafer."

Mrs. Shafer had a ruddy complexion and a friendly smile. I smiled back. She seemed somewhat uncertain, perhaps about renting to someone with a beard.

I told them where I was from. As I explained about my new job, they seemed to relax a bit and we moved on toward the little house.

"Interesting place, the asylum," Mr. Shafer commented. "Never been up there."

"Never had reason to," Mrs. Shafer added.

He swung the door open and they followed me in. I felt an instant affinity. The place had been deceiving from the outside, but the interior was warm, with honey-colored knotty pine paneling throughout. Not wood-grained plastic veneer, but real wood. The old-fashioned oak furniture looked comfortable and inviting. Very cozy. Right away I knew I was home.

Mr. Shafer nodded toward a fireplace of round fieldstones on one side of the living room.

"My brother laid these hardheads from the field out back. Did a real nice job. He was quite a craftsman . . . died three years ago."

I nodded and we all stood in respectful silence.

"You're not married?"

I hesitated. I still wasn't used to dealing with my new status.

"No, single. Divorced, actually."

They both looked apologetic. "Lot of that going around," Mr. Shafer said.

Silence again.

I was a little concerned about the rent, and when they didn't bring it up, I finally asked.

"Well, we thought around two-seventy-five a month. Plus utilities. That too much?"

I tried to cover my shock, comparing it with the $1000-a-month rent I'd paid for my small California apartment.

"No, no. That's fine. Certainly fair."

"Good." He stuck out his hand and we shook on it. A done deal. No complicated lease, no hefty security deposit. I felt as though I'd stepped back in time. I couldn't believe my luck, and glowed in the straightforwardness of these Wisconsin folk. This was another universe. One that I'd wanted, wished for, for a long time.

"C'mere, Dr. McGarry. I'll show you something else." He pointed down the short driveway. "You'll like that," he said.

What was he talking about? It looked like an ordinary driveway to me.

He grinned. "For snow shoveling, young fellow. We do have some pretty good blizzards in these parts, you know. But I'll come up with the tractor if it drifts in too bad. Make sure you get to work."

I gazed out at all the greenery, the woods, the spring wildflowers nestled beneath the trees across the road, the fleecy, white clouds against an aqua blue sky. I couldn't even begin to imagine it all buried under snow.

3

JUST A FEW MILES FROM MY NEW HOME, SCULPTED INTO THE craggy limestone bluffs that line the Wisconsin side of the Mississippi River, are the serene grounds of the Peace River Mental Health Institute. I drove there that first day marveling at the narrow road twisting through the hills, bordered by towering sugar maples and dignified northern pine. Refreshing pockets of white birch stood out amid the darker hues, and, from time to time, surprising glimpses through the woods revealed the Peace River, frothily dipping to join its mother, the Mississippi.

Nestled into a heavily wooded coulee is the hospital—a series of trim, two-story brick buildings that might be a well-endowed private college. Only a quarter of the size of the state hospital I'd worked at in California, Peace River is ten times more inviting.

Locating the Psychology Department was easy, but when I asked for Dr. Ben Farrell, I was told that he'd had to go back East—really East, not just Wisconsin East—on a family matter and wasn't expected to return for a couple of weeks. His secretary directed me to Cameron Hall, where I would be joining Dr. Richard Stacey's adult male service. This was another aspect of my new start: It had been six years since I'd worked on an adult ward, and I found I was looking forward to it.

At the nursing station, a ward secretary sat at the counter that ran the length of the narrow room. Above the counter large windows gave an unobstructed view of two long corridors. The ward secretary glanced up at me, smiled, and nodded toward a middle-aged woman, who turned and greeted me with a handshake.

"Hi, Dr. McGarry. I'm Joan Lindstrom, head nurse. They called and said you were on your way."

As we shook hands I sensed a stiff appraisal, with inquisitive blue eyes and discerning smile taking my measure.

I was beginning to realize that my being from California was creating a bit of a stir, as though I hailed from outer space. Ben Farrell had told me on the phone that no one could understand why a Californian would want to come to Wisconsin. It wasn't going to be easy to explain to people burdened by long winters of sub-zero temperatures.

Joan Lindstrom's smile softened. Evidently I passed muster. I sensed a tough, solid nurse—deferential to a point, but watch out. I'd need her as an ally, and I liked what I felt about her.

"Dr. Stacey's at a meeting this morning, so I'll do the honors, Dr. McGarry. Where shall we begin . . . with a tour?"

"How about by calling me Pat?" I suggested.

"Okay, fine. And I'm Joan. Let's see . . . Oh, yes, here are your keys." She handed me a metal ring with half a dozen keys on it.

"Thanks." I slipped the hefty key ring into my coat pocket and looked around. Immediately my eyes fell upon a very attractive young woman letting herself out of one of the wards. Slender, with rich auburn curls cut short and sporty, she was wearing a yellow blazer over a black blouse and skirt. Great legs, too, I noticed. There was a certain gracefulness as she walked toward us, a winsome smile lighting up her face.

"Brenda Warren, meet Pat McGarry, our new psychologist," Joan said.

"Hi. Welcome to Peace River, Pat." Brenda said, extending her hand. There was a wholesome quality to her, an appeal that went beyond her looks. Her expression was warm and direct, and so was her handshake. Her darkly lashed eyes were an unusual jade green, and they had a playful glint. My heart kind of skipped. That hadn't happened for a long time.

"Brenda's our star social worker. If you need anything done, she'll find a way. The impossible may take a day or two, but she can work wonders. A real whiz."

Brenda laughed in a delightful way, embarrassed by the compliment. "Right. I'm such a whiz I'm ten minutes late to a meeting." She breezed out with a cheery, "See you later."

Joan followed my gaze as I watched Brenda leave.

"She's practically engaged. You California guys don't waste any time, do you?"

Her voice had a slight edge to it. Oops. I wondered how Wisconsin guys behaved.

Joan cleared her throat quietly. "Well, I was about to tell you that we house up to one hundred and twenty patients here. Of course, they're separated according to the severity of their disorders."

She gestured to the left half of the "V" that stretched away from the nursing station. "This wing is Unit One, the admission ward. Usually we have about thirty people to evaluate at any given time—that's where Dr. Stacey would like you to begin." She paused briefly. "Most patients stay there for the first couple weeks, but occasionally very aggressive patients go to a ward with greater security. Is this what you're used to?"

"Pretty much," I said.

"Good. Unit Two here is the acute treatment unit for our

thirty-day wonders—people being regulated on their meds and those who have less severe symptoms and may just need a time-out."

She turned and motioned toward the back wall of the nursing station. "On the other side of the building are Units Three and Four—our tertiary or secondary units: Three houses long-term chronic patients, Four is the Security Unit —for predatory males. They're never out except under the tightest supervision. They even eat their meals there. We have women's wards upstairs and we have to protect them."

"How many patients are there on Unit Four now?"

"Probably about twenty-five. Too many."

I nodded. "They're a constant challenge, I'm sure." Now I was remembering some of the reasons I'd preferred working with children.

"That's one way of putting it," Joan said dryly. "Anyway, the charts are here, one for each ward," she said, pointing to two round carousels at one end of the counter. They contained the usual blue plastic three-ring binders universal to medical facilities, arranged in a lazy-susan type turntable for easy access. "We're very team-oriented here," Joan continued, "so each team member records anything special that's observed: If a patient has been mute for several weeks and someone hears him say something, it's charted. And if a patient takes a swing, whether he connects or not, it's recorded. That warns the other team members. All pretty standard, really. Let's walk over to the other side."

We entered another nursing station, the mirror image of the one we'd just left, but in contrast to the relative calm on the admission wing, here I found myself staring through the windows at the chaos of the chronic wards.

"These are our problem patients," Joan was saying.

I could see immediately that I wouldn't be nearly as relaxed as I'd always felt with the kids. It was a lot easier to deal with patients half your size.

Joan sensed my uneasiness. "We don't have many violent

patients here, but we do have a few, so be alert. And don't hesitate to ask one of the techs to go with you on the wards. At least until you're familiar with the patients, it's better to play it safe—

"Speaking of which," she added, and I thought I detected a tinge of worry in her tone, "we have a few HIV positives and hepatitis B patients. They're kept on the Security Unit. I'll point them out to you. Just be sure and use extreme caution when you're around them."

She broke off as a burst of laughter erupted from a room that opened off the nursing station. "Coffee break. Come on, I'll introduce you."

Two psychiatric technicians and a nurse sat around a small table in the anteroom. Joan made the introductions.

"Where you from, Doc?" asked a young tech named Terry.

"California. Merrick State Hospital, just north of L.A."

"You have criminally insane there?"

"Some. But I worked mostly on the Children's Unit."

"Yeah?" said the other tech, Joe, who was gray-haired and stocky. "Well, this ain't no kids' unit, that's for sure. You better be on your toes around this place. We got some pretty bad characters—"

" 'Specially Grunske," Terry broke in. "He's been wild as a hawk lately."

"Sure has," Joe agreed, watching me closely. "Don't *ever* turn your back on Grunske. He's totally unpredictable."

"Right. Thanks for the warning."

They were testing me, the inevitable struggle between the professionals and the techs. They were the ones in the trenches, taking the real risks and the brunt of being attacked. It wasn't hard to understand why they might resent someone new, who made a lot more money than they did and might try to throw his weight around.

We made small talk for a few minutes and then Joan and I returned to the nursing station. Just in time, it seemed.

"Telephone," said the ward secretary, holding the receiver out to Joan, who shrugged an "Excuse me" and took it.

Across the corridor, behind a large dayroom window, a very chronic-looking patient peered out, forehead pressed against the smudged glass. His eyes were badly crossed and his mouth drooped open. The moment he caught my eye, he began waving frantically at me. I waved back and a big smile creased his face. I smiled back; no mayhem on his mind. But the waving quickly increased in velocity and soon he was leaping up and down, both arms going like windmills. As his actions became more frenzied, I felt a distinct uneasiness.

"I see you've learned not to wave to Stanley," said Joan, suddenly beside me and observing the agitation across the hall. "He'll stop after a while if you don't look at him." She pointed toward a corner of the dayroom. "There's another prize. That's Wesley."

A red-faced man was seated in a bright orange fiberglass chair, rocking with grim determination. The way he rocked was riveting: Back and forth he surged, legs shoving with such force that the chair seemed certain to flip over. Each time it lurched backward, it reached a critical point where the patient faced the ceiling briefly before the chair reversed itself and then shot forward again with incredible momentum.

I could only shake my head.

"He does that for hours on end."

Just watching him was making me queasy, but Joan was moving on.

"I'll be tied up for a while now, Pat," she was saying, "and Dr. Stacey won't be back for an hour or so. There's a ward meeting starting in a few minutes, though, and that'll be as good a way as any to meet Stanley and friends. You game?"

"Sure." I fumbled with my keys.

"It's the one with the green tape," she said.

"Thanks."

As I approached the ward's locked door, the occupants of the dayroom converged on the other side, apparently intrigued by a new face. Looking as nonchalant as possible, I unlocked the door and eased inside. Immediately the welcoming committee surrounded me, and I was struck by the pervasive odors of perspiration and other aspects of enforced human closeness. Trying to override it all was some kind of hospital disinfectant. It was a potent combination.

"You my lawyer? I been waitin' for you," snapped a scowling man with a clean-shaven, bullet-shaped skull.

I shook my head "no" and he cursed, then stalked off, muttering angrily and making angry slicing motions in the air with his arm.

"You a new docterr, you a new docterr?" asked Stanley the Waver, tugging on my coat sleeve. As I tried to pry his fingers loose, he planted himself directly in front of me.

"Yes, I'm—"

Nodding happily, the Ward Crier abruptly let go of my jacket and skipped around the dayroom pointing at me and chanting:

"New docterrr, new docterrr . . ."

"Simmer down, Stanley," instructed Terry, one of the techs I'd met outside.

Across the room another patient, arms tied to the sides of a wheelchair, grinned idiotically at me. Near him a very obese man lay across three chairs, snoring loudly. I was fascinated by the way he was sprawled, numerous folds of fat draping over the molded fiberglass. It looked terribly uncomfortable.

For the first time, I became aware of the din. I moved toward the far side of the room and took a seat near a large fellow intently watching a soap opera on a television perched high on the wall. It was bolted securely to a metal platform, high enough to be out of harm's way.

An extremely tall, thin man, eyes glazed with medication, collapsed like a spent puppet into the chair beside me. Looking straight ahead, he leaned slightly toward me.

"Who are you?" he whispered furtively from the corner of his mouth. His lips had barely moved. As I started to tell him, he abruptly got up and ambled away. I closed my mouth.

"Ward meeting," called someone. "Chairs in a circle."

Some sluggish movement ensued. A tech near me got up, cautiously tapped the Sleeper, and then stepped back. With a loud snort, the fellow came awake and laboriously pulled himself erect. As he glared at the tech, I watched with a growing unease.

The two stared heavily at each other for several moments, and then the patient shifted his gaze to me. His immense displeasure seemed to grow. I smiled and nodded. He looked at me a little longer, then grunted and looked away.

A commotion seemed to be brewing somewhere down the hall. Then Joe, another of the techs I'd met, came into the dayroom leading a vehemently protesting man. The patient's arms were held tightly in front of him by leather cuffs which encircled his wrists and were then strapped to a wide leather belt. His legs also had large cumbersome leather hobbles; he could take only short, shuffling steps. Fastened to the strapping that restrained him was a leash, which was looped twice around Joe's hand. Joe drew his charge to a halt in front of me.

"Dr. McGarry, this is Mr. Grunske, the fellow we were telling you about."

I found myself looking into one of the fiercest and most malevolent faces I had ever encountered.

"You can sit here next to the doctor if you like, Harry," said Joe.

Thanks a lot, I thought, beginning to resent the initiation rites.

The confining leg straps forced Mr. Grunske to swivel slowly and then, with an explosive grunt, he fell heavily into an adjacent chair. Slowly, he pivoted toward me, his face scowling and twisted, the ponderous leather straps creaking as he moved. His toothless mouth opened as he made a final lurch. I was galvanized to move out of range.

"How d'ya do, Doc?" croaked Mr. Grunske, a big, crazy grin breaking across his face. A pussycat.

After a ward meeting in which the patients said little and the staff not much more, I was introduced to Dr. Stacey, the unit psychiatrist and service chief. A tall, trim, middle-aged man, he apologetically explained that this was his afternoon for consulting at a local clinic.

"We'll get together tomorrow. In the meantime, just wander around, meet the patients and staff, and learn the routines so you can go into rotation next week." He was out the door.

I gulped. This meant that, starting next week, every third or fourth patient admitted to the unit would be primarily my responsibility. I could see I wasn't going to be given the luxury of adjusting gradually to my new circumstances.

Later that afternoon, Joan suggested I interview a newly admitted patient who was quite paranoid. "I think you might find Mr. Teesdale interesting, Pat. Would you like to see his chart?"

I shook my head. "I'll see what I get from him first. Which one is he?"

Joan nodded toward a figure seated in a strategic corner of the dayroom, from where he could observe the activities of the nursing station. He was a slender man with hair graying at the temples. He would have been handsome if not for the intense frown he projected. He was wearing the regulation hospital gown, robe, and slippers.

I approached him gingerly, sat down, and introduced myself.

His response was to lean toward me and whisper, "Don't say my name out loud—there's a microphone in that thermostat over there. Keep your voice down. *They're listening!*" The last phrase was a ferocious hiss. Mr. Teesdale's eyes gleamed with self-righteous assurance.

I smiled at him and shook my head. This seemed like an opportunity to introduce some appropriate "reality testing."

"No, Mr. Teesdale, there are no microphones planted in here. That's just an ordinary thermostat for controlling the temperature." As soon as I said "controlling," I realized it was the wrong word to use.

He swiveled in his chair and glared at the thermostat. Then he swung back to me. "You're wrong. *It's got a microphone in it*—I know that *for a fact!*" There was a razor's edge in his voice.

I tried to back off.

"Uh, Mr. Teesdale, it really doesn't have a microphone. Go over and look at it more closely. It's just a regular thermostat."

My efforts got me a very paranoid glare. He was beginning to view me as part of the plot.

I stood up. "C'mon, let's take a look at it. You'll see there's nothing at all sinister about it."

I walked to the thermostat and gestured for him to come over.

He got up warily and cautiously approached the shiny aluminum box.

"Examine it as carefully as you like. I'm sure you won't find—"

Suddenly Mr. Teesdale lunged forward. With one smooth arc of an uppercut, he caught the bottom of the thermostat with the heel of his hand. Springs, washers, screws, and broken pieces of metal and plastic rained about the room. When the debris settled, two springs, still attached to the base, waved languidly from a gaping hole in the wall.

Mr. Teesdale bent down, collected each shattered part, and examined them minutely. Then he peered into the hole, carefully fingering the springs. Finally he turned to me.

"You're right, there's no microphone here." His voice seemed a tad friendlier. Then he began scrutinizing the room, his eyes narrowing when they came to rest on the ceiling. "They must have put it in the lights." He began to circle the room, squinting up into the light wells.

I was feeling sheepish when Joan came upon the scene, acutely aware that this would not create a positive impression. I caught a smirk or two from the techs and knew the story would go around the hospital, starting with: "The new psychologist goaded a patient into attacking a thermostat . . ." Being the new kid on the block, I was fair game. What could I possibly do for an encore?

I suspected the answer had just waltzed across my desk, hellbent on flying out the window.

4

AS JOAN HAD SAID, MOST NEW PATIENTS WERE OBSERVED on the locked admission ward for a few weeks while social history information was gathered and a treatment plan was formed. Then, depending on the team's recommendations, they were transferred either to an open ward or a locked one. The day after The Confetti Kid's admission, the treatment team met for staffing.

Dr. Stacey began by summing up what little was known about our latest admission: ". . . Caucasian male, late teens, early twenties, name unknown, place of residence unknown. Picked up for resisting arrest after disturbing the peace early last Thursday morning in La Crosse. Held in jail over the weekend. Patient carried no identification, his clothing has no laundry labels to work from, fingerprints reveal no prior La Crosse arrests.

"He came to the attention of police because of his dangerous behavior on Interstate 90: He was waving his cape, stepping in front of cars, challenging them as if he were a matador fighting a bull. Many cars swerved to avoid him. Luckily, he didn't cause a serious accident. When apprehended, the arresting officers reported all he would say was that he was 'The Confetti Kid' and that he was hitchiking to Minneapolis. He kept throwing confetti on them until they took his pouch away.

"When they did that the patient clamped his mouth shut and refused to answer any other questions, although he would occasionally shout, 'Stave the arrogance, Stave the arrogance, I say!' He was uncooperative and refused to give his name and address or explain why he was wearing the costume.

"In jail he became agitated and abusive, threatening to dissolve the building if they didn't let him go. Because he seemed to be having command hallucinations—voices telling him to do things—he was considered a potential danger to himself or others and Judge Hearns signed observation and commitment orders.

"As most of you know, the patient had a major breakdown on admission. He became floridly psychotic in Dr. McGarry's office and was taken straight to seclusion. I would have preferred to withhold medication for a few days to see if his psychosis is being caused by cocaine or another drug. But he was so totally blitzed we went ahead and started him on two milligrams of injectable Haldol, twice a day. This morning his condition remains unchanged." Stacey turned to Joan. "Let's up the dosage to five milligrams."

Joan made a note and looked up. "La Crosse General has had some kids experimenting with designer drugs. C-balls seem to be big right now."

"That's certainly a possibility," Stacey nodded. "And a bad drug reaction is certainly preferable to paranoid schizophrenia. But actually," he hesitated, "this doesn't feel like a drug reaction to me. We won't know for sure until we see whether he bounces back from psychosis and get a social/medical history on him. A few days should tell us something."

He paused, studying his notes, then looked at Dr. Ramsden, the older and rather grizzled M.D. who conducted the intake exams. "What's his physical status?"

"He was fairly bizarre when I examined him. His health seems good, although he's about ten pounds underweight. Neurologicals all checked out. Of course, he was too agitated and out of contact to give me any kind of a medical history, but I saw nothing to indicate organicity, like a brain tumor."

Stacey nodded. "Okay. Do you have anything on him, Brenda?"

"Not yet, I'm afraid, but I somehow doubt he's from this area. I've called around a bit. My guess is he was just passing through. We're checking missing persons reports in the Twin Cities."

"Right," nodded Stacey. "Okay, for the time being, let's continue as we've started: We'll keep him in seclusion, continue the Haldol, and observe the Watch Order. For now, because of his age and our lack of history, the working diagnosis will be Brief Reactive Psychosis. Can we agree on that?"

There were murmurs of assent. Brief Reactive Psychosis was generally the diagnostic category used for teenagers and young adults who had encountered some overwhelming psychosocial stressor that led to the collapse of the personality structure. With no information as to whether The Confetti Kid had a psychiatric history of a more pervasive disorder such as Schizophrenia or Manic-Depressive Psychosis, Brief Reactive Psychosis was the most conservative diagnosis. It gave him the benefit of the doubt. If that was what we were dealing with here, the duration of the psychosis would be fairly brief. Two weeks at most.

In psychosis, the senses play bizarre tricks: People are convinced they see and hear things, believe their food is poisoned, or sometimes smell unusual and disgusting odors. None of this can be verified by an outside observer; it all resides in the mind of the tormented individual.

What The Kid had experienced the previous day in my office was personality decompensation. Such raw aggression is similar to what takes place in mob behavior and panic, when the veneer of civilized conduct is peeled away, exposing primitive behavior that is entirely unpredictable and often violent. The law of the jungle takes over and it's survival of the fittest—or meanest. That was why Dr. Stacey had warned the team members, especially the techs and nurses, to be very careful around The Kid.

"Other than that," Stacey was saying, "we'll just have to see what comes next, whether the meds dissolve the delusional system enough for him to tell us his real identity. And if he can't do that soon, we'll have to hope Brenda can come up with some news about him. Now let's move on . . ."

A few days later I was watching The Kid through the porthole window of the seclusion room, torn between empathy and marveling at his antics as he alternately beseeched, argued, grew serious, and laughed mockingly. Then he lapsed into an eerie silence. After a while, he stretched out on the floor and babbled gibberish. What was going on inside his brain? Something had certainly scrambled it badly.

"Patrick McGarry?" came a vaguely familiar voice over my shoulder.

I turned. "Dr. Farrell, welcome back."

"Make it Ben. Welcome aboard, Pat." He stuck out his hand and gave me a firm, crisp shake. "I understand you've had an unusual introduction to Peace River in my absence." He nodded toward the seclusion window. "Is this where 'The Confetti Kid' resides?"

"Yes." I stepped back so he could look inside.

While Ben peered in, I matched my memory of him against our one meeting earlier. Of moderate height, probably in his early sixties, he was in good physical condition. His hair was a dove gray, his eyes direct and penetrating as they took in the action of the seclusion room. He had a kind face, with an element of wryness, a kind of amused irony that had furrowed the corners of his mouth in a pleasant way. There was something about him that was reassuring. When he spoke again, his tone was surprisingly thoughtful.

"Fascinating . . . utterly fascinating." He turned toward me. "I'd like to examine him up close. Is he combative?"

"Not really. Only when they give him a shot."

I opened the top and bottom locks of the double-bolted door and swung it open. Ben walked in and I followed, pulling the heavy door closed behind us. The Kid was standing in a rigid, upright posture, arms raised, face pale. He was ready for liftoff.

Ben stepped up to him, stopping just beyond the reach of his arms. "I'm Dr. Farrell. We're here to help, if we can." His voice was soft, calming. I liked that.

"I know your world has gotten pretty scary lately. Can you tell us how you're doing? Are things better for you now?" He paused. "Or worse?"

The Confetti Kid was rocking on his heels, staring out the small window. I wondered if he even noticed the fading afternoon sun. Slowly he turned toward us. His handsome face reflected bewilderment at our presence, as if he had just returned from some great distance to find us standing there. His eyes moved morosely, searchingly, from Ben's face to mine and back again. Tears welled up, then spilled over and down his cheeks, tracing their way to the edge of his jaw before dropping onto his gray-striped hospital gown.

His lips moved. Soundlessly at first, then with effort he whispered, "Manslaughter? . . ."

He turned to me. Again the whisper, only this time he said, "Man's laughter?"

And back to Ben. "Manslaughter? . . . Man's laughter? . . ."

Tears were streaming down his cheeks. Softly he repeated this again and again, his eyes glistening. There was excruciating pain in his voice; it was heart-rending to hear it.

Ben looked at me and shook his head sadly. I moved

closer, placing my hand gently on The Confetti Kid's arm. I murmured, "Yes, manslaughter causes pain, doesn't it? And man's laughter can, too. It's all very confusing right now, isn't it? But we'll help you. Please try to believe that. And trust us. It will get better."

The Kid was staring down at his shirt front. The spots of wetness from his tears had begun to spread and he touched them tentatively. Again he whispered, "Man's laughter? . . . Manslaughter? . . . Man's laughter? . . . Manslaughter? . . ."

The words formed a rhythm and he swayed as he repeated them over and over.

"You're safe here," I said. "Everything's going to be okay. Take it easy now."

I touched Ben's arm, motioning to withdraw. As we eased out into the corridor and closed the door, The Kid retreated to a corner and crouched there, rocking. We left him there, whispering, his arms clasped tightly around his knees.

In the hospital coffee shop a few minutes later, we filled a couple of mugs and Ben nodded toward a table by the windows. He seemed as fascinated with The Confetti Kid as I was.

"Where else," he asked rhetorically, "could you hear someone do that with language? Take a word, break it up, and it becomes something entirely different. Psychosis can be so brilliantly creative. And yet it defies comprehension." He stirred some cream and sugar into his coffee.

"Have you done psychotherapy with anyone like this?" he asked.

"No. I've never seen anyone quite like this—even in L.A." I'd meant it as a joke, but Ben was so preoccupied that it went right past him.

I tugged on my beard, a habit I had whenever an idea excited me. One of my therapists had commented on it—and ruined it for me by making me conscious of it. But it was enough of a habit that I kept on doing it anyway. My mind was racing.

"I think he'd be a fascinating therapy case. I can't imagine the origin of all this confetti stuff. At the same time, I'm not at all sure where you'd begin."

Ben nodded. "Yes, it's difficult to say at this stage. He's pretty rough. But if The Confetti Kid decides to stick around once the psychosis recedes, and he's willing to try therapy, you're right—you don't get many chances like this."

"So I should grab it, huh?"

"It's a marvelous opportunity, Pat. If you like, I could be a sounding board. And that way I could follow the case a little more closely."

"Sounds great. I'd welcome your perspective."

"It's a deal, then. If—and it's a big if—he stays." He took a sip of coffee and set the cup down. "There's something about him that reminds me of the few patients I've seen who were in spiritual crisis."

"Really?"

"Yes, you don't encounter them often, but they do turn up. Issues like meaninglessness and isolation propel them into psychosis."

"Existential journeys that crashed?"

"Exactly. There's a lot of that in our society today. People at loose ends, no meaning in their lives. The loneliness and hopelessness are very painful."

I nodded. "I saw plenty of that in Southern California." While I was saying this, it occurred to me that I hadn't been doing too well in that category myself. Ben seemed to read my thoughts.

"You have some recent firsthand knowledge, Pat, what with your divorce and all. Did you find all that pain got you any closer to yourself?"

Ooooof. A heavy turn in the conversation.

"In a way it did, I guess," I began. "But about the only

thing I found out so far is that all these great catchwords about recognizing and appreciating what's really important in life, and so on—well, those things are much more difficult to define after you've just been psychologically broadsided. I'm still sorting through the debris, Ben."

I definitely didn't want to pursue this personal route, so I threw out a generality:

"A lot of people are uneasy these days. Especially now, when everything seems so tenuous and uncertain."

"Sure. Everyone wants answers, some structure underneath them," Ben agreed. "But as you've no doubt learned, it's one thing to know the destination, and another to get there." His tone softened and he touched my arm.

"Look, I know you're still pulling things together. You came here hoping for a new beginning. When we met, you were at a crossroad, ready to take a few risks in the hope of greater accomplishments. So, here you are. And remember, you've got a couple of big strengths to fall back on."

I looked at him questioningly.

"You have a Ph.D. And you've worked successfully as a child therapist."

"I know. But I'm still feeling a bit shredded. And my self-confidence took a big hit."

Ben considered that. "What about therapy?"

"I've been in and out, off and on. I saw someone during the divorce and I've made some progress, but now it seems I have some whole new issues to work on."

"I see."

By this time Ben was no doubt having some strong second thoughts about me. But he might as well know right off what he was up against.

"Well, I can't be your therapist, of course," he said. "But I can refer you to someone. And certainly serve as a source of support to you here." He paused. "May I be straight with you, Pat?" he asked.

"By all means."

"I liked what I saw the first time we got together. I wouldn't have offered you the job if I hadn't. And I like to think I'm a good judge of character." He smiled. "My impression is you've got more going for you than you think you do. Start building on that. And recognize there are some pretty severe tests ahead. For you as well as for The Confetti Kid. You two may have a bit in common. There's a lot of anguish in that young man—"

"Dr. Farrell, dial four-one-four. Dr. Farrell, dial four-one-four." The page broke the moment.

"Excuse me, I'd better get that," said Ben. "Let's talk again soon."

I nodded, then sat a while longer. If The Confetti Kid and I had something in common—a sobering thought—were we going in the same direction? And if so, where?

5

DAY AFTER DAY, WE WATCHED THE KID FOR SIGNS that the tranquilizers were working. A week passed. Nothing changed. He spent most of the time exploring the confines of the seclusion room, stalking from one wall to another and back again like a caged tiger. Finally, approaching exhaustion, he'd retreat to a corner and fasten his burning eyes on the big door. He hardly ever slept.

Sometimes he swore loudly, furiously berating the world at large, the pitch of his voice rising higher and higher as a steady stream of incomprehensible gibberish spewed out. And sometimes he cried for hours, rocking back and forth, holding his stomach with a terrible gut-sobbing pain that left him gasping. A few times a day I went in and sat on the floor next to him, but he never acknowledged my presence, or seemed to notice the arm I rested on his shoulder.

Then he began challenging us. He assumed a judo stance and backed around the seclusion room, making guttural, primitive sounds unlike any I had ever heard before.

This pugnacious period lasted for four more days, during which the acts of administering the shots of Haldol became a full-scale war. On the morning of the fifth day, he almost casually submitted to the injections, and our hopes jumped that the steadily increasing doses were finally having an impact. We had begun to think he might be one of the small percentage of people who simply don't respond to chemotherapy, or else that he had an extraordinarily high tolerance for the medicine: What he was on by then would almost have sedated a young elephant. But time and again, any thoughts that he'd turned a corner were dispelled by more tirades of verbal mishmash. After four weeks of this the whole staff was discouraged. We hated to see someone this young not coming around, for we knew that his chances for recovery worsened by the day.

The fifth week after his admission, The Kid's diagnosis was changed. The bible of psychiatric diagnoses—*The Diagnostic and Statistical Manual of Mental Disorders*—limits the diagnosis of Brief Reactive Psychosis to one month. What follows that describes a time-related continuum of psychological deterioration: Such a disorder sequentially becomes "schizophreniform" and, after six months, if there is still no abatement of symptoms, "paranoid schizophrenia."

I had thought he couldn't get any worse. I was wrong.

Nearly a month and a half after his admission, The Kid took another psychological plunge: Into the deep, dark pit of catatonia—a highly unusual and dramatic form of psychosis.

When Joan Lindstrom and I entered the seclusion room on rounds early one morning, we found him facing the far corner, his back to the door. He was standing with his arms raised above his head, his hands together as if in prayer. His posture was completely frozen.

"A tech found him like this when he checked him at three this morning," Joan said.

"*Just* like this? You mean he hasn't moved since?" I asked incredulously.

"Apparently not."

These days it's rare to see the catatonic state, with its emblematic and bizarre physical rigidity and accompanying mental stupor. I had read about catatonia, of course, but this was the first time I'd ever seen it.

I squeezed into the corner in front of him. He remained absolutely rigid. He didn't even blink.

"Kid," I spoke into the waxy, pale face, searched the unseeing eyes. "What's happened to you?"

I moved his arm down a bit, let go, and watched it return as if by some eerie remote control to its former position. He was like a zombie. I couldn't imagine the sheer tension of holding my arms up like that for even a few minutes, let alone hours on end. Just watching him exhausted me.

I sighed.

"If only you could tell us what's going on so we could help you. . . ."

"I'll have Dr. Stacey take a look at him," Joan said, anticipating me.

Later that morning we had our monthly meeting of the psychology staff. Afterward I told Ben about the latest development.

"Really?" he said thoughtfully. "That's an interesting progression—or regression." He turned to me. "You know, catatonia can be an extreme adaptation to overwhelming fear. Some people have suggested that a catatonic state is the last stage of a genuinely biological defense against death—you go comatose to avoid being violently killed."

I shook my head and kind of laughed. It sounded preposterous to me.

"No, really, Pat. The idea is that the terror is so great the mind shifts into an altered state of consciousness. It's kind of a last-ditch effort to survive."

"But we're a hospital," I countered. "At some level, he must understand that he's not in physical danger here."

Ben gave me his wry smile.

"You're being too rational, Pat," he said. "This is an act of desperation. You've seen films of an animal caught by a predator? It goes limp, just hangs there being chewed on, and sometimes the killer loses interest, drops it and walks away. And then the darn animal—frog, rabbit, possum, whatever—gets up and miraculously hobbles off. The worse for it, certainly, but still alive. I'm sure that's where the expression 'playing possum' came from, come to think of it." Ben leaned back and looked up at the ceiling. "Now all you have to do is figure out who or what has chewed on this fellow. And convince him that you're going to protect him —and that he'll survive. . . ."

"You make it sound so easy. But when we have to have five or six techs hold him down for his shot, it kind of undermines our credibility doesn't it?"

"True, but that can't be helped. And you're not part of that, anyway. Just keep talking to him as if he can hear you. Some patients in catatonic states have accurately reported afterward what people said to them—or about them. They couldn't respond at the time, but they were somehow aware of what was going on around them."

"It's similar to someone in a coma, then?"

"Seems to be. Although catatonics probably have an edge. Have you ever come across Fromm-Reichman's report on catatonic patients?"

I shook my head.

"After they came out of the catatonic state, some of her patients told her they had been afraid if they moved they would die."

"Really?"

"Yes. So in case at some level he can hear you, keep reassuring him that you're his ally, and that you'll protect him."

So I began stopping by a few times a day to do just that. Over and over, I told The Kid that he was totally safe and that we were watching out for him while he couldn't defend himself. There was never the slightest trace of reaction, but I kept at it. Who knew? At least it made mc feel as if I was doing something.

After a few days, The Kid's face began to take on the distinctive pallor of the dying. He'd stopped eating and the nurses started feeding him by tube, but it had little effect on his cadaverous appearance. His skin tone turned a yellowed ivory, his eyes glazed over from not focusing, and his cheeks became even more sunken.

Since seclusion was no longer necessary, we decided to move him to a room where there was more openness and light, hoping that might help somehow. One morning, bracing The Kid between us, Brenda and I guided him down the hall and into his new quarters. He moved in slow, mechanical steps, not resisting us, but not really walking either. His gait was tottering: When we hesitated or stopped, he stopped. And tried to resume his statue-like pose.

It took only a short time for us to see that the change of scenery had absolutely no effect.

"Got a moment?" I poked my head around Brenda's office door. She was at her desk, chewing on a pen, staring at some forms in front of her.

She looked up and the surge of pleasure I felt reminded me again how much I was attracted to her. Stifle, I told myself sternly. The woman is practically engaged, remember? And even if she weren't, you're not ready, not ready at all. So cool it.

"Sure. I've been wanting to see you, too." She sounded like she really meant it.

"Okay, you first," I said.

"Do you know Mr. Gorman on Four? Kind of roly-poly. We call him 'Murray the Mattress Eater.' "

I laughed. "You're kidding. He eats mattresses?"

"Not exactly. But he is the ward billygoat. That's why he's put in restraints from time to time. He'll just start eating everything in sight—matchbooks, styrofoam cups, towels, and yes—one night he slipped his cuffs and actually did chew off a whole corner of his mattress. Dr. Stacey was wondering if you had any ideas for a behavior modification approach to him. Being in restraints means a lot of nursing time goes toward feeding and changing him. Would you check him out? See what you can come up with?"

Brenda fastened her lovely green eyes on me and I couldn't imagine ever saying "no" to her about anything.

"Sure. Sounds interesting."

"Good. Now, what did you want to see me about?"

"Three little words," I said, pausing for effect.

She raised her eyebrows. "The Confetti Kid?"

I nodded.

"I feel so bad, Pat. I've scoured all the counties anywhere near here, but not a clue has turned up. Not one person of his description has been reported missing. I've sent his fingerprints to the State Crime Lab, but their mainframe has been down for a week and they're still not sure when it'll be up again. When it is, they'll have a backlog that'll take weeks to run."

"And I'm sure we won't be a priority."

"You can count on it. Anyway, I gave them all the information I could on our Confetti Kid and they promised to get back to me. Sometime. So I'm afraid that's all I've got for you." She looked very disappointed.

"We'll find out who he is eventually. About the only time this happens is with amnesia victims, especially when they've left their home territory."

Brenda reacted quickly. "Hey, I should have thought of that. Maybe we could run his picture in the papers and on the news—a missing person bulletin."

"Except he looks so bad now, Brenda. He's really deteriorated. Would anyone recognize him?"

She shrugged and we fell silent.

Then she perked up. "Let me work on it a while longer, Pat. This is the kind of challenge I like." She looked at her watch. "Hey, how'd it get so late? Staffing's coming up. Let me just grab a few files here."

In triple time, she selected several folders and pages of notes from the clutter on her desk and we set off for the ward.

In staffing a few minutes later, Stacey paused a long time after he read off The Kid's name. Then he sighed. He was as perplexed as the rest of us were.

"I think at this point we'll do a pharmacological about-face. This is about the most entrenched, resistant psychosis I've ever seen." He massaged his temples, thinking. "We'll switch him to Navane. It's constituted differently and the absorption runs a different route. It's got a good track record with intractable, persistent delusions. If that doesn't work, we'll see," Stacey went on. "We could do a course of electro-convulsive therapy, give the neurons a good shake. Joan, let's give him a few days to clear the Haldol out of his system and then start him, maybe Sunday, on the Navane. You people will have to watch him closely, okay? Anything could happen. And we'd better have a seclusion and restraint order ready—in case he gets agitated again."

Another week passed as we watched for some sign that the psychotic siege was lifting. Nothing happened. The Confetti Kid was now the subject of most staff coffee breaks, and some of the techs had a lottery about when—and if—he'd ever come around. It was gallows humor, but we needed the release. We felt enveloped in a shroud of frustration.

The Kid did nothing for himself. If the staff put him in bed, he stayed there, lying taut and rigid until someone got him up again. Once up, he resumed his unmoving stance, as if he were in an upright coma: standing or sitting for hours, his expression blank, his eyes unblinking, staring into nothingness. After a time his muscles began to atrophy and a physical therapy program was launched. But he looked worse every day. It took a real leap of imagination to recall the handsome, solid-looking fellow we'd admitted.

It is deeply upsetting to see anyone in the grip of such psychic malignancy. And we felt more and more discouraged.

I still stopped in to see him a few times each day, often taking my clipboard with me to make notes and reminder lists while he stood silently by the window. There was nothing to do but keep talking reassuringly to him, hoping the companionship and my friendly voice would somehow penetrate and perhaps lay the groundwork for a future therapeutic alliance.

For his part, The Kid appeared lost in a continuous internal dialogue. Everyone else was excluded, of course.

One afternoon, as I sat on his bed, my back propped against the wall, I carried on my own inner dialogue: There has to be so much you want to say. How do I break through the silence? I shook my head and sighed. Isn't there something you'd like to say, Kid? About how much you must have been hurt? Wouldn't it help to let the pain out? Please, Kid.

I sighed again, and set aside my reverie to jot down some notes on my clipboard. Occasionally I glanced at The Kid, who was standing at rigid attention, his stiffened arms at his sides today rather than up in the air. I decided to take that as progress.

For perhaps five minutes I was absorbed in my work, and when I looked up again I did a double-take. His left arm was now extended slightly in front of him, his right arm stretched out behind.

I hadn't seen him move, but he had.

Though I wanted desperately to watch him, I forced myself not to. I didn't want to frighten him, and I was hoping he would move again. After two or three interminable minutes, I allowed myself a little peek and was stunned to see that he was now a good two or three feet closer to me. I hadn't heard so much as a rustle, but he was actually coming toward me! Imperceptibly, in agonizingly slow motion, but he was definitely moving. My whole body tensed as I waited to see what he was up to.

At last he was right in front of me. Slowly, ever so slowly, his skinny, white hand reached out to pick up the extra pen on the bed next to me. His tormented eyes fixed on me. Then, inch by inch, his gaze moved down to the clipboard in my lap. Carefully, so as not to spook him, I flipped to some blank sheets and held the tablet out to him.

"Is this what you want? Here—"

Solemnly he took the board and laboriously seated himself cross-legged on the floor a few feet away. This took about three whole minutes. Then, in a clumsy, twitchy fashion, he began to write.

Had he somehow tapped into my thoughts, my wondering if he had anything to say to me? The idea sent chills down my spine.

For nearly ten minutes—deliberately, painstakingly, barely pausing—he wrote. When he was finished, he gently laid the clipboard and pen on the floor beside him. Then, without so much as a glance in my direction, he rose languidly and took up his old position.

I got up, retrieved the board, and, with some difficulty, read the herky-jerky writing:

> Death always gouges the spirit. The funeral coughs coffins and vaporizes a vast void of universe containing hordes of horrors and antlers of anguish. This is the cosmic debris of existence, the absolute rule that while life is half-witted, death is freedom to enter the cosmos, the harshly haphazard hall of mirrors which travel the carnival of Time, accursed by the razed circus tent of Death. This patent paradox links fruitful logic with

> metaphysical banality and our swing from the sperm to the worm consecrates the asymetrical amorality that accompanies the knife thrust of soul saboteurs and raconteurs. The cocaine infidels know not of the earth's glorious demi-gods, but only of a slapshot of grave cadavers grimacing at midnight. The pale horse approaches, the skull saddle glowing, the Grim Reaper raping and roping the pictorial platitudes from where? Only the fairy tale exists, the artist is lacerated, exposed in repose, his blight to be extinguished in a pernicious sunset pyre. A testimonial to the connoisseurs of sewerdom. The squeal of evil, the stained skull of stench, the dense metaphor of artistic purpose all bequeath an elaborate hoax.

My first reaction was to be disappointed that the message offered no clues to his identity or what had happened to him. Then I understood that Ben was certainly right on one count: The Kid was defending himself against death. It was all pretty crazy stuff, schizophrenic word salad. But so creative, and what a vocabulary. The Confetti Kid was a very bright guy.

I had an idea.

"Kid, I'll leave the pen and few sheets of paper, just in case you feel the urge to write some more. Okay?"

I set them down beside him, hoping no one would decide to take the pen away on the assumption that it might be dangerous for him to have it. It might be. Still, I was hoping hard that he wouldn't be able to resist writing down more of his thoughts.

"And Kid—" I said softly, "I'm glad you felt safe enough to share these thoughts with me. My promise still holds—we'll take care of you. Remember, this is your sanctuary."

There was no movement at all from the apparition by the window, nor any sign to indicate he had heard me.

When I visited him early the next morning, there was a drawing that revealed another dimension of his ominous preoccupation with death. And considerable artistic talent as well.

These were the first steps. Garbled as the messages were, they were attempts to reach out. Resurrection seemed to have begun. About time. The Kid had been in the hospital for two months.

The Shafers were wonderful landlords. They'd practically adopted me. It started after Mrs. Shafer noticed how many Palooka Pizza boxes I was recycling. They took to inviting me for Sunday dinner, and there was always a foil-wrapped package pressed into my hand when I left. During the week I often came home to find makings for dinner by the back door: a basket of vegetables from their garden or a loaf of homemade bread, sometimes still warm from the oven. Later in the season, we fired up the barbeque and grilled freshly picked corn on the cob and hamburgers or "brats," wonderful Wisconsin bratwurst that were unlike anything I'd ever had.

All that summer I learned about the unpredictability of the region's climate. It alternated between days of relatively dry, moderate temperatures when Canadian fronts prevailed, and hot, sticky, humid days when the Gulf of Mexico shoveled up thunderstorm conditions. I discovered I'd traded year-round earthquake fears of "The Big One" for the prospect of no less frightening summer tornadoes.

At Peace River, we held regular drills for such potential events. One particular afternoon, a savage thunderstorm struck during a group therapy session I was conducting. We had just gotten underway when the high winds swept in and splintered limbs from three huge trees that, unfortunately, could be seen from the group therapy room. Never having witnessed a storm of such magnitude before, I was hardly in a position to be reassuring anyone of anything, but I had to try. When the lights suddenly blinked out, the generally high level of tension in the room surged to near panic. To my enormous relief, everyone managed to stay calm until the emergency generator kicked in with its dim half-lights, but the rest of the session was a washout, so to speak.

That evening when I got home, I had a couple of drinks to settle my frazzled nerves. And called Brenda to see how she'd survived the fray.

"It was exciting, wasn't it?" she asked.

She actually seemed to have enjoyed it. Very strange person. But when she heard where I'd been trapped, she was sympathetic; she'd been dictating in her office, so she took a break and watched the storm with some other social workers and secretaries likewise interrupted by the power outage. Stacey hadn't been that fortunate. He'd been caught in one of the tunnels between the buildings and had had to literally grope his way back to his office in total darkness.

Mrs. Shafer's garden fared amazingly well, but it took the hospital maintenance crew several days to clear the downed limbs and other storm debris. I gained new respect for Mother Nature that day.

6

THEN WE LEARNED THE CONFETTI KID'S IDENTITY, BY A total fluke. I mentioned our mystery patient to a number of people at a mental health conference and a week later one of them called. Tricia Cooper was a psychiatric social worker at Meredith Mental Health Institute, on the other side of the state. The hospital served a catchment area of Milwaukee County and northeastern Wisconsin. Trish thought she might have a lead for us.

"I interviewed a new patient yesterday, and he mentioned staying at a mission on the east side of Madison two or three months ago. It sounded like a mixture of street people, mentally ill, you name it. Anyway, he said there was a guy there who was crazier than he was—a fellow who threw confetti on people and told them it would 'cleanse their greedy souls and bring them rapture.' He said that the guy wore some kind of glittery suit under his street clothes—"

"Wow! Sounds like our guy, Trish. By any chance, would your patient remember the name of this place?"

"Yes. It's got a peculiar name. It's called the Church of Cosmic Revelation. Run by someone named Father Paul. I think it's near the Five Corners area, in the old hippie section. Madison Social Service should know about it."

"Well, I happen to be going to Madison this weekend. I'll stop by and see Father Paul. Thanks, Trish. I owe you one."

When I told her, Brenda was excited. I pushed my luck.

"Want to check out the Church of Cosmic Revelation with me? Saturday?"

"Ohhhhh," she said, "any day but that. I have to work that day. I have appointments with some families who can't come in during the week."

"Any possibility of postponing them?"

Brenda made a face. "That's what my boyfriend wanted me to do. He had some plans for us in Chicago this weekend, and he was miffed when I said I couldn't make it. When he leaves his job at the end of the day—he's a tax attorney—he leaves it. He thinks I should do that, too. No one really understands the goofy hours we have to put in here." She sighed. "I could reschedule, but it would be a nightmare. And I have to see these people soon."

"Hey, don't worry about it. I'll check it out myself, Bren. Another time, maybe."

"Sorry, Pat, I didn't mean to get into all that. I wish I could go. I'd really have liked that."

Me too, I thought. Me too.

So on the last Saturday of that hot, humid August, I drove languidly along I-90, marveling at the deep green, tree-covered hills, the neat farms, the incredible symmetry of the cornfields running right up to the tree line where the slopes became too steep to cultivate. I collected the materials I needed at the university library, and then headed for Madison's east side.

Driving across town I absorbed the beauty of the city. Madison is unique: The dominating capitol, patterned after its Washington parent, is the hub, with streets forming spokes that radiate out in each direction. State Street stretches west from Capitol Square to Lake Street at the edge of the university. Its entire length is a mall—no cars allowed—with a steady parade of students and other interesting characters and an intriguing array of shops. It reminded me of the boutiques along Union Street in San Francisco, and I hoped I'd have time later to explore.

Madison is made up of many distinctive neighborhoods, each with its own park. I'd never seen so many parks, and all of them were filled with people having picnics. The town's shape is determined by five lakes, with the urban and residential areas neatly tucked around them. The well-kept homes and lush greenery are typically Midwest, small-town America—very Norman Rockwell. It all felt very comfortable to me.

The place I was looking for was on the east side, a working-class neighborhood with smaller, more modest houses, all very old-fashioned. On Williamson Street I spotted a food co-op that seemed a likely place to start. The soft-spoken pony-tailed clerk turned out to be a good choice. He knew where it was.

"Three blocks along Atwood, in an old movie theatre." He accompanied me to the door to be sure I was pointed in the right direction. Evidently concerned about what official business I might have with the Church of Cosmic Revelation, he volunteered a reference for the place: "Father Paul does a lot of good for a lot of people," he said.

I nodded and thanked him.

A few minutes later I pulled up to the neglected marquee, a few determined letters still clinging to it. In the glass case was a faded poster for "The Last Picture Show." Nice touch. The front doors were locked, so I walked around the side and found another, more promising entrance. The scarred metal door was propped halfway open with a rock. Behind it, a thriving vegetable garden stretched into the alley. A rusted-out van, apparently used for storage, had taken root nearby.

Inside, old doors reclined on sawhorses stretched along

one wall. These makeshift tables were stacked high with cartons of what I recognized as surplus government food. On the other side of the room were neat rows of cots, each with a khaki army blanket and a pillow. One was occupied by an elderly man with skin like burnished leather. His searing eyes watched me fearfully. I greeted him, but he didn't respond.

From beyond the arc of dim light in the doorway I heard several distinctive hacks of a smoker's cough, then a long wheeze. I blinked in the semi-darkness but could see no one. Then from somewhere in the gloom a deep, resonant voice asked, "May I help you, Brother?"

As my eyes adjusted, I saw a figure seated at a desk in the far corner. Skirting a row of old theatre seats, I walked toward it.

"I'm looking for Father Paul."

"You've found him. What can I do for you?"

He was a grizzly bear of a man, an African-American with gentle eyes and a woolly beard strewn liberally with gray. He was wearing an old flannel shirt, a navy ascot, and a beret angled jauntily on his head. He looked like he'd just stepped out of the French countryside.

I introduced myself and told him why I'd come.

"Have a seat. What makes you think this person might have been here?" he asked.

"Because I understand that a while back you had someone who was doing things with confetti. There can't be too many around like that."

"Not likely. But a lot of people come through this place. Most of them have problems of one kind or another—we get alcoholics, homeless people, and quite a few just on the bum. They get some pretty strange ideas."

"Yes, I'm sure. But this was a young fellow, early twenties. Would've looked like a college student. You probably don't get too many that young." I pulled out a Polaroid I'd taken and handed it to him.

"Do you recall this fellow? He looks a lot thinner and rougher here than when you would have seen him."

Father Paul studied the picture for several moments.

"Maybe." He looked up at me, his eyes narrowing slightly. Was he sizing me up as a member of "the system?"

"What did you say you do at that hospital?" he asked.

"I'm a clinical psychologist there." I hoped this reassured him a little that I was as protective of my charges as he was of his. "Look," I said, "we're both in the same business. I need to get through to this kid. It'll help if we can find out who he is. And what happened to him before he came to us."

"Won't tell you his name, huh?"

"Not *won't. Can't.* I don't think he knows for sure who he is. Anyone who's psychotic—which he is—is more or less amnesic. But for the last few weeks, he hasn't talked at all. Unless we can find someone who can identify him, he may end up being a long-term client of yours someday."

That plea opened a small wedge.

"I get your point." Father Paul rubbed his beard thoughtfully and stared at the picture again. "Well, I remember him all right, but I'm afraid I can't help you much. He was here quite a while ago, March maybe? On and off. Pretty confused. He'd say odd things—referred to us as the 'Salivation Army,' for instance. I do remember that. I knew something was wrong with him, but—" He shrugged.

"Were you able to get a name from him? Or any indication of where he was from?"

"No. They called him 'Joe' around here, but that wasn't his name."

"Was he a student at the university?"

"Don't know. He never said. Mostly he just sacked out here, ate a few meals, and disappeared during the day. Usually he was very quiet, but sometimes he'd jump up and start rambling about the world being on a dangerous course. Then he'd dart out and be gone for several hours. One day he just didn't come back.'' He shrugged again. ''People come and go here.''

''Do you think any of your other clients might know anything about him?''

Father Paul shook his head. ''I doubt it. He was pretty much a loner.''

''Any trouble with the police?''

''None that I'm aware of. It's possible, though.''

''Well, did he seem particularly disturbed, delusional? The commitment papers we got identified him as 'The Confetti Kid.' It's what he called himself.''

Father Paul sat back. ''Yes, I remember the confetti stuff, but I didn't know what to make of it. Of course, I hear a lot of stories from these people. You know what alcohol does to the brain. We have at least one case of DTs a week. Some of our street people are really chronically mentally ill, and they spend most of their time in some kind of dreamland. I talk with them, try to reassure them. But this kid zipped in and out. He didn't talk to me much. I think I may have intimidated him.''

''And you never saw him with anyone else?''

''No, he kept to himself. Some of the guys razzed him about the confetti business, so he just avoided everyone.''

''I see. Thanks for your help, Father.'' I started to get up.

''Just a minute.''

''Yes?''

''With someone as disturbed as that boy was, I usually try to get them to see Kayla.''

''Kayla?''

''She's a counselor, too. Like you. Only she's a special one.'' A smile was playing under the big beard.

''In what way?'' I asked.

''Well, she's not your ordinary therapist. She's psychic.''

''Really?'' A psychic therapist. So, I thought, aren't we all?

He paused, savoring my perplexity. ''Yep. She sees auras,

can tell when the colors around you are negative, stuff like that. She's the best damn counselor I've ever known. She can actually *feel* what's happening in you.'' He frowned. ''But I don't know if the kid went to see her or not.''

''Where can I find Kayla?''

Before he could answer, the phone rang.

''Excuse me.'' He lifted the receiver and listened for a few moments. ''Hold on a second,'' he said to the caller. Then he hurriedly scribbled an address and a small map on a scrap of paper and handed it to me. ''It's not far, he said. ''A few blocks that way.'' He waved and picked up the receiver again.

''Thanks.'' I placed a few bills on the desk.

''All donations gratefully accepted,'' he smiled. ''Tax deductible, of course. Want a receipt?''

''No thanks, that's okay.''

''Good luck,'' he said.

While Father Paul and I were talking, I'd heard the percussion of distant thunder. When I got outside the sky had turned ominous. I still wasn't used to the ferocity of Wisconsin's hit-and-run summer thunderstorms. I'd driven barely two blocks before huge raindrops splatted against the windshield, accompanied by strobes of lightning and artillery cracks of thunder. Within another block, gusting winds pulled me to the curb and then a driving, pelting rain engulfed the car.

Ten minutes later the rain eased, the skies brightened, and the sun began to reassert itself. To the southeast the fleeing storm teamed up with the sunlight to create a vivid rainbow. The gutters were flooded, so I inched my way along until I saw the sign for Kayla's street. All the houses along the street were the same: 1920s, cookie-cutter bungalows. Kayla's was a daring blue.

I climbed the steps and rapped at the old wooden door.

I had never met a psychic. The word conjured up images of gypsies and crystal balls, though I knew that was probably simplistic. Still, like most people, I was desperately curious about the future. Especially my own.

The door was opened by a rather modish woman, in her fifties, I judged. Her features were gentle, and her smile revealed even, white teeth. A dashing silver forelock drew my eye; it was a sharp contrast to the jet black of the rest of her hair, which curved in a long braid around her shoulder and fell onto the faded, ankle-length madras dress she was wearing. She seemed simultaneously old, venerable, yet somehow very young. The incongruity made me hesitate.

"I'm sorry to bother you. Is Kayla in? Father Paul said I might find her here."

"Yes," she answered. Her voice was unusually soft. "I'm Kayla. Won't you come in?"

I had an odd notion that she was expecting me.

She stepped aside and motioned toward a curtain of glass beads that led into a small parlor. The whole room was a time capsule. A royal blue overstuffed couch and matching chair faced the entryway. An old wicker rocker sat at an angle, its back toward the door. Above the sofa hung a Victorian picture of snorting gray horses, their nostrils flared, in an ornate gold frame. Heavy, dark purple velvet drapes bracketed the only window facing the street. Plants flourished everywhere and a rotund Buddha sat on the old trunk that served as a coffee table. The beaded curtain was still clicking faintly as I sat down on the couch.

"What can I do for you?" Kayla asked, a southern lilt barely detectable in her voice. She seated herself in the chair and her azure eyes, with an unusual grayish tint, settled on me.

A different kind of woman, I thought.

Briefly, I explained the situation. She nodded when I showed her the picture.

"Yes, I remember the young man. His name is Stephen.

I don't know his last name. He was quite distraught when he came here. The colors surrounding his aura were very bad—browns mostly—and very dark. His energy was almost exhausted, his psyche very precarious. There was much pain. The image I had was of someone on a wet river boulder. People were reaching for him, but they couldn't save him . . . the water was swallowing him. . . ." She paused, then said, "I didn't tell him this because I could see that he was mentally ill."

She closed her eyes and sat quietly for a few moments, her eyelids fluttering slightly. Then she spoke again.

"The hospital is a good place for him. Stephen needs a sanctuary right now. You said you're his doctor there? Yes, that is as it should be . . ."

She opened her eyes and again I felt the power of her gaze. I also felt a little bubble of anxiety. Actually, a medium bubble. This was weird.

"You have an interesting aura," she said.

"Thank you—" I didn't know what else to say. "I guess I have to plead ignorance. I don't really know what an aura is."

"Most people don't." Kayla smiled. "We human beings are complex, as I'm sure you would agree, and certain energies, whether positive or negative—or both—are given off. An aura is the array of colors, the hues that these energies create. Some of us are sensitive to this light energy—we can see the colors that radiate from a person. The energy field is very uniform in healthy people, but it's irregular in someone who is ill or in pain."

"People giving off colors—it's hard to believe. Seems pretty far out." I was getting more uncomfortable, feeling completely out of my depth.

"Yes, I know. Many people believe only what they can see. And they regard what I say with great skepticism. But since I've always been able to see auras, I've never needed any proof that they exist. When I was little I thought everyone could see them. I was amazed when my grandmother explained that it was a special gift. Many times since then I've encountered a certain . . . prejudice. . . ." She sighed, then gave a delightful chuckle, a wonderfully soft, rippling laugh. "It would be so much easier if other people could see these things, too."

"I'm sure it would."

Funny, I thought. I believed her. I was very aware of how little the behavioral sciences understood such phenomena, or even recognized them.

"I will send Stephen healing energy," Kayla was saying.

"Healing energy—how do you do that?"

She smiled. "The curiosity of the scientist. A person with an open mind—good for you." When her pleasure faded she said thoughtfully, "I send healing energy by visualizing Stephen, then surrounding him with white light. Particularly his head."

She closed her eyes. She was apparently engaging in this now, and while I waited, I studied the enigmatic expression on the Buddha. When I looked at her again, Kayla was watching me. I guessed the transmission of energies had been completed.

I cleared my throat. "Do you have any idea where I could find out more about Stephen? Did he ever mention where he lived, or the names of friends? Anything at all?"

"No. When he came here he was quite confused. And terribly distraught, as I said. The colors of his aura were such that all I could do was bathe him in light. There was enormous pain and hurt, and I had to be very careful not to intensify it and cause him more pain—or to take on too much of that negative energy myself. You know, when you open yourself up you become very vulnerable."

"Yes, I can appreciate that. Believe me."

"I've seen a number of young people like this. They feel desperately alone, isolated from society. Sometimes they resort to extreme measures, Dr. McGarry. They begin to explore evil, Satanism, not so much to understand, but to try to harness the sense of power they lack, to use it as a tool of vengeance. They plunge into the subconscious with little knowledge and no one to guide them. Sometimes they find themselves caught in a vortex of destructive feelings. When hatefulness and malevolence consume the spirit, the spirit becomes diabolical. That's when people commit violence, destroying others as well as themselves. It is a vile karma. . . ."

I let out a low whistle.

Kayla went on, "I didn't think Stephen had gone that far, but I knew he needed treatment. He seemed overwhelmed by life, in so much pain. He was so guarded it was very difficult to talk with him. I doubt that anything like this has happened to him before." She sighed. "I wasn't very optimistic."

"Stephen didn't say anything about his family, then?" I asked.

"No. I'm afraid that's all I can tell you about him."

Kayla made no move to get up. She seemed to be appraising me, her gaze steady, unrelenting. It was a bit disconcerting.

"Would you like a demonstration—a reading—so you can experience what I've been describing?"

"I guess so—" I smiled uneasily. "Yes, I'm really curious about what it is you do."

"May I have permission to enter your aura?"

I nodded. I wasn't at all sure what that entailed, but maybe it could make the path to Stephen's past clearer.

Kayla settled deep into the chair, her feet tucked under her, her hands folded in her lap, her eyes closed. Her breathing became rhythmic, almost trancelike. Her expression was serene. I watched her closely, wishing I'd learned at least something about ESP and psychic phenomena. They were topics that had been virtually ignored at the university, though every now and then I'd come across an article that referred darkly to how the CIA, as well as the Russians, were experimenting with them.

Kayla cleared her throat slightly and began, "You have many strong colors—and a great deal of gold, white, and yellow in your aura. Reach out and hold onto that part. It is very good. Know that it's there. It's healthy, healing energy. If you ever step into a demon's place, the forces there can be so strong they can obliterate the good energies. If you find yourself in a place like that—and you have to deal with real demons, lower worlds, evil—remember to trust that old part of yourself. The goodness. Open your eyes in the dark and see the darkness as your brother.

"I'm picking up some things ahout Stephen now. . . . It appears your paths have crossed before, in a previous lifetime. But now it is you who must help Stephen." She stopped, frowned, and began again:

"I've been instructed to tell you that there is a density of energy close to the earth, and that is where the ghosts come from. It's a confined space, a plane of existence. And it frightens people who sense it but don't understand it. I believe that Stephen, in his journey to find self-expression, touched on this plane. And he was not ready for it."

Far out! I thought.

"May I touch your hands, please?"

Kayla held her hands in front of her, palms up, and I placed mine gently on them. Her thumbs held my hands firmly, and after a minute or so she pulled hers back so only our fingers were touching. Finally she dropped her hands into her lap. I did the same. Strange, I'd actually *felt* something—a slight vibration, or something warm flowing between us.

"You have a gentle spirit . . . and a deep sensitivity toward others. But at the same time you have a very strong will . . . and determination. Those different forces cause conflict at times. . . . You're deeply committed to people, yet there's a part of you that requires aloneness, solitude. It's been hard for you to find a soulmate who can accept those contradictory forces. . . ."

What a cryptic statement. But true. Kayla opened her eyes and gave me a long, discerning look. She closed them again.

"There is a large expanse of water, an ocean? . . . hills . . . an older couple. There's a deep love, and concern . . ." She paused, a frown knitting her brow. "You're divorced?"

"Yes." Did it show that much?

"I thought perhaps you were because I was getting a very strong image of a young boy. Your son? But no . . . like a son, but not. There is something different about him, but a special closeness is there . . . a strong bond. Does that mean anything to you?"

My mouth dropped open and I stared at her. The ocean, the hills, my parents, Mike . . . There was no way this woman could know about that part of my life.

"I'm amazed that you could know that." I answered. "I'm from Southern California. My parents—the older couple you saw—live near the ocean. I do miss them very much. And that little boy . . . Mike Harris. I worked with him for three years in a hospital near Santa Barbara. We were, we are, very close. He was my first real patient and it was hard for me to leave him."

"Yes. But you were ready to move on to new experiences. You have an interesting karma, Patrick McGarry."

"Karma?"

"Destiny. Your life will have an impact on many others. I don't often tell people things like that, but I believe it's something you should be prepared for. You have much to share. . . ."

Kayla paused, then looked gently at me.

"I sense . . . a certain pain—a loneliness—in you. You cover it well, but you never felt as if you really fit in. And you've never known what to do with the feelings you take on. There's a sensitivity. You feel things acutely—other people's anguish and despair. When you see it in their faces you take it within you. Even their pain. That's too much. You must learn to let go, to protect and shelter that sensitivity, not allow it to get tangled up in a world that contains so much misery."

This was definitely spooky. What she said was absolutely true, but I had never thought of it in quite that way. I do tend to react strongly to the pain I pick up from other people. Big cities are particularly hard on me: Instead of seeing the sights, I see the desolation in people's faces.

I shrugged. "I'm trying to let go of that. I suppose that's one of the reasons I moved to Wisconsin. So far it's been much better. Easier on me, a lot less intense."

"Good. You were ready for a respite. It was very important."

"So I've learned. I was burning out."

Kayla was watching me closely. Evidently she agreed with that assessment.

"In many ways," she said, "you've been through a period of severe disharmony. Now you must undertake the task of rebuilding. And that takes commitment, purpose. But first you must heal. . . ."

"Yes. I know."

"I can reassure you of one thing: You will find your soulmate. Be open, and be willing to reach out. Don't push her away."

I stared at her. I should have felt encouraged, I suppose, but I was feeling numb. I knew I didn't want, couldn't deal with a "soulmate" yet, and I didn't plan to search for one in the foreseeable future.

Kayla smiled warmly and went on, "I thank you for sharing yourself with me—and not closing me out. The mind has a most difficult time grasping what lies beyond immediate reality. Many people are frightened and put up energy to protect themselves. You tried not to do that. Even though you have doubts, you are at least open to other possibilities.

That tells me that if anyone can help Stephen, it will be you. As I said, there have been other lifetimes you've shared. And now your lights have found each other once again in this one. Perhaps you can teach him what he needs to learn about life."

"I hope I can."

"There is one other thing I can tell you about Stephen. I had the distinct impression that he'd had some contact with the police. You could check with them. They may be able to help you."

"Yes. I'm going there next, actually. Thank you." I hesitated. "What do you mean, 'other lifetimes?' "

"Most people find it hard to believe that they've lived before. But our souls return again and again, each time learning more in their search for enlightenment." Kayla paused. "We can talk more about this another time, if you like." The blue-gray eyes came to rest on me again. "We do share the same work. That may sound odd to you, but you and I have more in common than you might think. I hope I'll see you again. I would very much like to know how Stephen progresses."

I promised to be in touch.

As I circled the Madison Police Department in search of a place to park, I kept thinking of what Kayla had told me. She had churned up some real issues, all right: ones I preferred to avoid. I knew I was steering away from relationships, not wanting to make another mistake. She had nailed me there. Psychologist, heal thyself.

At the front desk of the police department I explained my mission and was directed to Records where, after convincing her of my need to know, a computer technician punched in various key words from my description: Male, caucasian, age 18-25, first name: Stephen, aka "The Confetti Kid."

The computer searched and soon an arrest report

scrolled up on the screen. Another key brought a printout. I scanned it eagerly.

MADISON POLICE DEPARTMENT
Madison, Wisconsin 53701

Name: Stephen Parker
Aka: The Confetti Kid
File Number: 009175046

March 30 — Unit 3 Report: 2:30 a.m.
Calls from 5 different citizens in 200 block of Regent Street complaining of a subject dressed in a Halloween costume climbing fire escapes and jumping from roof to roof. Complainants state that subject is throwing confetti from rooftops and disturbing the peace. Subject is reported to be a male Caucasian teenager, dressed in a multicolored suit and cape. Officers searched neighborhood, but could not locate subject.

April 3 — Unit 3 Report: 1:05 a.m.
Two citizen calls. Young man throwing confetti reported on rooftops again. No trace when officers arrived on scene.

April 5 — Unit 3 Report: 2:35 a.m.
Citizen report. University Avenue. Subject wearing brightly colored costume seen climbing from a tree to a rooftop, then scattering confetti. When citizen called out and asked what he was doing, subject replied, "Bringing joy to the world." Officers searched neighborhood. Could not locate subject.

April 9 — Unit 3 Report: 1:50 a.m.
6 citizen calls between midnight and 1:50 a.m. Subject seen changing clothes in ATM booth, observed on fire escape at 257 University Avenue, then moving along business and apartment roofs on University Avenue. Subject gone when officers responded. Confetti found on sidewalks. No evidence of breakins or vandalism. Subject is either prankster or a nut.

April 15	Unit 3 Report: 12:35 a.m. Arrested young man who has been subject of many complaints. Confetti in his possession. Seemed confused and incoherent. Refused to give name other than "The Confetti Kid." Charged with disturbing the peace and littering. Taken to lockup. 1:10 a.m. Subject agitated and uncooperative. Desk Sergeant called University Hospitals, where subject was transported by patrol car. Subject hospitalized on Acute Treatment Unit. Dane County Mental Health Center has had contacts with subject, whose name is Stephen Parker. They will coordinate inpatient and outpatient followup treatment.
April 16	10:04 a.m. Dane County Mental Health Center reports that subject checked out of the Acute Treatment Unit AMA (Against Medical Advice), taking his confetti costume with him. Charges referred to District Attorney's office.
April 30	Charges dropped. Subject's whereabouts unknown.

That was the final entry. So The Kid's name was Stephen Parker! What a break. I tucked a copy of the report in my pocket and set out for State Street, where I did a lot of mindless browsing. Then I headed back.

That night I called Brenda because I thought she'd be dying to know what happened. But she sounded subdued, distant, so I gave her the condensed version and cut the conversation short. The next morning she called and apologized, saying she and her boyfriend had had a quarrel just before I called. I told her I was sorry to hear that, and we talked a little longer about the demands of our jobs. Yes, they did tend to raise havoc in relationships.

The office of the Mental Health Center in Madison had been closed over the weekend, so on Monday I asked Brenda to make arrangements for a court-approved Release of Information. Then I called and talked with Myrna Landau, a psychiatric social worker there. She outlined her dealings with Stephen Parker, then faxed me a summary later that afternoon:

Dane County Mental Health Services
Madison, Wisconsin 53701

Patrick McGarry, Ph.D.
Staff Psychologist
Peace River Mental Health Institute

RE: Stephen Parker

Dear Dr. McGarry:

Thank you for your telephone call regarding Stephen Parker. Your description fits him perfectly and I am relieved to hear he is hospitalized and being cared for. Our agency lost track of him in late April when we were told by his landlord that he had disappeared. As I indicated to you, we had sporadic contact with Mr. Parker for nearly a year. The circumstances surrounding this young man are as bizarre as they are detailed and I will try to present them here as succinctly as possible.

Our first contact with Stephen occurred almost a year ago when his estranged girlfriend, Jennifer Bates, sought counseling here. She had been living with him for a short while; she described their live-in arrangement as an impulsive act and said she was almost immediately aware that they were not compatible. Jennifer was a senior, a nursing major, while Stephen, I believe, was a humanities major and in his junior year. She came to our Center because Stephen continued to deny her decision to move out. Once she finally left, she was concerned about his safety because he seemed deeply depressed.

She said Stephen refused to take part in counseling so she was provided with supportive individual counseling, which was terminated when she graduated and left the area. She is now living in Minneapolis.

On one occasion Jennifer called and asked me to accompany her to the apartment while she collected her personal belongings. I thought that this would also afford me the opportunity to meet Stephen so I could urge him to come to the Center for counseling. On the way there, Jennifer told me Stephen would refuse to answer the door or the telephone. She was quite sure he was there, because the next-door neighbor was leaving food outside his door and it was disappearing.

After Jennifer pleaded for over ten minutes through the closed door, Stephen relented and opened it a crack. I was struck by how frail he looked. He was highly suspicious of our motives and I sensed a tremendous vulnerability.

He finally allowed us in. The apartment was extremely cluttered. There was almost no furniture: an unmade, very dirty bed; a formica table covered with bulging paper and plastic garbage bags, and a small black-and-white TV with a beanbag chair in front of it (reminded me of "Peanuts"). Dirty dishes filled the sink and the wastebasket was overflowing with aluminum TV dinner trays and Seagram's bottles.

Numerous paintings were stacked around the room against the walls, facing in so I could not see them, but several sculptures and figures caught my eye. One was an old department store mannequin dressed in long underwear, part of which was covered with sequins. This seemed to be a "work in progress."

It was impossible to administer any kind of mental status exam because Stephen became quite upset and tearful as Jennifer tried to find her things. I suggested that he visit the Mental Health Center, but he ignored me. When I tried to determine if he was suicidal or whether he could be a danger to anyone else, he clamped his mouth shut and refused to speak. Shortly after that he barricaded himself in the bathroom. Jennifer and I then said goodbye through the closed door and left.

My supervisor at the Center agreed that Stephen needed psychiatric care, but his status did not meet the letter of the law for hospital commitment. I did conclude, however, that he was potentially delusional and nearing a psychotic break. Jennifer continued to express great concern for his safety and said the building manager had reported to her that he was increasingly bizarre. At her request, she and I then returned to the building and the manager let us into the apartment. Stephen was not there. The refrigerator door was ajar, and we saw that the mannequin had been stuffed inside. The confetti suit, however, was gone.

I advised Jennifer and the manager that we still did not have sufficient grounds for a court commitment, but as Stephen did seem to be deteriorating, something might soon bring him to the attention of the authorities and we could then petition the court. The manager agreed to continue his surveillance, but two weeks later he called and reported no sightings of Stephen. Because the rent was two months in arrears, he had placed the few belongings in storage and changed the locks.

I can only surmise that the breakup with Jennifer was too much for Stephen to tolerate. I'm sure you'll want to contact her as she may be able to give you personal information and family history. Her address is enclosed. She works as a nurse at Methodist Hospital in Minneapolis.

From what Jennifer told me, Stephen is a talented, very sensitive young man. Good luck with him. If you have any questions or need further information, please do not hesitate to contact me.

Sincerely,

Myrna J. Landau

Myrna J. Landau, A.C.S.W.
Psychiatric Social Worker

Now that he was in clearer focus, I felt an even deeper sadness for Stephen Parker. What struck me particularly was that there had been a number of people in his life who tried to help him. But none had been able to.

I hoped I wasn't about to join the crowd.

7

"OKAY, THINGS ARE STARTING TO BREAK FOR us," Stacey said, addressing the assembled team the next day. He opened The Confetti Kid binder. "We finally have a name—" he paused and consulted the page, "—Stephen Parker, college student. We have a primary source, an ex-girlfriend in the Twin City area whom Brenda will be contacting shortly. And best of all, we're finally having a positive response to the meds we've pumped into him for the last two months. Although now he seems to have gone overboard the other way."

Stacey was right on that score. I had seen Steve earlier and the classic signs were there: sluggish, plodding movement and very prolonged speech. It took him nearly thirty seconds to say, "Good," when I'd asked, "How's it going?" But there was no doubt that Stacey's medicating skills had cleared the delusions and the catatonic regression. We'd made contact.

"Now," Stacey was saying, "we have a few problems to iron out with Mr. Parker. The first is the easiest. Joan, let's cut his Navane back ten—to thirty milligrams—and work toward a maintenance dose. The second is that his Observation period extension will be running out about the time we get the psychosis wrung out of him. I don't think he'll be a clear danger by that time, so it's possible he won't be here much longer."

Everyone was nodding. It was a familiar scenario now: Psychotics tend to get better on medication, which clears their major symptoms. But then they are often unwilling to undergo the rigors of intense treatment, especially psychotherapy, to get at what caused the break in the first place. So they frequently sign out or run away from the hospital, only to lapse back into psychosis as the medications wear off. Eventually, many have to be re-hospitalized, a cycle mental health workers witness over and over.

Stacey was looking at me. "I haven't spoken to him about it yet, but I'm going to ask Pat McGarry to be lead therapist with Mr. Parker. Which means, among other things, talking him into a voluntary commitment. If you can do that, Pat, it'll give us some time."

I nodded. "I'll see what I can do."

"He may be a tough one, but we've got to do something fast for this young man. Otherwise . . ."

He didn't have to finish. We all knew Stephen could one day lapse into the oblivion that shrouds the chronically mentally ill.

After the meeting I found Steve sitting by himself in his room.

"Can we chat a few minutes?" I asked.

He nodded slowly and started to get up.

"Let's just talk here. That okay with you?"

He eased stiffly back into the chair.

"How are you feeling? Any problems?"

He looked at me with a vague stare. ". . . I . . . think . . . I'm okay . . ." Even that minimal reply was an effort for him. Like a record playing at the wrong speed, his voice was very deep, his speech very slow and somewhat slurred.

"Things probably seem very strange for you right now. It's mostly because of the medication you're taking. Dr. Stacey has adjusted it and you'll be feeling better soon. We're glad to have you back."

He looked at me quizzically.

"Was . . . I . . . away . . . somewhere?"

"Yes, Steve, you certainly were. May I call you Steve?"

He nodded laboriously. "That's . . . my . . . name. . . ."

"Right. And your last name is—"

His head bowed in concentration.

Then, so low I had to strain to hear, he mumbled, "Parker . . . . My name is . . . Stephen Parker . . . people call me . . . Steve. . . ."

"Good! Do you remember who I am?"

He stared at me for the longest time, as if he'd never seen me before. At last he shook his head "no." Once again, I introduced myself and explained about the hospital and what had happened over the last couple of months, brushing lightly over the details of his psychosis. When I finished, he asked,

"Will I . . . be here . . . long?"

I hesitated, not really knowing how to answer. Then I told him it would most likely be a while. That he had a very serious illness, but that I hoped he would be willing to work with us. I wasn't about to get into the voluntary commitment thing yet.

All the time I talked, he watched me, his eyes narrowing in concentration.

"We'll be getting together regularly now, Steve." I smiled. "I hope you'll be feeling more like your old self soon."

"I . . . hope so . . . too. . . ."

As I left him, his eyes settled solemnly on a framed print that hung on the wall across the room. No doubt intended to infuse serenity to the occupant of the bed, it was a beautiful wooded scene with a reflecting pond in the foreground. I hoped it would bring him some peace.

Brenda cornered me later that afternoon. "Oh, I'm so mad about missing it! I knew you'd get lucky down there!"

"You don't know the half of it," I countered, teasingly.

"What? Tell me."

"I didn't put the most interesting part in the report."

"Oh?" She raised her eyebrows.

"Yeah. Kayla, the counselor who helped identify Steve, is a psychic."

"Really?"

"Uh huh. She did a reading on me, Bren."

"You're kidding. What did she say?"

"It was eerie."

Brenda's green eyes got bigger. "I want to meet her. I've always wondered about that stuff. What did she tell you?"

"About Stephen?"

"No, about you."

I stammered something and she laughed with delight.

"That good, huh? She must have been right on."

"Pretty close," I agreed. "She told me some things about myself that she couldn't possibly have known anything about."

"Hmmm." Brenda had picked up on something in my voice. "Tough though, huh?"

"Yeah."

"Well, sometime if you need a friendly ear—"

"Sure. Me too. I mean, if *you* ever want to talk," I stammered. Damn, this wasn't going well. "Anyway, I'm around." Immediately I thought better of that. I hoped she wouldn't get the wrong idea.

She gave me a long look. It was an awkward moment. Then she said, "Thanks, Pat. I appreciate that." Then she smiled. "So anyway, can I meet her sometime?"

"Kayla?"

"Yes, of course, Kayla. When will you be seeing her again?"

"I'm not sure. She wants to know how Steve does, so I told her I'd be in touch. She may come up here sometime."

"Great. Let me know if she's going to. Or if you go to Madison again, I'd like another chance to tag along."

"Okay." Yes! I thought to myself.

"Oh, before I forget, after staffing I reached Jennifer Bates. She's very concerned, but she's glad Steve's in the hospital. I didn't tell her much, just asked if she could come down sometime soon and help us fill in the puzzle. She's coming day after tomorrow. One o'clock. You free?"

"I'll make it a point to be."

"She told me one blockbuster piece of information: Both Steve's parents and his younger brother were all killed in a car accident about three years ago."

"Wow, what a blow."

"Yes."

"Hmmmm. And then the breakup with Jennifer."

"Uh huh. Two precipitating stressors."

I whistled and shook my head.

Two days later, Jennifer Bates was in Brenda's office, right on time. She was in her early twenties, and her most outstanding features were attractively waved blond hair and lovely hazel eyes with a melancholy turn. She wore a serious expression, and though she had a want-to-please quality, her low, modulated voice was tight and anxious. I immediately felt protective of her.

To help her relax, we made small talk about hospital work. Jennifer had considered psychiatric nursing, but then she'd taken this job in pediatrics instead. I could picture her comforting frightened children—she'd be good. After a time, she asked how Steve was and we told her. We laid it out for her honestly, trying not to alarm her any more than she was already, but not minimizing his situation either.

Jennifer appeared increasingly perplexed as I summed up Steve's condition. She was frowning, so I stopped, wondering where I'd lost her.

"Is something unclear?" Brenda inquired.

"I don't understand. Steve is very smart. In some ways, he's brilliant. It doesn't make sense to me that someone as smart as he is would really believe he's someone called 'The Confetti Kid' and end up on a psych ward. That confetti suit was part of a new piece he was creating." She shook her head and sighed deeply. "Highly intelligent people don't *go* crazy—do they?"

Brenda and I exchanged glances. She nodded at me to go ahead.

"Unfortunately, they do, Jennifer. It doesn't really have anything to do with how bright a person is or how much talent they have. We're all vulnerable. Given enough stress, anxiety, isolation, whatever, anyone can lose touch with reality. In this case, Steve's high intelligence means his chances for recovery are probably better, but it's no safeguard against his or anyone else's becoming severely depressed or schizophrenic or developing any other psychiatric disorder."

"Can you see that, Jennifer?" asked Brenda.

"I guess. It just seems like he should have been able to stay on top of things better. It's hard to accept that he couldn't."

"Well, it's taking him time to absorb everything that's happened," Brenda said. "Don't feel like you have to understand it all right away."

Jennifer nodded and took a deep breath. Poor thing, I thought.

We sat in silence for a while. Then I asked, "What can you tell us about Steve?"

"I really don't know where to begin—"

"It doesn't matter." Brenda's voice was soft. "Start

wherever you want and just tell us what comes to you."

She gave Brenda a grateful, if wan, smile.

"Well, I met Steve a little more than a year ago. At an art fair. He was selling his paintings. He was such a gentle person, so soft-spoken, and his paintings were . . . well, unusual. Powerful. The colors were so intense, yet diffuse at the same time. I was fascinated by them.

"Anyway, we got to talking. He was explaining things to me about art and I remember thinking, 'Gee, he's a lot like his paintings.' And he is—he's very complex. He's a deep person, full of contradictions. And he feels things very strongly. In many ways he's brilliant. But in other ways he's so naive, like a little lost puppy or something. My heart just kind of went out to him. He really touched something in me.

"So later that afternoon, when the show was almost over, I came back to his booth and helped him pack up. He had sold only one small painting. And given away four. Five, with the one he gave me that night." Jennifer smiled in a vaguely distant way as she recalled the happy moment. "I still have it," she said.

"How did Steve seem to you at that time?" Brenda asked.

"Oh, he was wonderful," Jennifer said. "He was the most unself-conscious person I'd ever met. He just turned me around completely. I come from a small town in Minnesota, you know, where my life practically revolved around studying and sports. Not even much dating—marriage and kids were off in the distant future. I was career-oriented, independent. I wanted to establish myself before I got seriously involved with anyone." She shook her head. "It didn't quite work out that way."

"How so?" I asked.

"I fell in love with Steve and the way he lived. Or the way I thought he lived. My life—which had been so routine up to then—suddenly became exciting. I'd been such a goody-goody before that all my nursing professors thought I'd gone stark raving mad. My parents were appalled, of course, and so were all my friends, but being with Steve was so . . . idyllic—picnics, talking 'til dawn, sleeping with this gentle person who knew my every thought, anticipated everything I was going to say or ask. I never thought it could be so good.

"Before long, we were living together. We were also barely surviving. I had a part-time waitressing job after classes, but Steve felt he had to work two jobs as well as go to school full-time. He drove himself too hard—like a lunatic, I was going to say."

"What can you tell us about his parents?" I asked.

"Not much, I'm afraid. He hardly ever talked about them."

"You mentioned that his parents and brother were killed in an accident," prompted Brenda. "How long was that before you met him?"

"A couple years, I guess. He never told me exactly what happened, or when. It was pretty clear he didn't want to talk about it, so I didn't push."

"Did you have any sense for how he'd adjusted to the suddenness of so many losses?" I asked.

"I—" Jennifer shook her head solemnly. "I don't think he'd dealt with it at all, really. That was my impression, at least."

"Why do you say that?" asked Brenda.

"Well, in some ways he acted as if they were still alive. It was very strange. He seemed to blame them for everything that was wrong with his life. His childhood must have been very unhappy."

"What can you tell us about it?"

"Nothing specific. He never brought it up, except for oblique comments like, 'Parents are supposed to make sure things like this don't happen.' "

"Referring to what?" I asked.

"I think it had something to do with preparing him for life, teaching him to take care of things adults have to take care of. But whenever I asked him what he meant, he'd get vague and if I pushed him, angry. So I just dropped it.'' Jennifer shrugged and then went on, ''Anyway, at first being with him was wonderful.''

''When did things start to change?'' I asked.

She sighed deeply. ''It wasn't long—two months, maybe—and then we started to disagree: He wanted a frugal life; I didn't want to live like a hippie. We got on different schedules: I lived by day; he'd be up all night—painting, sculpting, sometimes just reading or . . . well, I honestly don't know what all he did. Before long we were living totally different lives. And the few times we were together, he withdrew from me. When I tried to talk to him, he brushed me off.

''About then his paintings got strange, *really* strange. Very dark, weird colors. Abstract, you know. He'd never paint landscapes or pictures of things you could recognize, just these bold splashes of color. But the colors went from being beautiful and bright to murky and kind of scary. Anyway, he'd disappear into the back room—his studio—and I'd hear him working in there hour after hour. He would just exhaust himself.''

Jennifer paused and wiped away a tear. ''I think he was avoiding me. Between our opposite schedules and his painting, it got so we didn't speak for days, sometimes. Even when we were both home, hours would go by without one of us acknowledging the other. It was pretty weird, now that I look back on it. We were living in the same apartment, but we weren't really living together, if you know what I mean. It's sad. What we had was so beautiful, and then all of a sudden it was like somebody pulled the plug and our love just drained away. Neither of us could stop it.''

We sat in silence a few moments before Bren and I asked, virtually in unison, ''Can you tell us anything else?''

All three of us laughed and it brightened the room briefly. Jennifer looked slightly more positive again.

"Well, one thing about Steve, he needs people around him who are worse off than he is. You know, people in trouble or having some sort of personal problem. He filled the emotional vacuum in me—he rescued me. Except that as I grew stronger, and got myself together, my strength seemed to squeeze him. It took me quite a while to see what was going on. It was like he needed me to be very dependent on him and, as long as I was, things were okay. But when I began to question how we were living, or try to take part in a decision, he felt threatened. And he'd pull back from me.

"As I look back now, I think the qualities I found so fascinating at first became so exaggerated I got scared. And then something odd happened. Not long before we split up, Steve did an about-face: The more I pulled back, the harder he tried to hold on. He got frantic—painting me pictures, writing me poems, notes, letters, pouring his heart out. He bought me little gifts or flowers. And all the time I was miserable. I knew I had to get away, but I was terrified of what he'd do if I left. He was acting so . . . strange—"

Jennifer's voice broke and tears trickled down her cheeks. Brenda handed her some tissues and after a time, she went on.

"He would get terribly depressed and say things like I'd be better off without him or it'd be better if he was dead, too. I was afraid he was thinking about suicide. Then he'd switch and be the complete opposite—he'd talk about trying for a show in a Chicago gallery, or getting a loft in New York City, and on and on like that. He was trying so hard to cover up, but I could see his pain oozing out of every pore. It was horrible.

"I told you Steve feels things very deeply—I've never known anyone so sensitive. And he's always expecting to be rejected. He's so talented, but he has absolutely no confidence in himself. Toward the end there, he'd go at his work in a frenzy. It was like he was possessed." She stopped for a minute.

"I didn't see it, but—he was going crazy then, wasn't he?"

"Sounds like it," I agreed.

"How were you doing at the time?" Brenda asked.

Jennifer sighed deeply. Clearly it was a strain to relive all this. "Not well. By then I was totally depressed myself, crying all the time. I looked like a hag and didn't care. Studying was impossible. Finally, one of my friends suggested I get some counseling. That's ironic, isn't it? People thought I was the one going crazy—" She wiped at her tears again.

"Is that when you went to the clinic and saw Myrna?" Brenda finally prompted.

"Yes. I needed help. But Steve needed it more. He was drinking a lot then. You couldn't reason with him. Myrna really tried to get him to the clinic, but he wouldn't go. That's why I finally took the job in Minneapolis. I was so frustrated and depressed around Steve, for my own sanity I had to get away."

Jennifer shivered slightly. "I thought I'd put the whole disaster behind me. But when Brenda called on Monday, it all came flooding back."

"How do you feel about seeing Steve today, Jennifer?" Brenda asked. "Do you want to?"

"I'm not sure if I'm up for that."

"You don't have to," I said. "He's not expecting you. We just wondered if it was important to you to see him."

"No need to push it," Brenda added.

Jennifer seemed immensely relieved at that. We talked a bit longer, and then, as we began to say our goodbyes, Jennifer said,

"Oh, I almost forgot." She pulled a slip of paper from her purse. "I made a copy of this for you—it's the last poem Steve wrote to me. I still cry when I read it."

Brenda took the paper and read it, then soberly handed it to me.

Robert Lane

Last night when you said you were leaving . . .
It felt like some great giant
Was reaching down into me—
        Wrenching out my heart

The thriving young tree of our love,
Ripped out
Roots strewn all about
        The gaping hole.

I cried
For my mother—
Her voice
        Her touch

Funny how,
At a time like that
A grown man falls back
        On the love he first remembers.

And now
        I've
            lost
                you
                    both.

"You can see why I feel so guilty," Jennifer sighed shakily. "If it hadn't been for me—"

"No, Jennifer. Don't blame yourself. Steve's problems were a long time in the making," I said. "He was on the way down before you even met him."

"Still, I think I pushed him down faster."

We encouraged her to consider more counseling and promised to let her know of Steve's progress. Then Brenda walked her out to the reception area. I wanted to take some time to think about what Steve's life must have been like during the last couple of years. But I pushed those thoughts to the back of my mind and went to the ward to pick up my next appointment, a middle-aged man with severe depression. I was feeling a bit melancholy myself.

Later that afternoon I was walking to the parking lot when Brenda caught up with me and fell in step.

"Quite a meeting, wasn't it?" she said.

I nodded.

"And quite a poem—calling out to the feminine, a good Jungian would say." She stopped walking, and when I turned she was looking at me with concern. "That was very difficult for you to read, wasn't it, Pat?"

I nodded grimly. "Do you think Jennifer noticed?"

Brenda reached out and gently brushed my arm. "No," she said softly, "she was far too wrapped up in her own feelings."

"But you—"

Brenda nodded. "I knew it would touch you. It did me, too. Very personally."

Her voice became husky and her face looked very sad. I saw that she was near tears. What was going on with her?

"Hey, what's wrong?"

Brenda shook her head and moved away, crossing the lot to her car.

"Bren?" I called out.

"I'm okay, Pat." Her voice choked. She didn't sound okay. "See you tomorrow." She ducked into her car, flipped a quick wave, and sped away, leaving me staring after her.

8

AS THE EFFECTS OF THE MEDICATION ADJUSTMENT BEcame more pronounced, Steve's alertness improved dramatically. When it was time to make my move, I scheduled an appointment for him. Once he was settled in the recliner beside my desk, I handed him a box.

"First off, I want to return something that belongs to you, Steve. Thought you might like to have this back."

He took the package and carefully folded back the tissue paper. Inside was the spangled underwear suit and cape in all their multicolored glory. And the glitzy tennis shoes. His fingers moved lightly, caressingly over the material. He looked up at me and smiled.

"Thank you."

"You're welcome. It's special to you, isn't it?"

"Yes." He was smoothing the creases almost reverently.

I asked him the standard query: "Steve, what's your understanding of what happened to you?"

He fidgeted a bit and then, in a low voice, he said, "I guess I had . . . some sort of nervous breakdown."

"What does that mean to you, Steve? What's a 'nervous breakdown?' "

"I don't know exactly. My nerves were shot—I was tired and depressed. Just wasn't myself for quite a while."

"Uh huh. Anything else?"

"Not really. I kind of went off the deep end. I remember feeling pretty confused . . ." His voice trailed off, and he looked at me questioningly. "So that's it? I had a nervous breakdown?"

"In a sense, yes, Steve, although we don't call it that anymore. You had a severe psychotic break."

"Right. I went crazy."

I nodded. "Actually, your personality structure—the mind part of your brain—collapsed. Everything got terribly scrambled, you began believing you were someone called The Confetti Kid—" Here I motioned toward the uniform he was holding in his lap, "who apparently had extraordinary powers. Actually, the day you came here, you tried to fly out that window." I gestured toward the big thermopane.

He glanced quickly at it, then resumed smoothing the creases in his confetti suit.

"Do you remember any of that?"

He shook his head "no," but avoided my gaze.

"Well, that's not surprising." Then I added, "You haven't been very communicative, either. We had to rely on a bit of luck to find out who you are."

He looked up, perplexed. I explained how we had identified him, ending with, "And finally, we talked with Jennifer."

"Jennifer?" He was stunned. "She was here?"

"Yes, earlier this week."

"How come she didn't see me? She probably wants to get back together, huh?" he asked hopefully.

"No, Steve," I said gently. "She didn't suggest either of those things."

"What did she say, then?"

"She told Brenda and me what happened before she left Madison. And that leaving you was very difficult for her."

He stared at the floor.

"I'd guess the breakup with Jennifer was probably one of the things that pushed you over the edge."

"One of the things?" He looked up sharply.

"You've taken some pretty hard hits the last couple of years. Your parents' and brother's deaths, college not going well, having to work two jobs—that's a lot of stress. And, from what everyone tells me, you have a deeply sensitive nature. The effect was cumulative."

Steve seemed unconcerned. Offhand.

"So, how long do I have to stay here?" he asked.

None of what I said had penetrated.

"That's somewhat up to you. You're coming to the end of your court-ordered commitment, but we'd like for you to stay on as a voluntary patient for the time being."

"You mean I can leave any time?"

"No, not quite. You still have a couple weeks left on your commitment. Besides, Dr. Stacey is still getting you regulated on a good maintenance dose of medicine."

"But that shouldn't take long. And then I can leave?"

"Steve, wait a second." I held up my hand. "What I've been telling you isn't registering. It would be a big mistake for you to leave too soon. You have some serious weaknesses in your personality. They need to be strengthened or this may happen again—"

"It won't happen again," he interrupted. He shook his head decisively.

"How can you say that, Steve? You're just coming out of a major break. You've been completely bonkers for weeks, crawling around the seclusion room, grunting like an animal. You don't even remember most of it—" A touch of exasperation made the remark more sarcastic than I'd intended. I could sense he was wanting to seal it all over, deny that it had happened at all.

"That's just it—if I *was* that crazy, don't you think I *would* remember? I can't believe I wouldn't."

"Steve," I tried again, making a real effort to be patient. "Trust me. You completely lost it. You were flat-out nuts. In fact, we videotaped you from time to time while you were in seclusion and later during your catatonic state—"

"You taped me?" he demanded.

"Yes. For training purposes. But perhaps it would be a good idea if you saw the tape. Would you like to?"

"Sounds pretty weird." He fell silent. Finally he looked at me. "Yeah, I think I would. I don't believe—"

"Okay, maybe sometime next week. If that'll help convince you to stay, great. We need to talk about what happened to you, and your delusion about being The Confetti Kid."

"Delusion? What do you mean? You saying I'm not The Confetti Kid?" An edge had come into his voice now.

I backed off. "Well, I realize The Confetti Kid is part of you, Steve. An important part. But it got a little scary when you tried to fly out that window. That's a delusion—thinking you have special powers. Were voices telling you to do that?"

He looked up at me sharply. I'd guessed right.

"That's an auditory hallucination. The mind playing tricks on the senses."

"What kind of tricks?"

"You start hearing imaginary voices, or believing that you feel odd things: bugs under your skin, or your food tastes off so you think it's poisoned. Or people are talking about you, or they're after you. Or you smell strange odors. They're all symptoms of psychosis."

"How do you know those things aren't real?"

"Maybe, but I would guess the voices were seriously interfering with your artwork, because psychosis causes very peculiar jamming and distortion. Of vision, hearing, touch. The mind gets so confused it starts making up its own dialogue. Then it's hard to know what's real and what isn't. Do you remember these kinds of things happening to you?"

He nodded slightly. "Yeah, but I can take care of myself now. What happened was just a freak thing. It won't happen again."

"Steve, right now all the really crazy stuff is being suppressed by the medicine you're taking. But that doesn't begin to deal with the root of your problems—the way you think and the way you get along with people. If you were to stop taking the medications now, crazy thoughts would zoom right back in again. We don't want that to happen."

He was shaking his head, obviously not accepting what I was telling him.

"I'll be okay. Besides, I don't really need to get along with other people. They leave me alone, I leave them alone—"

"Steve," I interrupted, "if you think I'm going to believe that for one moment, you'd better think again. Your need for others is very obvious. Who are you trying to con, anyway? Yourself? That's part of your problem. You're not fooling anyone else."

He shifted uncomfortably. I sat back, telling myself to cool it. I'd probably pressed too hard.

Finally he broke the silence. "I really don't understand what happened. Lots of guys break up with their girlfriends, right? Have their family die, get hassled. And they don't end up in the nut house. Why did it happen to me? I really want to know that. Can you tell me why?"

This was a hopeful sign and I pounced.

"There are a lot of ideas on that, Steve, but no one knows for certain. Some people think a person inherits a kind of genetic timebomb that clicks down to a precise moment and then goes off in the personality. One day they're fine, and the next things start to change drastically in the way they perceive the world. Others, like Dr. Stacey, believe there's a chemical imbalance, where the communication between the brain's cells—the neurons—is badly disrupted. Or maybe the brain's structure changes somehow—some agent makes cells change or die off somewhere deep in the brain, so eventually the mind can no longer function."

He seemed interested. "But no one knows why one person goes crazy and another doesn't?"

"No. Dr. Farrell and others believe that an illness like yours is a heroic attempt to survive. A way of preserving and renewing the creative spirit. So there's even a philosophical explanation, if you will. Those are the kinds of issues we'd explore together in therapy."

"Unreal!" Steve was shaking his head. "It's a whole world I never knew existed. It might be a kick to do it sometime, but I don't have much time right now. How long would I have to stay for that?"

"That's everyone's first question the minute they start to feel better. They can't wait to bail out of this place."

"Can you blame us? So—how long?"

"It's difficult to say. All I can do is give you our recommendations and hope you'll negotiate with us."

"I'm listening."

"You've got a serious psychiatric disorder. Your personality structure is still very brittle. I don't mean to be evasive, but the length of time will be determined largely by your progress in therapy. We want to make sure this doesn't happen again. It's not good for people to have repeated psychotic attacks. When they do, the mind's chemistry seems to change, for the worse. That may be how people become chronically mentally ill."

"You're not implying I could become chronically mentally ill, I hope," he said. "You're just trying to scare me."

"Not at all, Steve. But at this point there's no way to predict what might happen if you go back to Madison and try to pick up where you left off. What really concerns the psychiatric team is that you were pretty delusional and it took a lot longer than it should have for your psychosis to respond to the meds and begin clearing. That's a real negative.

"On the positive side, though," I went on, "you've got some real strengths: You're young, probably in the superior range of intelligence, and you've got a lot of artistic talent.

From that standpoint, you're in good shape. But unless you do something now, there are no guarantees that in a few months, or maybe a year, you won't become psychotic again."

"But what good would staying here do?"

"As a voluntary patient, you could begin intensive psychotherapy. Take a hard look at your personality structure. Try to find the flaws and correct them. You'd dive deep, with me as your guide. I'd help you learn as much about yourself as possible so you're stabilized and strengthened enough to withstand future bouts of stress. This state is pretty foresighted, realizing it's better to invest intensive therapy and care in someone your age rather than turn you into a thirty-day, pill-popping wonder who bounces in and out of hospitals the rest of your life. Take advantage of it, Steve."

"And how long would that take?" he pressed.

"Depends on a number of things—how hard you work at it, what you find when you get in there, and how long it takes for you to make the necessary changes. Figure at least six months—"

"Six months!"

"At least."

"Are you kidding? You want me to stay in this prison for another six months? You're the one that's crazy if you think I'm going to stick around this place that long!"

"Hold on, Steve. I didn't say you'd have to stay in the hospital all that time, though you'd have to be relatively close by. And as soon as you're ready, we'd help you find a place to live in town, and you would continue therapy with me and stay in touch with the hospital's outpatient program."

"But what about school? I have to go back to Madison."

"That probably wouldn't be a good idea right now. You should get some therapy first, then perhaps you could attend college around here for a semester or two before going back to Madison. We'd be monitoring and working with you as long as we—and you—felt you were learning from the experience.''

Steve said nothing. He looked stunned and resentful, but I went ahead.

''Bear in mind that it took years for all this to build up to the point of a psychotic blow-off. You can't expect to repair all the damage in a few days or weeks. To do it right will take time. And a lot of effort on your part.

''So now, just think about it, Steve. Consider very carefully what may be a major crossroad in your life.''

He glared back at me.

Things didn't work out quite the way I intended. I made arrangements for Steve to view the tape, but whenever I ran into him he made excuses about not having time. Then he seemed to be avoiding me. I chalked it up to his ambivalence about staying and decided not to pressure him.

Several days later I was paged to Cameron One and Two. When I got to the nursing station, Joan and Brenda were conversing quietly. They looked concerned.

''What's up?''

''Steve's evidently been learning the ropes from some of our resident experts,'' Joan said. She held out a sheet of paper.

It was a handwritten note, addressed to the hospital superintendent:

> I, Stephen Parker, being of sound mind and body, do hereby demand immediate release from the Peace River Mental Health Institute.

The signature was a rather grandiose flourish.

''I thought this might happen,'' I said. ''Still, I was hoping.''

"We'll have to schedule a hearing with Judge Hearns within three days," Brenda noted, always the planner.

I nodded. "Any refusal of medication?" I asked Joan.

"No," she replied, "Not yet, anyway. If he does go off it, for sure he'll slip back into his delusional system."

"But that may take too long," I said.

"Longer than two days," she agreed.

Brenda was shaking her head. "I have a bad feeling about this. Steve's a savvy guy. He can look pretty good on the surface, at least for the duration of a hearing. Now that he knows how to play the game, I doubt we'll be able to keep him."

"You're probably right," I said. "It'll be hard for Judge Hearns not to let him go at this stage. Even though he saw him when he was really crazy and knows he's likely to revert to that."

"Yeah, unfortunately it doesn't matter what he was like before," Brenda replied. "By law, all the judge can rule on is Steve's present condition. Is he a danger to society? Or to himself?"

"Protecting the patient's rights really hampers us sometimes," Joan sighed. "I see it all the time—not being able to hospitalize someone who desperately needs it, and having to discharge people too soon."

"Yeah, it's tough," Brenda said. "Families have to watch someone deteriorate and can't do a thing about it."

Joan nodded.

"Judge Hearns is sympathetic. He's a good judge." Brenda frowned. "But Steve's probably gonna walk."

More like run, I thought.

9

BY MID-SEPTEMBER, STEVE HAD AN HOUR OF LIBERTY A day and he usually used it to wander around the grounds. Over the past couple of weeks I had occasionally caught sight of him from my office window, sitting on a bench at the edge of the woods, aloof and always alone. Other times he just walked, a solitary figure, his hands plunged deep into the pockets of his faded cords, his Levi jacket collar turned up.

He continued to avoid me, so the day before the hearing, I timed it so I was on the ward as he signed out. When I asked if I could tag along for a while, he didn't say no. I fell in step, making small talk until we'd left the building and reached his bench by the woods.

"So tomorrow's the big day, huh?" I said.

"I guess."

"What do you think your chances are?"

"Good. Probably great." His voice was flat, devoid of emotion.

"You may be right. But I have to tell you I'm deeply concerned."

"Yeah? About what?"

"You need treatment. And this is a good place to get it."

"Yeah?"

"Yes. We can help you—if you let us."

"I don't need help." His voice was low, resentful. "I want to get out of this place, back to my old life. Back to my art."

"I can understand that, Steve. Maybe it's only our timetables that are different. I'm just not comfortable with your leaving now."

"Well, I'm not comfortable being here, okay?" he said sarcastically.

"I know it's hard, Steve. But really, you're not ready to leave."

"Why not?"

"Being The Confetti Kid was a fantasy that got away from you. Your real self, like the real world, got too painful. So you reinvented yourself and gave yourself special powers. Trouble is, magical thinking doesn't work—it's only make-believe. You need to understand that and be able to live in the real world, get on with having some happiness in your life—"

"Happiness?" he snorted, a short, bitter bark. "That's a laugh. There's no such thing as happiness!"

"Of course there is," I countered. "You just haven't had much of a chance to experience it."

He didn't answer, just sat gazing through the trees toward the thin ribbon of river that glimmered in the distance.

"Will you let me help you?" I asked gently.

"It's stupid. Useless to even try." The tone was caustic, bitter.

"You've been badly hurt, Steve. There's so much pain—"

He whirled toward me and his mouth opened, then clamped shut. His eyes were tearing up and he seemed on the verge of either exploding or crying.

Then he got up and strode quickly away into the woods.

What else could I have said to get through to him? Nothing, I told myself. It was up to him now. A deep resignation settled in on me as I walked back across the grounds to my office.

The next day, Friday, Judge Hearns and his court reporter arrived promptly in the Peace River conference room, followed by the attorney ad litem, who'd been appointed by the Court to represent Steve. Quite a few staff members were there for the hearing, and Ben Farrell was conversing with Stacey. Looking uncomfortable, Steve was sitting alone in a corner. I pulled up a chair and sat down next to him. He nodded stiffly.

The Judge opened with a brief description of the hearing, where it was being held, for what purpose, and who was present. The precipitating events were reviewed in sterile form. Then Brenda presented a quick social history, after which Stacey and I summarized our contacts with Steve, the diagnosis, and our treatment recommendations. When we were finished, the Judge turned to Steve.

"You seem to have responded well to the treatment here, Mr. Parker. The last time I saw you, you told me to call you 'The Confetti Kid.' Do you remember?"

Steve smiled sheepishly and shook his head "no."

"You're not using that name now, is that correct?"

"No, Your Honor," he answered in a soft voice. "I mean yes, that's correct."

"And what are your plans if you are released from the hospital?"

Steve gave a brief explanation of what he would do: Return to Madison, register for classes, pursue his artwork.

I had to admire him. He'd pulled himself together amazingly well. This was a pretty stressful event, yet he was conducting himself with aplomb. His metamorphosis wasn't lost on Judge Hearns, either. I could tell that he was impressed by Steve's appearance and demeanor. And by how much change there had been since he'd last seen him.

"Well, Doctors—" Judge Hearns addressed Stacey and me, "for the record I need to hear opinions as to whether the patient, Stephen Parker, can provide for his own basic needs. And does he present a danger to either himself or to others? Is there any risk that he might become violent and injure himself or others?"

Stacey and I exchanged looks.

"Your Honor," I began, "at this time it is our opinion that Mr. Parker is not potentially assaultive or, for that matter, suicidal or homicidal. There is, however, a question in our minds as to whether he can care for himself. At the moment, the antipsychotic drugs are controlling the symptoms. Our concern is underlying pathology. He says that he no longer believes he's The Confetti Kid. I'm not sure I believe him—I think he may be telling us what he thinks we want to hear. He says he's cured. I'm equally sure that he's not."

I paused and let the court reporter, whose fingers were whipping over the little keyboard, catch up. "It is the opinion of the treatment team that Mr. Parker needs further treatment. In particular, he needs in-depth, uncovering-type psychotherapy. He needs assistance in understanding what has happened to him and he needs to learn to cope more effectively with the inevitable conflicts of life."

Out of the corner of my eye, I could see Steve staring at me, using all his concentration to appear calm.

Judge Hearns watched him for a few moments, then asked,

"Dr. Stacey, do you concur with Dr. McGarry's opinion?"

"Yes, Your Honor, I do. I think it will be only a matter of time before Mr. Parker's psychosis reasserts itself."

"And is it your considered opinion that this treatment you feel Mr. Parker needs cannot be provided on an outpatient basis?"

"For the foreseeable future, I believe that it cannot be, Your Honor."

The judge turned to Steve, who coughed nervously.

"Have you anything further to add before the Court makes a ruling in this matter?"

Steve's voice was low. "I do not agree that I need more treatment. I admit that I was pretty screwed up when I came here, but I'm back on track. Now I just want to go back to Madison. Start living again. I'm fine—they've done all they can for me. It's up to me now to prove I can make it on the outside."

The room was totally silent for about four minutes as the judge shuffled some papers and pondered his decision. At last he said, "Well, gentlemen and gentlewomen, I don't know what to say. As you know, I'm bound by law to continue commitment only if the patient presents a clear and present danger, or cannot care for himself. I respect the expert medical and psychological opinions that have been offered here today, and I am inclined, from my own experience with similar cases, to agree with your assessments as to the probable outcome of release at this time.

"However, under the circumstances, I do not feel we can force treatment on Mr. Parker. He has turned a deaf ear toward your pleas and there is nothing in his testimony today to suggest the presence of a psychosis. If anything, during these proceedings he has made a convincing case for his recovery and release. Furthermore, it is the Court's opinion that until such time as Mr. Parker can appreciate the need for therapy, and becomes willing to cooperate in his treatment, there is absolutely nothing anyone will be able to do for him.

"Therefore, I must rule—"

"Excuse me, Your Honor."

"Yes, Dr. Farrell?"

"I wonder if I might ask Mr. Parker a few questions?"

Steve's head jerked up and his eyes fixed intently on Ben.

"For what purpose?" asked Judge Hearns.

"I believe that the Court should have certain other information before making a ruling."

The judge looked perplexed. He turned to Steve. "Would you be willing to answer a few more questions, Mr. Parker?"

"I guess so," he answered.

"Very well, then, Dr. Farrell. I will allow some additional questions."

Ben smiled at Steve disarmingly.

"Well, Steve, I'm glad to hear you feel we've been able to help you."

"Yes," Steve replied cautiously. "I'm cured, and I do have you people to thank for that."

"I see," said Ben, leaning forward in his chair. "And what has happened to 'The Confetti Kid?' "

Steve shrugged.

"If I recall, Dr. McGarry returned the confetti suit to you a couple of weeks ago. Is that correct?"

"Yes, that's right. He gave it back," Steve answered slowly, uncertain as to where the questioning was leading. We all were.

"Well," continued Ben, "Would you go down to your room and get it, please?"

"Uh," Steve was puzzled and glanced uneasily at me. I raised my eyebrows. What was Ben up to?

Steve looked across the room at Ben. "But why? What's my confetti suit got to do with my discharge?"

"I'm just curious. Seems to me that if you're not The Confetti Kid any more, you don't need the suit any longer, do you? So run down and get it, will you?"

Steve turned to Judge Hearns. "Your Honor, do I have to do that?"

The judge addressed Ben. "Dr. Farrell, I fail to see the relevance of this line of questioning."

"Please bear with me a few more minutes, Your Honor. I believe my reasons will become apparent shortly."

"Very well. This is somewhat unusual, but you may retrieve your suit, Mr. Parker."

Looking irritated, Steve got up and left the room. We waited in silence, Ben scribbling a few notes on his pad. In a few minutes Steve returned with the confetti suit folded neatly in his arms, sneakers on top.

Ben motioned him over and took the suit from him, although Steve was visibly reluctant to give it up. While Ben carefully examined the costume, the cape, and the shoes, Steve shifted nervously from one foot to the other.

As Ben inspected the suit, he seemed to affect surprise that Steve had stayed next to him and was hovering there. Finally, he looked at him and nodded.

"Thank you, Steve. That's all. You can take your seat again."

Steve looked confused.

"But I want my suit back. I can't leave without it."

"Oh? Why not? You won't need it now, will you?"

"No, but—"

"I mean, you've told us you're no longer The Confetti Kid, right? So I thought you might want to donate it to the Institute Museum. You know," he said, giving Steve a warm smile, "Peace River has never had a Confetti Kid before. You're the first."

"But it's my suit, *my property!"* His voice rose.

"Yes, yes, I know that, Steve. But you won't need it any more, will you? Only The Confetti Kid can wear it, isn't that right? But it's so . . . beautiful and unusual, it would be a shame to throw it away. After all your work to make it. And it would make a fine addition to the hospital mu—"

"No! It's ***my*** suit. You have no right to it! Give it back!" He lunged for it, but Ben pulled it away.

Steve's face flushed. His expression was panicky, and threatening.

"Give . . . me . . . back . . . my . . . Confetti . . . suit!" he snarled menacingly. "You have no right . . . ***give it back!***

I'm the ***only person*** in the world who has a right to it!!'' he said with contempt. ''It has ***power!*** It ***protects*** me! ***I NEED it—it's mine!''***

Suddenly, with his fists clenched, he boxed the air threateningly, the whites of his bloodless knuckles like ivory bullets. His eyes were wild. The only sound in the room was his gasping breath. The rest of us were holding ours. Then he screamed in mounting hysteria:

''I am a man of destiny—how dare you tamper with the way things are meant to be?''

Knowing he had made his point, Ben held the suit out. ''Okay, Steve. Here, take it,'' he said softly.

Steve didn't move. He stood stock-still, all color drained from his face. His arms descended to his sides, fists clenched. His eyes were riveted to the confetti suit.

Ben bore in gently. ''You do still believe you're The Confetti Kid, don't you, Steve? That you have special powers. Isn't that right?''

After a long moment, Steve nodded dispiritedly. A single tear formed and rolled down his cheek. I saw it drop onto his shirt. The stress had put him in shock, and I was afraid it might also tip him back into psychosis.

I got up and crossed the room, took the suit from Ben, and offered it to Steve. He was like a robot as he took it from me. Then I put my arm on his shoulder and steered him back to his chair. Head on his chest, shoulders slumped, he collapsed, pulling the suit close to his chest.

I knew that in his mind, The Confetti Kid was the stuff of drama, of legends. He'd buried his identity in his splendid warrior costume. As I watched his pathetic, hunched figure, I felt the bond all of us share in our deep need to vanquish chaos and keep ourselves safe from the frightening randomness of life.

Steve's inspired creation of a belief system that would fight the forces of evil, so carefully contrived and so symbolic, was what had drawn me to him in the early days of his hospitalization. Even then, I must have sensed what he stood for, that collective dream of humanity for a peaceful world, safe from harm. But for Steve, the twin forces of good and evil—perennially clashing within the individual as well as the universe—had shattered him. And now Ben had shredded his delusional refuge.

Judge Hearns cleared his throat.

"I hope you understand, Mr. Parker," he said, "that everyone in this room wants to help you. No one would like for you to leave this hospital more than these people would. They truly care about you, no matter what you may think. But at the same time, they know that if you leave now, it will be only a matter of time before the delusion takes over completely again, and you are out doing whatever it is you think you have to do when you throw confetti—"

"No, *nooooooo,"* Steve howled. *"Noooooo!"*

It was a primitive, forlorn, excruciating moan.

Judge Hearns paused until the wailing subsided.

"Mr. Parker, please listen to me. This is a most difficult call to make here. What the Court has witnessed just now supports the need for further treatment. On the other hand," the judge addressed the rest of us, "the Court is not convinced that Mr. Parker is unable to care for himself. And no evidence has been submitted to substantiate that at this time he presents a danger to himself or anyone else."

Uh oh, I thought. Here it comes.

"So, although the Court would strongly recommend—as strongly as possible—that Mr. Parker remain in the hospital to continue treatment, it is not within the purview of the Court to mandate this."

The room was very still.

"Therefore," Judge Hearns continued, "Mr. Parker's involuntary commitment to this hospital is hereby revoked. The patient is to be discharged at his request."

He looked at Steve. "Do you understand the Court's finding, Mr. Parker?"

Steve remained hunched over, immobile. At last he looked up. "You mean—I'm free to go?"

"Yes. Unless, of course, you decide to stay on as a voluntary patient. On the basis of what we have seen here, it is my strongest recommendation that you do that."

"I can leave?"

He looked over at me, amazement written across his face.

Judge Hearns sighed and tapped the gavel lightly on the table.

"This hearing is adjourned. Good luck, Mr. Parker."

Steve was rocking slightly back and forth, staring unseeingly ahead.

Chet and I practically carried him back to his room. We left him curled up on the bed, hugging the confetti suit almost ferociously with both arms.

I fully expected to find Steve packing his few possessions when I looked in on him a few hours later. Instead, he was pacing the room, arms folded, an intent look of concentration on his face. He barely acknowledged me.

"Are you okay?" I asked.

He shot a quick glance at me and kept walking. Then the words came in a rush, laden with a tension that was just beneath the surface.

"That was so close, my god that was close, I came so close, so close, oh, I can't believe how close." He repeated this several times.

"What, Steve? What was so close?"

"Ohhh, I almost—it's a good thing for Dr. Farrell that The Confetti Kid stepped in."

"Oh?"

Again, the agitated look. "Yeah. Dr. Farrell was just this close—" he held his thumb and index finger up, nearly touching, "—this close." He stopped, highly distraught.

I sat down on his bed, and after a time I prodded him, "What almost happened, Steve?"

His eyes were wild. I felt my anxiety rise a notch as he covered the space between us in three big steps and sat down beside me. His voice was a terse whisper:

"Dr. Farrell could have been destroyed if The Confetti Kid hadn't saved him."

Wow. I realized that Steve's sense of reality was torn in a way I'd never understood. How should I respond? If he'd assaulted Ben, the outcome of the hearing would have been entirely different. Now I was more concerned than ever about his leaving.

"Steve—" I began.

"I came so close! I almost killed Dr. Farrell. I wanted to. I really wanted to—"

And then he practically dissolved before my eyes. He hurled himself face-down on the bed, his sobs muffled as he buried his head in the pillow. I put my hand on his heaving shoulder and just left it there.

A few minutes later, the sobbing subsided and he came up for air. He was still weeping, but more quietly now.

"Is there anything I can do, Steve?"

He pressed his head into the pillow again and shook his head back and forth.

"I hate to see you leave like this," I said. "But any time you get in a jam out there, or want to talk, I hope you'll call me, Steve. Collect if you have to. Okay? You'll remember that?"

He nodded into the pillow.

I gave him a card from my wallet. "My number's on here, okay?"

He nodded again.

"See you then, buddy." I gave his shoulder a squeeze. "Take it easy. I hope things work out for you."

I got up in the half-light and headed toward the door.

"Mac?" A muffled voice from the pillow.

"Yes?" I smiled. Only my best friend in high school had ever called me that.

Steve raised his head. "I'm scared . . . so scared. ***I am so scared."***

"I know, Steve. Believe me, I know that."

"Mac? I've been thinking." He rolled over, but I could barely make out his face in the late afternoon shadows.

"What?"

"Maybe I should stick around awhile."

"Oh?"

"Just until things are a little better."

I couldn't believe what I was hearing.

"Could I? I mean, the judge said I could go. But does that mean I have to?"

"Not at all, Steve. You're free to stay as a voluntary patient. But it has to be your decision."

"Well, okay then. Maybe I'll stay. Just until I get over this scariness."

"Sounds like you'd better stay on then, Steve. It's asking too much for you to try and go it alone right now."

"Yeah."

"You take it easy then and Monday we'll sign you in, okay?"

"Okay."

"And give some thought to therapy, will you please, Steve?"

"Maybe."

"Just think about it. And Steve—"

"Yeah?"

"Good decision, buddy."

The sobbing resumed.

That weekend, on an impulse, I decided to drive to Madison. Before I left I called Brenda to see if she wanted to go with me, but she wasn't home. Too bad. I left a message on her machine and took off.

Once I hit Madison I called Kayla from a pay phone on

campus. I was relieved when she answered, and then asked if I had time to stop by. Actually, she was the main reason I'd come.

A few minutes later Kayla met me at her door and ushered me into the Victorian parlor. I briefly recounted the events of the last week and asked if she had any suggestions. The intense blue eyes were troubled.

"I don't have Stephen's permission to enter his aura . . . " she paused, frowning, "but let me see if I can contact his guide."

"His guide?"

"Yes. Guides are spirits that protect people. Everyone has them."

"Oh?"

"Yes. They often act in our behalf. Stephen had a guide with him when I saw him."

Kayla closed her eyes, meditating. I was glad, because I was clearly skeptical and was afraid my face would betray me. As I watched, her breathing slowed, and her expression became tranquil.

All was quiet for several minutes and I began to fidget. Then she frowned slightly and leaned forward. Abruptly, she opened her eyes and leveled them on me.

"Stephen's guide agrees—Stephen should stay in the hospital. There is so much negative energy inside him that it's going to be touch and go for quite some time."

"Does the guide have any explicit suggestions—" I stopped, feeling completely foolish. I couldn't quite believe what I'd asked. Here I was, a trained Ph.D. scientist, acting as if some kind of supernatural entity could tell me how to treat a patient.

Kayla sensed my hesitation. "It's all right. The only way you learn is to inquire." She smiled in her benign way. "According to Stephen's guide, much of what has happened is his karma. His fate, if you will. There are powers operating here that—"

She stopped, as if listening, and then gave me a long, steady look. Unnerving.

"I am to tell you this . . ." her voice sounded different and I felt myself tensing. "When Stephen's world started breaking up, he was very distraught. The severity of this experience released other forces from the depths—dark energies that burst forth and overwhelmed him. Many urgent, uncontrollable impulses—hatred, rage, evil thoughts toward himself and others—reached such intensity that his young mind could not fend them off. That's why he became insane."

"Incredible," was all I could muster.

"Nevertheless, it is true. It happens more often than people know." She hesitated. "But you have doubts." It wasn't a question.

"Well, not exactly," I hedged. "You're using different words, but many psychologists acknowledge primeval, base energies and their potential for destruction. I think of them as hostility, selfishness, malice."

Kayla smiled. "Those are all dark forces, Patrick. Negative energies. They can be very powerful."

"Yes. I guess anyone who's worked in a mental hospital or a prison would have a tough time denying what you say. I have a colleague, a forensic psychologist, who says when he examines a serial murderer or a sexual psychopath, he feels a force of evil and cruelty so pervasive that it almost engulfs him."

Kayla nodded.

"So I guess it is a kind of energy," I said. "I just never thought of it quite that way before."

"What we say," Kayla continued, "is that all human beings have an arsenal of powers. Some are positive and beneficial, others are potentially malevolent, and sometimes destructive. The negative ones must be gradually understood, so they can be acknowledged and mastered. Just as you are a teacher, a psychotherapist, so do we have our teachers, or shamans, as they are called. The shaman serves as protector, making sure the beginner does not try to go so far as to be hurt."

"So you believe that Steve went in too far alone?"

"Yes. Without knowledge or guidance. The journey into deep understanding is an arduous one, fraught with danger if the power is not properly channeled. Or if the negative energies somehow prevail. A person must learn to handle all the energies in a constructive, enlightened way. With study and concentration, growth and inner harmony will follow. Then it becomes power from within, rather than a manipulative power over others. Manipulative power leads only to a core of hollowness."

I nodded. "Psychotherapy does much the same thing. It's an inner exploration, too. You talk about energies; we talk about strengths. You talk about inner harmony; we talk about integration and balance—learning to balance and understand, develop that inner strength."

"There's one other piece of information I have for you, Patrick."

Kayla's smile was a little mysterious and I tilted forward again, well conditioned by this time. I was entranced.

"This persona Stephen has developed—The Confetti Kid. It is necessary for now. Allow him to seek protection there. When the negative energies overwhelmed him, he took refuge in that identity because it allowed him to retain vestiges of his constructive energies—decency, truth, compassion. You have understood some of this.

"He is a gentle person—a humanitarian at heart—who wants to devote his life to people. And contribute toward making the world better. This psychosis, as you call it, is just one of the ordeals he must endure, learn from, and overcome."

I nodded again. Wasn't it a lot like what I'd been telling Steve?

Kayla leaned forward. "During a lifetime each of us must

complete certain tasks. There's not much time and it goes by quickly, so we have to pack a lot into it—move up the spiritual ladder as fast as we can. We have to make the moments count, learn what we must do, and then do it.

"And you, Patrick, are one of the people chosen to help him accomplish this. As I told you last time, you have had previous lives together. As strange as that must sound to you, this time you must serve him, as he has served you in the past."

I wondered why that idea didn't sound quite so preposterous anymore.

10

WHEN I SAW BEN THE FOLLOWING MONDAY, HE readily acknowledged his role at the hearing as the bad guy. But he'd been convinced that the potential outcome justified the risk, he said. "Otherwise we would have lost him for sure, Pat. Sometimes we have to manipulate a patient in his own best interests. It had to be brought home to Steve just how crazy he still is, and I certainly didn't want you to have to do it. You're going to be his therapist, the one he has to connect with. He'll remember your supporting him through all his trials. You can build on that."

"So I'm the good guy, huh?"

"Right," he agreed. "But now you have to start prying him open. Even though he's agreed to stay, you may not have much time."

"I know."

We lapsed into silence.

"Something else bothering you?" Ben finally asked.

"I think so, but I'm not sure what."

"Talk about it."

"I'll try." I paused to collect my thoughts. At last I said,

"I guess I'm concerned about how all this is going to play out, Ben."

"How so?"

"If he agrees and I begin helping him peel off all those layers, open him up, I'm also making a commitment to helping him reconstruct himself in a healthier way."

"Go on."

"Well, I'm not sure I can do that. Don't you think he should have someone more experienced in long-term, uncovering-type therapy?"

"Not necessarily, but we seem to be back to the confidence issue again. And trust. You'd like guarantees." Ben leaned back in his chair.

"I guess so. Yes."

"Unfortunately, there are none. Not as a psychotherapist, certainly not as a person trying to come to terms with life."

"I know. I guess my own problems keep getting in the way."

"Don't use them as excuses, Pat. Or let them undermine your self-confidence. There's no reason you can't help Steve and at the same time work on your own dilemmas. Season yourself."

Intellectually I knew Ben was right. But the flashes of anxiety I'd been feeling since I'd come to Peace River felt very near the surface now. Would I be opening a Pandora's box that I couldn't close? And was it Steve's or mine?

Ben leaned forward.

"Look, Pat. The world itself is a minefield. You have to constantly watch your step. If you get too bold, or careless, sure, you may step on a mine and it may blow up. It may have a small charge or a big one. The big ones leave bad scars. Sometimes somebody else sets off the detonation and you get zapped by remote control. Sometimes you even step on one when you know better: You get into a situation that's doomed from the start, and you knew it would be. The majority of people never step very far into the minefield. Fear stops them—fear of themselves, of others, of bad things happening to them."

"You're describing my life, Ben. A minefield."

"I'm describing a lot of people's lives. You have to learn to study the terrain, step cautiously, and keep moving. But plan those moves. Now, you can do that with Steve, can't you?"

I smiled. "Thanks for the pep talk. Yeah, I think I can."

Then I told him of my encounters with Kayla. I wanted to see how he reacted. When I finished, he said only, "That's very interesting."

It was about what I expected. Ben was at ease with the world, and I knew he meant it. The rest, as I was learning again and again, was up to me. I hoped I was up to it.

Later that afternoon I went looking for Steve. I found him sitting in the dayroom, mindlessly watching a soap opera. He looked forlorn, perhaps still stunned that he'd agreed to stay. But he seemed pleased to see me. I suggested we go up to my office.

"Sure," he said.

I tried not to show my excitement as we made our way upstairs.

He sat in the recliner and I rolled my chair near him, resting my forearms on my knees.

"I'm sorry the hearing was so rough on you, Steve. And I do want you to get out of Peace River as quickly as possible. But even more I want to do everything I can to make sure you never have to come back. Here or to any other psychiatric hospital."

"That makes two of us. I don't want to come back either."

"The responsibility for that will be yours, mostly. It'll take time and a lot of hard work on your part, but I'll back you all the way. And just as soon as the staff thinks you're ready, we'll release you and continue therapy on an outpatient basis. Just try and meet us halfway—"

"I don't know, Mac," he said softly. "I just want to get out of here and be my old self again, have my old life back. Is that too much to ask?"

"It's asking a lot right now. It'd be great if you could turn the clock back and start over again. But at the ripe old age of twenty-one, you've been hammered with a catastrophic illness. It's not life-threatening from a physical standpoint, but it is in terms of the quality of the rest of your life."

"How do you know any of that?"

"Probabilities, Steve. The chances are two out of three you'll have another psychotic break, especially without therapy. And if that continues to happen—"

I had an idea.

"C'mon. I'll take you on Unit Three, show you some of the other patients I work with. The real toughies, mostly chronically mentally ill. But keep one thing in mind: They weren't born this way. Most of them developed some form of psychosis early in their lives, just as you have. And it went untreated—perhaps it happened before we had the right drugs or maybe the person refused treatment, or treatment wasn't available. Or maybe it was such a malignant form of, say, schizophrenia, that the only treatment was to control the more overt symptoms with medications. In any case, these guys had one psychotic break and then they either never came out of it or they got better but had more episodes until they reached the point where this is as good as they get."

Reluctantly, Steve followed me down the stairs to Unit Three. When I unlocked the door and we stepped in, a horde of patients swarmed around us. I answered a few of their questions and then steered Steve into one of the dayrooms. I introduced him to Stanley, the Waver. And Wesley, the Rocker, who stopped only long enough to stare vacuously at us before he resumed his rhythmic humming/rocking routine.

I pointed to a patient working with a tech. "That's Murray—he eats everything in sight. We have him on a behavior modification program now and it's beginning to work. He's different, though, in that he's not only schizophrenic, he's also retarded. A double whammy.

"Jack, the one watching television over there, was in graduate school—dentistry—when he broke down. He just went totally downhill, became terribly delusional. If you talk to him, he'll tell you he's dead and then, in the next breath, tell you he's married to God. Shall we ask him?"

Steve vehemently shook his head "no."

"Okay." I nodded toward a fellow who was methodically rolling a cigarette. With great care he licked the long end of the paper and pressed it into place, ran his nicotine-stained finger back and forth along the edge several times, and tamped down one end. A skill borne of experience. He stuck it in his mouth and sucked it defiantly, staring back at us with unveiled suspicion. Smoking was no longer allowed anywhere in the hospital, but some patients were still being weaned off tobacco. This fellow was down to two a day now, which he was allowed to suck but not light.

"Arnold was about your age when he had his first break. He's in his fifties now and he hasn't left here for years. He has no family, and whenever they try him in a group home he withdraws and thinks everyone is after—"

"Let's get out of here," Steve whispered hoarsely. "Now. I've seen enough."

"Okay."

I caught up with him at the door and let us out. Back in my office, he was silent.

"What are you thinking?" I asked.

"That was a dirty trick, Mac," he said. "I didn't appreciate it."

"I'm sorry. I thought you needed a dose of reality."

"Yeah, like Tough Love, where they take delinquents into a prison and give the inmates a chance to scare 'em."

"Something like that."

"Well, you made your point, okay? I was terrified. But that's them, and I'm me. That could never happen to me."

"I hope you're right. But you know, Steve, you could be wrong. Given the right—or wrong—circumstances, anyone can become mentally ill."

He shrugged and I saw him swallow. "No. I can't believe there's even a chance of ending up like that. I'm caught in the middle here, Mac. Seeing those guys up close scares me to death, okay? It's bad enough just to go in there, but to think of becoming one of them—I can't. How can *you* even think about me that way?" Steve shook his head.

"I know it's disturbing. But that's why we want to get to the bottom of this thing right now, before it's too late."

"Yeah, well, first off, I don't really understand what it is you want to do to me, and what you expect me to do for myself. Everything's so twisted."

"So let's untwist it. Where can we start?"

"I don't even know that."

"What's important to you right now? What are your feelings?"

He was silent for several moments.

"Scared. But getting out of here is the most important thing, Mac."

"Besides that. How else do you feel?"

He sighed. "Mainly, confused. Like, what is therapy? What does a psychotherapist do?"

"Good place to start. Those are good questions."

Steve straightened slightly in his chair.

"Just think of me as a teacher. A special kind of teacher. I help people learn about themselves so they can get along better: be happier, have more satisfying relationships. Be true to themselves and find contentment with their lives." I paused, remembering something Kayla had said. I smiled.

"I'm also something of a guide. I know roughly how the mind works, but again, people have such special experiences that each of us thinks differently. I can only point in a general direction. You'll have to take the lead. You and I will be talking, with you trying to put the bits and pieces of your life together while I listen and make suggestions. Then between us we'll see if we can figure out what caused the blowout and what can be done so it won't happen again. We'll be covering a lot—"

"Like what?" He looked very apprehensive.

"We usually start with childhood experiences, family interactions, school, friends. Looking at all that allows you to begin to understand the connections between various childhood experiences and the ways of thinking and acting that you rely on now. When you start really digging into those memories—push down into the nitty-gritty of fears and doubts—we call it 'working through.' And when you begin to see how everything fits together to make you the person you are, we call it 'insight.' "

"But what good is all that?" Steve asked.

"Just the act of recognizing those connections raises your awareness of how you're thinking, and you begin to connect that with how you feel, and how you act. Instead of reacting out of habit—say an automatic response of avoiding conflict or not expressing anger—all of a sudden you're aware, conscious of the situation and your reaction to it. And if it's a reaction that doesn't work well—stuffing angry feelings inside, for example—you can make a determined effort to change it by doing something different. Perhaps expressing your anger to the person who caused it."

He looked slightly relieved. "Well, I guess it doesn't sound all that bad. I mean, how hard can it be to just talk?"

"Uh, Steve—" I held up my hand. "Don't for a moment underestimate the difficulty. Psychotherapy will probably be one of the toughest things you'll ever do in your life."

"Why?"

"Lots of reasons. Delving into memories that are locked out of your awareness—down in the unconscious—will be painful. And scary. The mind has blocked many of them out of memory, so unearthing them is very tough work. The mind can really resist. But it has to be done because those memories are exerting powerful influences over how you think and act. They have a great deal to do with what's happened to you."

For several moments he pondered that. Then he said, "Well, I suppose I could give it a try." A grudging capitulation if ever there was one.

I didn't care. He'd said the magic words.

"Okay, fine. In light of what's happened to you, what do you feel led up to your being here?"

"Oh, boy!" He let out a big sigh and kind of collapsed back into the recliner. He pushed his legs up and closed his eyes.

I waited.

Finally, he looked at me and kind of shrugged in defeat.

"I don't know what to say," he admitted.

"Sometimes it'll be hard to collect your thoughts and then express them. But one trick is to free associate. Just let whatever pops into your mind come out, whether it seems to make sense or not. The idea is to get the flow going. Like you do when you get an inspiration for a painting. You just let that creative process go, don't you?"

Steve smiled and his eyes sparkled. "Yeah, that's what happens. I lose all sense of time, get completely caught up—"

"Okay, this is similar, a thoughts-and-words flow. So tell me what comes to your mind when you think about yourself and your life."

He started to shake his head, so I prompted:

"What descriptive words come to you when you think of yourself and your immediate world? How would you describe it?"

He stared ahead a moment, then blurted, "Confused, chaotic . . ."

"How so, Steve?" I asked.

"The world. It's just too complicated, you know."

"Like?"

"Well, everything from stuff like how to scrape together enough to pay the rent, or which bills to pay and which ones can be put off. Wondering how I'll ever pay back my college loans. How am I going to make it as an artist?"

"Is money a problem for you, Steve?"

"It shouldn't be. I shouldn't have to scrape. My folks left me some money, but see, there's this attorney—Andis. He hassles me every time I try to get money from my parents' estates. It's my inheritance, dammit. *My money!* But he says I should invest it, not spend it. He says I should get a degree in business so I can make a lot of money. Well, he doesn't say it like that, but that's what he means." He smiled grimly. " 'Course I take his advice about as much as he takes mine. It's a question of standing my ground."

"That must be difficult. Your work as an artist is very important to you, isn't it?"

"Yeah. But I don't want to be a commercial artist doing deodorant ads and crap like that, for god's sake." He sighed. "Anyway, I never have time to think about that stuff because I'm just trying to survive, worrying if the money'll last till the end of the month. It never does, of course, and I end up charging stuff. It's a never-ending rat-race. And I can't see that it'll ever get much better."

"Okay, Steve, but you've just acknowledged something important that we should focus on in therapy. Know what?"

He sat back. "No, I don't have a clue."

"Your reference to not having enough time to think. You're so caught up in the ordinaries of life you don't have time to think about what you want out of it. What your life plan is. Or your philosophy of life. The spiritual dimension seems to have eluded you."

And me too, I might have added.

He sighed audibly. "Yeah, I know. I've read a little about that stuff from time to time, but I've never hacked out much of a philosophy for myself. A life plan, huh? So we can talk about that kind of thing in here?" For the first time since we'd met, he sounded hopeful.

"Sure. That's a definite area for exploration. Plus, do you know what else you could consider?"

"What?"

"Keeping a personal journal."

"A journal?"

"Sure. Use it to focus on what's important to you. We'll be meeting together only two or three hours a week, so you'll have lots of thoughts in between."

"A journal?" Steve repeated.

"Uh huh, I've kept one off and on and found it very helpful. I'd like you to use it to record your dreams, questions, dialogues, whatever occurs to you to write."

"Can I draw?"

"Sure. Whatever you want. It's your journal. Draw, paint, write poetry, express feelings, memories. Make of it whatever you want."

"Can I complain about the lousy food here? Or that my room doesn't have a phone or tv?"

"Of course. See, you're already getting into it. Wait a minute—"

I rummaged around in my desk until I found a red spiral notebook that had worked its way to the back of the drawer. I flipped through the first few pages and tore them out, then handed it to Steve.

"Here, you can use this." I'd brought a spare in to the hospital, foolishly thinking I'd have time for occasional journal entries. I'd made exactly two. Now I wrote every third or fourth evening at home. It smoothed out the rough spots. I hoped it would begin to do that for him.

"I don't know," he sighed.

"What don't you know, Steve?"

"What good is a journal?" he asked. "What hope is there for me? Like, without Jennifer? I've been so alone since she left."

"That's exactly the sort of thing you could use a journal for. Write about that and whatever else bothers you. See if you can cope with the challenges and gain some control. You'll be surprised. Sometimes you see a totally different perspective when you get it down on paper. And if you want, share your journal with me—or parts of it. I'll be glad to comment on it—constructively, of course. I'd do it in writing so you'd have it to look at outside our sessions."

He smiled back ruefully. "Well, how have you coped with the challenges?"

"Not too bad. Could have done better, I guess, but—"

"Yeah, well I heard you're divorced. Are relationships a hassle for you, too?"

I nodded. "You bet."

"You ever scared?"

"Sure. Especially in graduate school. But I figured I had to give it a try. Had everything to gain and not much to lose. If I hadn't made it, I had some alternate plans."

"Yeah, well, I don't have a main plan, let alone an alternate one. All the details of life screw me up—and screw up my art. Most of the time lately I go numb. Before I came here I was just going through the motions." He rubbed his forehead and shook his head. "It seems to me life is just one endless stream of hassles, total grief."

"And no control over any of it," I said softly.

"What?" Steve looked up.

"No control. Nothing seems predictable or certain to you, does it? When you have no influence over the outcome of anything, you feel you have no control over your life."

"Yeah. I guess. But how would psychotherapy fix that?" He was looking at me thoughtfully. "I mean, it'll all still be there. Even all-day and all-night therapy won't get my life in order, pay off my loans, get Jennifer to marry me, keep the hassles away. If it would, everybody would be in therapy."

I nodded. "You're right. The consequences of therapy won't be that direct. But some of those problems will be lightened indirectly. Therapy teaches you a different way of looking at things. Like how to be more effective. Most important, it helps you decide what direction you want your life to move in, what your priorities are, and how you're going to achieve them. The spiritual dimension."

Steve was still shaking his head, but he was a tad friendlier again. "You make it sound like the salvation of the world. Like everyone should go through therapy."

"Actually, I do think virtually everybody could learn something from it. And maybe then we'd have fewer problems—with divorce and drugs and violence, and so on. But no, therapy doesn't design a perfect world, nor a perfect you. What it does is give you perspective, a sense of belonging in the world. That's a balance that eludes a lot of people."

"Have you been in therapy, Mac?" He was looking straight at me.

"Yes. On and off for several years."

Don't follow up please, Steve, I said to myself.

"Did it help you? Did it do all the things for you that you've been saying it would do for me?"

Oh, boy. Trust a patient to cut to the heart of the matter. I had to answer him honestly.

"It has, Steve, and it hasn't. I went through the divorce last year and I've had my share of problems to work through. And I probably always will, to some degree. But therapy was one of the most profound experiences I've ever had. I had a pretty good load of neurotic baggage I hauled around for years. I'd have to say I'm a better person after therapy, and definitely a happier one, but I still have a ways to go."

He seemed satisfied with that and I said an internal "Whew."

"So you're convinced all of this will really, really help me?"

"That's the objective, Steve."

"I see," he said thoughtfully. "Or at least I think I see. It sounds simple in some ways. But very tough, too."

"It is. That's why I said it'd take a while. It's not going to happen overnight. Or without pain. I'll try to help you set the foundation, give you the tools. But understand, this is the beginning of a lifelong endeavor. You're going to be growing, changing, constantly adapting to new situations. All therapy does is give you a psychological jumpstart and get you going."

"Something has to get me going, Mac. Let's start."

"Good for you. See you here Friday at ten a.m."

What I didn't want to tell Steve just now was that my therapy was "on again." I'd recently started having sessions with Dr. Katherine Kertess, who was in private practice in the nearby town of La Crosse. It was a departure for me—my first female therapist. But it made sense because it would afford some good reality checks. As Freud said, "What is it women want?"

Happily, I was beginning to discover that what most of them want is not much different from what I want: companionship, loyalty, trust, love, friendship. For me, though, the tough task would be taking the risk to start the search again.

II

11

IT WAS TIME FOR ME TO SWITCH HATS. NOW I WAS GOING TO be Steve's therapist, so I didn't want to be making administrative decisions that could affect his life in the hospital: whether or not he could have liberty, move to a different ward, or go on excursions. If I had the power to withhold privileges, he might be tempted to hold back vital information because of his concern about how I'd react to it. In the service of building a therapeutic alliance with him, I had to become a neutral figure.

Instead of the recent normal give-and-take of conversation we'd shared, I now had to be a listener, offering occasional reflective comments on whatever Steve told me. The purpose was to place the responsibility on him for conducting his own exploration.

When the occasion arose, I would also want to point out to him various connections between early events in his life and how they might have influenced his present thinking. Sometimes tying together the more dramatic events is elusive because defense mechanisms do such a good job of protecting the status quo, no matter how miserable it may be. Ideally, Steve would be discovering these connections himself. I'd certainly be nudging him toward them, but the mind, and especially a mind as disturbed as his, has a great capacity for staying blind to reality, and an even greater fear of change. In Steve's terribly fragile state, even the prospect of change would be a frightening threat to what little control he had.

So he and I began meeting regularly, and I felt we were off to a good start. When his name came up in staffing a couple of weeks after the hearing, Joan summarized the nursing notes.

"We're giving Steve two hours of liberty now, but he doesn't go to the canteen or socialize with the other patients. He spends a little time outside in the park and then usually disappears into the woods."

"And I've noticed he takes a brown shopping bag with him, kind of crunches it up, maybe to hide it," a tech named Casey volunteered.

My ears pricked up. People were turning to me as if I might know something.

"I don't know what he's up to," I admitted. "I'll ask him." The next afternoon I was on a long-distance call when I saw Steve leave, and by the time I got outside, he was a small figure fading into the woods. I walked briskly across the park area. It was a warm day in early October and I was glad for the chance to take a walk. The leaves were turning orange and yellow and there was a crispness to the fall air that was invigorating.

I called his name when I reached the edge of the woods, although I knew he probably couldn't hear me. After I made a few downward turns in the narrow path the forest became more dense, and I was pleasantly enveloped in the rich muskiness of damp earth. Several minutes in, I was about to call his name again but a flash of color in the woods ahead stopped me. I was aware that my mouth was hanging open—as if to catch flies, as my mother would say.

I eased off the trail into a small stand of pines where the

gentle sighing of the wind in the needles played counterpoint to something else. A riot of dazzling colors, he was pacing across a clearing, his hands alternately on his hips and then waving around. ". . . my destiny . . ." I heard him say fiercely ". . . *forces of evil* . . ." and then ". . . commitment and renewal . . ."

For a long, full moment I leaned against a tree while my mind adjusted to what I was seeing. And tried to decide how to deal with it. Then I called out: "Steve?"

The colors froze. I clambered down the path to the small clearing where he stood, resplendent in the regalia of The Confetti Kid. I tried to behave as if nothing about the scene struck me as out of the ordinary.

"Sorry," I blurted out. "I tried to catch up with you before you left—wanted to tell you we can meet earlier tomorrow if you'd like," I improvised lamely, moving toward a fallen tree trunk where I saw he'd left his street clothes.

Steve seemed dazed, but then said, "I thank you, Sir." His voice had a formal lilt I'd never heard before.

I motioned for him to sit, but he seemed rooted to the ground.

"Can you tell me about all this? I'd like to know, to understand, The Confetti Kid."

There was a long silence, during which I couldn't help thinking of his lunging toward my office window, and the horrible struggle that followed.

"Why do you want to know?" His voice was familiar now. He'd switched off The Confetti Kid, just like that.

"Because it's the only way for me to understand you and what's happened to you. I'm on your side. Remember, we need to work on this together, as partners."

All my training and all my experience has convinced me that trusting another person, sharing something deeply personal, has to be the most fragile rope bridge there is, spanning the deepest chasm. Crossing over it means one frightening step after another, and the younger you are, the scarier it usually is. I watched as he weighed the dangerous options.

"Please, Steve." I was trying my best to make eye contact with him, but he wouldn't look at me.

Finally, he asked, "What do you want to know?"

"Everything, Steve. Anything you care to tell me."

He studied the ground, where two ants struggled with a piece of straw, together managing to drag it away.

"Do you remember how it started?"

He shrugged. "You want to hear from the very beginning? How I was chosen?"

I nodded.

"You won't laugh?" He eyed me suspiciously.

"I promise."

He began pacing again, back and forth, in front of me. The words came slowly at first.

"It happened last spring. I'd been up all night—trying to paint. But I couldn't. I couldn't sleep either because I felt so wired. So I went out walking along a bike trail by Lake Mendota. It was early and the sun was just coming up. I came around a clump of willows and the reflection on the water blinded me. All these colors were dancing around my eyes. And in that instant everything that had been bothering me so much became clear—why Jennifer left—why I couldn't get along with anybody—why I was so unhappy—why I could never fit in."

His voice trailed off and I waited.

"Suddenly I was filled with incredible excitement. I knew something awesome was about to happen—" He glanced over at me, checking my expression.

"Wow, that must have been something," I said, hoping my voice was reassuring.

"It was, because then the truth was revealed to me: I was special! Understand, Mac, I didn't ***choose*** to save the world. I was chosen to do it. To do something about the forces of evil. ***I was given a mission—to make the world a more joyful place.*** " He was shouting.

"And you know what?" he asked me, quieter now.

I shook my head.

"The reason everything had gone wrong—why I had to suffer so much hurt—was that the pain purified me. I had to go through it to understand and to be able to fulfill my true destiny," he said excitedly. He looked very happy. At peace.

"It was a spiritual revelation. On that day of days: ***I. Was. Transformed.*** " He looked down on me benevolently.

I nodded. "We call that a transcendent experience, Steve." To myself, I thought, McGarry, don't touch this delusional system now with a ten-foot pole.

"Yeah, I like that. Transcendent. There's so much bad in the world—greed, selfishness, hatred. Look at all the people who use their power in evil ways! Well, I was chosen to end all that."

"An admirable undertaking, Steve. Have you any idea how this task happened to fall to you?"

He stopped pacing and thought for a minute. Then he came over and plopped down beside me on the tree trunk.

I could see that the question bewildered him. It was probably the first time he'd considered it. But then, in a voice heavy with conviction, he declared:

"That doesn't matter. All I know is I can feel an incredible force infusing me with power. It kinda scared me at first, but now I've accepted it. The power is necessary because I have a mission of global importance to accomplish."

I caught the shift to present tense, and the formal lilt again. He was poised somewhere between being Steve and being The Confetti Kid. I realized that he didn't know where one stopped and the other began.

"Do you know if anyone else has received similar instructions?"

He looked at me sharply.

"Oh, no. Everything was revealed only to me. As the agent of change, I knew what must be done. And only I can do it. It's a tremendous responsibility, you know—to save the world."

"Yes, it is. Can you share with me how you'll be carrying out this mission, Steve?"

"Well," he paused, choosing his words carefully. "The vision I had was filled with colors. The most gorgeous colors exploding everywhere, merging and superimposing until they became one. But at the same time, each was distinct. Anyway, all philosophies and religions were merged by the colors—"

"The colors?"

"Yes. The colors are the key. Nothing can happen without them. They bring light to the darkness of evil. Certain colors are harmonious. They can change reality. Colors are the key to accomplishing the transformation."

"The transformation?"

"Evil to Good," he said impatiently. He seemed exasperated that I was too dense to understand. "I told you, I have to make the world better! Color can do that—if you know how to use it!" He was getting more and more excited.

"See, when other people look at a color, that's all they see: a color. Now when an artist looks at a color, it's absorbed for its true essence. You know, for symbolic meaning. The colors of the spectrum represent many things: love—generosity of spirit—compassion and tolerance for others—hope—spirituality—faith. And there are colors for knowledge, honor, truth, and understanding. The dark colors, of course, signal evil and treachery. You have to avoid them, be careful."

His voice took on an evangelistic fervor and again he looked intently at me. "Have you ever heard of auras?"

I nodded. "Yes, as a matter of fact I have. The colors that people give off."

"Yes, yes, you understand," he said excitedly.

"But where does the confetti come in?"

"Oh, it's very important. Later that same day—the day of my revelation—I walked by a certain store, and something—some force—just pushed me to go in. When I got inside, the first thing I saw was a rack filled with packages of confetti. All different colors and shapes—beautiful, shiny circles, gold stars, red hearts—hearts of love, circles of friendship, stars of the universe. I sensed immediately what they symbolized! I was supposed to use the confetti to take the pain out of people's lives—just soak it up like a bunch of little sponges."

"But why is it so special? Is there a reason?"

"Of course." He said it as if he were speaking to a real dimwit. "It's not ordinary confetti. It's special because I discovered it, and so it, too, has been given special powers—just like me. Together, I knew we'd be omnipotent. So I bought all the confetti in the store. And in all the stores I could find that had it."

Oh, boy, I thought.

He continued enthusiastically: "See, it's a channel, a means to accomplish my goal." His tone softened and became more instructive. "I researched it. 'Confetti' is the Italian word for candy. It was first used in medieval celebrations. The aristocracy showered the crowds with candy, sometimes money. But poor people threw little bits of paper. It was all they had, but confetti represented generosity, good wishes for one's fellow human beings, a sharing.

"You can see that, can't you?" He paused, observing me carefully to determine if I understood.

"Yes, a sharing. So then what?"

"I took the confetti back to my apartment, and that night I began my sculpture." He smiled self-consciously, a little embarrassed. "First I worked on a department store mannequin. I dressed it in the suit and painted these designs all over it. Then, each piece of confetti had to be properly placed, a correct order and special relationship of colors observed. Later on, I began using sequins, like these.'' He raised a glittering arm. ''They looked better.''

''That must have taken you hours,'' I said.

''Yes, weeks actually, even though I worked on it day and night.''

''I can believe it. Did you know at the time how it was going to be used, its connection to the better world? Were you thinking about what you were going to do once it was finished?''

''Not really. I lost myself in the creation of it. I was so hyper, I had more energy than I've ever had before in my whole life. Toward the end, I began to realize that making the suit was kind of a practice run, a way to test me to see if I was worthy of the next step.''

I nodded.

Again he seemed reluctant, rather self-effacing about his role.

''I had been selected. I had passed a test of faith. But a genuine commitment was needed.''

I raised my eyebrows. ''And that was?''

After a long silence, he shrugged. ''It's hard to explain. To begin with, priorities and values are all wrong now. They need to be changed. The hypocrisy, the push for material possessions, being super-competitive, doing whatever you have to to get ahead.''

''The 'me' mentality—''

''Right. It does terrible stuff to people. There's no caring or understanding anymore, only rudeness and arrogance. I truly believe people are empty on the inside and don't have a clue about why.''

Amazing. Especially to someone from Southern California, this part didn't sound so crazy.

''Why do *you* think people are empty inside, Steve?''

''Oh, they're so superficial, so blown around by image,

advertising. I mean, they're at the mercy of mindless appeals to their sexual, violent natures. There's just no appreciation—"

"Of?"

"Of finer qualities. Of an inner life built around love and understanding. And respect for the arts and creative expression. The celebration of the spirit."

"I see."

"I doubt it," he said curtly. "I haven't met many people who understand the artistic spirit. Artists are an endangered species, you know. Very few can make a decent living—can't get into galleries and even if they do, they're exploited. I know horror stories, believe me. They just yank your chain all the time. Poets, composers, actors, anyone who's an artist has the same problem."

"And you feel that deeply, I'm sure." Where was all this going?

Steve looked at me for a moment, then dropped his eyes. But not before I'd seen his tears.

"Yes, I feel it. I feel pain and anguish for every artist." His voice was tremulous. "But it goes 'way beyond that. Nobody's happy now. It's a desperate time. Look at the suffering of the poor, the homeless."

We sat in silence for a couple of minutes. Then he sighed, a sigh so heavy that it almost broke my heart.

"Anyway, that's my task, to cleanse our society. We can help those less fortunate, rediscover love and cooperation. We can live peacefully and joyfully together in brotherhood and sisterhood."

"That sounds like a tall order, Steve."

"Naturally, I know it isn't going to be easy," he said disdainfully. "But it's not impossible, if that's what you're suggesting."

He looked at me through veiled half-lids. I could see he was closing up. My skepticism had come through and a palpable change was going on between us. I tried to intercept it.

"What special powers does the confetti have, Steve? Is it magical?"

I'd barely gotten the question out before a haymaker swing came at me. I flinched, closed my eyes, and braced myself for the impact. An old image flashed by, me as an exuberant nine-year-old catcher, jumping up and getting cracked in the side of the head by the late swing of a bat.

Except this time no blow fell. Cautiously, I opened my eyes to find my hair, my beard and my sportcoat bathed in tiny pieces of bright confetti.

"There!" he said proudly. "Now you'll feel the magic, too."

"What will happen?"

"In time, you will change. Become more optimistic. The confetti gives me power over you. Whoever I throw it on undergoes a metamorphosis. Confetti is absolution. It is forgiveness. But most of all, it is renewal."

Methodically, he brushed the confetti that clung to his hand into a little pile in his palm and returned it to the magic pouch. When the last piece was safely in the bag, he smiled.

"Every day miracles are being performed, you know. I myself have been surrounded constantly by mystical experiences, a feeling of oneness with nature and the world. I have mastered the divine pattern of the universe. I see things like trash cans waiting to be picked up, and there is a message in their arrangement. Something I had never seen or understood—or even noticed before—is suddenly clear, revealed only to me. I am enlightened as no one has ever been before."

He shook his head and smiled in happy reminiscence. Then he cast an appraising eye on me.

"Well?" he asked. "Anything yet? Do you feel the magic?"

I considered carefully, afraid of alienating him, yet not wanting to lie.

I shook my head slowly. Little bits of color floated to the ground. "No, I don't think so."

Steve waved his hand dismissively. "Never mind. It's too soon, anyway." His voice had changed again. "But it's all part of my dream—a dream that's come true. The Confetti Kid can do things I could never do. I am a sovereign soul—my dreams are fulfilled."

A cloud of suspicion passed over his face.

"You're probably thinking this sounds crazy and you should lock me up and throw away the key—"

I interrupted. "No, Steve. Everyone needs dreams."

He considered this a few moments. "I agree with that. Without dreams, there's no hope. There are so many things I want to do, be, but I can't, unless I—" he faltered.

"Unless you what?"

"Unless I'm different. More powerful. I needed to be someone. When I was chosen to be The Confetti Kid, I became someone. Invulnerable. Distinctive. Unique."

"I can see that, Steve."

"The Confetti Kid has the power of the ages. And I use that power to enlighten."

"Can you tell me about that?" I asked.

He looked away.

"I'm not sure. In fact, it gets pretty vague at this point, Mac. I was on this tremendous high and everything was wonderful, and then all of a sudden it wasn't anymore. My brain starts hurting whenever I think about this part." He sighed.

"Well, maybe the two of us can piece it together."

"Maybe." He sounded very sad.

As he'd slid down the treacherous slope of psychosis, things had scrambled badly for him. Now, just sharing some of his crazy thoughts was probably making him afraid, at least unconsciously, of sliding again.

"Do you remember anything that doesn't hurt your brain, Steve?" I asked, trying to lead him out of danger.

He was quite subdued. Once again he sighed deeply. Now his voice betrayed the fear of where all this might be heading, and I had to lean forward to hear him.

"I remember working on the suit. The colors, all the confetti had to be done just right. When it was finished, I tried it on. It was incredible how much better it made me feel. It still does. And then—" he paused.

His anxiety was palpable, his voice a whisper as he continued, "One day Jennifer came back with a lady. They were telling me I had to do this and had to do that—take care of myself, get counseling, and like that. Me, with my special powers, needing counseling! How absurd! Ridiculous! And Jennifer didn't even notice—***she didn't even see***—how different I was. I was so sure she'd see how much I'd changed and . . . come back to me . . . because she needed me."

"That must have really hurt."

He nodded vigorously, his eyes filling with tears again.

"It hurt so much my stomach knotted up real bad," he choked. "I was so mad—at Jennifer for leaving, at myself, for being such a jerk. Then I got depressed. After they left I got mad again and just lost it. I was climbing the walls, drinking, raging, crying. My powers were in shreds."

"They made you doubt your powers?" I ventured.

"Yes. But not for long. Pretty soon I felt this calmness. Like, they didn't understand, but hey, I still knew what had to be done, and I was going to do it. I thought about how surprised Jennifer would be when she learned my true identity, and how much she'd regret leaving me. I knew we'd meet again someday when I was being honored with awards. I'd be gracious about it, and then when we were alone together, I'd forgive her. We'd be reunited. It would all be perfect." He took a deep breath. "That was my vision."

"What happened to it?" I asked.

Another big breath. "Well, then I became The Confetti Kid, fighter for truth and justice, for honor, for creativity."

"Those are admirable things to fight for, Steve. I don't

think anyone would disagree with what The Confetti Kid hoped to accomplish. But how did he go about it?"

"Well, I'd usually go out at night. I'd put on my suit, take my confetti pouch, and go to different neighborhoods. I'd spread confetti like the Sandman sprinkles sand." He smiled at the association. "If I ran into someone who needed renewal, I'd spray 'em with confetti," he gestured, "like I just did to you. Sometimes they'd get mad and yell at me, but I knew they'd be glad when they felt the magic. Sometimes I sprinkled it from the rooftops. I really don't remember all the places I went. Certain things I remember okay; others, I don't. It's kind of mixed up."

"I see. Did any of this seem strange to you, Steve?"

"Yeah. A little. There were times when I got confused—my thoughts blipped by, zip-zip-zip. I had trouble concentrating, thinking something through. My mind would be racing and all the colors would start flashing and I'd rub my eyes and it'd only get worse."

"Do you recall if during this time you had any other peculiar experiences?" I asked. "Did you ever hear voices speaking in your head?"

He nodded slightly, but didn't say anything. After a time I asked quietly,

"What was it like?"

He sighed. "It was very strange. My parents are dead, of course, but I kept thinking they were trying to communicate with me. Through my special powers and all, they'd say things to me, you know? Not especially good things, either." He paused a moment. "Other times I heard the Voice of Destiny. At least, that's what I named him. He was the one who told me to spread the confetti, have a world-class celebration that would bring love and goodwill to all. So that's what I did."

"And how long did all that go on, Steve?"

He thought hard. "I don't really know. It's all jumbled. I was protecting the sleeping citizens of the city, but I could see the forces of Evil were trying to undo my work. They were very strong. My apartment was being watched because of what I was doing. Enemies were keeping me under surveillance because they wanted to prevent me from completing my mission. I saw the manager looking at my apartment, talking to strange people. They were planning to steal my confetti, you know. And my suit . . . they were trying to steal my power. So one night I just left. Put my confetti suit on under my regular clothes and took off."

"For?"

"I don't know. I had no place to go, so I just walked. I stayed in an empty garage for a few nights, then at a kind of safe house. They let me stay there. I had no money, and food and bed there were free. But I didn't like it much. I tried to make friends, but they laughed when I told them about my vision and asked for their help. Even after I threw confetti on them, they laughed at me. I couldn't understand why. It was the first time the confetti hadn't worked.

"I kept going as long as I could, but then my mind started fading in and out, playing tricks. Parts are clear, but others I don't know if what I remember really happened or not. I got panicky a couple of times when I didn't know where I'd been or what I'd done. All of it was very dream-like. Surreal."

"What other kinds of tricks did your mind play, besides fading in and out? Do you remember any?"

"There was this lady. I was trying to talk to her, tell her about my powers. She was listening, interested and all, but then I saw these colored lights in her hair, flickering on and off. It was really weird, like she had a Christmas tree on her head—and she seemed totally unaware of it! You'd think that'd bother her, wouldn't you? I don't know who she was, but I do remember she was nice to me." His voice trailed off.

I waited in silence.

"And then," he turned triumphantly, "there was the time I rescued someone."

"Really?"

"Yes, a black woman, about my age." He smiled in happy reminiscence."

"What happened, Steve?"

"One night, very late, I was on a rooftop throwing confetti and I saw her get pushed out of a car. She fell down and just lay there on the sidewalk, crying. The car pulled away, then it stopped and I could hear some men's voices arguing. Very fast, I climbed down the fire escape, jumped to the sidewalk, and landed right in front of her. She looked real scared, especially when I threw confetti on her, but I reassured her that I was a champion of the people and that I would rescue her. And then I did." He beamed.

"What did you do?"

"The car had turned and was circling back, so I helped her up, took her down an alley, and we hid behind some trash cans. The car stopped where they'd dumped her out and a couple guys got out and looked around, but then someone yelled from the car and they got back in and took off.

"The woman kept asking who I was and was I going to hurt her. I told her 'no,' I was The Confetti Kid and that I protect people from Evil. I don't think she believed me at first, but after a few minutes she relaxed and told me she'd met these guys in a bar and they seemed all right. But then they turned nasty. She said I saved her. I told her it was what I was chosen to do: She needed help and so I was there."

He smiled proudly, then frowned.

"What?" I asked.

"A night or two after that the police saw me and put me in jail. I asked them if they knew who I was, if they knew how important I am to the future of the world. They didn't. Didn't believe me." He sighed. "I don't know—" He put his hand over his eyes.

"What don't you know?"

"It all swims together. Ohhhhh—"

"What is it Steve, what's happening?"

He pressed his fingers to his forehead and massaged it.

"I'm getting a bad headache."

"I know this is tough on you," I said. "You'll probably remember things a little bit at a time. As they come back, we'll try to figure them out. But enough for today."

I stood and brushed the rest of the confetti off my coat, then tried to get it out of my hair and beard. Steve watched impassively.

"I'd better be getting back. You planning to stay here a while?"

"Yeah." Naturally, he didn't want to change out of his confetti suit.

I walked to the edge of the slope and peered down. Below, through some breaks in the trees, I could make out the Peace River, the muted fall colors mirrored in the water. It was a beautiful spot. Over my shoulder I said,

"If you'd like, Steve, we could come here every once in a while for our sessions. Would you like that? Might be good for your spirit."

I turned and looked at him and our eyes met.

"I'd like that, Mac. I'd like it a lot. This is hallowed ground, a magical place. Mystic powers nourish my soul here. If I stay a while longer, maybe they'll heal my headache."

"Okay. Take it easy. I appreciate your taking me into your confidence."

He shrugged self-consciously.

"See you later, buddy."

He didn't respond and I sensed that he was drawing back into character again. A few steps up the path and I thought I heard something. Then he stood and paced across the clearing again, not just back and forth, but in a pattern of some kind. He was mumbling something, but I couldn't catch the words.

Later that afternoon I slid deep into the lounge chair in Ben's office.

"Steve?" he asked, smiling.

"You got it," I agreed, shaking my head. "I've heard of people smuggling chocolate chip cookies or booze into hospitals, but I just got showered with magical confetti. You better watch out. He's still got a supply and if anyone needs a dousing—"

I gave him a quick summary. He was surprised. As I finished, he was nodding and his eyes sparkled.

"Fascinating! It never ceases to amaze me. Once you get a patient to tell you just a little bit about his delusional system, it's as if the floodgates open. They've kept it all inside so long."

"I had that sense, Ben, as if it was a tremendous relief for him to finally get some of it out."

"It's a big step, too. Because somewhere deep inside, he knows it's crazy, but it's all he has. Now that he's shared it with you, acknowledged its existence, it's a sign that he may be willing to let you lead him out."

"I know he needs the delusion now. I guess that's why the meds haven't touched it."

"Hmmm, yes, his delusional system runs very, very deep."

"So?" I asked.

Ben leaned back in his chair, gathering his thoughts. This seemed to be the kind of challenge he savored.

"Steve's a classic, the heroic figure, the personification of the hero myth. Taking upon himself the titanic concerns of society."

I was shaking my head. "What are you talking about? I thought he was psychotic."

"He is psychotic. The Confetti Kid is right out of his unconscious: the prototype hero, the Luke Skywalker-Superman phenomenon. All cultures have heroes in one form or another. What Jung called archetypes, universal themes—birth, death, resurrection, renewal, power, demons, the earth mother—to name a few. The hero is legendary, whether it's a scowling Clint Eastwood or a Medal of Honor winner. Isn't that why we love them so much? Why we find them so appealing?''

''How does that apply to Steve?''

''Steve may well be one of those people for whom the psychotic experience is a plunge into the depths of the unconscious—a very mystical and potentially messy place. For some people, though, the journey is necessary for their psychological rejuvenation. It's been called a flight to health.''

''But why such extreme measures?''

''He told you that when he shared his delusional system with you. And he's said it before—in the picture he drew and what he wrote. He's been quite lucid about how alienated and fragmented he felt everything around him was. And by extension, how alien and fragmented he was. He felt powerless in the face of overwhelming forces. So when his immediate world became more and more intolerable, he compensated by retreating into inner experiences. Which meant he had to spin out this elaborate fantasy. And that, of course, only increased his isolation. Young people are especially vulnerable—feeling things so acutely, then overreacting, overcompensating. That's when they fly out of control and head for a crash somewhere down the line. Steve's salvation was an elaborate fantasy couched in a magical identity.''

''But he's right, Ben,'' I said. ''Our society does have a lot of problems, awful ones. He's certainly not crazy there.''

''No, those are valid points.'' Ben leaned back, choosing his words carefully. ''You're doing well. He's talking to you, explaining himself, even pelting you with confetti. Those are all positive signs. He's accepted you into his delusional system.'' He paused.

"Why do I feel like there's a 'but' coming here?" I asked.

He looked pointedly at me. "Because there is one. Be very careful, Pat. You can put one foot at a time into his delusional system. But never both. And be ready to pull out again. Fast."

That made the hair on the back of my neck stand up.

12

"DOCTOR McGARRY, DOCTOR McGARRY. PICK UP on seven." The switchboard was paging me for a long distance call. I was in the nursing station on One, so I took it there.

"This is Kayla. Stephen has been in my thoughts lately. How is he?"

"Better, but he's not doing as well as we'd hoped. He's turning out to be a very tough nut to crack." I said it with a smile in my voice.

Kayla chuckled. "That's terrible. You should be ashamed of yourself, Patrick McGarry."

"Hospital humor," I replied. "We get a little strange up here."

"So it would seem. The reason I'm calling is I'll be over that way next Tuesday. I thought maybe I'd stop in to see Stephen. And you, of course. Would that be okay?"

"Should be. I have to warn you, though, that Steve has some strange notions about you. I think you're the person he identifies as having colored lights in her hair."

There was a pause. Then Kayla said, perfectly seriously, "That's curious."

"I'll talk with Steve and let you know if there's any problem for Tuesday. I doubt there will be. I think he'd probably like to see you again."

"Okay, see you then unless I hear from you."

"Fine." Then I had an idea. "Kayla?"

"Yes?"

"I'd be interested in anything else you pick up on Steve when you're here. You know, he's still a real puzzle to us."

"Do you think he'd let me do a reading on him?"

"I don't know. I can ask him."

It was only after I hung up that I had some second thoughts about bringing a psychic in as an informal consultant. Most of the staff were fairly open to different approaches, but I knew summoning energies and auras might be stretching it a bit. More than a bit.

Steve agreed to see Kayla. He seemed intrigued, in fact. His memory for that period was pretty scrambled, but Kayla's kindness and warmth had pierced through the fog. And, he recalled, she definitely was the colored lights lady.

Brenda was excited when I told her Kayla would be coming.

"Won't this be a slap at your expertise? Who all knows you've called in a psychic?" she teased.

"I've told you, Stacey, and Ben. That's it. And it better stay that way," I warned her. "Besides, I haven't exactly called her in—she's just visiting."

"Oh, come on, Pat. Lighten up. It'll give people something to talk about," she laughed.

"No. Period. If you tell anyone about her, they'll never leave me alone about it. I get in enough trouble as the new boy around here without that."

Brenda sighed and shook her head. She considered me hopeless. "So anyway, she'll 'visit' Steve?"

"I'll sit in, too, if that's okay. I'll leave it up to him."

"Guess it'd be pushing it if I asked to be there, too. Is

there any chance I could talk with her afterwards? I have a couple of questions—"

"I'll ask her. Leave your schedule open after four. Want me there?"

Brenda squinched up her nose. "I don't know, it's kind of personal."

"So much the better." I grinned.

Brenda swatted my arm and turned to leave. "I'll stay free after four, Pat. Call if she's up for another reading. Call anyway. I want to know what happened. Please?"

"Of course."

"And I promise not to say a word." She did a beautiful pantomime of going into a trance and took off down the hall.

The following Tuesday afternoon Steve looked almost relaxed as he entered my office. He greeted Kayla like a co-conspirator.

"Are they treating you okay here?" she asked.

"Pretty much. Everybody but Mac here, anyway." He cast a sly glance at me.

"Don't be a troublemaker," I told him.

"I'm glad you came," he said to Kayla. "I wasn't sure I'd ever see you again."

"You remember coming to see me, then?"

"Yeah. A lot of things are muddled, but I remember you. I appreciate your being so nice to me when I was getting—well, pretty far out." To me he said, "I told you about that—we talked a few times and I'd feel better for a little while afterward."

Kayla listened, nodding as he spoke. She reached out and took his hand.

"You're better now, young Stephen. More at peace. It shows. And the colors of your aura are better."

"They are?" he asked, obviously pleased.

"Do you remember the readings I did for you, some of the things I told you?"

"Not very well."

"Would you like me to look again? Perhaps I can tell you some things that might be helpful to you."

Steve glanced at me, then back at Kayla. "Sure, I guess."

"Do you mind if Pat stays?"

"No."

"Give me both your hands, then . . . . Now I want you to close your eyes, clear your mind and relax. Think of some pleasant scene—water, a lake, the woods. Okay?"

He nodded and Kayla closed her eyes and began to concentrate, breathing deeply in the rhythm I remembered. During the silence I took out my notebook and pen.

After a while a smile creased Kayla's face. "Dear Stephen, Dear Bright Soul, you have so many colors in your aura, so much energy, vibrancy, creative powers, and—" she stopped and Steve's eyes immediately fluttered open, "—that deep sensitivity . . ." she continued, and shook her head. "Your aura is definitely stronger now, but it must become stronger still, strong enough to protect your sensitivity. You are slowly rebuilding, but you must learn to blend your energies so there is harmony among the creative forces and the others, the physical, mental, and social currents. Now you feel all of them tugging at you and you don't know which to follow, but, with time, you will learn to balance them out."

"But how long will it take?" Steve asked.

Kayla stirred briefly but then the rhythmic breathing resumed. Soon she spoke: "I cannot tell you that, Stephen. No one can. First, you must learn patience, that all things come in their own time. All I can tell you, Dear Bright Soul in Search of Truth—" and she gave Steve's hands a squeeze, "is that no one makes the journey alone, and no one makes the journey together. All paths are the same . . . and all paths are not the same. . . ."

Steve looked over at me with a puzzled expression and then back at Kayla.

"I'm not sure what that means."

Kayla opened her eyes and smiled at him. Then she glanced at me. "Can you tell him?"

I wasn't sure I knew, either. I shrugged. "I guess we each have to find our own solutions. No one can tell someone else exactly what the answers are. They'll be different for different people. So each of us has to discover for himself. Be a seeker. Close?" I asked.

Kayla nodded.

"I still want to know how long it'll take," said Steve.

"I would hope it would take your whole life," Kayla responded.

"What?" he asked.

"Kayla is talking about the search for some kind of meaning in your life," I said. Steve looked puzzled and Kayla continued:

"Your soul must be guided through the wilderness of the inner self. Pat's right, this is a search for fulfillment—a meaningful life. I sense enormous energies at work in you, dear Stephen. Some positive and constructive, others negative and destructive. There is so much confusion and hurt in you now. And yet so much that is vibrant and healthy. You have to learn an awareness, how to channel those negative energies into constructive modes. You bring a great deal from your past lifetimes—"

"Really?" Steve drew away and Kayla released his hands. "I used to dream I'd lived before, but—you're saying I really *have?*"

"You have lived many lives, Stephen. And in each one you have been a person who felt deeply, acted strongly, spoke out against injustice. The Confetti Kid is actually very much in keeping with your previous lives."

"Wow. I'd like to believe that, but I'm not sure I can."

"It's not necessary for you to believe or even understand, for that matter," Kayla said calmly. "What is necessary is that you not be confused by your inner idealism when it runs up against what others tell you to do. You are on a vision quest, seeking, but you must trust your heart: Listen to it, listen to the depths of your soul. You are a pilgrim who has a long history of defying those who would control you."

"Tell that to Mac. Maybe you can convince him to spring me out of here."

"Patrick is your teacher, dear Stephen. Your teacher and your friend. And the hospital offers the sanctuary you need for now. You went to great measures to avoid pain. You separated yourself, tried to create a parallel universe. It can't be done. So this is a time and a place to realign yourself. You must learn to center your energies, take the cosmic perspective. You must decide which paths you wish to follow. And then do so."

We were silent for a few moments, Steve apparently pondering cosmic paths.

"Do you sense anything else, Kayla?" I asked.

She closed her eyes again and resumed the deep breathing. Finally she spoke again: "You must learn forbearance, to attune your dark interior so there is harmony. In time you will develop a more tolerant sense for your self and for others. This is very important for you to do. There are many complexities and cruelties in the world. Suffering stalks everyone. You must learn to absorb the blows of life. Otherwise they will devastate you."

Steve looked a little frightened.

Kayla opened her eyes again with that penetrating look she had so often given me. "There are things spiritual in your aura—the butter-yellow of a creative, growing spirit. But you must learn to use your power, live your life so you have no regrets. Then you will understand the secret, the meaning of life. Your life. Only then will you be ready to leave your friends here, and be prepared to resume the journey on your own."

Steve grasped the arms of his chair and looked thoughtfully at her.

"Well, I'll have to think about this," he said. "But Kayla, what's the big deal about my having to stay in the hospital? Tell Mac it's stifling for creative people to live where they don't want to. Especially a place like this."

"But it's necessary for now." She nodded slowly. "You have been through much agony and suffering, Stephen. Your insides have been torn apart. There is still much pain there to be healed. It is the creative spirit that fights its way out of agony. Then you must learn to accept the craziness that you have had. Not be frightened by it, but learn to humor it. Harness it, rather than allowing it to control you. As it did."

"But the pain—" he said.

"I know," Kayla replied softly. "But you must fight back, not indulge the hurts you have suffered. Reach out to the hand that reaches for you. Do not forsake others, dear Stephen. Overcome your great fear, grasp the extended hand, seek out the truth."

Steve sat motionless, eyes on the floor. Kayla continued. "The magic, Dear Bright Soul, is only in the nature of our seeking. Will you reach out? Accept my friendship?"

For a long moment, Steve didn't move. Then, slowly, he raised his gaze to meet Kayla's. He nodded tentatively and blinked. There were tears in his eyes and he was visibly choked up, but Kayla gave him a warm smile. And a hug. Steve shyly returned it.

Kayla said she'd be happy to meet with Brenda before she left that day. I introduced them and then excused myself.

The next day, all Bren would tell me was that it had been "very revealing." Her tone was so serious, and so sad, that I backed off and let it ride. I was afraid it had to do with the guy she was going with. And the last thing I wanted was to be the consoling friend who catches her on the rebound.

I had learned that lesson my first time around.

13

"SOMETHING'S BOTHERING YOU." OUR SESSION HAD just started and Steve was restless. "I have to stop taking these pills. I feel just rotten. I'm tired and sluggish, my concentration is shot, and my mouth is so dry all the time that I'm always thirsty. And I can't draw at all."

"Okay, we'll talk with Dr. Stacey about that, Steve. I'll set up an appointment."

He settled in, mollified, then looked over at me.

"Kayla's different, isn't she?"

"Yes, she is. What did you think of the reading?"

"It was interesting." He lapsed into silence.

I dropped my voice. "Anything else?"

He shook his head "no."

Silence.

"Nothing much going on today, huh?"

Another shake of the head and more silence. I finally had to break it.

"Steve, therapy is up to you. I'll meet you halfway, but you have to at least make an effort. Take the risk."

He looked over at me. "What kind of risk?"

"The people risk. As in trust. As in opening up, as Kayla was encouraging you to do. That's the only way we're going to get anywhere."

"There's just nothing to talk about."

I decided to be a little more confrontational. "It may be, that with the exception of your parents, you've never really trusted anyone. But you have to learn to, Steve. Sometime."

He was staring blankly at the opposite wall. He inhaled deeply and then let it out as he said, "Well, I sure didn't trust my folks. But I did trust Jennifer. And look where that got me."

"I'm not sure it's fair to blame Jennifer, Steve. My guess is most of this started long before she came on the scene. And I wonder if you ever did really, truly trust her, in a mature, loving sense."

"What do you mean by that?"

"I got the impression that you were fairly possessive, that you didn't want her to be her own person."

He shot a sidelong glance at me. "Why wouldn't I?"

"Only you can answer that."

"You're the psychologist. You tell me."

Confronting him was making him defensive, but I decided to play it out a bit longer.

"Maybe you don't trust yourself, care enough about yourself."

"Come on, what are you talking about?"

"Just that if you don't trust yourself, it's virtually impossible to trust and love another person."

"That's not true. I mean, I did love Jennifer. A lot. No matter what I may feel about myself, I loved her."

"All right. Then how do you feel about Stephen Parker? You tell me."

He was silent and I waited. "I don't know," he said.

I rolled my chair closer to him. "Steve, these are issues you must look at. You've got to have a much better understanding of yourself and feel a heck of a lot better about yourself before you can even begin to think of the happy marriage and wonderful life that you've dreamed about."

He kept his eyes down, not making eye contact. His chair could just as well have been empty. He was giving nothing.

"Steve," I implored. "Stop fighting me. I'm in your corner. But we have to be a team. We have to work together on understanding what makes this talented, sensitive guy run. Come on, give it a chance."

When he spoke now his voice was bitter, and there was a sneering anger in his tone. "Tell me this—how come you're divorced? Did your wife leave you? Is that what trusting got you?"

I sat back, feeling deflated by the hostility of his attack. And surprised at his ability to identify one of my core issues and bore in on it. Never underestimate the marksmanship of a patient, I thought. They can intuit a therapist's vulnerabilities and be all over them in a second. The best defense is a good offense.

"Steve, I'll answer that in a minute. But first, let me explain something. I realize I'm probing sensitive areas in you. And that when I do it frightens you, and sometimes hurts you. Your gut reaction is to get back at me for that hurt. Which is okay. But we both need to be aboveboard. Honest in what we say to each other. If I hurt you, tell me. If you get angry at me, tell me. This is a safe place. Nothing that takes place here goes outside that door unless you want it to. But the main thing is: We have to be honest and open with one another. Okay?"

He was silent.

"Now you asked about me. If I'm such an expert in human relationships, why the poor track record?"

He nodded slightly, but didn't look at me.

"Relationships, finding the right person, have been a problem for me. You'll be interested to know that I've spent a bit of time in therapy discussing that. I've had my own share of maturing to do. I held off making a commitment because of college and graduate school. Nice big rationalizations, really, but I felt like I couldn't handle too many things at once. I was scared, too. When I did get married, I thought I'd found someone to spend the rest of my life with. Unfortunately, it didn't work out that way."

I stopped. I was saying far more than I'd intended to, and Steve glanced up. Now he was waiting for me to go on. So I'd share a little more, I decided.

"We were two nice people who never should have gotten married. We had very little in common. In a way, it was too bad. In other ways, maybe it was good for me—I learned a lot from it. And I'm still learning. For many reasons I wasn't ready for everything a good marriage entails—giving up a part of yourself, making the other person's needs at least as important as your own. Now I understand better what happened, and that's helped. And one of these days I'll be ready to try again."

I smiled at him, but he didn't smile back.

"So, will you get married again?" He studied my face.

"Sometime, probably. Friendship, companionship, is all I want now. I'm not in any hurry. I'm still reeling a bit. It's scary for me, just as your opening up to me is scary for you. But it comes back to that risk factor again. Both of us have risks to take."

He seemed thoughtful, so we sat in silence for a few moments before I added, "Any time you want to ask questions about me Steve, I hope you will. It's only fair. Okay?"

He nodded, then looked sharply at me.

"Are you interested in Brenda?"

I let out a strangled gasp. "What?"

"Are you dating Brenda?" he asked.

"Is that what the patient grapevine is saying?"

He shrugged, smiled, and waited. Guess I'd asked for this.

I sighed. "Steve, this is your therapy hour, not mine. Yes, I'm interested in her. But believe me, we're just good friends. She happens to be going with someone else. Now, may we get back to the therapy of one Stephen Parker, alias The Confetti Kid?"

"Okay. But I bet if you asked her out she'd go. She's pretty cute."

He grinned and I just rolled my eyes. Talk about losing control of the therapy hour.

That afternoon I spoke to Stacey and told him about Steve's medication complaint. We set up an appointment for him and Steve to meet, and when I informed Steve he surprised me by asking if I would be there, too.

"You want me to sit in?" I asked.

"Yes."

"Okay. Any particular reason?"

"Psychiatrists scare me. He seems, I don't know, formidable."

"Okay. He's not, Steve, but you'll find that out."

The following day we met in Stacey's office. I'd warned him of Steve's fearfulness and I saw right away that he was making an extra effort to be cordial and reassuring. The better I got to know Stacey, the more I liked him. I thought I knew what Steve found intimidating; Stacey had a brusque, no-nonsense style about him, and yet at the same time a casual offhandedness. They were conflicting signals and could be misconstrued.

He was a congenital organizer and everything in his world was rendered orderly, logical, sensible. His compulsivity drove him to keep voluminous notes in a packed calendar book. His shirt pocket drooped with three Mont Blanc pens and a variety of cards containing long lists that he consulted frequently. A couple of times someone on the team had teasingly threatened him with stealing his lists to see if he'd collapse without them. He'd made it very clear to everyone that we should never try it.

Even the way Stacey moved fit his personality. There were no superfluous motions, just a fluid, loping walk on a tall spare frame that ambled effortlessly from the nursing stations to the wards and back to his office again.

As Steve listed complaints about the medication, Stacey leafed through the chart, occasionally looking up, nodding, asking a question. When Steve described the blurry vision he was having and how it affected his drawing, Stacey reacted quickly.

"We'll cut back then, Steve, and see how it works. Let me know if you continue to have side effects and how disruptive they are."

"How often should I tell you?"

"As often as you have something to report. Joan or Pat can usually track me down. Or write me a note and leave it at the nursing station. But keep me informed."

"Okay. How soon will I notice a change?"

"You have to understand, Steve," and here Stacey closed the chart and set it on the desk, "you're taking one of the most powerful mind-altering drugs we have. Navane strikes right at the core of brain activity—the neurotransmitters, which integrate thinking, feeling, behaving. That's what it took to get you out of psychosis. And you're not operational yet. Most of you is back in reality, but a big part is still stuck off somewhere else. We've got to get you past that."

Steve recoiled. As usual, Stacey wasn't mincing words.

"Do you know if there's been any schizophrenia in your family?" he asked.

Steve shook his head. "Not that I know of. My parents drank quite a bit. My father may have been an alcoholic. But—"

I looked sharply at Steve. This was the first I'd heard about it.

"Well, what's happened to you, then?" Stacey asked

him. "What's all this Confetti Kid business?"

Steve looked helplessly at me.

I nodded encouragement to him.

"I'm not sure," he began. "Mac says the glue that holds my personality together dissolved, under stress and stuff. That I'm not put together too well."

"And what do you say?"

He thought a moment.

"I really believe in The Confetti Kid. What he stands for: goodness and decency in a world that's a total mess. But I'm not sure what's real and what isn't any more. We've been talking about when sanity becomes insanity, and where you draw the line. But it's not easy. Right, Mac?" he asked hopefully. I nodded.

"Yes, I like the way you put it," Stacey replied. "You want to hear my ideas?"

"Sure." He seemed relieved to have the pressure taken off.

"In spite of what some people say about glue holding your personality together," and here Stacey stopped and winked at Steve, "there's some very exciting research into the possibility that people may have a genetic predisposition to develop a schizophreniform disorder like yours. That's why I asked about your family history."

Steve nodded and Stacey continued.

"A person's DNA is composed of genes that program not only physical characteristics like body build, hair color, and all that, but psychological ones as well—temperament, motivation, even talent, like your artwork. We think some of those genes click on and click off all during a person's life, programming all kinds of physical functions—aging, diseases like diabetes, maybe even cancer. And it's quite possible, though we don't know this, that some genes click on for psychological disorders as well, like depression, and possibly Alzheimer's."

"So what do you think happened to me?"

"You probably have a genetic predisposition to psychosis. When stress continues to build, most people bend, and bend some more, but you didn't. You broke. If you did once, more than likely you will again. That's why we want to help rebuild you so you'll be tougher. We want your personality to be like the broken bone—once it's healed, it's stronger."

"Is that what the medicine is for? To make me stronger?"

"Partly. We hope so, anyway. Maybe during your lifetime someone will be able to fix that faulty gene, or whatever it is that happens. But in the meantime you'll probably need to take medications. Not all the time, maybe, but whenever you feel yourself slipping, losing control. So actually, the responsibility for getting better—and staying better—will be in your hands."

Sometimes Stacey laid things out with painful honesty.

"So sometime in the future, there'll be a cure for all the people at Peace River?"

"That's the hope. Down the road quite a ways, but it may well happen sooner than we think. Right now a whole coordinated research project—the Human Genome Project—is being carried on in laboratories all over the country. In the next decade or so, researchers should have a pretty good idea about what each gene on the chromosome does, and what its specific function is. Which one gives you brown or red or curly hair, which makes you a musical genius or a gifted painter, and which sets off a clinical depression like some of the patients here have. The potential is enormous. And the psychoses will, in all likelihood, be in there, too."

"But how would it work?" Steve asked, genuinely intrigued.

"At this point it's pure speculation, Steve. It may be that a majority of these illnesses will be traceable to a defective gene or a cluster of genes. The next step will be altering it very early on—in the embryo, even. So that what was supposed to happen never does. I prefer things that way—

structured. Put it on the electron microscope. Let me see it. Cause and effect. If something's wrong, find out what and where and fix it." Stacey paused. "Have you ever taken a good biology or genetics course?"

"Not since high school."

"Well, the thinking now is that a gene may trigger a mental change by giving instructions to the body to make less of a given biochemical substance, or perhaps more. So in the brain, where all activity is regulated by electrical-chemical transmissions, interruptions in the messages going from one part of the brain to the other would disrupt thought processes. Specific genes may very well program one group of people to have depression and another group to have the symptoms of schizophrenia.

"If a gene kicks off those changes and they last for a period of time, at some point the cells that make up the brain's structure seem to adjust to those changes. And then you have the person who becomes chronically mentally ill.

"That's why," Stacey added, "we want to put those brain cells of yours in as good working order as possible before we turn you loose. Does that make sense to you?"

Steve met Stacey's eyes and for a moment I thought he was going to object, but then he nodded.

"Yes," he said. "I guess it does." A tinge of excitement, of maybe-things-will-be-all-right-after-all, lingered in his voice.

Two steps forward, I thought.

"One other thing," Stacey said. "I want you to become as well informed as possible about what happened to you. Go to the medical library. Read the psychiatric journals. It's your mind and your life we're talking about. Be the kind of patient who is knowledgeable. That'll give you greater control over your illness."

Steve nodded. "I'm beginning to feel like I'm back in school again. Should I be expecting an exam in here somewhere?"

"You've already passed it, Steve," I said. "You decided to stay."

He shot me a look—as if he were about to be dropped behind enemy lines for a dangerous mission. Then he made a thumbs-up gesture. And smiled.

14

A WEEK AFTER KAYLA'S VISIT, STEVE VERY TENTATIVELY handed me his journal. I thanked him and promised to return it in a few days. But something was on his mind.

"You seem uncomfortable."

"I'm wondering what you're going to do with what's in there."

"I'm going to spend some time reading it, think about it, and try to understand you better. Then I'll write you some comments. Nothing more."

He didn't seem reassured.

"I won't criticize you, Steve. At worst I may encourage you to explore something in more depth, maybe suggest a book you might read, but that'll be about it."

He still looked doubtful.

"Trust me," I asked, holding my thumb and index finger closely together, "just this much?"

He shrugged and took off for the ward.

Robert Lane

I got to the journal as soon as I could. As I'd anticipated, it almost vibrated with his artistic sensitivity. There were comments about our early fall and, here and there, a poem or a sketch. I quickly scanned the first two poems, then read:

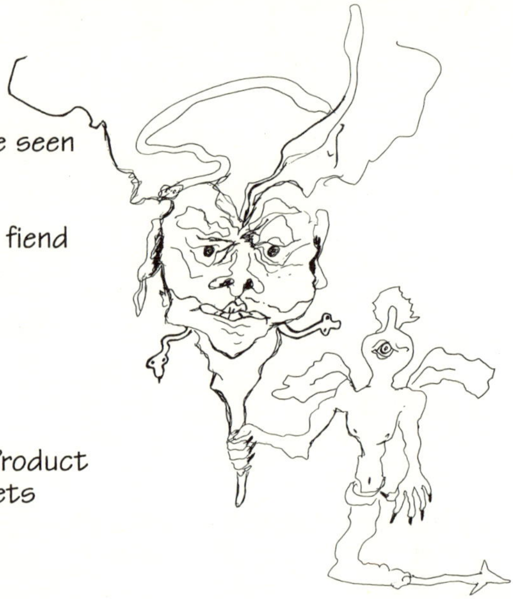

Horrific
    Goreific
        The things I have seen
Monolithic
    Paleolithic
        The home of the fiend
          And now I rest
        And now I die
    And now
And

Our Gross Domestic Product
Which art in the Markets
Hallowed be Thy name
Thy machinery hum,
Thy profits come
On earth, that's considered Heaven . . . .

Mother Teresa
Do you ever have a little nip now and then?
Otherwise how would you endure the pain you see?
The starving children
The sick, the dying
The world leaders you have to meet
And shake the hands of deceit
Mother Teresa
Would you like to share a bottle some night
Over a smoky oil drum fire
And tell me how . . .
                    . . . to survive

The majority of the journal entries were fairly guarded. The one exception dealt with the attorney Steve had mentioned who was described with great frustration and some of the anger he had so much trouble expressing. He seemed to be using the defense mechanism of projection—placing the blame for everything that had gone sour for him on someone else.

October 18 2:30 p.m.

I keep thinking about that jerk Andis. He's responsible for most of this. I mean, I didn't need any more financial pressures. He's always so self-righteous, lecturing me on how I should live my life. He says the same things in a hundred different ways. Sometime I'm really gonna let him have it—tell him exactly what I think. Wonder what he'd do if I did. Probably never give me another dime! What an idiot! Why the court left everything up to him. I'll never know. It's a royal pain . . . .

He did not refer to anyone else, nor to any other feelings. Fairly well-defended, Steve had woven himself into a psychological cocoon. Unwrapping it would be slow going. Although I found the poems and drawing startling, I didn't comment on them, but pressed him to dig deeper, to try to discover the real Stephen Parker. When I returned the journal to him, he flipped immediately to my commentary, scanned it, and seemed relieved.

"Thanks, Pat."

"One question I did have, though, Steve, about this attorney—Andis. Does he know you're here?"

"My illustrious lawyer? With all the lustre worn off? No. He doesn't."

"Shouldn't you let him know?"

"Why should I? I don't want to talk to him. Besides, he doesn't need to know. Until I need money—"

"Do you have an inheritance coming?"

"Yeah. But it's all locked up in a trust. It amounts to about eighty thousand dollars or so, but I'll never see most of it. I needed some to finish school, but the dork wouldn't hand any over."

"Why not?"

"I don't know. He doesn't like me. He doesn't approve of the courses I'm taking. Kept stalling me with one dumb excuse after another."

"Still, he should probably know you're here. Do you want me to call him?"

"Sure, go ahead. Then you can see for yourself what a total moron he is. He has a Teflon brain—nothing I say sticks to it."

I smiled tolerantly. "He can't be all that bad."

"Right, Mac," Steve said sarcastically. "He couldn't be."

I got Andis's number in Milwaukee from Information and was told by his office to call back at exactly 3:20 p.m. Okay, I did. At 3:20, Attorney Andis was still in court, so I was asked to call at 4:05, which I also did. Still not there. After two more abortive attempts, I finally reached him. But before I'd finished identifying myself, he broke in.

"Who's paying for this?"

I explained I was calling on the hospital line, which was taxpayer supported.

"I don't mean the phone call. I mean my time. My fee is $250 an hour, which translates to a little over $4 a minute. Who's going to pay that?"

"This really shouldn't take that much of your time. Or mine. I'm calling as a professional courtesy."

An explosive bark erupted from the receiver, presumably Mr. Andis, Esquire, clearing his throat or bringing up a hairball. I held the phone away from my ear for a moment.

"Okay, okay. Let's get on with it. Who are you calling about?"

"I'm calling about Stephen Parker," I said evenly. "He's a patient here at Peace River Mental Health Institute. I understand from him that you're the executor—"

Another explosive bark. This time I yanked the receiver away and waited for the spasm to pass. I'd never heard anything like it. God, what would it be like to be in court with this man?

"I knew it!" he roared. "I knew Parker was a loser. I've spent a lot of my valuable time talking to that young man. Not that it's done any good. He was a great disappointment to his parents, you know. It's a blessing they've been spared further heartache. And he certainly won't listen to a thing I tell him. Don't think I haven't tried to get through to him. Majoring in art and philosophy. How ridiculous! How's he going to support himself? I must have asked him that a hundred times. Of course, he never had an answer—"

I could feel myself bristling. Steve was right: Andis was an arrogant jerk. Worse. He motor-mouthed on until I finally heard him say:

". . . So now he's in trouble, locked up in a mental hospital, and he decides to come to me—"

"He's not in trouble, Mr. Andis," I interrupted. "And he's not locked up, either. He's undergoing treatment for a psychological problem."

"He's got a psychological problem all right. He is totally unrealistic. If I told him once: business, accounting, finance. That's where the money is."

"Mr. Andis, listen to me: What Steve needs far more than criticism and anger is your understanding and compassion. And your prayers.

"Goodbye, Mr. Andis." The line was silent as I hung up the phone.

Steve came to our next session waving a letter at me. It was the most animated I'd ever seen him.

"She answered my letter! Jennifer! She'll come see me if I want her to! *If I want her to!* How could she think I wouldn't? The sooner the better, as far as I'm concerned." He was euphoric.

All during the following week I tried to calm him down, pointing out that a visit hardly signaled a reconciliation. But he wouldn't hear of it. He was so high that I considered asking Stacey to evaluate his meds.

The shock came when Brenda asked if I'd read Jennifer's letter. I hadn't, of course. After thrusting it in my face, Steve had tucked it back in his shirt pocket. It seemed that he had written Jennifer several very poignant letters, begging her to visit. Jennifer had called Brenda and said she would agree to meet with him only if it would be helpful in his recovery. And only if we—Brenda and I—were present.

I presented Steve with Brenda's description, but he denied badgering Jennifer. And refused to produce her letter. When I told him the four of us would be meeting together at Jennifer's request, he stalked away. He'd so convinced himself that Jennifer was coming back to him that he wouldn't even consider any other scenario. And the distance he now established between us showed me he was furious with the messenger who brought him the news—me.

The morning of Jennifer's arrival, Steve did a flip-flop and decided he didn't want to see her after all. "Just tell her I'm sick," he said.

I told him it was pretty crummy of him to expect us to make excuses for him. Jennifer was coming all this way just to see him, and only because he had pleaded with her to do so.

At last, he relented. But as we waited in my office, he still searched for escape clauses—"I can't go through with this, I look like hell" . . . "I don't know what to say to her" . . . "I really feel sick. . . ."

I told him to settle down. "You started this, Steve. You have to see it through."

Eventually Brenda knocked and entered. Jennifer hung back at first, then appeared in the doorway.

"Nice to see you again, Jennifer," I said, standing.

"Hello, Dr. McGarry—" she began, then broke off as she met Steve's gaze. They stared at each other like two little kids, shy and afraid. Both were dreading this meeting.

"Hi, Jennifer, nice to see you," Steve said breezily, trying for a certain bravado that didn't come off.

"Steve—you look good," she said, a crimson blush rising in her cheeks. She really was a beautiful young woman.

I caught Brenda's eye. We smiled like a couple of matchmakers.

"So how've you been?" Jennifer asked.

"Good. Food's lousy, almost as bad as the commons. And there's not much privacy around here. But otherwise I can't complain."

He glanced at me with a pleading where-do-we-go-from-here look. Brenda picked up on it and said, "Why don't we all sit down?"

Jennifer gravitated to the chair beside Steve. Brenda closed the door and took the last chair, next to my desk. After more small talk, she turned to Jennifer:

"Were there some questions you had for us, Jennifer? Or something you wanted to tell us?"

"Well no, not really. Steve wanted me to come." She shot a quick look at him and then dropped her eyes.

Steve shifted uncomfortably. "Well, yeah, it's been a while," he said. Then, to me, he said, "I wanted to see her again."

"Did you have something to say to Jennifer, Steve?" Brenda asked.

He shrugged. "You're putting me on the spot here. What can I say?" He couldn't bring himself to look at her. "I want her back."

Jennifer sighed. Since Steve seemed to be talking through us, Jennifer did too. "Steve and I were close. Very close. I think the world of his talent. He's very gifted. But as I told you last time, there's a side of him I don't understand. And it scares me. When we were together, some of the time he was so confident, just bubbling over with all these wonderful ideas. And then seconds later, for no reason I could ever figure out, he'd swing over to the other side and get really down and hate himself. And when things got bad, he'd disappear into the room he used for a studio and not come out for hours."

Steve had sunk down into his chair, trying to remove himself from the conversation. He still didn't seem to be able to look at Jennifer, but he didn't try to stop or dispute her either.

Jennifer's eyes glistened with tears. "Toward the end he would say really spiteful things to me. Things that hurt—that I didn't love him, and stuff like that. And he'd get so angry with me, but I never knew why. I always figured he was upset about us and was just taking it out on me, but that wasn't fair. It made me miserable.

"And everything had to be perfect. His standards were so high they could never be met. *I* certainly couldn't meet them. Not even Steve himself could, really. I think he knew that, but he just couldn't admit it. He was so terribly afraid that he would be a . . . a failure, I guess. He took everything out on me until I just couldn't take it any more—"

Jennifer was weeping silently and Brenda took her hand and gave it a squeeze.

Softly, I said, "How did things seem from your perspective, Steve?"

There was a long silence. Then he practically whispered, "I have nothing to add."

"Steve. Please try. We need to know what went wrong between you two." I paused. "Jennifer needs to know."

He rubbed his forehead, hiding his face. "I don't have

anything to say. You heard her. Nothing I ever did was right. That's the way it always is for me . . . with people."

"You mean they always hurt you, Steve?" I asked quietly.

"Yes. Always."

"And that hurt wrecked whatever trust you had?"

He straightened abruptly.

"Ask *her!"* he demanded, pointing at Jennifer.

"Ask her what, Steve?" said Brenda.

"Ask her what she did to me. She knows. God, she hurt me. I trusted her, and she—all she did was use me—"

"Steve! I didn't! How can you say that? I *didn't* use you!" Now the accusations came fast. "Your ideas of love are so weird! You have all these great dreams, how life is going to be so perfect, how famous you're going to be. But you reject even the simple comforts of life because you don't want to 'sell out.' You turn down help because you're too proud. You sneer at every job and act like you don't have to lower yourself to work because some day you'll be a millionaire."

"I will be. You'll see—"

"Steve, you're living a fantasy. You act like a super-macho male one minute and a scared little kid the next. You go from one extreme to another and you expect me to go along with you. And then you have the gall to tell me that *I* used *you.* Of all the hateful, spiteful things you've ever said, that's the nastiest. And you know it's not true."

A heavy silence descended. Bren and I exchanged looks, deciding by tacit agreement to be still and let things sink in.

After a time I said, "Steve?"

He looked as if he were coming out of a deep trance. He shrugged.

"There's nothing more to say. You can see how she hates me."

"Oh, Steve! How can you say that? I don't hate you. If anything, I still care for you too much. And I hate seeing you in this place. Can't you understand? I wish you could make your peace—with people, with yourself, with life—"

"I have, Jen, I really have." He was earnest now, pleading. "I've accepted the fact that even when I get close to someone, like I did with you, I'm still alone. I always will be—I'm a solitary person. There's something about me, I'm different from anyone else. I know that now—and I accept it. It doesn't bother me anymore."

"No, Steve," said Jennifer. "That's not the inner peace I'm talking about. For your sake, I hope they can help you here. And find out why you're pulled in so many directions."

"What do you mean? I know I was acting a little weird before you left, but that's over now. I've changed. What more do you want from me?" His voice was hoarse, guttural.

"I would like to be your friend, Steve. That's why I came here today. Because I care about you and I want you to get well—" Jennifer stopped. Then she said, haltingly, "Steve, forgive me if I've hurt you, but the doctors have to know these things if they're going to help you. You have to open up to them, let your hurt out. You have to trust—"

"That's easy for you to say," he interrupted. *"Trust!"* He spit the word out in pure disgust. A cauldron of rage was down there somewhere, bubbling away. But he caught it before it boiled over. When he spoke again his voice was cold, resigned.

"Jennifer, let me tell you about trust. Remember that poem I wrote for you? About how it felt like some great giant was reaching down my throat and ripping out my insides and everything we had was being pulled out by the roots? I still feel that way—ripped apart, withered. Dying. Well, enough is enough. I'm not going to feel anything for you—or for anyone—any more. It's just not worth it. I don't need you. I don't need anybody."

"Oh God, I'm so sorry, Steve." Jennifer's voice choked and she started to sob, burying her face in her hands. Brenda moved to comfort her.

Sorrow and anger enveloped the room like a heavy fog. Brenda and I, equally caught up in their twin agonies, were silent. I was working to keep a cap on my own emotions. When I looked at Brenda, she gave me a brave glance, but her eyes were watering.

I cleared my throat. ''Steve, do you really think Jennifer meant to hurt you? That she hates you? Is that what you honestly believe?''

He shrugged but said nothing.

''Are you sure you're not the one doing the hating?'' I asked gently.

He shook his head. ''No, I don't . . . oh, I don't know—'' he said softly. Then he moaned, ''Ohhh, it wasn't supposed to happen this way. This isn't how things are supposed to be—''

Suddenly he leaped out of his chair and bolted from the room. I went after him, but he refused to come back.

15

FOR THE NEXT FEW DAYS STEVE AVOIDED ME. OCCASIONally I caught sight of him on the grounds, his neck scrunched down into his jacket, kicking at fall leaves as he plowed along, an agitated, unhappy figure. Once I thought I saw him staring up in the direction of my window. But whenever I was anywhere near the ward, he was nowhere to be seen. The ward staff reported nothing unusual, but I worried that he might not show up for our Friday session.

My apprehension proved groundless. On Friday afternoon he was prompt to the minute. He dispensed with greetings, and I noticed he had his coat with him.

"You told me this is my hour, right? To do with whatever I want?"

"Yes, within reason," I smiled.

"Well, would it be reasonable to walk down to the river?"

I did a quick check of my schedule. "Sure, we can do that. Just so I'm back by three. You've been doing a lot of walking lately, haven't you? And thinking?"

"Yeah."

We headed for the path we'd used before, and soon we passed the spot where Steve had donned his confetti suit that day. Down here the leaves were wet underfoot, muffling our steps. Somewhere ahead the harsh notes of a bluejay announced our coming.

When we reached the Peace River, I was surprised to see how high the water was. A fairly swift current tumbled amid the rocks, and gnawed resolutely at the banks. A little farther on we stopped in a small clearing. I commented on all the erosion taking place.

"That's the way I feel," said Steve. He was pointing to a beautiful but dying clump of paper birch. Precipitously tilted, the roots had been undermined and laid bare by the rushing water.

"Uprooted?"

"Yeah, and about to be swept away."

"We won't let that happen, though, will we, Steve?"

He gave me a long, intense look. As we stood there, gazes locked, I had the eerie feeling of a window open to his soul, revealing fear and pain so intense that I almost flinched. Utter aloneness radiated from his eyes. It was all I could do not to look away.

At last, Steve did. And then, his voice trembling, he asked, "Do you . . . do you think Jennifer will ever come back to me?"

I could only shake my head. "I have no idea. But you're still hoping for that, aren't you?"

His face said it all. He wanted her back more than anything else in the world. He shivered, and I was sure it wasn't from the chill of the air; he was easing away from the intensity of his feelings.

"I know how deeply painful this is for you, Steve. And that it's not easy to share with me."

He nodded and moved toward a large boulder near the water. When he sat down, I chose a rock nearby. His gaze fastened on the swift current.

"It'll be okay, Steve," I said. "You won't be swept away. Whether or not you and Jennifer get back together, you can hang onto me. No matter what we encounter."

He shook his head and sighed resoundingly.

"It's all so scary, Mac. I'm completely confused. I don't understand what's happening to me." He sighed again. "When I saw Jennifer the other day, I realized how much I still love her. You know, I was building my whole life around her. She was my reason for living."

He looked at me, assessing my reaction. I tried to look encouraging.

"Go on."

"Well, when she said she was leaving, my life just unraveled. But it was a mistake to think I could even halfway please her. I mean, somebody like Jennifer? Loving me? Come on! All the while we were together I kept expecting her to leave. And I sure as hell don't want her coming around now, feeling sorry for me because I'm in the nuthouse." He paused, then said more softly, "But I don't want her forgetting about me either."

"What do you want from her, Steve?"

He shook his head and whispered, "I don't know. I care about her so much, I don't think I can stand that I've lost her."

I waited a while, then asked, "What does caring mean to you, Steve?"

He hesitated. "I'm not sure—lots of things, I guess. Wanting to share things with her. Just *be* with her. She was so special to me. We had something so . . ." He lapsed into a long silence.

Finally I said, "Something unlike anything you'd ever experienced before?"

"Totally."

"But you're remembering only the best parts. You've forgotten the worst, when the anger and the blaming began."

"It just about tore my guts out, Mac, it hurt that bad. And it's been hurting ever since. God, when you love someone like that, the pain really cuts deep. Why couldn't it have worked out? You know, I just can't imagine what kind of plan God has for me, to give me so much pain. Am I that bad? Have I done that much wrong? They say you don't get more than you can handle, but I just don't know how much more I can take."

Questions like these were always hard for me to respond to. I'd asked them all myself too many times. All I could muster was, "It must all seem terribly unfair to you, Steve."

So we sat in silence again, watching the eddies swirl among the shoreline rocks. Finally I asked,

"Are you ready to start rebuilding?"

"Will it get Jennifer back for me?"

"You know I can't predict anything like that. What I'm talking about centers on you. Maybe you can learn something that will help next time around, whether it's with Jennifer or someone else."

"Yeah, well there won't *be* a next time. I'm not gonna get shot down again, Mac."

"So you won't even try?"

"Why should I? Give me one good reason."

"You've been alone and hurting for a long time. You've talked about how much you want someone to share your life with."

"Yeah, well, maybe I don't. Maybe it's not worth the trouble. Maybe I'm better off alone. I don't know any more."

"You just told me you wanted Jennifer back."

"Huh. Who am I trying to kid? Jennifer doesn't want anything to do with a psycho. She's never coming back." He gave me an anguished look. "It hurts like holy hell!"

"I know, Steve, I know. You're like everyone else on the face of the earth. The most precious hope you have is to find that one special person who'll love you deeply."

"I tried," he moaned. "I tried so hard. I really did. If Jennifer had tried as hard as I did, accepted me for who I am—"

"And who are you?"

He turned, perplexed.

"Who are you? Do you know who the real Stephen Parker is?"

"Of course I know."

"Are you sure? Steve Parker? The Confetti Kid? The rebel, the artist, the poet, the lover, the would-be millionaire, the student, the husband-to-be—even the 'psycho,' as you put it. An awful lot of roles there. We've got to narrow them down."

He shrugged.

"Come on, Steve, give me a break. I'm on your side. Level with me. You convinced yourself that Jennifer was the person you were looking for. But when she broke away, you shoved all your hopes and dreams off a cliff. As you said, you'd built your whole life around her. Actually, you made your whole identity contingent on her being there. Right?"

"Yeah, I guess."

"So without Jennifer, who are you?"

He shrugged again. "I don't know. Do you think that's why I flipped out?"

"Well, I think it accelerated the feelings that pushed you over the edge. By basing your whole identity on Jennifer, you gave away your power. And put a terrific responsibility on her, which she couldn't take. Now you have to learn to cope with that reality, rather than racing back into your fantasy world."

I knew I was pushing him, but he hung in there with me. To my relief, the meeting with Jennifer had jarred his make-believe life. I was hoping the dislocation was the wedge that could get me into his psyche. But I knew it could go either way.

He was staring thoughtfully at the water again. Finally, in a voice so quiet I could barely hear, he asked:

"So what should I do?"

"You already know what I think, Steve. You have to make a choicc. A real battle is going on inside you—whether to continue your 'I'm okay' charade and hope that your situation miraculously rights itself. Or take the risk that I may have something to offer that will have a substantial impact on your life."

He was silent. I waited, listening to the gurgling waters and the gentle soughing of nearby pines. Finally Steve sighed.

"Believe it or not, I have been trying it your way. A little bit, anyway," he said simply.

"Yes, I've sensed it, Steve."

"You know—" his gaze was on the river again.

"Yes?"

"This river—the Peace River—that's a lyrical name. Peace is such a beautiful word. It's so calming. World Peace —peace among nations, among people, or, like Jennifer said, 'inner peace.' "

"What does 'inner peace' mean to you, Steve?"

He sighed again.

"Inner peace. Peace of mind. Harmony. Being satisfied with what you are, whatever you accomplish. Peace makes me think of words like thoughtfulness and consideration, being able to live without conflict, bitterness, misery." For the first time since I'd met him, he seemed completely untroubled, almost serene.

I sat quietly. Not wanting to break the spell, I reflected on what he was saying, matching it against feelings with which I was all too familiar. It was a rare moment of shared solitude. I was pleasantly aware of the dank smell of the woods, the occasional splash of the water around the boulders.

"This is a beautiful spot," he said.

"That it is, Steve. Serenity itself. Sometimes I think more healing can take place in a natural setting like this than anywhere else."

"Yes," he said. "It heals the spirit."

"I agree. The river is a good metaphor for life. There are areas of turbulence, as you said, when the shores of our lives are eroded and torn away. And there are stretches of relative placidness, the calm pools where we can concentrate on enjoying life and regenerate. The important thing is adapting, using whatever nature gives us to prepare ourselves for the high waters. Becoming resilient enough to prevail. That's what I want you to learn."

He was studying the water, watching it curl around the rocks along the shoreline.

"I don't know, Mac. It just scares the hell out of me. Opening up, you know? Anyway, if the genetic connection is true, I'm pretty much programmed to be the way I am, aren't I? Maybe I should just start accepting that."

"Well, that's an option. But why roll over and surrender? Why not try my way first? Even if you do have a constitutional defect, why couldn't it be offset, compensated for? You may have been born with artistic talent, but you certainly weren't born knowing how to draw perspective. I would imagine artists are like therapists—you never stop reading, experimenting, learning new methods. There has to be tremendous mastery involved to being an accomplished artist. There definitely is in trying to be a decent human being."

We sat silently for a time before Steve turned away from the river and looked directly at me. Then he kind of chuckled.

"You know, Mac, in the last half hour you've made more sense to me than in all our previous times combined."

I smiled and shook my head.

"That's because you're listening now. You're giving me a chance."

I looked at my watch. "As much as I don't want to leave what we have here, responsibility calls. I've got to get back."

"Okay." Steve smiled sadly. "But I'm never ready to leave here."

Reluctantly, he stood and followed me back to the path. As promising as this session had been, I knew better than to get my hopes too high.

16

"WHERE SHALL I START TODAY?"

"Wherever you'd like, Steve.

He shifted in his chair several times.

"You seem fidgety, restless."

"Yeah. I am."

"What's up?"

"I don't know. I guess . . . part of it is, I don't want to bring up what I know needs to be talked about."

I waited, trying to send him some mental courage. I figured if Kayla could do it, I could at least try.

Finally, his voice barely audible, he said, "Remember once you asked what my childhood was like?"

I nodded.

"Well, I've been thinking about it. A lot. Remembering things I haven't thought about in a long time."

"Uh huh."

Another sigh.

"I don't know where to begin."

"Sometimes the very first memories are a place to start."

He looked at me. His hands were gripping the arms of the chair, his posture stiff. The pressure was intense.

"What comes to mind when you think about being a kid? How would you describe yourself, your childhood? In what words?" I kept my voice low, reassuring, my tone warm, comfortable.

He was getting increasingly anxious. "I don't know."

"Close your eyes for a few minutes, Steve, and take some deep breaths. Rest your head against the back of the chair, and let the tension drain out." When his eyes closed and he had breathed deeply a few times, I said, "Imagine the tension flowing out of your fingertips, your toes. Starting with your feet, move up through your body, letting each muscle group relax. Clear your mind. Think only about breathing deeply and relaxing each muscle."

He followed my instructions and soon his breathing slowed, his grip on the chair relaxed, and some of the tightness subsided.

"Maybe I'll just start talking," he said, opening his eyes.

I mouthed an encouraging "okay."

"From as early as I can remember, I've felt . . . like an outsider, as if I didn't belong. Sometimes I wonder why I'm so different." His voice trailed off.

"How so, Steve?"

He sighed deeply. "I've always felt so alone."

Another long silence and I primed the pump again.

"Your parents? Were they—"

"Mostly gone." He looked over at me and I nodded.

"Did you blame yourself, think you were at fault in some way?"

He nodded in a slow, resolute way. "Yes. You know, I think my childhood wasn't so much innocence as it was a . . . kind of oblivion."

"That's a powerful word, Steve."

"That's how I felt, though."

"Can you talk about it?"

He raised his eyebrows and shrugged. "My parents were never there. When my brother and I were little, a string of sitters took care of us. Some were okay, but they were all strangers. After a few months, one would leave and another would take over. A lot of the time we were by ourselves. I was expected to take care of Brad when I was only six or seven.

"Actually," he smiled ironically, "he always handled it better than I did. He had the kind of personality where he just fit in, whoever came to the house, or whatever daycare center we were stuck in. People always liked him 'cause he'd just go with the flow."

"And you?"

His voice turned bitter with self-contempt. "I was the problem kid, the one always messing up."

"How so?"

He shook his head slowly. "I don't know. It was . . . well, the message at home was, 'I've done this for you, now you owe me that.' There were strings attached to everything, and it bothered me because nobody ever did anything just for the sake of doing it because it was the right thing to do. It seemed my folks did things only with ulterior motives. And I never felt I could keep my end of the bargain.

"I mean, I know Mom probably figured that since she'd given me life and cared for me when I was a baby, I owed her. But how can a kid pay that back? How *could* I? By not causing trouble, I suppose. But I couldn't help it. If they wanted me to do something, I wouldn't. Not without a hassle, anyway. I'm sure they didn't know what to do with me. So here I was, this rotten, ungrateful kid who lived in a big house, had all these toys and things. But was desperately unhappy and lonely all the time."

"And they didn't understand where all that unhappiness was coming from?"

He shook his head.

"Tell me about them. What were they like?"

He took a deep breath. "I never understood my parents. Maybe kids aren't supposed to. They got along better than most couples, I guess—a lot of my friends' parents got divorced. Mine argued sometimes, but not very often. Mostly they agreed on what was important."

I nodded.

"Both your parents worked?"

Steve smiled wryly. "Did they ever."

"Tell me about that."

"Dad was an insurance company executive. He made a terrific salary and earned every bit of it. He was as hard-driving and competitive as they come. The company was everything. He was always on the go. My mom told me right before they were killed that he had high blood pressure and that I should try not to upset him. She told me the doctor, who was also a friend of theirs, was trying to get him to take it easier. And quit smoking and drinking so much."

"So he didn't spend much time with you?"

"Nope. He was always in a hurry. 'Hi, Steve, bye, Steve.' Life was one big push for him. If he hadn't had the accident, he probably would've had a heart attack before long. He was only fifty-one, but he seemed a lot older."

He described all this in a surprisingly matter-of-fact tone, as if he were telling me about a television program he'd watched. I couldn't imagine the amount of energy it was taking for him to block out all the underlying emotions.

"It was ridiculous," he said. "Why was he always pushing like that? I never understood him. He was like a stranger."

"It sounds as if he left you with a lot of unfinished business, things that needed to be said but never were."

Steve stared at the floor.

"We'll have to deal with that sometime, Steve."

"Yeah, sometime maybe."

"And your mother?"

"Same story, practically. They fed into each other. Mom had incredible energy. She was busy all the time too. It's just as well they all died together because I don't think she would have wanted to live without him—and he'd have been lost without her. And if it was just Brad who was killed, it would have blown Mom away."

"When did they die, Steve?"

"Three years ago last month. They'd just dropped me off for my second year at Madison and they were driving back to Milwaukee on I-94. They got into this huge multi-car pileup. They might have survived, but there was a semi behind them . . . Mom and Dad died instantly. Brad died the next day."

It was my turn to take a deep breath. I couldn't imagine such a tragedy. "Wow, the three most important people in your life, going down that quickly. It must have knocked you for a loop."

Again, I was surprised at how well defended he was.

"Yes and no. At first, I was so caught up in all the details. I went home as soon as I heard, of course, and ended up having so many things to take care of I had to drop out of school for a semester. It sounds weird, but I never thought much about what had happened. It's like it was someone else's family, I was just a bystander. This is the first time I've really thought about it."

"It's a good start, then, Steve." I decided I'd better keep things at a relatively intellectual level for the time being, so I asked again about his mother.

"What was she like?"

"Mom?" He deliberated before answering. "She was great. Very kind. And funny. She had a great sense of humor. Her name was Marcy. Whenever Dad got edgy she just made a joke and he'd settle down. Brad took after her that way. He was a very witty kid, and quick like she was. But the last year or so, Mom was under a lot of pressure at work. She was an art director at an advertising agency. Very creative, expressive, she really loved it. But there were always deadlines coming up, clients demanding one thing or another, make-or-break presentations. It was tough on her."

"I see why you said your parents were well matched."

"Yeah. My father, my mother, even my brother—he was president of his junior class. They were always on the cutting edge, in the fast lane. I was just the opposite, cautious, careful, very shy around people."

"How do you mean?"

"Oh, well," again the wry smile, "when we were little I can remember how Brad always galloped off to daycare—I was dragged there kicking and screaming. It never bothered him when we changed schools or moved to a bigger house. To him, it was just another adventure. For me, it was having to wrench myself away from the one or two friends I'd managed to make, having to deal with a strange new school, being scared about new teachers. I got teased a lot because I was so shy."

"Anything else you remember from back then?"

He pondered for a time, looking anxious. "The very worst times were when I got sick. I'd want Mom to stay home with me, and sometimes she did. For a while. But then she'd have to get back to work and I never could bear that. I'd beg her not to go, then have a tantrum, throw up, do whatever I thought might keep her from leaving. Tried to make her feel guilty, I guess. But nothing ever worked with her. And I always ended up screaming at her, telling her I hated her."

He shrugged. "Eventually I figured it out. I came in a distant fourth—after her job, my dad, and Brad. I just wasn't as important to her as other people and things that needed to be done."

"So how did you feel about all this?"

A slight hesitation, then, "Helpless. Utterly helpless."

"Frightened?"

"Yes. And very . . . resentful. Nothing ever went my way and there wasn't a damn thing I could do about it."

"Do you feel cheated?"

Steve nodded.

"No one there to love you, no one to take care of you, comfort you when you needed it."

"Uh huh . . ." His eyes were tearing.

"And so you just swallowed all that hurt."

A tear coursed down his cheek. He flicked it away and made a monumental effort to regain his composure.

"What else could I do? I've always relied on myself. You can't count on anyone else, can you? I've learned that, believe me. If I depend on me, I'm in control. Even my art is controlled—at least, that's what my teachers have always said. Controlled creativity. Sometimes I wish I could open up, be more spontaneous, but something holds me back."

"Maybe there's a connection."

"Between what?"

"Between some of what you've been telling me about your childhood and your wanting to be, what, more inspired?"

"Yeah, inspired—I like that. I want to push my work out where no other artist has gone before. But I'm too much of a perfectionist. Jennifer was right about that. Maybe there is a connection. You know, I think I can see some similarities —between Jennifer and me breaking up, and losing my family."

"Those losses were a gigantic shock to your system. Grieving takes a long time."

"Yeah, but . . . you know, I don't think I have been grieving," he said.

We sat in silence for a bit and then I said softly, "Talk about it, Steve."

"Their deaths? Well, now that I think about it, I never did deal with it. And believe me, I don't want to think about it now either. Not ever."

I nodded.

"Like I say," he went on, "things had to be taken care of—and I was the only one left to do it. That clown Andis helped with the legal stuff, but I had to take care of all the personal effects and junk. It was just too much. Too much."

"I'm sure. And no feelings ever came out, Steve? No grief?"

"Not that I remember. No."

"So then what happened?"

"Oh, the whole thing got so messed up. Dad and Mom were both making high salaries, but they owed a lot on our house, and on the condo we had in Florida, and all the cars. We had four. I really wanted to keep the BMW convertible, but I couldn't. Everything was 'heavily financed,' as they say. Plus, Mom and Dad were always very generous with Brad and me. We lived pretty well.

"Too well, as it turned out. All they left was a lot of debt. And it was a worse mess because neither one of them had a will. I couldn't believe how complicated that made it. I mean, how could they not have had wills? I guess Andis was right—they worked so hard they couldn't be bothered with managing all the money they made. So they spent it and borrowed whatever they didn't have for whatever it was they thought they needed. But they had no idea of their assets and liabilities. Someone at the bank said they must have thought they would live forever. I think that's true."

"A lot of people live that way."

"I'm never going to."

"Oh?"

He shook his head. "Uh uh. It was very . . . disillusioning. Besides, one thing I do know: Nothing lasts forever."

"True. What else have you learned?"

He leaned back in thought. I liked that about him. He seemed to consider things carefully, a mature quality for someone so young. At last he said:

"I guess I began to question a lot of things. Their deaths made me look at life more seriously. I began to think maybe I wasn't as wrong and out of step as I'd always thought I was. I read a lot, and the more I read, the more I felt some of the things I thought were important really were important after all."

"So your perspective began to change?" I asked.

"Only a little. Having to settle the estate took a lot of time. But it really opened my eyes. When all the properties were disposed of, the debts paid, and the lawyers' and accountants' fees settled, there was about eighty thousand left. Andis got himself appointed trustee and he's doled it out to me like it's his money. I'm sure my parents would never have wanted him to have the last say, but that's how it turned out. It's really ironic."

"Oh?"

"Yeah, Mom and Dad had lots of ideas about what was best for me, but all I know is, I don't want to live the way they did."

"So how do you want to live, Steve?"

Again, I got the wry expression.

"That's the problem, I know pretty much what I don't want, but I'm not sure yet just what I do want. Or how to get it."

He brooded a while.

"Heck, planning my life seems impossible. The rules keep changing. I hate that. I like things to stay the same. But, of course, they never do. And it's gonna get worse. I mean, my generation is inheriting chaos. I don't know how you plan for that."

"Plan for what?"

He shook his head. "The future. This country is morally and financially bankrupt. The economic system we're inheriting owes trillions of dollars. I can't begin to imagine how much that is. And the national debt keeps going higher, and higher, and higher. That's going to be with my generation all our lives. It's gonna mess up our standard of living—at the very least. The whole thing is totally screwed up. Things just keep getting worse, and no one does anything."

He looked over at me.

I nodded. He was right.

"I didn't think about it till just now, but that's pretty

much the way my family was, too. Appearance was the important thing—acting as if everything was great when it was really rotten deep down." Steve sighed. "To me," he went on, "life should be about being together, sharing ideas, experiences. I mean, that's how a family's supposed to be, right?"

I nodded again.

"Yeah, well, the only time I even saw my parents was when we were playing tennis or eating pizza, or maybe watching a football game. Even then, their beepers would go off. We never talked."

"Did you try?" I asked.

"Nah. No one was ever around. They were too busy keeping everything going. Even at home they were busy, on the phone or something. Handling some crisis or other. That's one of the reasons I don't know how to act when I get around people. I'm always wondering if they think what I say is stupid. So I just don't say much."

"You're not very sure of yourself, are you?"

"That's an understatement."

"It's tough on your self-esteem, Steve."

"I don't have any 'self-esteem,' Mac. My opinion of myself is pretty lousy." He looked over at me.

I motioned a "go on."

He appeared to be taking an internal inventory.

"There's not much of anything I like about me: I'm very average, or below. Manny Mediocre. I've always wanted to be exceptional, but I'm really very common." He said it all with terrific finality.

I could only shake my head. "You sure are hard on yourself. Probably twice as hard as anyone else would be. How come?"

"I just have high standards, that's all. I expect a lot of myself. I don't want to be a failure."

"So you're either a success or you're a failure? It's that all-or-nothing?"

"Yeah, when you put it like that, it is. You either do something well or you fail."

"And what happens when you fail?"

"Even the thought of failing makes me feel a little sick. That's why I push myself so hard. I want to innovate, try out new things, be what Sartre calls an 'active agent.' "

I started to reply, but he rushed on:

"This reminds me of something! When we studied Nietzsche in philosophy, I could really identify with him. He was a renaissance man with a strong social conscience, a real awareness of the underclass. Totally committed to searching for truth. The more stuff of his I read, the more I realized how similar we are. His family was just like mine—all messed up. He was super-upset because nobody cared about anyone else. And there was this big gap between the aristocracy and the poor, just like there is now." Suddenly, he stopped.

"What?"

"If I tell you, you're gonna think I'm crazy."

I smiled.

"I know, I know. You already think I'm crazy. But this is *really* crazy."

I shrugged and smiled again, intensely pleased at how he was opening up before my eyes.

"A while back, I believed I was the reincarnation of Nietzsche. And I thought I could find the answers to life by locking myself in my room the way he did. For over a week I hardly ate, didn't watch TV or listen to stereo. I just read, thought, and waited for something big to happen." He frowned and fell silent.

"So what happened?" I asked.

"Bad news." He shook his head sadly. "Nothing happened. Except I got super-depressed. By the end of the week I was totalled out, absolutely convinced that there was nothing to live for, no hope." His voice trailed off.

I murmured, "Quite a downer."

"Yeah, it was. I crashed in flames."

I left him with his thoughts again. After a while he glanced over at me. "I just remembered something else about Nietzsche. He went crazy, too, you know. Just like me. Died in the asylum, I think."

Silence again. He studied his hands. Then, his voice hushed, he said, "Maybe I'll die here."

"Why do you say that, Steve?"

He shook his head. "Death pops into my mind every now and then."

"Oh? How long has that been going on?"

"Years."

"How often?"

"Depends . . ."

"On?"

He shrugged. "If things are going well, I don't think about it. But like, when nothing seems to go right—"

I waited. Silence.

"Have you ever thought about suicide as a way out?" I asked.

Steve nodded silently.

"Can you share that with me?"

He shook his head slowly.

"Have you ever tried to kill yourself, Steve?"

A pronounced sigh. Then a whisper. "I don't want to talk about it."

"Okay, Steve. But sometime we have to unearth this stuff. This is part of the heavy load of baggage you keep dragging around."

"I know. I'm just not ready."

Silence stretched out again. At last, speaking softly, he said, "The first time was when I was about thirteen, and then I tried again when I was sixteen."

He checked me to see if that might be enough. It wasn't. I motioned to him to keep talking.

He sighed. "The first time I took a bunch of pills, but I

threw them up. The second time they stayed down and I woke up sicker than a dog. I didn't know how much to take to do the job." He looked at me again.

"You didn't have to have your stomach pumped?"

"No. Mom and Dad never knew anything about it."

"How serious were you?"

"Serious. Neither one was just a gesture, if that's what you're wondering, Mac. *Gesture,"* he sneered. "God, what a way to describe an attempt on your life."

"Why did you want to die, Steve?"

He shook his head. "I was miserable. Nothing mattered. I was sure nobody'd miss me anyway and I was tired of being alone. The second time I was drunk and just figured things were never going to get better."

"You've been hurting a long time, Steve," I reflected.

"Yeah."

"What was it like for you before you tried to kill yourself? What led up to the second attempt?"

"I mostly remember nothingness, deadness. Everything inside shut down because everything outside caused too much pain. Like, I'd get choked up seeing a homeless person pushing a shopping cart down the street. All I could see was me, ending up like that. Or like a blind man tapping along. It was unbearable. Once I saw a little kid in the mall being slapped by his dad, and I couldn't stand it, I wanted to punch the guy out. There's too much hurt and sadness. Death in living color on 164 cable channels—car and plane crashes, families incinerated in fires, assassinations, homicides, serial killers, awful civil wars. It goes on and on."

He looked over at me and I sensed he wanted confirmation. Were these perceptions valid? Did he have a right to retreat?

"I agree. Everything you say is true. It bothers me, too. A lot."

Steve was looking directly at me. "The Confetti Kid is

our only chance to put it all right. Only he can end the suffering."

"Well, it's true, his message is one of hope, of something better, something to live for."

"Yeaaah," he said, drawing it out. For the first time, I thought, he was seeing how the real world connected to his delusional one.

"I have a lot of admiration for The Confetti Kid, Steve. He's a crusader who believes in principles and lives by them."

"He tries to—"

"Well, he does more than try. He's devoted to bringing back values that have been missing for a long time. Is that close?"

"Yeah, I guess so. I've seen stuff on TV about the fifties. Things seemed a lot less complicated then. People were happier. They had less, maybe, but they didn't seem to mind. There was more togetherness, people kept the same friends, shopped in neighborhood stores. In our neighborhood, people were always moving in and moving out. Some of them we never even met before they moved, or we did. I never wanted to have a best friend because I knew it couldn't last."

He looked over at me.

"Any of this making sense?"

"Yes, it is, Steve."

"It's not crazy?"

"Not at all."

"You'd tell me if it was?"

"Bet on it, Steve."

He gave me a long look. "Then how does a person like me get along?"

"You can learn ways. That's part of our work together."

We sat in silence for a while. Then he said:

"I want to know what you think, Mac."

"About?"

"What I've been talking about. You just sit there and

listen all the time. I want to know what's in your head, okay?''

''Okay. I agree with a lot of what you say. There's a great deal of suffering in the world. Life is very often unfair. It certainly wasn't fair to your family, it hasn't been fair to you, and it isn't to a lot of people. But everyone suffers, gets slugged from time to time, just by the chaotic nature of life. No matter how we try to protect ourselves, there will always be situations that we have no control over.''

''So what does a person do about it?''

''I guess you learn to tough it out. Be resilient enough to absorb the blows. Pick yourself up and come out scarred, but tougher and wiser. You work through the pain, the loss. You try to learn as much as you can from each experience, and then you carry on.''

''Yeah, but what if you keep getting zapped?''

I had to think about that one. ''I guess I can answer that best from a personal point of view. It may not be right for anyone else, but I'm trying to develop a rhythm—having periods of active engagement with the world, but recognizing that I need to pull back regularly. I need solitary times for reflection and renewal, and for deciding what course corrections I need to make.''

''That sounds tough.''

''It is at first, Steve, and it doesn't always work. But once you get the rhythm down, my sense is that's how we come to endure life. By fully grasping it. Actively sometimes, passively others. But always staying engaged.''

Steve smiled. ''Sounds a little like Sartre's active agent.''

17

IT WAS OCTOBER, AND I WAS FEELING GOOD ABOUT STEVE'S progress. Then something happened that made me wonder if I weren't deluding myself.

Halloween is the only holiday on which a bit of lunacy is sanctioned, when it's all right to dress goofy and act outrageously. In a mental hospital, it can be a particularly daffy time. It's also a good excuse for a party.

On Halloween night, barely controlled pandemonium prevailed in the large dining room where most of the patients from Cameron Hall were gathered. The atmosphere was festive. Paper cut-outs of ghosts and black cats dangled from the ceiling, and the tables and windowsills were decorated with grinning pumpkins. Nearly everyone wore a costume. Even Mr. Grunske was there, in his restraining leathers to be on the safe side, but nevertheless painted up like a clown and wearing a fright wig. He seemed to be enjoying himself. Chet, dressed in a cowboy outfit, hovered nearby, escorting Wesley The Rocker to a seat at one of the tables, where he began mini-rocking. No matter where Wesley sat, he rocked. To an outsider, the scene would have looked a bit surreal, but it delighted me.

In the middle of the crowd, I noticed a tall black witch's cap, moving constantly. Joan Lindstrom turned out to be under it. A number of other techs and nurses were also decked out, some with great wit and creativity.

People bobbed for apples, played pin-the-tail-on-the-donkey, and drank apple cider. Then the inevitable bingo game began. Hospital bingo games are a world unto themselves. Every patient wants to be a winner, so whenever a letter-number combination is called out, arms shoot up and two or three people simultaneously yell, "Bingo!" just as a matter of course. Considerable discussion then ensues but eventually the game gets underway again until the next bingoes are challenged. In our hospital's version of the game, there can be no losers, and the rules are flexible enough that there never are. Before long, the players' pockets were filled with candy bars and other small prizes.

Suddenly there was a stir at the double doors. When I looked, I saw an imposing figure clad in a black sheet, a stark white skeleton mask for a face. The garish features had been painted on with some sort of chalky substance. I actually shivered. It was not your fun figure.

"Who's that?" whispered Brenda, who'd joined me near little Murray. I had just substituted a big pumpkin cookie for the napkin he'd been munching on. With so much stimulation he was relapsing slightly into his former tendencies. So were a few other people.

"Beats me," I said.

"It's creepy."

"Yeah, bizarre," I agreed. "Who'd do something like that?"

We looked at each other.

"I think we're about to find out," Brenda said quietly. "It's coming this way."

The figure approached and paused in front of us.

"And who might you be?" I asked the apparition, trying to keep my voice light. By now I had a pretty good idea.

"I—" and my suspicions were confirmed as soon as I heard the alter ego voice, "—am the personification of Death—the *Grim Reaper*. I have awaited this day with great eagerness. My appetite must be satisfied. And I will not be denied! Take heed!"

With that the black sheet whirled and stalked off to the punchbowl.

"What was that all about?" asked Brenda.

"I don't think we want to know."

Later that week my schedule had a respite when an inservice meeting was cancelled. I stopped by the nursing station and joined a small group on break, drinking coffee and helping to demolish a large box of great-tasting doughnuts. People were looking ahead to the weekend and the mood was light and a little silly. Gradually they drifted back to their duties and only Brenda and I remained. Just what I'd been angling for. It wasn't often I got her alone.

"That was a spooky bit with Steve the other day. Was it connected to his therapy?" she asked.

"I'm sure it was. He's really working at it, very on-task."

"That's good to hear."

"He's smart, too. I'm picking up a bit from him. Between my own therapy and listening to him, my learning curve is in a power climb." I swooped my hand into the air, palm down, like a plane. I was half kidding.

"You're in therapy?" Brenda seemed surprised.

"Oh, sure," I said casually. "For a few months now. Learning to cope with the trauma of adjusting to the slow pace back here." I kept a smile in my voice.

She stared at me, evidently not sure if I was serious. I decided to level with her. I told her about the situation in California. And my hopes of finding a way of life that was more in keeping with my identity and the future I wanted.

"And what have you found since you've been here?"

"A lot to like," I smiled. "The pace, the people. It was the right decision."

Brenda's clear green eyes continued to study my face, and I felt the magnetism between us. She really was beautiful. A nice mix, very refined and feminine, but at the same time spontaneous and feisty, always ready for some new adventure. And there was a gentleness, an openness about her that I really admired. No gamesmanship or hedging. With Brenda, you knew instantly where you stood. She projected an I-can-take-care-of-myself image, but right on the surface there was also a vulnerable side to her that people sensed and responded to. It was no accident that the patients revered her and were very protective of her.

Now she smiled at me and cocked her head.

"So do you miss California?"

"I miss absolutely nothing about California except my family, friends, and a special little buddy from Merrick State Hospital."

"Then why are you in therapy?" She blurted it out and then clamped her hand over her mouth, blushing in embarrassment. "Oh, how terrible of me, Pat. Talk about nosy social workers. I'm really sorry. I didn't mean to pry—"

"Bren, stop." I put up my hand. "There's nothing wrong with asking. It's simple enough: I just think therapists need to experience therapy themselves. And it's a good idea to go in for a tuneup every now and then. I was overdue."

She raised her eyebrows.

"Actually, I've been examining what went wrong in my marriage. What led up to it, what I contributed to the breakup, what I'll do different next time."

"Oh." Brenda looked perplexed. Why? I wondered.

"Anyway," I said. "I don't mind telling you. The main thing I'm interested in is understanding certain parts of me that I obviously didn't before."

"I never would have guessed. You always seem so, I don't know, together. Is it helping?"

"Yes, definitely. Being a client is tough, though. Not just the hard work, but sometimes I tune into the technique being used and it sidetracks me. All in all, though, I think I'm coming around."

"Well, good." She paused. "You like it here, then?"

"Very much so. Of course, I haven't been through a winter yet, but I really like the hospital, and our team. And my neighbors have been wonderful—just kind of adopted me. I had my first vegetable garden ever this summer, I've refinished a nice old oak desk chair, and I just signed up for a ceramics class. Which I've always wanted to do—work with all that gooshey clay."

"You *are* busy."

"You know what, though? The biggest plus I've found here is leisure time. I never had any before. In California, I spent hours of every day on the freeway, and just generally running around. Here I do twice as much and still have time to do other things I want to do. And I love the fall. It's been another whole new experience for me. The colors, the crisp air, the smell of burning leaves—I can't get enough of it."

"Sounds nice," Brenda said wistfully. "I can't remember the last time I took a walk."

"Well, you should make it a point to. It's good for the soul."

"I know. But I never have time for stuff like that."

I smiled encouragingly. "You have to allow for some 'Brenda time.' At least once in a while." I paused. "There. Now we're even. I promise, no more unsolicited advice."

She smiled pensively. "I asked for it. And you're right on, Pat. I almost never do something just for me."

"Make the time," I said again. I swallowed the last of my coffee. "You know, it's strange. I'm more relaxed here, too, than I ever was in California. Ever been there?"

"Just once. San Francisco for three days. I loved it."

"San Francisco is totally unlike anywhere else. Great town. But you didn't see the real California."

Brenda didn't respond. She seemed preoccupied.

"What?" I asked.

"Oh, nothing," she said. And then, "There's a chance my boyfriend may be transferred to L.A. He's in Chicago now, but his firm is considering opening an office out there."

"My sympathies."

"Yes, I have doubts."

"About?"

"Oh, about everything, I guess. Maybe I should be seeing a therapist, too." She laughed, but in kind of a sad, resigned way.

We looked at one another, a long, deep look. Then Brenda glanced at her watch. "Uh-oh, I was supposed to be in a meeting ten minutes ago."

The following week I was in Madison for a workshop on "Schizophrenia: Flight and Creativity," and when it ended early, I gave silent thanks. I'd have time to see Kayla before heading back. I called from a phone booth on the university campus. Luckily, she was free and said to come right over. After I quickly brought her up to date on Steve's progress, I said, "The real reason I'm here is to ask you some questions."

Kayla smiled. "I sensed that."

"I guess this whole business confuses me, that there's another dimension of existence somewhere out there—energies, auras, spirits, ghosts, guides, different planes—that can be contacted by someone like you."

She nodded but said nothing.

"I'm not saying it doesn't exist. But a western, rational mind—especially one like mine that's trained to look at the data, analyze it to hell and back—wants some evidence. And I know that's not possible, at least at this point. But I'm really curious, and I like to stay open, explore new topics. I don't want to exclude this whole thing just because I can't collect any data on it. Maybe psychic powers haven't been verified in the laboratory simply because there's no way yet to measure them."

"You can count on that, Pat."

"I haven't mentioned anything about this to people at the hospital—except Brenda and Ben—because I'm afraid of their reactions. A lot of people reject psychics out of hand, and have contempt for people who don't. You must have experienced that."

Kayla smiled. "Yes, Pat. Many, many times. Some people are very afraid of psychic abilities. But the more open and secure they are, the more willing they seem to be to accept the possibility that there are forces they're not familiar with."

"Well, I'm afraid I have to confess to being one of the doubters. Not the contemptuous ones, because I want to know more. I want to know how you do all this. But first—" I paused and sat back.

"Yes?" Kayla asked.

"Do I understand this correctly? That people with psychic powers can not only tell a lot about another person by looking at the aura or listening to the guide you described, but they can predict the future? Because if they can, that has tremendous implications: It means that our futures are already in place. That we have no real choices to make—no free will—because whatever decision we make was already set. It was going to happen anyway. So Steve was going to have a psychotic break. I was going to go through a divorce. Do you know what I mean?"

Kayla nodded, waited for me to continue.

"Trouble is, I have a pretty firm belief that each of us, within certain limits, controls our own destiny. I can't square that with predestination."

Kayla eased forward in the big blue chair. "Would you consider the idea that there may be something in between, Pat? That rather than a lockstep lifespan with no free will, there are strong tendencies that pull us toward certain choices? When I speak of the future, I'm drawing upon the energy of the universe, energy that exists from the tiniest atom up. And much of this energy can be measured.

"Psychic energy is very complex, though. Just as there are people who can hear a wider range of sounds, some of us can see and sense a wider spectrum of colors. And when we see that colored energy surrounding someone, it gives us clues to the person's health, his level of tension or contentment, even impressions of a disordered state like Stephen was in. Still is in."

I looked sharply at her. "Then you could see Steve's illness in his aura?"

"Oh, yes. The aura of psychosis is a chaotic one, the colors are more concentrated, all mushy and dark, out of control. The aura clearly reveals the devastation of the human spirit."

A mushy, dark aura? Come on. I didn't mean to, but I shook my head in disbelief.

Kayla was patient. "If you think about it, Pat, you'll realize that you don't rely exclusively on your five senses. I'm sure in many instances you've trusted your intuition. Haven't you ever gotten a strong urge not to go somewhere because of a vague sense of discomfort? And said something like, 'It just doesn't feel right?' "

"Sure."

"Okay, everyone has. But when most people get premonitions like that, they tend to discount them. They look for a rational reason, because they couldn't possibly know something before it happens, they think. They're usually even embarrassed to tell anyone what they're feeling. So they wonder why they feel they shouldn't do something, but then they shrug it off and do it anyway."

"Yes. I've done that."

"Then there was something psychic operating, Pat. You just suppressed it."

"But how can you say you can take these auras and whatever else you pick up and somehow predict what's going to happen to someone?"

Kayla was shaking her head vigorously. "That part you're mixed up on. I can't predict the future, for many of the reasons you stated before. All of us do make choices—good ones, poor ones. And each choice affects subsequent ones. Particularly at a major crossroad, we have the freedom to choose dramatically different paths. Our lives are the summation of our choices. All I can do is pick up certain tendencies, and perhaps vulnerabilities. In other words, based on a person's aura, and other information that comes to me, I can make intuitive guesses as to what kinds of choices a person will make."

"Why does that sound familiar to me?" I said, smiling.

"Because you do the same thing as a psychologist. You make predictions about a person's future based on judgments about personality styles. Or you use psychological tests. Then you try to predict how a person might behave in a given situation."

"Well, we can tell pretty accurately whether a person might be violent and act out, or be depressed and suicidal."

"Those are extremes, but yes, tendencies within each of us lead us to make specific choices that determine the next choices."

"So you believe people do have the power to make choices, to control their futures?"

"Absolutely, but only if they take that power. And don't let others, or fads, or cultural messages like materialism, decide for them. Many people go through life like ships adrift, moved by whatever currents happen to come along. Fears may paralyze them. Another person may control them. Jobs dictate how others live. So outside forces end up determining the choices, the decisions, and therefore the course of their lives."

"Do the people you see ever want you to predict what will happen if they do one thing or another?"

"Oh, yes. And many times clients want me to make

choices for them. I have to tell them I can advise, but I can't decide for them."

I nodded.

"I encourage each person to approach life with a purpose," Kayla said. "To be realistic and truthful with himself and others. To discover what is wanted out of life and then use imagination and determination to go after it."

"You know, I'm telling Steve essentially the same things, though it's more an ideal that we strive for."

"Of course," Kayla agreed. "And for Steve, it's even more difficult. He's had more than his share of adversity. I'm afraid it could still go either way for him."

"How do you mean?"

She shook her head. "His future is a terribly cloudy one." She closed her eyes in a meditative way. Then she told me she had Steve's permission to call up his aura whenever necessary. "I've been checking in on him every now and then, sending him energy." She paused. "Our Stephen is probing deeper and deeper. The colors around him are getting more vibrant, but they are still quite dark and mixed. He is tapping into some very dangerous areas and his energy is being sapped by the turmoil. There is such agony, and he is so weary of fighting. He fights everything, you know. The world, you, himself.

"He is still very vulnerable. He doesn't yet realize that the fighting is threatening to destroy him."

Kayla lapsed into silence, but her eyes remained closed, so I waited.

"May I have permission to visit your psyche, Pat?"

"Yes," I said without thinking. I gulped audibly, but Kayla gave no sign of hearing me.

After a few moments of silence she said, "Let me have both your hands."

I complied.

Her face was peaceful, relaxed. Then she frowned. "You must be very careful, Pat. Your work with these people carries a certain . . . inherent danger. You try so hard, put so much of yourself into their negative forces, that you run the risk of being sucked down with them. When you climb into that dense cloud of misery, it can be very dangerous for you."

She opened her eyes and looked deep into mine. I nodded that I understood. I was only too aware of how intensely I sometimes felt the suffering of certain patients. Too much so. And she sensed it.

Kayla's eyes closed again and she breathed deeply.

"Yes, I see," she said. "Did you know you have a special guide, Pat?" She smiled. "You'll be pleased to know he's an Irishman. He refers to the relationship between a psychotherapist and his patient as a sacred experience. Sacred because you are helping that person to touch life again. He indicates that there is an exceptional beauty in such a bond. In the case of Stephen, he had died a spiritual death, but you are bringing him back. There is still a long road to be traveled, but he is following you.

"Your guide suggests that you focus on the darkest part of Stephen. There is a burning rage, an inferno, within. This is very destructive. The energies need to be dispersed."

I listened intently, and with an odd sense of resignation. I knew Steve needed to probe those hidden, forbidding spaces. But I also knew you can't push anyone faster than they can handle it, that to do so could be very risky. And according to my estimates, we had a long way to go before Steve would be ready to journey more deeply.

Kayla went on. "The guide says you must teach Stephen to accept the crazy part of himself, rather than allowing it to frighten him so badly. When he begins to slide into the black pit, he panics, as though he's entering a freefall into oblivion. He is not. He can be safe. You must teach him to accept this and not be afraid. To use this negative energy in a constructive way—" She nodded, as if to someone else.

"The Confetti Kid," she continued after a few moments.

"Study The Confetti Kid. There are some clues there. Look for a grain of sand that is an irritant. Usually it's found where it's least expected. Nearby will grow a tiny pearl—the symbol of the inner search. We all must learn to absorb the irritating agent and turn it into a beautiful pearl. That is growth. . . ."

As always, Kayla's words had unexpected meaning for me. But I was wary. I couldn't lead Steve into a depth he might not be able to come back from, even in search of the irritant that had done him so much harm.

Steve's journal was in the brown envelope sitting on my desk when I got back from group. I meant to just scan it, but ended up reading it in detail:

November 5

This afternoon I walked down to my sitting rock on the river's edge. It's a place where the brownish water moves very slowly, the wind ripples the pools, the waves lap at the pebbly shoreline. Geese are flying over me, honking their way south. Forest trees surround me. I can recognize birch, but the rest I don't know—a bunch of gray-brown trunks, shiny red, yellow, and orange leaves, all crowding each other but still getting along okay. There's a softness to the ground here, I guess from having eons of leaves and stuff pile up and decompose. I like to sit on an old granite hardhead and wonder how long ago some glacier left it here and what stories it could tell.

A fish just jumped and scared me, and when I looked up I saw a chipmunk freeze, watching me with curious little brown eyes. Then he went on hiding nuts for winter. A pair of gray birds just hopped down to the water's edge. The female did a little sideways dance, then dunked herself and they both flew off together. Don't ask me how I knew it was a girl bird—she just acted kind of feminine. It made me sad, because it reminded me of Jen, but pretty soon the solitude of the woods soothed me. It felt good.

When I come down here, I feel at peace, alone with nature. I am a participant and an observer, watching the bees, the beetles, the ants, listening to bird calls and sparrow squabbles, studying the incredible detail of a rust-colored fernleaf. A little while ago three deer walked by. They stopped, looked at me, and moved on. It was like they accepted me as just another fellow creature, nothing more or less. In my thoughts I thanked them, thanked the earth and trees, the air, the water, the forest floor.

When I walk out here I try not to step on any plants or insects. They are my brothers and sisters. I've come to appreciate how deeply related we all are to each other. Why can't I feel that way all the time? When I'm not here, it feels like I'm going to shatter, or maybe just blow up.

Steve's journal was becoming an anchor for him. If he could continue to use it as a way of centering himself, it could help prepare him to return to the world he found so terrifying.

18

MY OFFICE PHONE RANG AND I PICKED IT UP ON THE second ring. "Dr. McGarry? This is Jennifer Bates in Minneapolis. Do you remember me?"

I had to smile. "Of course I remember you, Jennifer. How are you?"

"Fine, thank you." She sounded a bit breathless. "How is Steve?"

"Not bad, but we still have a way to go. Were you thinking of coming down?"

"Uh, not exactly. Actually, I'm calling to ask your advice. I'm not sure how to tell Steve this, but—well, I'm engaged. I met someone a while ago and things have moved faster than I planned."

"I see. Yes, that will be a problem for Steve," I agreed, thinking about how to prepare him for this announcement.

"I dread telling him," Jennifer said.

"Tell you what. Why don't you write Steve a letter, but send it to me. I'll give it to him at our first therapy session of the week. That way I can give him whatever support he needs." And prepare the staff, too, I thought. We'd have to watch him after a shock like this. "Thanks for letting us know first, Jennifer."

"That's okay. It's the least I could do. Thanks, Dr. McGarry. I'm so relieved. I'll get the letter off this week."

I offered my congratulations and we hung up.

I was glad she was relieved. No one else would be.

In our next staffing we discussed how to ease Steve through the ordeal ahead of him and agreed that he would need close monitoring. Stacey wanted to put him on a locked ward in case he fell apart and became suicidal, but I was reluctant. I didn't want him to have to deal with two rebuffs at once. And I wanted him to know we trusted him. We could always move him later if necessary. My view prevailed, but I knew Stacey was not happy with the decision. I was uneasy myself.

True to her word, Jennifer's letter arrived that Friday. I stuck it in my top desk drawer for Monday's session with Steve.

Try as I might, I couldn't put the situation out of my mind all weekend. Over and over I replayed how the conversation might go, fantasizing the reactions Steve could have. It even occurred to me to be on the alert in case he headed for the big thermopane window again. I had absolutely no idea what he might do.

On Monday morning, Steve opened the letter eagerly. As he read it, his face contorted, and then he stared at me in disbelief.

"You know what it says?" he asked, his voice breaking.

"Yes. Jennifer called last week."

"She's *engaged?"* He rubbed his forehead, the news slowly seeping in.

An extended silence. Then I said, "Don't shut me out, Steve."

He shook his head sadly, but said nothing.

"Disappointed?" I asked.

He nodded.

"Bitter?"

He nodded again.

"Tell me what you're thinking, feeling."

He exhaled a long sigh and shrugged. "Another dream bites the dust."

Then he clammed up. All I could get out of him were some flip jokes. He'd sealed over. Near the end of the session I asked whether he'd be okay until our next meeting on Wednesday.

"Oh, yeah," he replied nonchalantly.

"You won't do anything foolish?"

"Like what?"

"Like suicide."

He looked incredulous. "Are you kidding? Kill myself over her? No way. Not a chance."

I sighed. He was taking this far too well. It worried me. And it didn't get any better. During our two remaining sessions that week, nothing more emerged. He continued to maintain that he was getting over Jennifer by himself and didn't need to talk about it. He filled the sessions with superficial bantering, and I told myself to be patient. When he was ready to deal with it, I'd know.

On my way home Friday afternoon, I stopped at the market and ran a few other errands. By the time I finished, it was late and I was too tired to fix dinner, so I stopped at a little café in town. I was looking forward to building a fire when I got home and just relaxing. It was not to be. The light on my answering machine was blinking, signaling a terse message from Joan to call as soon as possible. This wasn't my weekend to be on call, and a sense of foreboding surged up as I dialed the ward.

"Pat? Good, we've been trying to reach you."

"Oh?"

"Sorry to be the one to tell you this, but Steve's disappeared."

"Oh, no," I groaned.

"Security is searching the grounds now, including your river spot. No sign of him anywhere so far."

"Damn."

"Plus—"

"Let me guess. The confetti suit is gone."

"Yup. Seems to be, anyway. We've looked in his room. It's not there. Would he have kept it anywhere else?"

"No. He's got it with him. Probably wearing it."

"Do you have any idea where he might have gone, Pat?"

"My hope is he's on his way to Minneapolis to try and talk Jennifer out of her engagement."

"That's what Dr. Stacey thought."

"Better call and alert her, Joan. Jennifer Bates. Her number's in the chart somewhere. Reassure her as best you can, but ask her to please let us know the minute she hears from him. Wait, give her my home number and ask her to call me collect if he shows up there tonight, okay? Or whenever. I don't even want to think about the other possibility."

"Yeah, we're all afraid of that."

"Well, it's on my shoulders. It's the risk I decided to take. There's a chance that he may have decided it wasn't worth talking to Jennifer. I just don't know. Have the police been notified?"

"Yes. Wisconsin State Patrol."

"Maybe their Minnesota counterparts should be, too. He'll most likely be hitchhiking. Guess I should have listened to Stacey."

"Don't blame yourself, Pat. All of us on the ward thought Steve was taking it all in stride. He's been friendly, almost happy-go-lucky—"

"Uh huh. Too much so."

"Hindsight, Pat. We saw no signs that he should've been put on a locked ward."

"I know. He fooled us all. I just wish—well, let me know if you hear anything, okay, Joan?"

"Of course. I have a hunch he'll turn up shortly."

Unscathed, I hoped.

I hung up and called Brenda and we tried to convince each other that Steve was fine, just enroute to Minneapolis.

When the fire burned down to coals I finally turned in. It was a little after midnight.

Sometime later the phone chirped into my ear. I managed to find it before the machine kicked in.

"Dr. McGarry."

"This is Jennifer. I hope it's okay. The nurse said to call."

"Yes, Jennifer. I told her to. Have you heard from Steve?" I sat up and squinted at the clock. It was 3:10.

"Yes, he's here, asleep on my couch. We talked until a little while ago and then he finally fell asleep. He's completely exhausted."

That made two of us. "How does he seem?"

"Okay. He was very reasonable and calm, but he kept asking why I was doing this to him. I explained in as many ways as I could think of and he finally seemed to accept my decision. He talked a lot about The Confetti Kid, though, and I can see he has the costume on under his clothes."

"Did he threaten to harm you in any way? Or himself?"

"No, no. He's very rational, almost detached. I think he's in his Confetti Kid mode, like he's above it all. But he's kind of wild, too. Underneath I know he's badly hurt. But he says he isn't going back to the hospital. He was very definite about that. What should I do?"

"We'll take care of it, Jen. The police will pick him up."

"They won't hurt him, will they?"

"No, don't worry. Just sit tight. And thanks for calling."

I called the hospital and was assured the necessary people would be notified. Then I fixed a cup of hot chocolate and drank it slowly, savoring the good news that Steve was okay. I'd convinced myself that he was halfway across the country and that I might never see him again. Or worse.

The return went well. A groggy Steve was checked into

the Minneapolis city jail, picked up late Saturday afternoon by the Minnesota State Patrol, and brought as far as the state line. There he was transferred to a waiting Wisconsin State Patrol car and transported back to Peace River by early evening.

He went straight to a locked ward.

As soon as I finished rounds Monday morning, I went to find Steve. He was sitting in the dayroom, playing cards with three other patients. Letting myself onto the ward, I came up behind him.

"What's the game?"

"Crazy Eights. What else do you play in a looney bin?"

This produced a high, nervous giggle from one of guys at the table. Steve stared momentarily at him and then turned around.

"How about taking a break?" I asked.

He sighed deeply and folded his hand. To the others he said, "See you later. I gotta get my head shrunk."

When we got to my office, he immediately took the offensive. "I should have known she'd turn me in. I mean, I knew I couldn't trust her." His voice was bitter. "Now I suppose I'm restricted for the duration and I'll be getting long lectures about responsibility and maturity and how that relates to my taking off and not dealing with things."

I smiled and held up my hands. "Hold on. No lectures, Steve. Though I suppose I could work up a couple so you wouldn't be disappointed," I said. "Actually, in an oblique way, I'm pleased. That you took off."

"What?"

"I know it sounds strange, but I see your running away as a healthy sign. I prefer your acting out, rather than in."

"Glad I didn't get crazy again, you mean?" He seemed unprepared for my being so reasonable. "Actually, I did. A little, anyway."

"A little is okay. I was more worried about a lot. You could have decided you couldn't go on without Jennifer."

"And killed myself?"

"It was a possibility. I was concerned about it."

"I told you I wouldn't do anything like that."

"Well, when you disappeared, I wasn't sure. Let's just say I was relieved when Jennifer called."

"Yeah, well, if I hadn't stayed there, you'd never have seen me again. But I couldn't stay awake. All I needed was a few hours' sleep. I told her I'd be gone when she got up. She said okay. I still can't believe she'd do that to me. She turned me in, Mac."

"She was concerned about you, Steve. And we'd called her; she knew we wanted to know if you showed up. Anyway," I reached into my desk, "here's your confetti suit. I keep ending up with it. Maybe I should hang onto it, so you won't take off again."

My kidding fell on deaf ears. Steve's eyes were riveted on the suit and I passed it over to him. He thanked me and said with great seriousness, "I won't run again. She's out of my life forever. But I had to talk to her one last time. After all, she was my only chance in the world for happiness."

"That's a bit melodramatic isn't it, Steve? Your only chance? Why do you say that?"

He shook his head sadly. "She was just so . . . so precious to me." Tears welled up in his eyes. He continued, his voice husky.

"I told you, with Jennifer, life was wonderful. She gave me all the reassurance I'd ever hoped for, what I never had as a kid. I felt really loved. All those daydreams I had, of finding someone who enjoyed and needed physical touch as much as I do. Well, with Jennifer I didn't need daydreams anymore. It was wonderful. I felt so secure when she held me. Having her made such a difference in my life, just being with her. She'd look at something I'd done and say, 'That's neat,' and I'd glow inside. She appreciated me and cared about me. We fit together so perfectly, Mac, there was never a question in my mind that we wouldn't be together the rest of our lives. Stephen and Jennifer Parker. It just sounded right, you know?"

"Yes, she was a kindred soul."

He took out his handkerchief, blew his nose, and wept silently. It was a few minutes before he regained his composure.

"There are still things I want to tell her."

"Use your journal, write her a letter. Get it out of yourself somehow."

He nodded.

"Jennifer is still the most incredible thing that ever happened to me. When I met her and we hit it off, I couldn't believe my luck. She thought and felt just like I did, and she wanted to spend every moment with me."

"It must have been super-intense for both of you."

"Yeah. It was very, very intense. Looking back, I felt a lot of pressure. Pressure from myself, mostly. I was scared. Petrified is more like it. I mean, for a long time I couldn't believe someone as beautiful as Jennifer would even go out with me, let alone live with me and love me."

"How so?"

"I'd always been afraid to let myself get close to a woman. And I had never opened up like that to anyone. I felt so alone as a kid." He swiped at his eyes. "And I feel so alone now—without her." Abruptly, he looked straight at me.

"You're here now, though, right Mac? You'll listen to me?" His voice was barely a whisper. "You'll help me?"

"Yes, Steve."

"You won't dump me," he pleaded. "Will you?"

"Trust me, Steve. I'll be here for you until you don't need me anymore."

He covered his face with both hands. After a few minutes he dropped them and said, "You know I told you how there wasn't much affection or love expressed in our family? Well, it was something I wanted, bad. But I had to cover the wanting up, because it just wasn't how things were done in my family. No one just went up and hugged someone, you know what I mean?"

I nodded again.

"So I just dreamed about it. And then I met Jennifer. But, you know, it was funny. I was always afraid Jennifer would turn out to be a dream, that I'd wake up and she'd be gone. Does that sound weird?"

"No."

"Anyway, that's why I needed her around all the time. So I'd know she wasn't something from my imagination. And now she's gone. My dream is really, truly gone. Someone else will have her for the rest of his life."

I sensed that Steve seemed to be working at tying something together, so I waited patiently. After a few minutes had elapsed, he picked up as if he'd never stopped.

"You know, Mac, I can see some things now. I felt like I was under a lot of pressure with Jennifer—to make things work, you know—but really, I put even more pressure on her. And I'd go back and forth on her. A few times after we had really bad fights, I wanted to break up with her, but I couldn't bring myself to do it. Then we'd make up and it'd be okay until the whole thing started building up again." He sighed. "I guess I didn't treat her very well."

"Go on."

He thought a while. "I think I was scared."

"Of?"

His brow knit. "I depended on her too much. Even though I knew it wasn't healthy, I wanted her to take care of me. But then again, I couldn't stand it when she did. This sounds crazy, Mac, but when I had it one way, I'd want it the other. Most of the time I liked having her there to lean on, but other times I wanted my freedom. I didn't want to have to answer to her. So I'd pull back."

"Like how, Steve?"

"Like a yo-yo. Goofy. I'd be distant toward her and then switch to the other extreme, get super possessive, want to be with her every second. Then I didn't want her out of my sight. I'd think silly things, like I'd be terrified she'd be kidnapped or hurt in an accident. If she talked to another guy or something, I'd get real jealous. When I was like that, she said I drove her crazy. I was out of control."

He sat, palm under his chin, eyes down, mulling over what he'd done. "You know what I think? I think maybe I wanted to break up with her before she had a chance to dump me. But then I'd chicken out, decide I didn't want to lose her, and flip out. Boy, was I a nut case."

I nodded in agreement, but he didn't notice.

"I guess I smothered us. That's what I did, isn't it? I suffocated her, us, our beautiful love. It's my fault she left me. I drove her away."

I just watched him, and waited.

"So why would I do that? I mean, I had it made, Mac. I had what I'd always dreamed of, a beautiful woman who loved me. My soulmate. And then I ruined it."

He sat back in thought, staring out the window, but he was looking inside. And again I waited, watching the changing expressions that crossed his face as the internal dialogue moved along. At last he spoke:

"All I can think is that I must've got royally screwed up when I was a kid. See, I never let myself open up, love someone. Now I'm beginning to wonder, do I even know what love is?" He sighed. "I sure don't know what life is all about. What do you think?"

"I think," I said, "that you're on to something."

"But what?"

"You're the only one who can figure out what it all means. And what you can do about it. But Steve—"

"What?"

"You're searching, and these are the kinds of things that will begin to make sense to you sooner or later. Probably sooner."

"Yeah?"

"Yes. You're making progress. Keep after it."

At our next session, Steve was primed. He whipped an envelope out of his pocket as he sat down.

"I wrote a letter to Jennifer, Mac. I haven't decided whether to send it or not. Read it and tell me what you think."

He handed me the envelope. I took the letter out and unfolded it.

Dear Jennifer,

It was strange being in Minneapolis, but I was glad to have one last chance to see you. It was very difficult for me, but you know, it helped me figure out a couple things about us and, mostly, about myself.

The worst part about our breakup was that I was still very much in love with you when you left. I still am. Seeing you, seeing how good you look, what a neat person you are, brought it all back again. It made me realize that it was the biggest failure of my life that I wasn't able to get you to love me the way I love you.

Saying goodbye the way we did was really tough. I felt bad and humiliated when they put me in the police car. Like I was a petty criminal. It was tough for you, too, I know. I could see the hurt and concern in your face. You have such a beautiful, *caring face, Jennifer. I'm sure you're a wonderful nurse and all your patients love you, too.*

When we were talking, I sensed some of the leftover feelings from our times together. We shared something very special. Knowing you love someone else hurts, but I want you to be happy. You deserve to be. Happiness is all I've ever wanted for you, and I wish you well. You've made your choice and even though it's not what I want, I'll have to learn to live with it. Somehow I'll survive.

I'll always feel I owe a lot to you. You believed in me as a person, and you believed in my work. Most important, you made me feel worthwhile. I think it was the one and only time in my life I ever amounted to anything.

So even though things didn't work out for us and I got kind of crazy for a while, I really thank you for all those good times and all you did for me.

I love you, Jen, and always will.

Steve

"Well?" he asked.

I handed the letter back to him, a lump in my throat.

"It's a beautiful letter, Steve. Right from your heart."

"Yeah, but what do you think? Should I send it, or what?"

I shook my head and smiled. "Only you can answer that. Look inside yourself, Steve. You decide what it is you want to do."

"But—"

"I'll be glad to listen while you thrash it out."

He frowned at me.

"You make the choice, Steve. You would anyway. No matter what I say, you'll do whatever you make up your mind to do, right?"

He grinned. "Yeah, I already decided to send it. I just wanted to hear you say it was the right thing to do."

"Nice try," I smiled back and nodded. "If it's what you want to do, then it's the right thing to do."

So far, so good.

The following week I flew to California to spend Thanksgiving with my parents. I was looking forward to the reunion, but after eight months in Wisconsin everything slid out of synch again the minute I stepped off the plane. Instant overload: the noise, the fumes, the quickened pace, the killer driving reflexes that reappeared even before my rental car hit the freeway on-ramp. My inner motor revved up to meet the stress and it felt strange.

My mother outdid herself with Thanksgiving dinner. My dad and I played a few rounds of golf and it was a welcome diversion. I checked in with three or four friends and savored the warmth of the sun. One afternoon I drove out to a group home in the San Fernando Valley and visited a special friend named Mike, a child I'd worked closely with for several years. He was doing well. Before I knew, it was time to go home.

It had been good to be away, but I was so glad to be back I almost yelled when I alighted from the little puddle-jumper that flew me the last leg from Minneapolis to La Crosse. My exuberance was swiftly tempered by a cold blast of wind and bleak, darkening skies.

I scraped a thin coating of ice off the windshield and breathed a sigh of relief when my car started on the first try. Within the hour, I was sprawled before a toasty fire, enjoying the pungent aroma of burning oak.

19

"I'M READY TO GET GOING, MAC. THIS WHOLE PSYCHOtherapy thing is driving me batty." Steve gave me a sly look.

I smiled at him. This humor was a healthy sign, some movement toward balance.

"Well, so what do I do?" he asked. "Walk in, sit down and bleat out my agenda, or what? What am I s'posed to talk about? How do I know if something's important? Can I just change the subject any old time? What if you think what we're talking about is real relevant stuff, but I know deep down I'm just doing it to avoid dealing with stuff that scares me? Do I tell you that?"

I was about to say something, but he barged ahead, so I closed my mouth.

"I can see where I could do a lot of wheel spinning here. Believe me, I can be pretty clever if I need to be. I do it without even thinking and then later it hits me what I've done. So who's gonna set me straight? I certainly can't. *You* don't—"

"Why is all this so important to you, Steve?" I asked.

He looked at me like I was asking a very dumb question.

"Because," he said in an exasperated tone, "I want to get *out* of here. I'm starting to think maybe I can take more control of my life, but—"

"Then you should be able to monitor yourself in here," I replied. "You can catch yourself when you digress from one of your digressions."

"No, no, Mac. I can't. I really can't. I'm feeling more and more antsy here. That's why I'm writing stuff down, keeping lists of things we need to talk about."

"Control again?"

"Yeah, the lists help."

"So keep them, and bring in topics if you want. But don't be surprised if you talk about something entirely different once you get here. Because as you're talking along, other thoughts will pop in that really need to be discussed and dealt with. At least that day."

"Okay, but I'm having a tough time with this self-exploration stuff. Thinking about Jennifer still rips me apart. And when I start thinking about my parents my insides get all jumpy."

"Of course, Steve. And that will happen for a while. We're stirring things up. By the way, what happened with your letter?"

His head dropped, along with his voice. "I sent it. And she wrote back. Basically she said, 'Sorry, Steve.' "

"I'm sorry, too."

"Yeah, well, I didn't really expect anything else." He sighed and shifted around in his chair.

After a moment, I said, "You're really wired today."

"The point is, I want to hurry up and do this therapy thing right. Maybe I can learn something I can't get anywhere else. That's why I said I'd stay awhile. But it's not working. The longer I'm here, the screwier my ideas get. I'm getting worse instead of better."

"I know it seems that way, Steve. There's a big battle going on inside you."

"Inside me, and outside me, too. I'm thinking about this stuff so much I'm going nutty. I can't talk to people, and when I do I'm constantly worrying about what they're thinking. That they can see how upset I am, the nightmare mess that's going on inside me. If I don't act the way people expect, I have the feeling they'll be furious at me, never want to have anything to do with me again. But I feel counterfeit. And I'm terrified of conflict. I hate it and I'll do practically anything to avoid it. So I just try to imagine what people want me to be, and act that way. But then I end up hating myself for being such a nerd. See what I mean, Mac? I'm one hugely screwed-up guy." He looked to me for affirmation.

"Let's work on that, Steve."

His gaze shifted toward the window. "Okay." A long sigh. "I want to talk about my parents."

At last! I waited.

"The problem is, nothing all that bad happened to me when I was a kid. It was more like what didn't happen."

The sentence drifted away and I finally asked,

"What do you mean?"

"The thing is, it was like my parents had these big rules, sort of unspoken laws that were never to be broken. You know, like no one was allowed to talk about the elephant in the living room. So we all ignored it. Know what I mean?" He glanced at me briefly, then dropped his eyes.

"Yes, I think so."

"So it wasn't like I was abused. I don't have a bunch of scars from being beaten with a two-by-four." Another peek at me. "You know?"

"What about scars on the inside?"

"Yeah, maybe." A deep breath. Then, softly, "The thing is, I don't think my mom and dad loved me." He couldn't bring himself to look up.

"Why do you feel that way?"

He shrugged. "I don't know. I've been trying to figure

that out my whole life. I mean, I wasn't a horrible kid who destroyed everything. If anything, I went out of my way to be nice, to get their attention. So maybe I was a pest, maybe they didn't love me because I bugged them too much. I don't know. But all I wanted from them was a hug every once in a while and to have them tell me they loved me." He gulped and forced himself to go on. "They never did."

His eyes filled with tears and he brushed them aside. I was hoping he'd have a good cry and begin to let go of some of the grief inside, but he recovered his control. He was still looking for the intellectual way out, trying to make sense of things rationally, which is typical of bright young people.

"I know, I know," he said, anticipating what he expected me to say. "Maybe they just couldn't express their love or something. See, when I was little, I thought parents were supposed to love their kids. Mine didn't. I kept trying, but they never noticed, so somewhere in there I decided it must be me. If my own parents couldn't love me, who else would? A defective like me? A loser?" He shook his head sadly.

"Could it be, Steve, that there are different kinds of love? That they did love you, but not in the way you needed to be loved?"

"What do you mean?"

"My sense is that while most children can make the adjustment to both parents working, to day care, whatever, others have real problems with it. They need the support of a full-time parent."

"For sure I did. I can remember literally hanging onto Dad, desperately trying to get him to look at something or do something with me. But he'd just pry my fingers off and tell me to grow up and stop whining."

"That must have hurt."

"Yeah, well, eventually I quit doing it. I grew up, all right. But here's the thing. Why did they have me in the first place? I mean, if I was so low on their priorities, why bother with kids? I used to wonder about that a lot."

"Well, maybe you should ask them, Steve."

"What?" He stared at me, dumbfounded. "You know I can't do that."

"Not literally, of course. But let's try something." I got up and shifted a couple of chairs so they were right in front of him. "Imagine that your dad is sitting in this chair, and your mother is in that one. Now go ahead, talk to them."

He stared unbelievingly at me, as if I'd taken leave of my senses.

"Ask them whatever you want. And tell them all the things you never had a chance to say."

"Well—" he began.

"Don't look at me, Steve. Look at them."

He squirmed and focused first on one chair, then the other. Silence. Then he addressed the empty chairs.

"Mom, Dad . . . I never understood why you left me alone so much. Let all those other people take care of me. Why did you do that?"

He paused, as though waiting a reply.

"Now take their roles, Steve. What do you think your dad or mom would say to that?"

"It'd probably be Mom who'd answer first. She'd say something like, 'When you were little, Steve, I tried to give you extra attention. You seemed to need it so desperately. But you have to understand that my career was very important to me, too. I simply couldn't stay home with you and your brother all the time. We thought we were providing well for you boys. And Brad managed just fine. Why was it so much harder for you? I didn't know what to do about it. We certainly didn't mean to neglect you, but I knew you felt we did.' "

"And your dad? What would he say?"

"Oh, something like, 'We had our lives to live, too, son. We had a lot of obligations—professional and social responsibilities. But why were you so clingy? I wanted you to grow up to be a fine, independent young man, but you were so hesitant and unsure of yourself. Your brother wasn't. What happened to you? You were so insecure you made me—uncomfortable. You wanted me to help you all the time, but I couldn't give you the kind of attention you always demanded. I was glad when you finally outgrew it.' "

"What would you say to that, Steve?"

He thought a minute. "Actually, I don't think Dad would ever have said that. I think that's how he felt, but he'd never have said it to my face. I wish he had. I might have been able to stop trying to make him into something he wasn't or never could be." He sighed and shook his head.

"Would you like to say anything else to your folks, Steve?"

He thought a few moments, then addressed the chairs again:

"I think you made some pretty poor choices, working as hard as you did. Dad, fifteen hours a day, Mom, probably ten, at least. And why did you have to smoke? You were both smart, educated people. You knew better. You'd talk about the research, say you were gonna quit. But you never did. Just like you'd talk about slowing down, cutting back, having more time for yourselves. But you never did that either. You had to have it all. Why? Was it worth it? Would you do it all over again?

"Remember when I started school, Mom? Even the very first day you just dropped me there and raced off to work. For you it was no big deal. But I was terrified there. I needed you."

He stopped, breathing harder, then began again.

"Remember the time you had to come to school and get me, Dad? A few days after I started kindergarten. Something was very wrong but I wouldn't tell you or the teacher what. You finally gave up trying to find out. Now I'll tell you:

"When the teacher told us we were going to have a fire drill, I thought she meant they were actually going to burn down the school. I couldn't understand why they'd do that, but it scared me almost to death. Next they'd be burning down our house! Then where would we live? I totally freaked. Screamed and cried, the whole bit. By the time you got there, I'd calmed down. But I was afraid to tell you why I was so upset. I thought you'd laugh at me. I knew you'd think I was a scaredy cat.

"That's the only time you ever came to school for me. Either you or Mom. You never went to talk to any of my teachers. You never came to any of my school activities. You went to some of Brad's, but none of mine. I know why. You told me and I'll never forget—'too many commitments. Mommy and Daddy would like to come, but we have other plans, things *we* have to do.' "

Steve looked morose, reliving it all over again.

"What else do you want to tell them?"

His eyes tearing, he said,

"I know you did the best you could for me. You gave me everything I wanted. Except what I wanted most—time with you, encouragement, love. And for you especially, Dad—to tell me you loved me, were proud of me. But see, you'd never say that 'cause I never measured up. I was a major disappointment to you, wasn't I, Dad? Nothing I ever did was good enough." He paused. Then, in an accusatory voice, "You made me feel so *worthless!*"

I almost winced as he said that. There it was, the idea behind so much of what came later. Perhaps at last this was the grain of sand, the irritant Kayla said to watch for.

"How do you think your dad might have responded to that, Steve?"

He shrugged. "I don't know."

"Try to imagine. What would your father have said if you'd ever told him he made you feel worthless?"

For some time we sat in silence. Finally, he sighed and said,

"I have no idea. None at all."

We were hitting big resistance. Straight out of the unconscious. I didn't want to leave it like this, so I moved to the chair Steve had designated for his dad.

"Well," I said, "might he have said something like: 'Son, you're right. I was too caught up to notice you. I didn't mean to make you feel worthless and I'm sorry if you felt that way. I did love you, very much. I just didn't know how to express it in the right ways. The ways you wanted me to. For that I'm truly sorry, Steve. I deeply regret whatever we did to hurt you. Obviously we did a lot. But it was unintentional, believe me. If I had my life to live over again, there are many, many things I would do differently. I hope you can find it in your heart to forgive your mother and me."

Steve listened quietly and by the time I finished, he was blinking rapidly, brushing his eyes with his shirtsleeve. At last he gave up and let the tears roll down his cheeks. Then he put his head in his hands and wept softly. I leaned over and put my arm around his shoulder as the years of grief and pain rose to the surface.

Eventually the choking and sobbing subsided. He took some Kleenex from the box on my desk and wiped his eyes and blew his nose.

"What are you feeling?"

He glanced up at me. "I think . . . relief. But it still hurts so bad."

"It will, Steve. Like a bad splinter. We have to get in there and dig it out. Then it's going to take time to heal."

As the Christmas season approached, I pretty much let Steve take the lead as long as he stayed the course. When he got too far afield I would nudge him back. All these excursions were exploratory probes during which I tried to judge the strength and resistance of his defenses.

I knew that with such a deeply entrenched delusional system a frontal attack would be useless. Trying to convince him that The Confetti Kid was just a crazy fantasy that he had to give up would have been a waste of energy. Worse, it would destroy the trust I'd worked so hard to build. The time-honored strategy was to find receptive spots in his personality, employ them by appealing to the rational side of his mind and, piece by piece, build an alliance of stronger personality segments that would ultimately be bridged by healthier thinking. Only then would his need for The Confetti Kid recede. All this seemed sensible to me, and I prepared to be patient.

It wasn't unusual for Steve to divert us into intellectual waters that afforded him safe anchorage from the storms within. To a point I allowed this, recognizing that he couldn't tolerate our steady probing into his unconscious conflicts and deeply repressed feelings. I knew we were dealing with too many potential depth charges, and that if certain ones went off at once another psychotic break was possible. My plan was to spread the detonations out, to insulate him from his terror as much as possible while we explored its sources.

Sometimes he tried to turn the conversations back on me. He'd be the therapist, and I was to play the client. Often I went along because I knew he needed to see my own vulnerabilities.

The mind resists change in many ways. Achieving genuine, constructive change means altering entrenched premises of thinking that have taken a lifetime to build. The personality is much like an onion, with different layers representing the development of self-esteem and the habitual thinking patterns that govern everything from expressing feelings and opinions to choosing behavior. Embedded within are the memories of experiences that shape our thinking. But to give up control of these deep-seated thought patterns, the defense mechanisms have to relent enough to allow longstanding and unresolved conflicts to surface for examination. This is why therapy requires so much time, patience, perseverance, and courage. It's an enormous undertaking. Not everyone can pull it off.

Steve's inner life was very rich. He'd learned to retreat there from all the hurts in the world. Once he started to share more of his daydreams with me, he fell back on them often, repeating various versions while I tried to help him sort out craziness from reality. To a point, fantasies are adaptive. But in Steve's case, that point had vanished when he'd become delusional. Now, slowly, we had to re-establish the boundary line.

"I always dreamed that one special person would come into my life. I'd recognize her immediately and from that day on we would love each other forever. I'd imagine how she'd look at me, how she would kiss and touch me and tell me she loved me.

"And sometimes, late at night, I would imagine her lying in bed next to me, and how she would respond when I'd reach out and touch her, just to be sure she was there. And then we'd talk for a while." He gave me a sheepish look. "Imagining stuff like that helped when I was miserable."

"Dreams do a lot," I commented. "Jung said, 'Dreams are what pull us into the future.' "

"Yeah," Steve said pensively. "I hadn't thought of it that way, but it's true. Dreams were what gave me hope that someday my life would be better. But look what happened."

He paused briefly, then continued.

"Anyway, I'd dream about our marriage and the kind of home we'd have. A simple, super-modern house that I'd design, with woods all around it, a stream nearby, maybe a garden and a small orchard. I'd have my studio on one side, where it would catch the best light. And because I had all this happiness—a beautiful wife, a dream house, recognition—I'd be fantastically creative, breaking all kinds of new ground in art. People would hail me as the new Picasso. I'd receive international acclaim and be invited to meet the President. I'd move among famous people. Quietly, unobtrusively, always with humility, speaking softly. And amused that famous people were actually hanging on my every word.

"Of course, there'd also be other fascinating women —not only attractive, but sharp—and we'd have little exchanges and I knew that all I had to do was say the word, just indicate that I was interested. But I wouldn't because I had a person at home I cherished with all my heart."

He gazed out the window, almost in a trance, reliving his dream. He looked peaceful, and I sensed that he'd spent a lot of his life this way. After a few moments he resumed.

"I guess what appealed to me most was that all these beautiful women thought I was attractive. And talented and famous, but my fame hadn't gone to my head. I could still be gentle and sensitive to their needs. And as I talked with them, I always knew they were just wishing they could be my wife.

"I had so many dreams like that. I'd see a pretty girl who fit this image in my mind of what my ideal would look like. She might be in a restaurant having dinner with someone, or maybe I'd see her on a bus or in a store. I'd memorize her face, her features, and then maybe sketch her, pretend she was the girl who became my wife. I'd dream about how we'd meet, the kind of things we'd talk about, the first time I'd take her in my arms and kiss her. And within a few weeks —maybe after we'd enjoyed a beautiful afternoon together and maybe we had just kissed—she'd tell me she loved me. I'd think how scared she was at saying it and how I'd react to it and then how relieved she'd be when I told her I was about to say the same thing to her. And then one day, Jennifer came along and I actually thought I'd dreamed her up."

He looked sharply at me, trying to read my expression. "You're probably laughing inside, thinking, 'what a dork. Is he for real?' "

"Not at all, Steve. What's wrong with dreams like that?"

"Well, that's just it—they're only dreams. Ever since I was a kid I've survived through daydreaming. My teachers were always getting after me 'cause my mind was off somewhere else. Nothing ever came easy for me. I've tried hard. Too hard, maybe. Nothing's ever worked. But my dreams did. And if I didn't like them, I could change them around whenever I wanted, make them even better. I can always rewrite the script and do whatever I want."

"But it's a very tough way of maintaining control," I countered.

He frowned. "Why?"

"Why do you think?"

"Because it's all inside your head?"

"And?"

He thought a moment.

"Other people aren't involved?"

"Right again. Through daydreaming, you isolate yourself." This was important. I wanted to plant the seed, see if it would sprout. "And then sometimes a person can't tell where the dream leaves off and reality begins."

He nodded. I couldn't tell whether or not he made the connection, so after a bit I asked:

"Can you recall any other daydreams?"

He hesitated.

"I used to have one where I died. I'd picture people at my funeral saying things like, 'I didn't know Steve had accomplished so much' or, 'You mean *Steve* founded that school of art? I had no idea.' And I'd be lying in the coffin watching and listening. They'd leave the funeral home shaking their heads. When I was alive they'd had no idea they were in the presence of greatness." He smiled wryly. "Mostly, though, I liked the other dreams better."

"The hero dreams?"

"Yeah." He laughed sardonically. "Big hero I was with Jennifer, huh?"

He lapsed into silence and I waited.

"Hero dreams, huh?" He looked at me.

I nodded.

His gaze was intense. "You probably think that's how I hatched The Confetti Kid. From Steve Parker, starving avant-garde artist, failed lover, marginal student, psychologically destitute human being, to . . . *ta da* . . . The Confetti Kid, hero of our times! Given that choice, who in his right mind would pick jerky Stephen Parker?" He said his name derisively.

"Is that how you really see yourself, Steve?"

"Of course. It's obvious, isn't it? Steve Parker is a Class A Jerk. A nerd. A big zero. A nothing."

"Do you truly believe that? Deep down?"

"What I believe determines who I am."

"What do you believe, then?"

His face flushed and he looked down. "I don't know," he said softly.

I waited.

"I know some things I don't believe."

"Okay, start there."

He sighed heavily.

"It's a crazy world, and now I'm a crazy person. Nothing makes any sense to me."

"Uh huh," I agreed. "It can be very confusing. And frightening."

We fell silent. After a while he looked at me.

"There are no answers, you know," he said.

"To what, Steve?"

"Life."

"What kinds of questions are you asking?"

"Big ones."

"Sometimes big things can be broken down into small parts and dealt with that way."

"Not these." His face flushed and again his voice deepened with an anger that was visible.

"The really crazy people are out there!" He jabbed at the window. "The greed-heads, with avarice running out their ears, cutting deals to make more billions, selling weapon systems that will kill the planet ten times over, building huge complexes, accelerating crop outputs with dangerous chemicals, paving the beautiful fields with concrete and asphalt, selling drugs that destroy minds and bodies. All in the name of their gods—power and money."

He glared at me defiantly, daring me to respond. I thought I'd better.

"I can't argue with any of that, Steve. A lot of people are deeply concerned about it. Some do a lot, but many feel helpless to change the course."

He gave me a long look, then wearily shook his head. The anger had drained away as quickly as it appeared.

"You don't understand, Mac. Something heroic has to happen. That's the only way we can survive."

"Help me understand, Steve. I'd really like to see this from your viewpoint."

"There has to be a major shift in the way people think and live. They act like they can go on like this forever, but they're fooling themselves." His voice had dropped. "People consume so much. They spend so much time in malls—buying more, destroying what few resources are left. It's all so wasteful. What will happen to future generations?" His voice trailed away and I waited.

"Someone has to change the thinking in this country. And in the world. Someone has to lead us out of the mess we're in, get us to see that what's truly important now is living a simpler life, getting closer to nature."

"That sounds almost spiritual, Steve."

"It *is* spiritual!" he almost shouted. "Yes! You understand. It's being in touch with the universe. That's why I love to spend so much time in the woods, listening to the river, watching the wildlife. It gets me in tune with what I know is important."

"And what's that, Steve?"

"My inner life."

"I see."

"You know," he looked directly at me, "there is a power greater than us. I don't mean it in a strict religious sense, but more along the lines that something, someone had to organize all this."

I nodded.

"The only way to understand it, to really understand it, is to be close to nature, to shove aside all the junk the media, the advertisers, the politicians push at you."

"I certainly agree with that."

Steve snorted. "You're the first then. No one else has ever been able to see the things I see, feel what I feel."

I let my voice drop. "And that's where the loneliness comes in—the isolation?"

"Loneliness, yes, and futility. It's hell being the only person on the face of the earth who feels everything so acutely and is so in touch with the future. And no one will listen."

"A prophet scorned . . ."

He laughed, a harsh, bitter bark.

"It must be terribly, terribly painful, Steve," I ventured.

He studied his hands, the long slender artist's fingers intertwined.

"Is your life that much better?" he finally asked.

"How do you mean?"

"Don't the wrongs of the world bother you? I'd think just working in this place would get to you."

"Sometimes. But mostly it's rewarding to feel I'm making a small contribution toward easing some of the suffering."

"Is that why you became a psychotherapist?"

"One of the reasons. The other is that people fascinate me. Trying to understand why all of us do the things we do. It's a very small niche for trying to make the world a better place."

"You're doing a whole lot more than I am at this point. I'm not much of an active agent, and society says I'm one mean meaniac."

I laughed. "A 'meaniac.' That's a new one."

"Crazy people find new ones all the time. The other afternoon I was staring out the window at the sunset and a patient came up to me and told me to change the channel."

"Really?"

He nodded emphatically. "Would I make that up? If you aren't nuts when you come to this loony bin, you soon will be."

"Steve, it's nice to see your sense of humor coming out. You have a very expressive face. Did you know that?"

"Can't hide nothin' from my shrink, can I?"

But of course he could—and was. Not intentionally, perhaps. But there were many more painful memories where these had come from, and I knew it might be some time before they surfaced. A distinct uneasiness was beginning to gnaw at the edges of my mind. I couldn't quite put my finger on it, but I had the feeling I was missing something.

I sought out Ben in his office that afternoon. "I need to talk with you."

He pushed back from his desk and gave me his full attention. A model of patience, he listened quietly as I filled him in on the session I'd just had with Steve.

"So I see some potential problems in working with him," I sighed. "My problems, not his. What am I—eleven, twelve years older than he is—and yet as I listen to him, I find myself in total agreement with a lot of what he has to say, his assessments. So much of it blends in with my own experiences."

"And that bothers you."

"Yes. It's beginning to. The point is, I agree with him more than I disagree with him. I mean, he's very knowledgeable about things. He's got a much better handle on issues than I had when I was his age. Maybe he isn't so crazy after all. Maybe he's right. It's the world that's nuts. He's a decent, vulnerable guy trying to play it straight. All he wants is to live in harmony with the earth. Except that seems to be impossible.''

''Whoa, slow down,'' Ben admonished. ''You're getting way ahead of yourself here. Sure, Steve is bright, and certainly talented. And perhaps he has a solid understanding of our social problems. Most of us are pretty sensitive to the contradictions in our society. But just because we can identify them doesn't mean we understand how to change them, Pat.''

''Right,'' I said, ''but what is a psychotherapist supposed to do when the patient's so-called delusional system makes all the sense in the world—''

''Hold on, Pat. I'm glad you agree with Steve. That helps with the therapeutic bond. But from there on it gets pretty touchy. Some elements of mental illness can be very seductive you know, the euphoric high of the manic-depressive, the delusional system of the schizophrenic. But you wouldn't wish such agonizing states on anybody, even though at the same time you can see why someone might resort to it.''

''Well . . . maybe.''

''Really, Pat. In some ways going crazy is like using narcotics. Craziness numbs a person to what is really a pretty callous world. Steve's particular 'high' revolved around this wonderfully idealistic world that he believed his actions would create.''

I looked intently at Ben. ''But that's a dream many people have. Including me.''

''Sure, but most of us don't cross the line. We adjust our dreams, our vision, and do what we can without losing touch with reality.''

''Maybe that's too bad,'' I said, but Ben ignored it.

''You haven't endowed a confetti suit with some kind of nutty power, have you? Or thrown confetti in hopes of magically changing people? Of course not. You and Steve share a concern for world crises, I grant you. And rightfully so. But he hasn't learned to deal with the ambiguities and uncertainties of life, much less discovered a workable way to channel his idealistic energies. You have."

"I suppose."

"What do you mean, you suppose?"

"Well, yes, I'd have to agree that Steve hasn't learned to deal with the uncertainties of life. But I'm not so sure I have either."

Ben gave me a look of utter exasperation.

"You told me yourself, Steve's seen the materialistic side of life. And he's determined he doesn't want any part of it. But instead of integrating some of the realities of the world, he's been searching, looking for ground where there is no ground. And in the process he stepped off the edge, into a freefall. The Confetti Kid was his safety net. But now he seems to sense that there are no long-term solutions down that avenue either.

"And that's where you come in. Steve crossed the line. Now it's your job to help him cross back over again to the healthier side. He needs answers he can use, stability he can build upon, premises, a philosophy of life he can live with.

"So teach him, Pat."

Once again, Ben had put things in perspective for me. But how long would it last this time?

Brenda called to me just as I hit the bracing wind outside the entrance to Cameron Hall. We retreated back inside.

"I'm glad I caught you. It feels like winter out there!" She shivered and skeptically eyed the raincoat I'd brought from California. She'd long ago established that it didn't even have a zip-in lining. "No parka yet?"

"Maybe this weekend. I hate to shop."

"You'll hate freezing more."

I liked that she worried about me. More, more, I thought.

"Anyway, some of us are going out to a Christmas tree farm to cut our own trees. Tomorrow. I thought that might be some kind of first for the California Kid."

I didn't have to consider long. "Sounds neat. Count me in."

"Good. We'll meet here at ten. Dress warmly enough. It can be cold out in those fields."

"Aw, gee, Mom, do I have to?"

I got a warning look. Don't tease, it said.

That night I went out and bought a down parka. And some long underwear for good measure.

It turned out to be a lot of fun. Five of us caravanned forty miles northeast to a tree farm owned by the parents of Marlene, a staff nurse. Assured that we could cut any trees we wanted, we set out, saws and ropes in hand, down a shallow gully that wandered back into the hills. Out of the sun's rays it was, well, brisk, and I was glad for my new gear. But even bundled up, my teeth were chattering. And the frozen clouds my breath formed chilled me even more.

On we trudged, past Christmas trees of varying sizes, all pruned and colorfully tagged. Everyone coached me on how to spot a likely candidate, and then I was to stand back and study it minutely before moving on to a more perfect specimen. I did as instructed, but before long they all started to look alike.

Brenda soon found a tree with an abandoned bird's nest and that did it for her. I finally settled on a rather forlorn little white pine that I was sure no one else would ever take. Brenda inspected it briefly and gave me an appraising look.

"I bet you bring home strays and anything else that wanders by."

"Well, someone—" I started to say, but she put a mittened hand to my mouth and smiled.

"You're just an old softie, Patrick McGarry."

Softer than you know, I thought.

Suddenly I recalled Steve's daydream scenarios and I was

reminded once again that The California Kid had all too much in common with The Confetti Kid. I pushed Steve's fantasies —and terrors—out of my mind and tried to breathe deeply in the icy air.

20

AFTER WORK ON THE FRIDAY BEFORE CHRISTMAS, I drove Brenda to the airport in La Crosse. She would be spending the holidays with her folks in Ohio. On the way, she commented on how mild the winter had been so far. I looked at her quickly to see if she was kidding. She wasn't. She was laughing about having to go south to Ohio for snow. We wished each other happy holidays and parted. My trip back home was far too quiet.

I'd found Steve's journal resting on my desk that afternoon when I returned from group therapy and it was in my briefcase, along with some test reports I wanted to work on over the weekend. Despite my good intentions, it wasn't until around mid-afternoon Sunday that I retrieved my briefcase from exactly where I'd dropped it on Friday. I remembered the journal with a jolt. Grabbing a can of soda from the refrigerator, I plopped into my favorite chair and began reading:

Dear Mac,

I'm making this a journal entry to you because I still can't tell you all the things I'm thinking and feeling. We keep going over my childhood, dragging up old memories that I've kept buried for years. Talking about all this stuff, hashing over so much that hurt me, is making me real nervous. Uncovering all this junk, will I go crazy again?

Digging down is like peering into a black cave where there's a huge bunch of wild animals hiding. I can hear them in there. They want me, and I know they can tear me to shreds. And you're standing there saying, "Go ahead, it's okay, I'll be right behind you."

But I'm the one who has to go in, not you. I'm the one they'll maul, not you. You have nothing to lose. I have everything to lose. And the scary thing is, there's no way you can go into my mind with me. You have to wait outside 'til I come back out—*if I come out*—and say, "Well, Mac, here's the way it was, when I was a kid—"

But I told you I'd try and find some ways to do it and so this is another attempt. I hope it works. If you find my torn up body (and spirit?) by your door, you'll know it didn't.

So here goes. I'm incredibly wired these days. It reminds me of when I was around 16, and one night I woke up in the middle of the night and couldn't get back to sleep. I was thinking about how unhappy and alone I was, how I didn't have anyone to talk to, and then it got really weird.

As I lay there, suddenly I was aware of how quiet it was in the room, and I started breathing ever so gently, little bitty breaths, trying to be invisible because the silence was closing in on me. My heart started beating faster and faster, making this awful pulsating noise. I could actually hear the blood going through my veins. And feel it.

And then this gigantic slab of fear dropped on me, and pinned me to the bed. It was so intense I absolutely could not move. I felt this terrible sense of dread, and I was sure I was going to die. I was doomed, there was no hope. And everyone else was going to die, too.

Then these huge waves of incredible fear began washing over me, each one bigger than the last, each one almost sweeping me away. I was choking, sweating, shaking. But I still couldn't move. My heart was beating so violently I thought it was going to explode. The noise in my ears was so loud I tried to muffle it with the pillow. I prayed to die. The way my heart was pounding, I was terrified it would burst any second.

I don't know how long that went on, but finally it passed. I was wringing wet, absolutely limp, numb. And I was still convinced I was dying. Or maybe dead already, I wasn't sure. This wasn't the time I took the pills and got sick, Mac. It was like something else was killing me, my mind, maybe.

This still happens from time to time. I've gotten better at dealing with it, knowing I'll probably live through it because I always have before. But the terror is intense. I just grit my teeth and keep repeating over and over, "This will pass, this will pass."

So now you know what you're asking me to let myself in for, and why I really don't want to. But I'll keep trying. For awhile. No promises. You're the first person I've ever told about this. So here goes. A little bit, anyway. I'll see how far I can get.

My memories of school are mostly very unhappy ones. I was always trying to make friends, or just be accepted. I was one of those kids who never got chosen for a team. The few times I was taken, it was forced and nobody was happy about it. I usually did lousy and the other kids would yell at me.

When I realized what an outcast I was, I was really bummed. During recess I'd find an isolated corner in the schoolyard and talk to myself and play games I made up. Sometimes, though, when I didn't have the energy to keep up a front, I just cried. I was miserable. I'll never forget that. I can still feel a kind of ache in my gut from way back then. It's always with me.

When I was around 10, I finally accepted that I would never fit in and wouldn't ever have any friends. So I figured I better make the best of it. I told myself that since no one liked me anyway, there was no point in worrying about it. And maybe it didn't matter. So what if nobody cared about me?

At home there was the situation with my parents. I was so out of step with everything and everyone there I avoided them as much as I could. Looking back now, I think I was probably trying to protect myself. I mean I did care, but I couldn't change things, you know? I'm sure my mother knew I was unhappy. She probably tried to talk to me about it. I really don't remember. But if she did, it didn't help.

The other thing I remember from school is the day the Challenger exploded and the teacher was killed. We'd all studied what they were going to do in space and every television set in the school was on. It happened right around noon and I remember watching the countdown and the rockets launching and then *pouf,* all that was left was smoke and bits of the Challenger shooting off as it blew apart. It was horrible. Mrs. Henderson, my teacher, gasped and started crying. Everybody cried but me. I was terribly upset, but I couldn't cry. No one ate lunch that day. We just sat there in shock all afternoon.

Anyway, I got a paper route and started earning some money. I saved enough to buy myself a new bike, and that made delivering more fun. I had customers who were nice to me and I'd stop and talk to them. They made me feel better when I was with them, but I still felt empty underneath when I was alone, which was most of the time.

In school I just stayed by myself. During free periods I'd read. I avoided the other kids, never stayed after to play sports or anything like Brad did. Brad was always so popular and I knew he was ashamed of me. He pretended I wasn't his brother, and I couldn't blame him. But that hurt almost more than anything.

Even so, those years—from the time I was around 9 to when I was about 12 or 13—were, in a way, the happiest of my life. What I remember best is how great I'd feel on a lazy summer day, riding my bike down a hill somewhere out in the country. Feeling the wind in my face, enjoying the hot sun, stopping under some trees and lying on my back on the cool grass, staring at the clouds in the sky. Stopping at a stream and getting a cold drink. There was a carefree innocence to it all, a naturalness I still treasure.

Sometimes it didn't even seem that bad that I was always alone.

I used to pretend I was an Indian. Proud, stoic, able to bear any trials placed on me. And silent. I'd play in the woods, gliding around, putting my toe, then heel down—or is it the other way around? I'd practice moving in the dark. Got pretty good at it, too, planning hiding places and escape routes.

I had a very vivid imagination. That saved me. Without it, I don't know what would've happened to me.

Anyway, I felt there must be a reason for everything that was happening to me at home and at school. It was some kind of test of my character and determination. The Indian thing again, I suppose. I thought a lot about God, too, wondering if He was testing me like He tested some of the people in the Bible. I figured if He was, someday He'd even it all out for me and eventually give me a good life after such a bad start. Isn't it amazing that I was still so hopeful?

I dreamed that when the good part came, I would be rich and famous. I'd do it all on my own and then visit my parents and they'd have to admit they'd been wrong about me. I'd imagine how they'd apologize and ask my forgiveness. Maybe they'd be at a ceremony where the President was giving me an award for some distinguished contribution to the country or something and they'd be all teary-eyed as he described what a fine person I was and said how the world needed more people like me.

Or I'd dream I was a Marine on a dangerous mission. I'd save a lot of my buddies' lives but be killed in action, and the President would be giving my parents the posthumous Medal of Honor and telling them what a valiant, heroic person I was. And the guys I saved would give testimonials and tell my parents how they all looked up to me and what an inspiration I was to them. I'd picture my parents looking at each other after it was all over and saying, "Well, he wasn't such a bad kid after all. We should have treated him better."

But it'd be too late. They'd just have to live with the guilt and fear that someone somewhere would discover how they'd ignored me. Then they'd be disgraced before the whole country.

Anyway, when I became a teenager, suddenly everything began moving faster. My parents rode me a lot and the more they did, the more I pulled away from them.

In high school the only friends I had were outside the mainstream, too. We didn't fit in with any of the regular groups, the Brains, the Jocks, the Nerds. They called us the Options, which sounds better than it was. Quite a few of the guys were doing a lot of drugs, a few were gay, and others were into heavy Satan trips. Those guys dressed all in black and cut their hair off on one side. Most of 'em were bitter, turned off on everything. But they accepted me, I guess because I didn't fit in anywhere else either. And I was just as unhappy as any of them.

One big thing happened when I was about 13. A customer on my paper route was a college art teacher. He was an older guy, with gray hair and a beard. His name was Gene. During the summer when he was off he worked in a little studio behind his house. I'd take the paper to him back there. The first time I stood around a few minutes and watched him work. He didn't seem to mind, so the next day I ended my route there and we talked awhile. From then on, I stopped every day.

I remember how surprised I was that first time I watched him take a sheet of paper, make a few strokes here and there, and before long a whole picture sprang to life. Pretty soon, he gave me some paper and a pencil and showed me a few things about how to draw. That summer I spent quite a lot of time with him. He told me

I had a natural talent, a feel for things. He said if I worked at it I could be an artist someday.

For Christmas that year Gene gave me a big sketch pad and some drawing pencils. I couldn't believe he'd do that for me. He treated me like I was someone, like I was special. My voice choked up when I tried to say, "Thank you," but he just patted my shoulder and understood. After that I worked hard on my drawings, then I'd show him what I'd done. He always complimented me, encouraged me, suggested how I might do the trees or something else better, helped me get perspectives right. He could work miracles on paper.

For almost a year I spent as much time as I could in his studio. I pretended he was my grandfather.

Then one day the studio door was locked. I went to the house and a woman told me Gene had gotten very sick and died during the night.

I walked away in a daze. How could he be perfectly okay one day and dead the next? I mean, it just couldn't be. Next thing I knew, I was at this hideout I had in a culvert at the park. I climbed in and cried until my insides hurt.

My whole world ripped apart. I'd finally found someone who liked me and thought I was worth something. Then bang. I lost him, my first true friend. The one person who meant more to me than anyone I'd ever known. It left a huge, empty hole in my life.

I wanted to die, too.

It wasn't fair. There was so much more he could have taught me. He was a super teacher. And maybe someday I could have done something for him in return. I should have had that chance.

I'm crying while I'm writing this.

Took a break. Wow, did that bring stuff flooding back! You'll be proud of me 'cause I had a good cry and got some feelings out. Kind of drained me, but now I feel better.

I still think about Gene, Mac. He was a very special person. I wonder if he knew how much he helped me. I wish I could tell him, and thank him for all he did for me.

Can't write much more now. I need to walk around a little. I'm feeling real antsy.

Later

Just remembered something else. I think Gene was the first person I knew who died. It hit me then that people really do die. People who are healthy one day can get sick the next and bam, before you know it they're gone. I realized that that could happen to my parents. And sure enough, a few years later, it did. In an instant, they and Brad were gone.

Now I think, it could happen to me, too.

S.

I laid the journal down on the table next to me, stretched, and went out to the kitchen to see what I could find to eat. As usual, I hadn't been to the store for a while.

I opened the refrigerator door and sighed. Gene had been someone Steve needed badly. Someone he could admire, trust, count on. Someone who had literally drawn him outside himself and begun to tap into his talents. And who then had been wrenched away from him just when he needed him most. I flipped the door closed and returned to write a note to Steve at the end of the last page:

This is a beautiful entry, Steve. Your description of anxiety attacks is very real. They can be devastating. The rest is a truly poignant account, a moving tribute to Gene.

You've had far more than your fair share of tragic losses.

I know this wasn't easy for you to write about, but you did a great job of it. Thank you for sharing it with me.

Mac

The Confetti Kid

The few light dustings of snow we'd had since Thanksgiving made me dare to hope my wish for a warmer, gentler winter might be granted. Each storm, so I was told, had a character all its own, so much so that forecasters named them. According to local lore, the most memorable winter storms began far out in the Pacific, gathered strength as they moved across the northern tier of states, and then dipped into the plains states for additional moisture and ferocity before heading for Wisconsin's snowbelt. My informants seemed to take perverse delight in pointing out to me that the Peace River area was the belt's buckle.

The first real humdinger of a blizzard, Abner—the tradition was evidently to start with the beginning of the alphabet—headed our way two days before Christmas. A winter storm watch was announced the previous evening and a current of excitement buzzed through the hospital most of the day. I'd be talking with one of the techs and we'd both stop and stare out the window, watching the churlish dark clouds being driven in by the jet stream express.

"Do you have plenty of supplies? Food, candles, a flashlight?" Joan asked at coffee break.

"Yeah, I'm pretty sure," I told her, realizing that my procrastination was about to catch up with me.

By mid-afternoon the first snowflakes arrived, swirling against my office window. They looked harmless enough, so I went on about my business, going to the wards to write some last-minute orders before I left for the day. When I returned to my office a little later, the gusts of snow were looking more serious. Survival instincts finally took over and I left the hospital early.

I filled the gas tank, picked up a supply of Palooka Pizzas, then stopped at the market for the obligatory candles and a flashlight. And some schnapps, the traditional Wisconsin antifreeze. The market was doing a brisk business so I wasn't the only one who had waited until the last minute. Somehow, that reassured me.

I overheard someone at the checkout counter refer to a snowblower, so I decided I'd better at least have a shovel. One stop turned into three before I found the last one in town. Luck of the Irish. By the time I pulled into my garage, it was starting to drift over in spots but it was completely bare in others. The wind was whipping clouds of snowflakes around the house as I grabbed my purchases and dashed inside. Conditions were deteriorating rapidly and I was glad to be hunkering down.

Really, it was kind of exciting. I'd never been in a blizzard before. Darkness soon fell and the tempo of the wind rose a notch or two, coaxing me to the window again and again. I built a fire and pulled the recliner close to it for warmth. The wind reverberated in the chimney and the temperature must have been falling because the roof timbers groaned and cracked in complaint. One big difference I'd noticed here was how much sturdier Midwest houses are compared to those in Southern California. They have to be to withstand all this, I thought. Buffeted by the wind, mine seemed to be rocking on its foundation. All the huffing and puffing reminded me of the Three Little Pigs. Although my house wasn't brick, I still felt snug and safe.

Yellow-blue flames mesmerized me and I was somehow comforted by the soft snuffling of steam escaping from the burning oak logs. I put my feet on the hearth and the warmth of the coals penetrated my thick wool socks. It was all so basic, so elemental, almost primitive. And much more fun than a California earthquake.

I called my folks and described the storm to them, downplaying the scary parts. I thought about Brenda. Lucky she'd left before the storm. I was sure all planes were grounded by now. After a pasta dinner, I picked up a Lawrence Block mystery and tried to read for awhile. But I couldn't concentrate. I kept getting up, wandering to the window, gazing out, returning to the fire.

Abner was practically the sole topic of the ten o'clock

news—footage of snarled traffic, people struggling against the brutal wind, maps of the progression of the storm, snow advisories for ten to twelve inches. The snowplows had been pulled off the roads because of the high winds and blowing snow. Drifts formed again across the roads within minutes of being cleared.

By the time the news was over nearly every window in the house was covered with snow. A few had little oval circles in the center, which were slowly being obscured by swirling ice crystals. Off in the distance I could see a warm glow of light at the Shafers' house. It was heartening.

I turned on the outside lights and peered out, shocked to see what looked like a snow castle where the bare branches of the burning bush had been. A long rock wall now appeared like a beached whale. The only thing I recognized was the tip of a forlorn canoe sinking into a white sea. I was astonished at how quickly the snow was accumulating.

Then I was struck with a romantic notion: Take on the fearsome elements. I put another log on the fire so it wouldn't go out and bundled up in my new parka. Then I slogged down the short driveway to the road. It was heavily drifted, virtually impassable.

The lashing snow stung my eyes so I high-stepped through the drifts to a sheltered spot in the woods across the road. There I stopped. To listen. It was eerie, the wind howling through trees and clouds of snow rampaging horizontally against the dim glow of a lonely streetlight at the end of the Shafers' driveway. I thought of the Indians and the early homesteaders and wondered how they'd managed in storms like this.

For some time I just stood there, savoring the experience, until a whiff of fragrant smoke reminded me there were perhaps better places to be. I retraced my steps, now nearly totally obscured by a new layer of snow. Inside the garage I shook off, shed gloves and boots, and headed for the warmth.

I was sure I wouldn't be able to get in to work the next day. The snow would be too much even for Mr. Shafer's hardy tractor. And then an old feeling came back to me, the elation I always felt when school was cancelled. Whoopee! I had three more books I wanted to get to and was anticipating a day in front of the fire. Why, the way the snow was accumulating, it could be a week before they dug me out! I fell asleep, visions of a loafing lounge lizard dancing in my head.

Shortly after five a.m. my dream abruptly ended with the guttural growl of a straining diesel. The wind had stilled and the crews had evidently been called out again. Peeking out the window, I saw an immense orange Oshkosh Truck, topped by blazing halogen lights. Huge snowblade wing in flight, it chugged resolutely down the road, bashing through the drifts.

There went my Snowday.

In the morning I'd have to break in my new snowshovel. Then I could inch my way down the slippery, icy road to the hospital.

With a sigh I went back to a now-troubled sleep, the romance of the blizzard replaced by adult reality. By the time I was ready to leave for the hospital, my good neighbor had cut a beautiful path for me through the driveway drifts.

Many of the patients had scattered to their families and hometowns for Christmas, but some trips home had been thwarted by Abner. For a fair number of patients, the hospital was home, and the staff worked hard to provide a festive atmosphere for all who stayed.

I was enjoying my first white Christmas. In one corner of my living room, I put up my scrawny tree and the fragrant scent of pine filled the house. I decorated it with tiny white lights and frosted gold ornaments and garlands. I'd always wanted to do that, but my ex had had other ideas. Another first: On an oval track under the tree I set up my "dissertation train"—the old Lionel I'd given myself as a Ph.D. graduation gift. The train I'd had as a kid had long since disappeared, but I'd spotted this one at an antique shop and impulsively bought it. Now I was glad. It was magical to get down on the floor and watch the little train circle the track in the warm glow of light from the tree. This was back to the basics. Total regression.

The only thing missing was someone to share it with.

The Shafers invited me to join their family gathering, but I declined, and on Christmas Day I accompanied Steve and a number of other patients to the dining hall for a gala institutional dinner. Maybe I'd had too many Palooka Pizzas lately or was just awfully hungry, but this turkey dinner was exceptionally good. And there was a welcome camaraderie to it, the lines of division between staff and patients erased by a bond of fellowship. Even Steve seemed to enjoy himself for a time, though I saw him ask a tech to go back to the ward with him right after dinner. He looked very tired and lost. It was a struggle for me not to try to console him, but a powerful surge of intuition warned me away.

21

BRENDA RETURNED FROM OHIO LOOKING RELAXED AND energetic. I signaled a "welcome back" to her as I entered the dayroom on Unit Two her first morning back. She was seated at a table with a patient, conversing quietly, going over some papers she had set in front of him. It must have been a routine matter because they certainly weren't going to get any privacy here. A heavyset fellow with ferret eyes was pacing back and forth in front of the table and another patient, a smallish man, was hovering behind Brenda's chair. The usual level of commotion, halfway between a buzz and a din, prevailed.

As I spoke with Chet nearby, I watched over his shoulder as the hoverer sidled closer to Brenda, eyeing her pretty auburn hair with great concentration. For some time he just stared, and then, slowly, he reached out and placed both hands palms down, so they barely touched Brenda's hair. He poised there silently for a moment, then curled his fingers down and began gently parting through Brenda's hair, eyes intent on her scalp. About this time, the ferret whirled and yelled,

"Hey, get away from her!" He lunged toward the small

man, who hastily jumped back, covering his head in fright.

Chet spun around and moved to intervene.

"It's all right, Mr. Sanders," said Brenda calmly. "He wasn't trying to hurt me. Were you, Mr. Richards?" She turned toward the squat little man cringing behind her. "Cootie patrol?" she asked.

He nodded solemnly. Chet had Mr. Sanders by the arm and was guiding him to the other side of the room.

"It's okay," Brenda assured him.

"Yeah, well just leave her alone, you fruitcake!" Mr. Sanders growled.

Brenda waited a moment, then addressed the quaking figure in a firm but warm voice.

"You know you're not supposed to do that, Mr. Richards. People don't like it. And it bothers the volunteers who don't know you when you come up behind them and start playing with their hair."

He nodded sheepishly.

"So we can't have any more of that. Now you go find something else to do."

She watched as Mr. Richards turned and shuffled away. Then she noticed me, the innocent bystander. She smiled self-consciously and shook her head.

"Glad I washed my hair last night," she said. "Who knows what he might have found?"

The patient with her laughed and then they both went back to their paperwork.

Later that afternoon I collapsed with a "Whew!" into the big armchair in Ben's office.

"What's up?"

"Steve and I are getting down to nuts and bolts, Ben."

"How do things stand?"

I filled him in and he nodded.

"Is there a problem then?"

"It's me again, I guess. I'm having trouble seeing the road ahead. What do I do next? Where should I expect him to turn? Do we just keep dipping down to see what we can come up with? How much pressure do I keep on him? And for how long? When is enough enough?"

Ben listened patiently. He looked silently over my shoulder, his brow furrowing. It was a mannerism I'd come to recognize. He did it when he was collecting his thoughts. I relaxed, calmed by his quiet concern. Then his eyes focused directly on me.

"You're entering rarified air. You and Steve keep crossing and re-crossing this terrain, each time getting progressively deeper, like explorers following switchback trails into a deep canyon. The deeper you get, the steeper the trails become, so you have to stop and rest more often. As long as you're making some headway, you probably shouldn't push him too much. Allow him time to absorb what he's coming up against. He's slowly learning to account for his own life. That's a major undertaking. So why not let him keep taking the initiative, setting the pace, deciding which trail he wants to take and at what speed."

"Okay, that's fine for him, Ben, but what about me? I'm the one responsible if he missteps. Or worse, falls."

"Ahhhh, you want assurances?"

"That would be nice."

"Too bad. It doesn't work that way, Pat. You know that. You're helping Steve get to the core of his personality, but try as we might, no one can anticipate the outcome." He paused. "The unconscious, is that what's making you uneasy?"

"I'm not sure. Maybe."

"Do you remember the last time you encountered Steve's unconscious?"

I shook my head. Then I had a flash of a costumed warrior hurtling off my desk and the melee that followed.

"You do remember."

"Yes," I said slowly.

"That must have been terrifying for you too then, Pat."

"I'm not likely to forget it."

"Do you see the ramifications?" Ben asked.

"I'm not sure. Are you suggesting that my anxiety is somehow connected to opening up his core?"

"Go on," Ben encouraged.

I sighed. "Okay. When the hatchcovers blew off in my office and for those weeks when Steve was so floridly psychotic, that was his core, the raw core. Full-blown rage, violence. I suspect hatred underlies that. And there's sorrow, certainly, if not depression. Over the deaths and separations. Over the unresolved feelings toward his parents, the alienation, all the loneliness."

"So far so good. Keep going," he urged.

"I can see we're getting close to that rage. Do you think I'm afraid that when we get there he'll come unglued, go psychotic again? I couldn't prevent it the first time. Are you suggesting that shook my confidence enough so that I'm blaming myself for the break? And would blame myself if he has another one?"

Ben raised his eyebrows questioningly, but said nothing.

I sighed. "Maybe I do, Ben. I don't know. I do know that there was this young guy who needed me, but I couldn't come through for him. There are a lot of shared themes in our lives. Dozens of similarities have crossed my mind as we've talked. Sometimes I've been shocked by them. We've both lost women who were important to us. We're both struggling with issues of trust, getting close, opening up. God, the list is endless."

"Do my ears detect—" Ben stopped.

"What?" I demanded. "What?"

"You tell me."

I stared at him. He was giving me a taste of what Steve was up against with me.

"I seem to be hitting some resistance." He smiled benevolently. "Relax, Pat. What does everything you've told me so far sum up to?"

I put my head back and closed my eyes. Steve's unconscious . . . shared feelings, issues . . . psychosis, confetti . . . parents . . . me, my unconscious . . .

I opened my eyes with a jolt.

"Uh-oh," I said.

"What?"

"You don't mean . . . countertransference?"

He nodded. That honestly hadn't occurred to me. Talk about denial! I'd learned and heard all about countertransference, of course. Unlike transference, which occurs when a patient develops strong but unconscious feelings toward the therapist, countertransference works the other way: The therapist's unconscious emotions toward the patient interfere with his objectivity to the point they hinder treatment. I'd always felt if that ever happened between me and one of my clients it would be so obvious that I'd recognize it. Now I stared past Ben, scanning my feelings and motives with Steve. What exactly was my stake in him? After a time I looked over at Ben. He was watching me.

"Steady as she goes," he said.

"Ben, are you saying that I've overidentified so strongly with Steve—and with the Confetti Kid—that I'm getting anxious, too? That as we move into the core of his personality when he's at maximum risk for another psychotic break, I could identify with him so strongly that I might—" I stopped dead, stunned.

"—have one too," Ben finished for me. "Yes."

"I can't believe it," I stammered.

"It's unlikely, Pat. But it could happen. And the good part is that between the Navane and the intensive therapy, the psychotic element in Steve's personality is under pretty good control. So far you've helped him ventilate enough of the pent-up feelings that the pressure has been released a bit. But, of course, there's always a chance."

A wave of nausea swept over me. "So what do I do? Should I bring in a co-therapist, someone who can do some reality checks on both of us?"

"I'm not sure you need to do anything quite that drastic, Pat. What other alternatives are there?"

I shook my head. I was still so stunned to find myself in the throes of countertransference I wasn't thinking straight. This couldn't be happening to me. No one was more aware than I was that therapy can be a risky business. How had I lost so much perspective?

Ben pressed on. "What could you anticipate Steve might do if he falls apart again?"

I thought a while. "I suppose he may take off again. Run away. Or he could get very depressed. What worries me most is that core of loneliness, his intense sense of alienation. So when the final well-head of feelings is uncapped, I think he could get super-depressed, possibly suicidal."

Ben nodded agreement. "The closer you get to those deeper reaches of Steve's personality, the more possible those outcomes become. But what implications might this have for Steve's therapist?"

His tone was so serious that he was scaring me. What did he know that I didn't?

"I'm not sure," I began. "I suppose my overinvolvement with Steve is so strong that if he ran away, or hit a significant depression, I could be devastated, too. Which I would be."

"So how might you react?" Ben asked gently.

"I don't know."

Ben raised his eyebrows and cocked his head.

And then it hit me. Yeah, I could see it now.

"You mean if I'm getting more and more anxious as Steve nears this core area, I may try to—to hold him back from going any farther? That unconsciously I might impede his progress?"

Ben nodded. "Forewarned is forearmed," he said simply.

I sighed. What a shock. The sense of control over therapy I'd had was just an illusion, something I'd convinced myself of to allay my own growing anxiety about where we might be heading. The mind tricks operating in Steve, or anyone else for that matter, were also operating in yours truly.

Sensing what I was thinking, Ben cautioned, "Don't be too hard on yourself, Pat. Being a therapist is a very complex skill. It takes years of study and practice. Just stay open to your feelings and analyze yourself as you go along. You have to be as attuned to what's going on inside yourself as you are to what's going on inside your client. Check in with me from time to time. Let's monitor it together."

"Thanks, Ben. I think I've got a better handle on this now."

But did I? I wasn't so sure at all.

III

22

SO FAR JANUARY HAD BEEN MILDER THAN USUAL. AFTER hearing so much about sub-zero temperatures, I was convinced such talk was directed at discouraging outsiders from moving to Wisconsin. Then a twenty-five-degree-below-zero blast of arctic air, straight off the North Pole, settled in for a week.

My skin was blue, my thin California blood turning to slush as I trudged stiff-legged from the parking lot, half expecting my frozen ears and nose to drop off before I reached the warmth of Cameron Hall. A bad head cold completed my misery and laid me up for three days. Finally, both colds lifted and I was back in business.

Steve started to ask to be discharged. As a voluntary patient, he could have signed out at any time, but he said he wanted to do it with the team's blessing. I'd repeatedly told him he wasn't ready and his response was always the same.

"Why not? I've been here seven months. I'm doing well, I've done everything you've asked me to do."

"I agree, Steve. You've come a long way. But we still have a tough stretch ahead."

"But I'd be living nearby. I'd keep coming in for therapy."

"What's the big push all of a sudden? Why are you so anxious to leave?"

"Because my insurance ran out and I don't want to empty my trust fund on this. Besides, I'm getting buggy in here. My life is so pending. Everything is on hold, college, a job, my whole future—"

"Okay, but there's a pretty serious reason for the delay, Steve. You got your bell rung. We've called a timeout while you make some major changes."

"So I've made them. I'm fine now, or ninety percent, anyway. I can finish the rest of therapy as an outpatient. I promise I'll keep coming to sessions. But I need to get out of here!"

"Wait, slow it down. First, I seriously doubt the ninety-percent improvement. You're still in transition. If you make a major change right now, you may lose a lot of what you've worked for. It's too big a jump." He started to protest but I interrupted him. "Do you remember when you pretty much took everything—especially your health—for granted?"

"Uh huh."

"Mark it well, because you'll never have the luxury of that kind of complacency again. Now that you've hit the wall of having a chronic health problem, your life has been forever changed. From now on you'll have to guard against a psychotic recurrence, which means having an entirely different perspective, developing a whole new way of living. And that takes time." I paused, then said, "Let me ask you something. Do you still think you're The Confetti Kid?"

"Ohhhhh," Steve groaned. "That again?"

"Well? Do you?"

He didn't answer at first. After a few seconds he said,

"Not as much as I did, Mac. I still believe in what he stood for, but I know I used my imagination too much, you know?"

"That's a good way of putting it."

"Yeah. I guess it was pretty crazy to believe that throwing confetti could make the world a more peaceful place."

"Uh huh."

"So, okay, I'm not The Confetti Kid anymore. How come you won't let me go, then? Why don't you want me to leave? Mac, what kind of friend are you, anyway? I've told you all this stuff about me, we've gone over it and over it and over it. If you were really my friend, you'd get me the hell out of here!"

"I am your friend. But you have to remember that first I'm your psychotherapist. That means a very different kind of friendship."

"But I've told you way more than I've ever told anyone else. Even Jennifer."

"I know that. But it's been in therapy. My role has been to explore with you and confront you with certain realities. I've said things that have provoked you. I've made judgments, even hurt your feelings. That's all part of therapy. So it's fine for you to consider me a friend, but only in a context of the special therapeutic relationship we have. A social friend wouldn't have any say in your release from the hospital."

"You mean it's a one-way deal. I tell you everything about me, but you tell me nothing about you."

"Not necessarily," I said. "You've asked me personal questions and I've answered. But yes, it is a somewhat one-sided friendship. You're trying to learn what tipped you into psychosis and how to guard against it happening again. You're the focus here."

"I'd rather be a little less in focus."

"I know you would, Steve, but I can tell you from my own therapy experience that this bottom fishing we're doing takes a while."

"Geez."

"Well, it's not a bad metaphor."

"Bottom fishing?"

"Sure, we're trolling along the bottom of your unconscious, seeing what gets churned up."

He shook his head. "Come on, give me a break. You're started to talk like a Wisconsinite. *Bottom fishing.*" He shook his head disparagingly.

"All right, wait."

I took a tablet and quickly sketched a diagram of psychotherapy, talking as I filled it in:

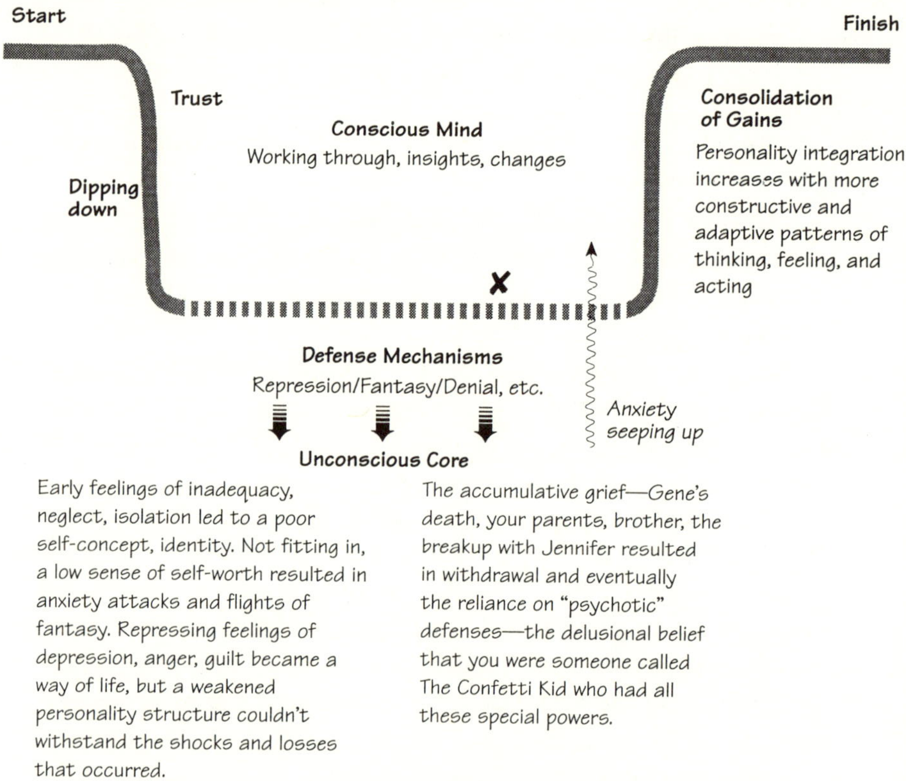

I retraced the line from the upper left corner down into the hollow. "Here's where we started. Trust was the big issue. Then you began dipping down, recalling events, talking about your parents, school, Gene, all that. That was the working through. When you began to see the connections between all those events and how they influenced the formation of your character, those were insights. Okay so far?"

Steve nodded.

I drew an "X" on the diagram, with the squiggly line and an arrow pointing up just after it. "My guess, Steve, is that you're about here." I tapped the "X" with my pen. "The problem is, we don't know what lies ahead or how much remains down there to be uncapped."

"Yeah, but I've got a good enough understanding of what happened—"

"To a point you do, Steve. But the maladaptive defense mechanisms you've relied on in the past aren't working very well anymore." I gestured to the squiggly line. "They've gotten so brittle that instead of sealing in the anxiety the way they used to, it's seeping up into your conscious mind and causing the agitation and anxiety you've been feeling."

"So how come I had those anxiety attacks before? Back when I was in high school? My defense mechanisms sure weren't working very well then, either."

"Because neurotic defenses like that are very unstable. They're a leaky dike trying to hold back an ocean of feelings. Every now and then a big hole will open and a flood of anxiety escapes out of the unconscious core. Too much pressure builds up, Steve. The pressure in high school was coming from your loneliness and alienation. Now, because of therapy, the pressure is coming from all over. Just one part of treatment is rebuilding those defenses into a more stable structure. And don't forget, you're still unearthing old feelings. Rejection is still a biggie. So you have to keep letting all that out, too. We're working toward integration, Steve."

He followed the line running from the "X" up the other side. "And this 'consolidation' part is what will take longer?"

"That's right. It took years to develop all those bad guys you relied on. We're trying to change the way you look at yourself—and the world—in a matter of months. That's a big order."

"You went through this stuff in your therapy?"

"Yes. And still am to some extent. There's no actual start and stop to it. It's a lifelong process."

"And it's made a difference in your life?"

"Definitely." Something in Steve's tone raised a flag in me. "What?" I asked.

He cocked his head and looked at me.

"You're still a strange kind of guy, Mac, you know that?"

"Uh huh," I agreed. "Why are you bringing that up now?"

He appraised me thoughtfully, then said, "I watch you around the ward a lot."

"You're not trying to change the subject, are you?"

"Nah. I don't think so. But it bothers me. You know everything about me, and I still know so little about you. California. Divorced. A few nurses and social workers interested in you, lots of rumors—"

"Is all this important to you, Steve? That important?"

"Yes, it is. I'd like to know more. You're always asking me all these heavy questions. 'What's your philosophy of life?' and like that. Now it's my turn. You've got it made. I want to know how you did it."

"It may seem that way to you, Steve, but no one ever has it made."

"I don't believe that. Rich people do."

"Wrong. It doesn't matter how successful or secure you are, or how many millions you have stashed, there's no way of knowing what life is going to spring on you from one moment to the next. Accidents can happen in an instant. No one knows that better than you. Nothing protects us. Jobs are terminated, businesses fail, marriages go sour, illnesses hit us. You're a case in point."

"Yeah, but it's easier for rich people."

"Sure, some things are easier if you've got money. But what I'm talking about goes deeper than that. I want to see you develop the resiliency to withstand the strain when events load up and hammer you. And a sense of appreciation and contentment with your life. Without that, none of the other stuff—being rich or whatever—matters very much."

He looked dubious but thoughtful. Then he grinned.

"I put people in nice little niches, you know. Have it made; don't have it made. Winners, losers. I like to divide the world up that way."

"A lot of people do, Steve."

"You, though, I'm not so sure about."

"Oh? How's that?"

"Well, for one thing, I was baiting you when I said you have it made. You don't. In fact, I think basically you're kind of unhappy. Lonely, anyway."

"Really?" I arched my eyebrows.

"Yeah. Since you said I could be the therapist today—"

"I did? I don't remember agreeing to anything like that."

"C'mon. It'll be fun. Shall I tell you what I see?"

"All right." He seemed to be enjoying turning the tables on me. And I was curious. So we'd burn a session.

He stared intently at me, as if weighing whether to go through with this; then he began tentatively. "Well, I think you've had a lot of pain in your life. And not just from your divorce. It's one of the reasons I trust you. I've thought to myself, he's been there, he knows what it's like."

"That's interesting. What makes you think that?"

"I'm not sure exactly."

He was watching me closely. "It's little stuff, I guess—your facial expressions, reactions. Mostly during unguarded moments, when you're thinking about something. I've watched you on the ward talking to one of the nurses or looking at a chart. It's a hard thing to describe, you know? I think sometimes you find human contact painful, the way I do. Like maybe bad things, stuff like what's happened to me has happened to you. It gives me some hope. But it also makes me curious."

"That's pretty good, Steve."

"Yeah? How close am I?"

"Pretty close. I haven't had anything on the scale you've had, but there've been some tough times for me along the way. The divorce, certainly. That really leveled me. I'd been burned before, too, and there've been other major disappointments. What surprises me is that it shows so much."

"I'm not sure it does. You have to look pretty close to see it."

"You don't miss much."

"Yeah, so tell me, what happened to you?"

I sighed. I didn't like the direction we were moving in. With the candor of the young, Steve was putting me on the spot. But I didn't think it was a ploy. I was a model for him and he had a legitimate claim to question and know more about me. I also knew he probably wouldn't drop it. He'd come this far, and he wanted answers. Maybe in the long run it would help.

"This is going to sound familiar, but I'm not sure what to tell you. Lots of things have happened to me, Steve, but there's no single catastrophic event. Most of what I learned about myself in psychotherapy had to do with conflict. When I was a kid, there was a lot of it—between my parents, between me and my parents, and especially between me and other authority figures like teachers and bosses. I detest people telling me what to do. I've never done well with that."

"I feel exactly the same way, Mac. I don't like conflict either, you know."

I nodded. "But the main thing is, I want people to get along and I want people to like me. That's true of practically everyone, I suppose. Someone once said that everything we do is an attempt to make others love us. I think there's truth in that."

"That's me, all right," Steve agreed. "But what I see in you seems more intense, Mac."

I smiled. "Okay. You're doing a pretty good job as therapist. Let me think a little harder here."

I tried to figure out what it was Steve was tuning in to.

In graduate school we were strongly encouraged to undergo our own psychotherapy and I had been over many personal issues in mine—difficulties with handling rejections, making commitments, taking risks, and all my problems with authority. During my teenage years I'd had a normal share of disasters. I'd flipflopped from being a nice guy to coming off like a manipulative jerk. And I had picked up a pretty good battery of defenses to shield myself. Through my twenties I'd continued to be troubled by relationships that went nowhere. In therapy I delved into a lot of escapades I'd felt ashamed about. Some of those still bothered me, incidents that I had semi-suppressed but which surfaced from time to time with their erstwhile recriminations and regrets. In therapy I'd learned that everyone has these experiences, but I'd evidently had more than most. And I'd carried them more heavily than most. Therapy had helped me accept a lot of this and move on. Or so I'd thought.

I sighed. "I don't know, Steve. Like you, I had to learn to balance my needs with those of others. Try not to do things just so other people would like me." I thought a minute. "I've had to learn to identify what I was feeling, especially when I was upset, and then deal with it directly. I'm still working on that."

"You mean you're not through therapy yet?"

I groaned inwardly. "Dealing with feelings is a continuing job, Steve. Besides, I'm cursed with being a melancholy Irishman—I'm moody and incorrigibly independent. My exwife couldn't put up with my moodiness. It's getting better, but it's still there."

"This all sounds awfully familiar. Basically what it comes down to is, you have the same problems I do, don't you, Mac?"

"We and millions of others. These are practically universal problems, Steve. Amazing numbers of people bump along through life trying to deal with these issues, and many never fully conquer them. So they despair, feel unappreciated, unloved. I see people like that all the time.''

''But doesn't that get to you? Hearing depressing stuff day after day? It drives me nuts to keep going over the same ground, saying the same things twenty different ways until I'm sick of hearing myself. How can you stand listening to the constant repetition?''

''You learn to handle it, Steve. It's part of the training. One of the first things they teach you is that the mind demands repetitious chewing. People do it all the time as they're making choices and decisions. So therapists have to expect that. And people are always second- and third-guessing themselves, too. Especially over important things that affect their lives. So you have to be willing to go along, really listening for as long as it takes to work things through.''

''Still,'' said Steve, ''I'd think all the negatives would drag you down after awhile. Maybe you're soaking up more of it than you should. You better be careful, Mac.''

I was touched by his concern. ''You're starting to sound like Dr. Farrell, Steve. And you're right. There's a fine line between caring and empathy, and overinvolvement. It's an occupational hazard. And it can lead to burnout.''

''Burnout? Maybe that's what's happening to you.''

''No, I don't think so. But I can't help absorbing some of the pain of the people I work with. And sure, it gets to me sometimes. But some of it I take on willingly.''

''Willingly?''

''Uh huh. I *want* to feel some of the pain, even if it's second-hand.''

''There's your problem, Mac. Why on earth would you do that?''

''It sounds absurd, but I think to be a good therapist, you have to feel some pain. If you insulate yourself too much, you get callous. Besides, that kind of hurting is a good reminder about what life is all about and what's truly important. Right now you can't begin to understand that because you've had a bellyful of suffering. But once you've conquered all this, you're going to have a greater respect for your own self, and for life, even. You'll savor life. You won't ever take a nice day or a beautiful sunset for granted again. With all the pain I see, I never stop saying, 'There but for the grace of God . . .' ''

''So you're trying to use suffering—''

''Yes, I'm employing it to keep myself centered. Or, to put it another way, you know how we all have these little dissatisfactions that gnaw away at us? If only I had a car, or if only I had more money. If only someone loved me.''

''Sure. I've got 'em all.''

''Okay. Have you ever noticed that whenever you get one of those desires satisfied, it's just replaced by another one? If only I had a *better* car or classier clothes. Or, as you experienced with Jennifer, you find this special person and then pretty soon you agonize about how to get your independence back, or whether to break up with her before she dumps you. So you're almost always disappointed—or at least dissatisfied—after you've gotten something you thought you really wanted. As soon as the newness wears off, you're bored with it, looking forward to the next want on your list. True?''

''Yeah, true.''

''The mind has all these desires, and they produce a constant underlying static of dissatisfaction. The trouble comes because we think all these wants have to be met or we can't be content.''

''Cut to the chase, Mac. What's your point?''

''Only that there'll always be unhappiness and suffering, whether it comes from our own dissatisfactions or from bad things that happen to us. But we free ourselves by rising above the wants, the underlying dissatisfaction, the disappointments, the defeats. We have to be open to them, observe and absorb the blows, and then learn from them. And somehow you make it through, you prevail. You learn to savor life. That's what I'm trying to teach you to do."

"Well, I've got a long way to go before I can step back like that."

"Sure. In a couple of years, though, you'll see how the rocky times made you stronger. When you've survived the wrenching kind of grief you've shared with me, and when your life turns around—when you meet someone who becomes a constant in your life—then you've got a basis of comparison, haven't you? With all that's happened, you're going to be much more appreciative of the things you always took for granted. Your freedom, for example. Being hospitalized stripped you of that."

"That's for sure. I hadn't thought of it that way."

"We usually don't. Until we lose it. The same thing with our health, or our families."

"You really believe I can learn to handle all the junk life will throw at me? The stress, the hassles? And everything I throw at myself?"

"You already are. Not only handling it, but using it constructively. You're chipping away at the deep stuff. And once you clear that out, you'll be in pretty good shape."

Steve looked down at the diagram again, following the line to the finish.

"But I have to stay here to do that?"

"Some of it, yes."

"So when do you think I'll be ready to leave?"

I sighed. "Let's just see how it goes, Steve."

"But give me a timetable. I need something to go on."

The whiny adolescent emerging.

"Okay. I'd like to see you start classes in summer school. How does that sound?"

"Sounds way too long to me." He shook his head.

"Anything would sound way too long to you," I countered.

"You're right," he admitted, sighing. "Okay, I suppose I can hang in there a while longer." He looked sharply at me. "But if we do it faster, I can leave sooner, right?"

"Let's just see how it goes," I urged. "Try not to think of time right now. Concentrate on resolving issues. Quit analyzing me so much and work on yourself."

"Okay, okay. Oh, by the way, Mac, the word is that Brenda and her boyfriend are ancient history. Finis."

I looked at him in surprise. "How would you know something like that?"

Steve grinned. "I have my sources," he said. "Who shall remain nameless. You better make your move."

"I'm not ready to make any moves, Steve. I need to know where *I'm* going before I ask somebody to go with me."

"You don't have to know where you're going to go to a movie or out for dinner, Mac."

"Maybe not. But I'd want to before I start dating anyone seriously. And definitely before I'd make a move on Brenda. She's a special lady. I'll wait 'til I'm ready."

"I don't understand. How can you not be ready to go out with Brenda? She's so cute."

I shook my head. "I've gone out very few times since my divorce, Steve. I haven't been up for it. Brenda and I are just friends. That's fine for now and besides, if she and her boyfriend really have broken up, she's going to need time to get over it. I wouldn't want to get her on the rebound."

It sounded remarkably wise. But was it? Enough therapizing the therapist, I decided uneasily. The lines had blurred a bit too much for comfort. I ended the session a little early.

I should have learned by now to ask Steve if I wanted to know anything about anyone around the hospital. His observations were uncanny. As I watched Brenda over the next few days, it was apparent that something had, indeed, changed for her. Subdued, preoccupied, and listless, she went about her job with no kidding or light-hearted banter. A couple of times when she caught me staring at her, she looked quickly away. No doubt about it, she was miserable. The pain in her eyes brought back the rawness of the pain I had gone through. It hurt to see her hurting.

But I kept my distance.

23

STEVE AND I CRISSCROSSED THE TERRAIN OF HIS CHILDhood many times over. Interpreting his parents' benign neglect as rejection, he had isolated himself at every turn, so his sense of identity had never progressed beyond an amorphous glob. His defense was to become a social chameleon who tried to be whatever he thought those around him wanted him to be, but this only increased his sense of isolation. As a result, Steve spent many of our sessions sobbing out his relentless confusion and despair as I helped him examine these past interactions in minute detail. Then resistance would set in as the painful feelings became too much, and he would retreat into safer, less threatening areas.

As Steve talked, I encouraged him to analyze and understand the implications of each event. For the most part, progress was so negligible as to be invisible, and the numerous deadends frustrated us both. Invariably, he would blame himself for the deadlock; I would just as invariably question him as to why he felt it necessary to always be so self-critical.

I am by nature an impatient person, but I kept my frustration to myself. I could have put together a fairly good approximation of Steve's personality dynamics within a couple of months and presented it to him. Shown him how Belief 1 lead to Thinking/Acting A, and then told him he needed to discard Belief 1, replace it with Belief 2, and move on to Thinking/Acting B. Nice, neat package, no batteries required.

But I knew better. And I'd learned to curb my impatience. Most of the time. If the therapy was to take hold, Steve had to take the lead in figuring himself out. I was a guide, a prompter, a cheerleader, a safety net. And, eventually, a safety valve. A player, but not *the* player. I was there to protect him.

What I was impatiently waiting for was more insight, how what had happened to him converted to how he thought and acted. I was waiting for him to experience Eureka, the first flash of so-*that's*-the-reason! comprehension.

Once that happens, the most difficult part of therapy begins. The journey into scary change, seeing the old neurotic patterns for what they are—pretense, imitation, a precarious house of cards. When the self-deception of the defense mechanisms is exposed, therapy probes further into the deeper reaches of personality to reveal the regions where the dark forces and their resident demons live.

Gradually portions of that darkened stage are illuminated. To look into one's psyche, to confront whatever one fears most, is daunting. That's why psychotherapists deal with the core issues a little at a time. Too much uncovering, too many demons set loose at once, and anxiety erupts. And when anxiety floods the personality, it can tip the scales into rage, profound depression, psychosis. Or worse.

It was all high risk with Steve. Yet I couldn't slack off. No matter how frightened he got, I had to keep a steady pressure on to be sure we unearthed the seeds of what had brought him here.

The week after I let Steve turn the tables on me, he arrived at our session looking very upset. Even before he hit the back of his favorite chair, he was off and running:

"I've been feeling real edgy today, Mac, like there's a lot ready to erupt. Mount Saint Stephen."

I nodded.

"Why do I feel like I'm losing it?" He sounded scared.

"It may be like that for a while, Steve. We're getting closer to all the toxins buried in you."

He shook his head morosely. "It's the pits."

"Just go slow," I cautioned. "Open your mind up a crack, take a quick peek, and close it up again."

"But how do I know it's safe to peek?"

"Trust yourself. Keep working to identify your inner voice. Listen to it and trust it. You'll be relying on it for the rest of your life."

"Yeah, but the inner voices I've trusted before haven't exactly helped, you know. Right now my insides are churning. Is that anxiety?"

"Probably. If it gets too bad or your thoughts start racing, we'll consider a med adjustment. Also, it may help if we meet more often."

He didn't look reassured. For the umpteenth time he asked, "Do I really have to go through all this? Haven't we done enough? I mean, I'm getting *worse.*"

I shook my head. "No, you aren't, Steve. It just seems that way. You may feel worse for a while until you start feeling better. But we're in a crucial phase now, where all that rancid gunk gets disposed of once and for all."

"Yeah, well, I'm tired. I just want to be finished so I can—" he stopped, a frown creasing his forehead.

I waited while the moments drifted by. Something seemed to have dislodged.

Then he said, "I just thought of something—" and stopped again.

We sat in silence for a few minutes before he looked over at me.

"I just got some images," he whispered, as if he were sharing a forbidden secret. "You know what, Mac?" A huge sigh.

"What?"

"You keep mentioning this core part of me. And I think I just got a glimpse of it."

I said nothing.

His face reddened, his breathing accelerated, and finally the words came, searchingly:

"There's a side of me I've never known about," he whispered. "No wonder I don't wanna deal with this."

"Take it a little at a time."

We sat in silence again, then he shook his head solemnly. "Wow. Double wow."

Excited, wondering what he had come across, I kept my impatience on a tight leash. Whatever was going on in his mind would not be enhanced by my intervening.

This was the skill that had been the most difficult for me to master. A psychotherapist is constantly attuned to the ebb and flow of conversation. The hard part is staying quiet, just listening, allowing the client to search his mind for events, connections, insights. Giving the maximum leeway possible. And being non-judgmental. A good psychotherapist just sits back and listens when the client is on this kind of a self-discovery roll.

At last Steve spoke again, slowly, feeling his way.

"I told you about the Parker charade." He smiled, but I could see tears welling up in his eyes. "I was always so conscientious, trying to please everyone, get along, get the love I craved. When I couldn't get it from my parents, I'd go after anyone else who'd pat me on the head. That's what I was—" he snapped his fingers, "—a damn puppy dog wagging my tail, licking everyone's hand, hoping they'd scratch my ears, rub my belly."

Tears rolled down his cheeks and he faced me with an anguish that wrenched me. His voice was filled with longing.

"I tried so hard to be loved . . . to be liked . . . hell, just to be accepted. And now I see what a gigantic hypocrite I was."

I waited an interval and then asked,

"Why do you say that, Steve?"

"Because ***I'm just like them!"*** he shouted. ***"I'm a fake, too!*** I've been every bit as hypocritical as they were. All that mattered to my parents was everything looking beautiful. So what if things were a mess inside? As long as no one else knew, all was well. Perfect parents, perfect children, living perfect lives in a perfect home! I played my part right along with them! To perfection! Anything else was unthinkable.

"But it was all so much crap! My dad was miserable. He hated his job, he drank too much. He tried to be an all-around guy who could do anything, be anything—all things to all people. The same with Mom, except when things got her down, she'd take to her bed with a wet washcloth on her forehead.

"It was all a lie. Everything . . ." His voice growled with anger. "And I bought into it. Totally. I just went along. And you know what? You know what I've just figured out here?" He skewered me with his red-rimmed eyes. "My whole ***life*** has been a lie. I never questioned. Just kept wagging my tail, waiting for a dog biscuit.

"God, how ***stupid*** can you be?" Now his voice was seething with venom. "You know what, Mac?" The question was demanding, confronting, and I could feel the underlying rage bubbling.

"What?"

"You want to know what kind of guy I really am? What I'm really like under these Joe College clothes? What's inside The Confetti Kid suit?"

I nodded.

He moved his body so he squared off, facing me fully, lips drawn back, teeth clenched. His tone was contemptuous.

"Are you absolutely sure you want to witness the real Stephen Parker, alias The Confetti Kid, alias Hypocrite of the Century? Are you ready for that?"

His intensity sparked a surge of anxiety in me, but I managed to keep my voice steady.

"Yes, Steve, I am."

"Okay, but you're letting yourself in for it, you know. You're not gonna like this."

"Go ahead, Steve." I dropped my voice as he raised his.

I stiffened as he shouted, ***"Okay. First off. I want you to know that deep, deep down I've got one hell of a mean streak. I am one very vindictive, hateful, spiteful bastard. You better not ever cross me. If you do, you'll regret it for the rest of your life! I've had it up to here with being nice, trying to be perfect. And for what? Tell me that, where has it gotten me?"***

When I didn't respond, he sputtered on, almost panting with exertion:

"I'm furious! You better believe it. I'm furious at Dad, who could never say 'good job, Steve,' or 'I love you.' Oh, no, never that! He never once told me that. And at Mom, who was never, never there when I needed her. Everything else in the world was always more important to them than I was. They treated us like grownups, not children who needed to be nurtured and loved.

"They had absolutely no understanding of how important love and attention are to a child. How important they were to me! They made me think I was weird for wanting them to take care of me. Or at least take me with them . . ." His voice was guttural and full of disgust.

He was silent for a long time, staring daggers at the floor in front of him, occasionally shaking his head. Then he looked back at me and continued, his voice filled with anguish.

"How can I ever get all this resentment and bitterness out? There's so much of it, and it gets stronger and stronger. It's taking me over!"

"Just keep talking, Steve."

He relaxed a little, allowing the tears to come. Then the rage erupted again.

"How could they have treated me that way? Why didn't they love me? Why was their damn work—and parties and tennis games—so much more important? How could they be so totally selfish? Why were our lives so stupidly complicated? We didn't need such a huge house, the fancy cars, all the obligations they kept piling on. That hurt me, too. Screwed me up. And what was the point?"

He slammed both of his clenched fists against the arms of the recliner. His face was livid, his voice venomous. His father and mother were in the room with us.

"How could you?" he screamed at the empty space in front of him. ***"How could you do what you did to me? Lies, neglect, hypocrisy! You never wanted me. You never cared for me! You never cared for anyone but yourselves. You goddam selfish hypocrites! You stuck your own parents in nursing homes because you couldn't be bothered with them. They were wonderful people. I loved to visit them when I was little and they were so nice to me, but then you put 'em away because they cut into your social life too much. And then you wouldn't even take me to see them—you always had excuses. But the real reason was you felt too guilty about what you'd done.***

"You denied us our grandparents! They were a drag on your lives so you just cut them off. Bam! They were an inconvenience for you, just like Brad and I were. But they didn't deserve to be treated that way. How could you have been so spiteful?"

His voice was seething, spewing out rage the likes of

which I'd never witnessed before. This was the mother lode we'd been searching for—and the father lode, too. At last he'd blown off the hatchcovers. Barely pausing to catch his breath, the blasting continued:

"You put our puppy to sleep because Brad and I couldn't train it not to poop on the rug. You murdered that helpless little dog and then you lied to us . . . said it got sick and had to be put to sleep! It wasn't sick! There was nothing wrong with it. The one thing we ever really wanted and loved and you waited 'til the two of us were gone and then you snuck out and had him killed! And then tried to convince us how it was better for everybody. What totally self-centered, selfish people! You're scum! You thought we bought all that crap, didn't you? But we saw through you! You lying, deceitful, sadistic bastards. And then you didn't even stick around 'til I could—"

Again, his fists slammed against the chair and then beat a regular tattoo on the arms, punctuating each explosive word.

"I hate you! I hate you, I hate you, I hate you! Both of you, for what you did to me! For what you did to Brad, for what you did to Grammie and Gramps, for what you did to Skippy. You wrecked all our lives. . . . You've ruined my life!

The rage that had consumed his soul poured out. His breath came in gasps, screeching out the years of frustration and confusion that had led up to this moment.

Suddenly he leaped to his feet, grabbed the fiberglass chair, and raised it over his head. ***"You deserved to die!"*** he screamed. With tremendous force, he smashed the chair to the floor again and again, bashing it until the spindly legs buckled and separated from the shell. At last he threw the pile of rubble into the corner in disgust.

And then everything transformed. He collapsed back into the recliner and broke down in unrestrained sobbing. The torment he'd throttled since childhood escaped in moans as he wrapped his arms around his stomach and rocked back and forth, gurgling and crying and gasping for breath.

I moved closer to him and put my hand on his arm, then gently laid my other arm across his back. As I touched him, he literally grabbed me and buried his face in my shoulder. I hugged him and let him cry.

"That's right, Steve, let it out. Get it all out, once and for all."

For a solid fifteen minutes great, wrenching sobs wracked his body. When he left my office that day he was totally wrung out. Limp as a dishrag.

So was I.

The source of our greatest joys, our emotions are also the basis of our greatest defeats. In the seeds of a love that has endured for decades lies the potential for a devastatingly venomous hatred. The passion that can compose an inspiring symphony can also spawn a fit of murderous jealousy. It is difficult for us to accept that the compassion of a Mother Teresa arose from the same part of the brain as the brutality of an Adolph Hitler.

At last Steve had uncapped the long-sought wellhead of his buried emotions, the reservoir of repressed feelings. Finally he was purging himself of the festering sores that had tormented his soul. This was core stuff, straight from the depths of his personality.

I was concerned about him. Before I left that afternoon, I noted in Steve's chart that he'd had a particularly rough therapy session. Typical. Today was Friday. People always seem to save an emotional breakthrough for the last session of the week. It worried me that I wouldn't be seeing him again until Monday. I talked with the night staff and told them he'd need additional support and attention over the weekend. And I asked the nursing supervisor to check on him as well. I'd sleep better that way. Maybe.

Brenda broke away from a group in the parking lot as I approached.

"Are you okay? I heard your office being demolished. What happened?"

"It was Steve, trashing his past with a chair. Breakthrough stuff, literally." I smiled.

"A chair, huh?"

"Purely symbolic."

"Of his parents?"

I nodded. "Probably Jennifer, too."

"That's one way of getting rid of old flames, huh?"

"Yeah, it's a good, if noisy way of dumping off emotional residue, especially anger. It's better than kicking the dog or putting a fist through a wall. The wall always wins."

"True." Her eyes flicked away and then back. "And what would you suggest for refined social workers who have 'emotional residues' to work off?"

"I heard once about a woman who bought cheap old china at garage sales and then when she was upset she threw it at her basement walls. Just seeing it shatter apparently worked off a ton of anger."

Brenda looked skeptical.

"Uh, Bren, is this refined social worker someone we both know?"

Brenda's eyes filled with tears and she bit her lip. "This is so silly! It's been over two months since Mark moved to L.A., but even before that we'd decided there wasn't enough there for us to talk about marriage. So it's not like I didn't know it was coming."

"Still hurts, though."

"Yeah. I guess it's getting better, but sometimes I still wonder if I made a mistake. He hasn't written or called, and neither have I. I know it's over, but I can't seem to let go."

She shook her head and the red in her soft brown curls caught the light. She looked so vulnerable I wanted to hold her, comfort her, tell her that somehow it would work out all right. That I'd take care of her.

Instead, I said, "Give yourself time, Bren. It took me months and months. Seemed like forever."

"I know. I keep telling myself that." She sighed. "One thing, though," Brenda drew herself up and her voice took on an emphatic tone I'd never heard before. "From now on I am going to be a very independent person. No more sitting in the weeds waiting for a man to decide whether he wants to commit, where he wants to work, how he thinks we're going to live. As far as I'm concerned, a relationship has to be a lot more reciprocal than that. Equal shares. So if the next guy isn't willing to meet me halfway, he's history!" Her eyes were flashing as she got in her car.

"Way to go," I applauded. "Bravo! Go get 'em, Tiger!"

I opened my car door and waved as she pulled away. And was surprised by how quickly I was back to what I'd been doing before. Worrying about Steve.

24

AS IT TURNED OUT, I NEEDN'T HAVE WORRIED. THE FUSILlade of anger seemed to release the pressure enough to give him a reprieve, though perhaps only a brief one. The rage was likely to erupt again, but I hoped it wouldn't be until he was ready to deal with it.

I saw Ben early Monday morning and told him about the breakthrough session. He was his usual, placid self as I recounted the details, nodding periodically as if what took place happened all the time. When I made a reference to Mount Saint Stephen, he stopped me.

"Where did that come from?" he asked.

"Steve referred to himself that way. Why?"

He rubbed his chin. "In a symbolic sense, it verifies what happened. I suppose it was a warning to you from his unconscious that he was close to erupting."

"How? You mean I should have known?"

"If you'd thought about an active volcano, you might have anticipated. In this case, it didn't matter, but sometimes it can make a difference when the patient's unconscious gives you a clue like that."

"Okay, but to me it just seemed like a fairly creative description: Mount Saint Helen's, Mount Saint Stephen."

"Sure. On the surface it seems picturesque, doesn't it?" Ben agreed. "Long periods of dormancy broken by terrific eruptions. But volcanoes also have deep mythological significance: A volcano is a source of creation as well as destruction. It can create life, like the Hawaiian Islands, or destroy it, like Pompeii. That's probably why native tribes call a volcano the fire of life, because inside it you find the primary forces of nature—air, fire, water and earth. All being intermingled, then explosively transformed."

"But how does that relate to Steve, Ben?"

"It's a stretch, I admit, but people can descend into the passions of their minds, where they confront both nourishing elements and destructive ones. And once they've come in contact with that spiritual source, they begin the process of mastering it. A volcano drastically changes the landscape, and so does a person who conquers deep-seated passions transform the landscape of the mind. And that's where I think Steve might be right now."

"You may be right, Ben. I'm going to watch him carefully. For sure, he's in a critical place. I think he needs some breathing room for now, but I'm bracing myself for the 'Big One.' "

Actually, Steve seemed to be in fairly good shape. Staff members were going out of their way to involve him in activities and keep him busy, and he was making a real effort to participate. At our session that afternoon I suggested that when people go through the kind of cartharsis he'd had, they sometimes get a kind of emotional hangover.

"Maybe," he said. "I've been kind of dragged out, not much energy. Yeah, I guess it is like a hangover. It hurt like hell last Friday, but in a way it felt good. I'm still zapped, though."

"That's to be expected, Steve, after a ventilation like that. Have you thought much about what happened?"

"Not really, Mac. I wasn't up to it. Sorry, but I just wanted to get away from it."

"That's okay." I'd already decided to play it safe and keep this session at a somewhat more neutral level, at least until I got a sense of how resilient he'd be. "A couple things occurred to me over the weekend, Steve."

"Like what?" Thinly veiled suspicion.

"Well, would you call yourself a perfectionist?"

He nodded vigorously. "Sure, no question about it. Both my parents were. I got it from them."

"Tell me about it."

He shrugged. "Well, whatever I do has to meet very exact standards. Like the confetti suit, you know? It had to be done just right. It really bothers me if things are crooked or messy. No matter what I do, it has to be neat. If it's not, I have to go back and do it over."

"What would happen if you didn't?"

"I couldn't do that, Mac."

"Why not?"

A big sigh. "Because it would bug me. Everything has to be perfect. I want things organized. Lines straight, whether I'm drawing or mowing the lawn. If something isn't right, I get nervous. It means I'm not in control."

"What about your down time? Do you keep the control going even then?"

"I don't have any down time. I can't sit for three minutes before I start feeling like I'm wasting time. That's why it's so hard for me here."

"So you never allow yourself to relax?"

"No, I guess not. I mean, I can't even watch TV without doing something constructive. Even when I'm down in the woods, I have to be sketching or working on a poem."

"Don't you ever do something just for fun?"

"Not really. Fun doesn't enter into it. I have to concentrate on what I'm doing or this little critical voice in my head starts accusing me of goofing off."

"Hmmm," I said. "Okay, I want a few journal entries on this, Steve. You're leaning on yourself too hard. Putting too much pressure on yourself, too many expectations. I want you to work on moderating that. Okay?"

"I don't know." He was shaking his head dubiously. "Anything worth doing should be done as perfectly as possible."

"You set yourself up for failure that way, though. Go for excellence, that's fine. But thinking everything has to be perfect is self-defeating."

"Maybe you're right. But I just don't know if I could ever do anything part way. Or if I'd want to."

"Not part way, Steve. Just be more realistic. Try to ease up a bit. Excellence rather than perfection, huh?"

He sighed and nodded.

"Good." I paused. "The other thing I wanted to bring up concerns your parents." I could tell he wasn't eager to hear, but I went on anyway. "When you blame your parents—their lifestyle, their values, whatever—for everything that's happened to you, and say they've ruined your life, what are you really doing?"

He shrugged and frowned at me, puzzled.

"What do you mean?"

"I'm wondering if you're not giving them too much power over your life. Aren't you turning yourself into a victim? Of course your folks had enormous power over you as a child, and you tried to live up to their expectations in order to gain their love. But even now, years after their deaths, it seems they're still wielding tremendous power over you and your life."

"No, they aren't. They can't be. What power?"

"The power to somehow reach back from their graves to make sure your isolation continues." It sounded a little more accusatory than I meant it to, but I couldn't take it back. So much for keeping the session neutral. I had to be more careful.

"Hey, come on," he protested.

I held up my hand. "The question I want you to think about is this: Do you want to allow them to keep that power? Or can you get past it?"

Steve sat thoughtfully for some time. Then he said tentatively,

"Let me try this out."

I nodded. Good sign. He was meeting me head on; he hadn't backtracked into defensiveness.

"You're saying that all this anger and bitterness I have is influencing how I think and act now? That even after all the stuff we've done in therapy, it's still messing up my life."

"That's my guess. We're making headway, certainly. I just want you to be aware of the blame element."

"But you think I have a choice about whether I let it go on or not?"

"Of course."

"So how do I stop it? What do I do?"

"That depends on what you want to do about it, Steve."

He thought again. "What do I want to do? Work it out, I guess. But how? Those feelings aren't going to disappear just because I want them to."

"No, but doing what you are right now will help."

"Analyzing, huh?"

"Right, and letting those feelings out the way you did Friday."

"Hard on the chairs, though." He smiled.

"Better that than keeping it all inside, festering." But he was right. There wasn't much left of the chair after he got through with it. I'd thrown the remains in the trash. And scrounged a replacement.

"Okay," he went on, "so I have to analyze and understand all these thoughts, actions, feelings—junk—and then figure out what part my unconscious plays in it all, right?"

"That's exactly what you have to do."

"One thing I've found out—"

"What's that, Steve?"

"This psychotherapy business is a lot tougher than it sounds. My mind keeps getting in the way. It doesn't really want to do all that analyzing stuff. If I'd known in the beginning what I know now, I probably never would have started this."

"Lots of big projects are like that, but especially therapy. You have to consciously push yourself to dig deeper. And as analyzing becomes more familiar, it eventually begins to happen as soon as things don't feel right. In a relationship, for example."

"Really? How?"

"You just get so attuned to your feelings that at the slightest hint of anxiety or irritation with another person, you slide into an analyzing mode. You turn within, explore the source of what you're feeling. When you think you've found it, you take the interaction all apart, try to get to the root—your part in it, someone else's part. From there you decide how best to deal with it: Can you sit down and discuss it with the other person? Can you make adjustments so that the situation is less conflict-ridden? You find a solution. If that one doesn't work, you try another—and you keep trying until the problem, and the feelings, are resolved."

Steve looked at me doubtfully.

"It's something for you to think about, work on."

"Yeah."

"This kind of dealing with conflicts up front is especially important in a relationship, Steve."

He nodded. He was aware that this had been one of his biggest pitfalls.

"Here's what I want you to consider: Do you think maybe you were trying to make Jennifer the mother you felt you never had?"

I hoped my timing for this pretty heavy interpretation was right.

He looked at me as though I'd taken leave of my senses. So I hit him with a right cross.

"And the follow-up to that: Is there a chance you might do that with any woman you get serious about in the future?"

"Oh wow, no way."

I shrugged. "Don't be too quick to deny it. I hope you see how trying to replace your mother could affect a marriage."

"Hey, Mac, back off. I sure didn't do that to Jennifer. It's too weird. It's sick!"

"Just think about it, Steve."

"You're 'way off base!" he snapped.

No, actually, I knew I'd hit fertile ground. The rest of the session went nowhere, but that was okay. I'd pried a couple of big issues loose. Now Steve could ponder them. Or repress them.

The next time I saw him, he was frightened.

"Mac, it's getting worse. I feel like I'm spreadeagled on some medieval torture device that's tearing my mind into little bits and pieces."

I sat up a little straighter. "Tell me, Steve."

"I'm going more and more out of control, that's all."

His mouth clamped shut, but his eyes gave him away. They were darting around, and his face was contorting with fear. He looked the way he had before his first blowoff. I swallowed. Not audibly, I hoped.

"Hang in there, Steve," I tried to reassure him—and me. "Keep talking. Don't close me out."

"Why do I feel like I'm going crazy, Mac?"

"Because you've peeled away layers and layers of crud and your mind is fighting it. Your mind would rather stay with the comfortable old self-defeating ways of coping rather than face up to dealing with things in a whole new way. You may feel like you're out of control, but it's just another tactic your mind is using to trick you into not changing. Why don't you try a relaxation exercise?''

Steve kicked back in the recliner and took several deep breaths. In a few minutes, a smile spread across his face.

''What?'' I asked.

''I was just thinking how much I *have* changed since I've been here.'' Now he was much calmer, back in control again.

''Oh? How?''

''Lots of ways. I've learned a lot of stuff about myself. How I got nutso. I used to think that anybody who was mentally ill was just weak, inferior. I thought if they wanted to bad enough, they should be able to stay in control, accomplish whatever they wanted to. Mind over matter, you know? And, of course, I was superior to all of them. Even though I had problems, too, I thought, hey, I'm not like *them.*''

''So what's changed, Steve?''

''Well, now I know that's not true. I mean, I've spent a lot of time talking to other patients. Nutcases, maybe, but they're really good guys. And, you know, they all accept me. Nearly everyone on my ward is interested in me, telling me all the time to go back to college, go as far as I can. They're so encouraging. And they all think I can go somewhere. Now that I think of it, I've made some of the best friends I've ever had in this place.''

''That's wonderful.''

''And you know what else? They may act crazy sometimes, but they're not dumb. I listen, and I watch. Most of them have years of experience on me, but they don't mind sitting down and telling me about their lives. I really enjoy listening to them. And they tell everything: Good parts, bad parts. They don't hold back much. There's a real honesty here you don't find on the outside. I like that. People here don't play games.''

''Most of them don't, anyway, that's true. They have no reason to. It's great you've made so many friends here.''

"Yeah, I'm surprised, too." He gulped hard. "Before I was so wrapped up in myself and my own problems I never really—I mean *really* cared that much about other people, you know? But I think here I've become much more understanding, more tolerant of differences. I used to pigeonhole people. Real simpleminded habit, Mac. Now I can't do that anymore, 'cause everybody's different."

Steve's interest in others was becoming so lively that he began to spend time on Four, the security unit. Home of the chronic and predatory males. For as long as the staff would let him stay, he would make sketches there and give them away. And the patients—who rarely had visitors and whose only knowledge of the outside world came from TV—responded. Soon they were looking forward to his visits, and some were even drawing with him. Steve loved it. Now nearly every one of our sessions began with a reprise of what had happened with his "buddies."

One day he came into my office with angry red welts on his arm. When I asked about them, he laughed.

"The Claw got me."

The Claw was Jeffrey Hall, an elderly man who was usually restrained in an invalid chair because he had an unfortunate habit of setting a deathgrip on anyone coming within arm's length. Evidently, he had worked his way out of a restraint just in time to snag Steve as he passed by. When I asked how he'd gotten loose, Steve laughingly acknowledged that he'd traded a piece of candy for his freedom.

"You should try a behavior mod program with him, Mac. He'd be a good candidate. He's crazy about candy—it'd make a good reinforcer."

It wasn't a bad idea. At all. Steve certainly was picking up a lot. I told him if he stayed here much longer, we'd have to hire him.

25

TOMORROW WAS SUNDAY AND I GAVE THE ALARM CLOCK a disdainful look as I turned off the light. In minutes I had drifted off, but it was a troubled sleep. I seemed to be looking for something, but it wasn't clear what. I was wandering around a huge estate that was crowded with a lot of people I didn't recognize. I had no idea what they were doing there, or why I was there myself. They were all deep in conversation, but I couldn't understand what any of them were saying. Just then I saw Steve standing on a balcony overlooking the courtyard where everyone had gathered. I waved, but he didn't wave back. He seemed to be in a trance. Then I became aware of an insistent tone that penetrated the dream. When it didn't stop, I groggily reached for the phone.

"Pat?"

It was Brenda. She was breathless, and sounded super-upset.

"What time is it?"

"It's three-thirty. Stacey just called me. He couldn't find your number. I told him I'd call you." Her voice choked. "Brace yourself, Pat, I've got terrible news."

"What, Bren?" I was wide awake now.

"It's Steve—" she wailed.

"What's happened? What?" All I could hear was muffled sobs. "Bren?"

"Oh, Pat. He hung himself."

I fell back into the pillow, my insides churning.

With great effort, Brenda went on, "They've taken him to La Crosse Memorial. Can you meet me there?"

"He's still alive, then?"

"He was. Barely. Now, I don't know."

"I'm on my way."

Brenda was waiting for me just inside the entrance to the Emergency Room lobby. She looked pretty rough, but better than I did. The lobby was deserted but all the lights were turned up full. The brightness made me squint.

"How're you doing?" I asked. What a dumb question. People in shock are prone to making inane comments, asking the obvious, but hearing myself fall back on such a cliché made me wince.

She shrugged.

"How is he?"

"They're saying he's comatose. They don't know if he'll come out of it."

I rubbed my temples, trying to keep up. "Do you know how it happened?"

"More or less. Apparently Steve was quite upset all day yesterday. He seemed better during the evening, though, watched television, and went to bed about eleven. At the one a.m. bed check he was missing and Chet noticed the closet door ajar. He'd hung himself on the closet rod."

"Ohhhh," I groaned. "How could he? Those things are designed specifically for psych wards. They're supposed to break when anything heavier than a few shirts is put on them."

"I know. They always have before. Not this time. Anyway, Chet cut Steve down right away and gave him CPR, but no one knows how long his brain was oxygen deficient. Even if he survives, he might have serious brain damage."

Suddenly feeling lightheaded, I sagged against the wall.

"C'mon," Brenda gestured to a couple of chairs. "They said they'd tell me as soon as they knew something. Stacey's inside. We might as well sit down."

I wanted to cry, but my mind couldn't gear up for it. All I could think of was how the circle of death was closing in on Steve. For the next hour every time someone in a green scrub suit emerged through the scarred steel Emergency Room doors, our heads jerked up. At last a weary Stacey approached us. I barely recognized him.

"Looking better but not good." He shook his head. "He's just barely responsive. He's in ICU now."

"Can we see him?"

"I wouldn't advise it. They're hooking him to the monitors and getting things set up. We won't know anything more for a while anyway. There's nothing more to be done here."

Brenda started to object, but Stacey took her by the arm and eased her toward the door.

"You guys take off now. I'm going home myself, but they've got orders to call me if his condition changes. I'll let you know the minute they do."

I left Brenda at her car and glanced around for mine. I was in such a daze when I arrived that I couldn't remember where I'd parked. I went home, showered, and headed out to Peace River. By the time I got there it was 7:45. Amazing that so much could have happened and I still wasn't late for work.

The first thing I did was scan my therapy notes to see what I might have missed. I'd known for years that some suicide attempts are virtually unpredictable, but I'd always deluded myself into thinking I'd be able to see one coming. I sure hadn't seen this one.

By mid-morning Stacey reported only that Steve was "slowly responding." Whatever that meant.

"He seems to be coming around," he assured me, but his grim expression said he hadn't much hope.

I spent the morning doing psych testing and then led a group therapy session. In between I called and asked Ben when he'd be free. Just after lunch I went over to see him.

"I feel like I've been body-slammed."

"You look like it, too, I'm afraid."

"Thanks a lot. But Ben, how could I have missed this? I should have been giving him regular Rorschachs. Maybe they would've given me a clue."

"Perhaps, but not likely."

"I just don't know. I told you we'd been down in some dangerous territory, but Steve seemed to be handling it. He really did." I heard my voice and it sounded hollow.

"He never gave the slightest inkling he was thinking of suicide?"

"None. In fact, he assured me he wouldn't try it again." I sighed. "I keep telling myself it was a typical young adult suicide attempt, one of those impulsive, spontaneous acts."

"I'd think so, too, Pat. The adolescent part is still very much there—so reactive, so glandular, so all-or-nothing. That, combined with all the aggressiveness that's been surfacing."

"Maybe. I just don't know. I keep feeling I should have been there for him, been able to prevent this."

"Of course. That's natural. You've tried for months now to teach him a better way. Usually, when a patient works at it as hard as Steve has been, things click. But there's always a risk—a risk we have to accept and tolerate. Remember, the decision was Steve's."

"But I'm still responsibile for not—"

"There's no fault to be laid, Pat. Not on you, not on Steve, not on anybody. These things happen. Life is full of improbables. It keeps right on challenging us."

The phone rang. Ben listened intently for a few moments, then said, "Hang on, he's right here." He handed the receiver to me. "It's Stacey."

I took the phone with dread.

"Pat, I'm at La Crosse. I just left Steve and he's alert, even said a few words. He's looking much better. CAT scan and EEG results were both negative for brain damage. He's not out of the woods yet, but things are definitely looking up."

I let out a big sigh.

"Great. I'll pass the word. Thanks."

What a reprieve. We had been given another chance.

After work that afternoon Bren and I drove back to La Crosse. Ground fog shrouded the low-lying spots and at one point we passed a line of huge willows, ghostly sentinels standing in formation on either side of the road. It was eerie and beautiful. We hardly spoke.

Steve had been transferred from intensive care to a private room in the general surgical wing. We stopped at the desk and identified ourselves.

"Any change?" I asked the charge nurse.

"He's making slow gains. Helps to be young." Maybe I was reading something into it, but her tone seemed to convey disapproval. Perhaps she resented that Steve had survived when only hours before he hadn't wanted to live.

"May we see him?" asked Brenda.

"Sure. But not for too long. He's very weak and his throat is raw. Don't make him talk."

We nodded and crossed the corridor to the door she indicated. I knocked lightly and we entered the semi-dark room.

Steve's eyes were closed. He looked asleep. We stood on either side of the bed and watched him quietly for a few moments. His face was ashen compared to the ugly purplish bruises on his neck.

Brenda took one of his hands in hers and his eyes fluttered open. A wan smile of recognition relaxed his face as he looked at her. Then his eyes shifted to mine.

"You sure know how to give an Irishman the fright of his life."

"Sorry," he mouthed silently.

He smiled again and started to say something, but Brenda shushed him.

"Don't talk, Steve. We'll just sit here with you for a bit, if that's okay."

He nodded and closed his eyes. We shoved a couple of chairs close to the bed and sat a few minutes, reassuring ourselves that he was really alive. In the half-light his face looked calm, almost boyish. Whatever demons had prompted all this were nowhere in evidence now.

On the drive back, Bren and I were giddy with relief. Neither of us wanted to think about how close to death Steve had come. We were both exhausted and ready to be alone, so I dropped her off at the hospital parking lot where she'd left her car and then went on home. I didn't sleep well that night, either.

The next evening Brenda had a meeting, but I felt compelled to check in on Steve again. When I knocked and swung the door open, he was staring at the television, watching a basketball game with the sound turned off.

"No wonder you wanted to come to La Crosse Memorial. Have a TV in your room, huh?"

He smiled weakly.

"Hi, Mac."

His voice was a hoarse whisper. I hoped it wouldn't be permanent. Might the larynx be damaged? Did that happen? If so, did it heal? I really had no idea what kind of residuals Steve might have. His color was better, but my eyes were drawn to the burnt orange and mauve abrasions that circled his neck.

He caught me staring. "Gross, huh?" he croaked.

"Yeah."

"Mac? Are you mad at me? For what I did and all?" His eyes searched my face.

"No, of course not, Steve. Angry with myself, maybe, because I didn't see it coming. But no, not with you."

"Mac . . ." Steve shook his head. It hurt to hear him talk. "Don't be angry with yourself. You couldn't have done anything. Even I couldn't do anything. I still don't know what happened. It came on me so suddenly. I didn't even think about writing a note."

He located the control and shut off the TV. He couldn't meet my eyes, but he obviously had something to tell me.

He whispered, "Mac, I went into a black hole. I was all alone. There was not another soul anywhere. Nothing but darkness. But I could sense I was absolutely, terrifyingly alone. The idea of existing in that void of nothingness was horrible. No answers, no questions, no nothing. And I had the sensation I would be floating there all alone for eternity. I couldn't stand it. I just freaked. I kept telling myself, 'Get away from here—*get away!*"

I nodded.

"That's really what happened, I swear to God."

"I believe you, Steve." I took his hand and held it tightly. He closed his eyes. Saying so much had tired him, but I knew it had been important for him to explain.

"Go to sleep now. I'll see you again tomorrow." I squeezed his hand goodbye. "I called Kayla. She'd like to come see you. That okay?"

He nodded weakly, his eyes closed.

I'd gotten to the door when he croaked my name. I went back and bent over his bed.

"One other thing, Mac." His eyes fluttered open. "Trying to kill myself this time was the worst mistake I've ever made in my life. Without a doubt."

"That's probably true."

"It's hard to believe I actually did that." He closed his

eyes again and shuddered. "I mean, I don't want to die. I really don't. Things've been tough, but I'm not ready to check out yet, know what I mean?" He smiled faintly.

"Yes, I think I do, Steve."

"I'm telling myself to do what you told me all those times—learn from it. I've been trying to figure out what led up to it, what purpose it might possibly have. And why I didn't die when I probably should have." He paused and took several deep breaths. His voice was deep and raspy.

"And?"

"I'm working on it. Just wanted you to know that."

I squeezed his shoulder.

"Good. Take it easy, Steve. I'll see you tomorrow."

"Uh, Mac, do you have to go? I mean, could you maybe just sit with me a little while? Like only till I fall asleep?"

"Sure." I pulled a chair closer and sat down.

" 'Night, Mac. Later, alligator . . ."

His voice trailed off. He closed his eyes, smiled dreamily, and fell fast asleep.

Staying with him like this was little enough to do, but somehow I was extraordinarily gratified to be there when Steve needed companionship. In a way, I felt I was standing in for his folks. Had they been alive, I was sure they would have been here now.

As I sat there, watching him, it all hit me like a sledgehammer. The call from Brenda, those indelible words, "Steve hung himself," my mind screaming, "No, *no!*" The devastation I felt thinking he was dead, or brain-damaged.

And it was my tampering that had precipated this. He would have been better off prancing around as The Confetti Kid rather than lying in his grave. Or sitting on some back ward, drooling all day. What the hell would it have hurt if he had gone around throwing confetti on people the rest of his life? I should have left him in peace. And in life.

And yet, I told myself, he wasn't at peace. Hadn't been

for some time. And living out his delusion would not have been any real life.

We had a covenant together. We'd made progress. Something had misfired, but now he regretted his attempt, was on the mend, was accepting and forgiving himself.

Could I do the same?

It was the end of the week before Kayla was able to come up from Madison. By that time Steve had recovered pretty well. He would be returning to Peace River later that afternoon. I met Kayla at the information desk and we walked up to his room together. She seemed somber, smiling in a sad way that I found unsettling, and speaking very little.

So far I'd held to an inner pledge: No lectures to Steve, no recriminations, no judgments. But I wasn't sure this was entirely the right thing to do, so I was curious about how a psychic would handle a suicide attempt. Steve apparently was, too. He bit his lower lip nervously.

Kayla stood by the bed, gazing at his bruised neck. Tears filled her eyes.

"Dear, dear Stephen. I can tell that you have been to the edge of death," she said sadly, shaking her head. It was almost as if she was reliving the terrible pain he'd been through these last few weeks. I could literally feel her suffering.

Steve was deeply moved. He couldn't bring himself to look at her so he just nodded. Kayla sat on the edge of the bed and took his hand, holding it in both of hers.

"There are some things I want to tell you. My hope is that you will remember them for the rest of your life."

Steve looked at her then and their eyes met. "I will. I promise."

"Stephen—dear, sweet soul that you are—suicide is no solution. When a person kills himself, all the worldly anguish that was supposed to be eliminated accompanies the soul. Whatever lessons are avoided through suicide must be faced and dealt with again in another lifetime. So there is no escape—one must fulfill one's journey, one's karma. Please, dear Stephen, never forget that."

Steve's eyes were fastened on Kayla's face and he nodded numbly. Tears were coursing down his cheeks, and he appeared very frightened.

"I know the past years have been excruciating for you. And that the last few months have been most difficult. But understand that great adversity also offers the greatest opportunity."

"I see that, now," he whispered. He was crying softly and she put her arms around him and hugged him. I could barely hear what she said next:

"I thank God that you stepped back from death and that this terrible thing did not happen. I thank God that when you threw the gift of life back in His face, He taught you how much He cares for you and gave life back to you. For that, you belong to Him. Your work here is not finished."

Steve closed his eyes. I saw his face contort with an emotional upheaval he was trying very hard to control. Kayla pulled away and held him by his shoulders. She looked him squarely in the eyes.

"Look at me," she commanded gently, and his eyes jerked open. Then her voice softened again. "We do not leave this earth, Dear Stephen, until we have learned all we must learn and have taught all we have to teach. If you ever feel these shadows engulfing you again, I want you to repeat this mantra: 'The Power of God is within me, the Grace of God surrounds me.' Can you remember that?"

Steve nodded vigorously and cleared his throat. But Kayla wasn't through.

"You must purify your spirit, and your body. Eliminate the demons so your thinking is clear, your purpose worthy. A lifetime here is so short, dear Stephen, and there is so much for each of us to do. You must not waste your talents."

"I know, Kayla, I . . . I don't know what to say—" He sighed. "I understand everything so much better now. I've thought about it a million times this week. That's *all* I've been thinking about."

Kayla nodded.

He went on, "I owe everyone an apology for letting them down so badly. You, Mac, Brenda, Chet and John—they saved my life, you know—and all the people who've tried so hard to help me. If I've learned anything from this, it's that a part of me did die in that closet. A part that needed to die."

"How do you mean, Steve?" I asked.

"I'm not entirely sure yet, Mac. I was looking at life so narrowly. I was so idealistic, I expected so much of everyone, and even more of myself. My problems were everyone else's fault—never mine. And I badly underestimated this wonderful world we live in. I thought solutions to problems should be so easy. You kept telling me otherwise, Mac, but it didn't mean anything—then."

He took a deep breath. "I think I've discovered the purpose of life—my life, anyway. It's to continually invent new purposes. And I'm going to do that by learning. By self-discovery, as I've been doing. But I want to go on, much farther on. I want knowledge. I want to know more about everything that happens around me. I want to know more about this great planet we live on, the universe that surrounds us. Everything I possibly can, I want to understand."

Kayla looked up at me and smiled. "I do believe our Stephen's wings are growing."

He nodded eagerly. "I hope so. I'm beginning to see that there don't have to be any final answers. And I think I can accept that, and live with it. I'm glad I have a chance to try again. I wish I hadn't had to come so close to dying, but maybe that's what it took to wise me up. I've finally made one major decision."

Kayla and I exchanged looks again. Steve seemed content to keep us waiting.

"What have you decided?" I asked.

"That when we're through with therapy, Mac, I'm definitely going back to school. I've thought about Gene a lot this week. My first art teacher," he said to Kayla, "but so much more, too. I've been thinking what an influence he was on me. He didn't want me to waste my talents, either, Kayla. And it's spooky, you know, but it's like he's come back now to show me the way to go."

"And where is that, Stephen?" Kayla asked.

"I want to be a teacher. An art teacher. I want to do for kids what Gene did for me. It'll be my way of giving something back. That's important to me now. Very important."

When I walked Kayla out to her car, she paused in the lobby. I thought she was preparing herself for the cold blast awaiting us outside. Instead, she put her hand on my arm and turned to me.

"Do you remember a couple of months ago when you asked if psychics could predict the future?" She looked troubled.

"Yes."

"This experience has been very disquieting. I could sense and tell you about Stephen's anguish, the precarious state of his psyche. But that was all that was available to my powers. I never had an inkling that he was going to attempt suicide. How I wish I'd known."

I felt oddly comforted that she hadn't.

26

I STOPPED BY BRENDA'S OFFICE TO FILL HER IN ON WHAT happened during Kayla's visit to Steve.

"That's quite a shift," she said noncomittally.

"Yeah, I thought so, too. Almost too good to be true. How can a guy do such a flip-flop after coming so close to killing himself?"

Brenda was silent for a few moments, deep in thought. This was a departure from her usual straight-ahead style. "I wonder," she mused.

"What?"

The steady gaze shifted back to me. "Did you ask Steve if he'd had an NDE?"

"A Near Death Experience? No, it didn't occur to me, Bren."

NDEs have been widely reported by people who are considered clinically dead and are then resuscitated. It happens most often with cardiac arrests, but drowning and other trauma victims relate similar accounts of observing their own lifeless body from above, while experiencing a feeling of tremendous peace and serenity. They also often sense a glowing white light that exudes comfort, love, and well-being. They frequently tell of having felt resentful at having to return to their bodies. What they all seem to have in common is that they never look at life in quite the same way again. Nor do they fear death. Poised somewhere between medicine and psychology, reports of NDEs have offered investigators a fascinating avenue of research.

"Actually," I said, "Steve's description was so morbid that I doubt anything positive could have come out of it. Certainly not enough to account for his current state of mind. He's almost rejuvenated now. But the whole suicide experience traumatized him."

"I know," Brenda replied. "But all the same, I think you should ask him. My recollection is that suicide NDEs have a pretty rough time. Anyway," she cocked her head and looked at me quizzically, "if anything like that happened, it should be dealt with, right?"

I sighed. Brenda had a way of cutting right to the heart of things.

The following Monday Steve and I resumed our sessions, and I asked him up front if he had experienced anything unusual the night of his suicide attempt. Was there anything other than what he'd told me before? As soon as I asked, I knew from his expression Brenda was right.

He was very quiet for a time. When he spoke, his voice was surprisingly soft.

"Well, yeah, there was something pretty spooky, Mac. I was afraid to tell you about it. I thought you'd figure I'd gone bananas again." He looked at me for reassurance.

I nodded. "Can you tell me about it now?"

"I guess. It was really weird. Not like when I've been crazy before—that was weird, too, but different. This was absolutely real, but at the same time, very dreamlike. But I wasn't dreaming. It really happened. That much I know. Without a doubt."

"So what happened?"

"Well, you know I told you about being pulled down into the darkness, being sucked into that black hole? That part was absolutely ghastly. I will never, ever, forget it. Then, I felt something even stranger."

"What was that, Steve?"

He was eager now, ready to share this experience. "It's hard to find the words to describe it. I remember the darkness of it all, and then suddenly I was engulfed by an almost ferocious energy. I could feel my—my life force draining away. I felt it going but I couldn't stop it."

"Then what happened?"

"Well, right as I was drifting off to wherever, I heard a voice say, *'Wrong move, man!'* I still don't know where it came from, but *it wasn't my voice.* And it wasn't anyone I know. It wasn't an ordinary voice, either. I was just sensing what was being said, you know?"

I nodded.

"Anyway, I was real scared then because I realized the voice was right. Dying this way would not be a good idea. So I started trying hard to save myself. Very hard. I mean, I really wanted to live. You have to believe me on that, Mac." His eyes were imploring.

"I do, Steve. What happened then?"

"I don't know. I have no sense of time here, but at some point the darkness lifted and the next thing I remember is being very, very scared. I didn't know why, or of what. Then I was aware of floating along in a kind of soupy fog. When the fog cleared, I could see my room at Peace River. I was looking down from the ceiling and there was a body lying on the floor. I looked closer and saw it was me. My body, anyway. It didn't look like me anymore, but I knew it was. This is really twilight-zone stuff, Mac." He shook his head.

"Was anyone in the room with you?"

"Yes. Chet and John—you know, my two favorite aides.

It was so confusing. I couldn't remember what happened, but it was definitely me down there on the floor. And Chet and John were frantically doing CPR on me: Chet was breathing for me and in between John was thumping my chest. The strange thing was I couldn't feel anything—nothing hurt. I just floated around up there—detached, but afraid of what would happen if I didn't wake up. But somehow I sensed things much more keenly, and I knew that I was going to be alone and drifting forever and ever. That just about blew me away. They worked so hard on me and I didn't come around. And my fear turned to terror.

"They were real worried, too. I could hear John cursing the ambulance for not being there already. I tried to tell 'em I was there, not to give up, but they couldn't hear me. I was afraid they'd get tired and quit, but they didn't. Then a young guy came racing in—he was the doctor on call, I think—and took over for John, but they still couldn't get a pulse. I knew I was going to die." He shuddered.

"And then?"

He shook his head. "Then I heard this very resonant, firm voice. No, again, it wasn't so much a voice as something I just sensed—***knew.*** I was being told, ***this is not your time. You must go back.*** And then in a rush I was back down in my body again—Yuck!—and feeling sicker than a dog. The pain—" Steve put his hand on his neck and his eyes teared up. At last he looked over at me. "What happened? Did I go crazy again?"

I looked him right in the eye. "No, Steve. You didn't. What you've described is called a Near Death Experience. An NDE. Did you have any sense of a loving presence, perhaps God, or a feeling of well-being, rapture? Anything like that?"

"No. Believe me, Mac, there was no rapture. There was nothing pleasant about any of it." He sighed.

"You said you sensed things more keenly. Can you recall any other impressions?"

"Overall, I'd have to say what I felt most was a deep

regret about what I'd done. And a horrible ache that it might not be undone. I felt lousy about how I've lived so far, and I wanted another chance to do it right."

I could only nod.

He looked at me the way a loving parent looks at a child. "A life is not something to waste, you know. Our growth depends on our choices."

I blinked. "Oh? How do you know that?"

He didn't respond and I began to wonder if he was going to. At last he said, "I can't tell you how I know it. I just do. It was like, whatever happened to me in that room that night will affect me for the rest of my life. I hit bottom. And then, for whatever reason, I got a second chance. I don't intend to waste it."

Steve's demeanor continued to surprise me. He was very different now, much more serious. At our session later that week he said, "There are still some things I need to talk about. About my suicide attempt. Okay?"

"Sure, Steve."

He settled back, elbows resting on the arms of the recliner, and took several deep breaths. He was willing himself to relax, almost meditating.

"Mac," he finally said. "That was the worst day of my life. By far."

I waited.

"All that Saturday, the day it happened, I could feel myself losing it. Incredible stuff kept shooting up. And the harder I tried to stop it, the worse it got."

"What 'stuff' was shooting up, Steve?"

"The same old crap, except it was incredibly intense. I couldn't get the anger and bitterness out the regular way like I've done with you. It just kept churning around inside. I thought I was gonna explode."

"But we've been dealing with those feelings for a while now. What happened then to tip the balance?"

"That night something snapped. I was watching an old movie on TV and all of a sudden I was slammed with revulsion for how totally, completely empty I was, how my life is just one big sham." He looked over at me.

"Go on."

"I was a stranger to myself. That night when I finally blew apart, everything inside collapsed. The walls caved in and I saw my center, my very core. And, Mac, I hated what I saw: I'm hollow, a shell made up of what I thought other people wanted me to be, what I thought I had to do to be a man. So others would notice me—and like me. And I even saw clearly what a game I've played here at the hospital, and with you, trying to be the perfect patient.

"That's the word, Mac: *perfect!* Mom and Dad's pursuit of perfection became so ingrained in me it's practically an obsession." He paused and I waited. "I mean, this is going to sound stupid, but I think The Confetti Kid was just an extension of that need to be perfect: If he was perfect, he could build a perfect world. At least in his mind. In my mind, I mean. I thought I could be perfection personified.

"What a joke! No wonder I'm a nutcase! And you know something? What terrified me that night was, without The Confetti Kid, who was I? Take away The Confetti Kid, and what's left?"

He hurtled on, not waiting for an answer. *"Nothing!* Absolutely nothing's left. I asked myself: 'What do I believe in? What do I stand for?' And I couldn't come up with a damn thing! All I saw was a mirror image of what other people thought I was. And I wasn't perfect at all. I was nobody."

After a time I said softly, "So you felt there was nothing to live for."

He nodded slowly. "Exactly. It seemed the least I could do was end the fraud. Do the first honest thing I've ever done in my life."

"Don't be so hard on yourself, Steve."

He shrugged. "This is tame compared to some of the

things I told myself that night. Do you think The Confetti Kid was . . . a way of being someone?''

''That seems likely, Steve, yes. Something inside you needed to invent him.''

He looked at me curiously.

''Pull deeper. Figure it out.''

He reached in his pocket and extracted a few pieces of confetti. He cradled them in his palm, staring at the glints of color as the light played off the tiny shapes.

''I stuffed so many feelings, I guess I stuffed my own sense of self. So maybe The Confetti Kid was sort of an escape valve, so I could get away from my problems. Trouble is, The Kid didn't express any feelings either. Actually, he did just the opposite. He was so benevolent and forgiving. I mean, really, he was worse than me that way. I guess he was my ideal—what I thought I should have been.''

He looked at me for affirmation and I nodded.

''Deep in my mind, I must have made him into some kind of superhero. He was supposed to make me worth something, because I was ashamed of how inferior the real me was. Do you think that's what happened? That I thought I was incapable of holding my real self together? So I used The Confetti Kid to keep from going over the edge, even though I eventually did anyway?''

''That sounds right, Steve. That's what The Confetti Kid would have done, split you off from all the pain inside. He drove a wedge between your bottled-up feelings and your awareness of them.''

''Okay, but then why did the bottom drop out? Why did I try to kill myself? Wait a minute, don't tell me.'' He held up his hand. ''I want to figure this out.''

I stifled a smile.

He crept ahead, as if he were feeling his way along a curved, narrow ledge where he couldn't see more than inches ahead at a time.

''At some level, therapy must have wised me up that I

couldn't rely on The Confetti Kid anymore. That must have shook up all kinds of . . . uh-oh, I'm getting warmer. I can feel the anxiety in my belly. Something's going on again, Mac."

"Step carefully, Steve. This is the same minefield you've wandered into before," I cautioned.

"I'm okay this time. I think. Glad you're here, though. I wouldn't wanna be in there alone again. Remember when Kayla mentioned something about a 'dark, mysterious center?' I've caught glimpses of that from time to time. I'm peeking in now, kind of teasing myself here. I feel like I'm right on the edge of understanding something. Ah—I remember now. When things were falling apart that Saturday night, this enormous blockbuster, this rush, hit me and I was revealed. Wow! Was I ever."

"Revealed how, Steve?" I said it more to reassure him of the reality of my presence.

"I'm not exactly sure. You know the darkness Kayla saw? It's the deepest part of my soul—all the agony, the loneliness I've always felt. And it's all twisted together with . . . there's a lot of bitterness, vindictiveness, and a . . . *wickedness* that runs all the way to my core." He sat back in the chair, trembling.

We sat in silence for a while. Then I asked,

"Do you want to go on?"

Steve didn't respond immediately. When he did, a look of wonder radiated across his face. "Yes, I do. I'm not afraid anymore and I do want to go on. I've got to get this off my chest. There's so much, Mac. I keep getting lost in it. But the main thing, ohhh—" he trailed off in a sort of a groan. "God, I'm ashamed to admit this."

I moved my chair over and put my palm on his shoulder.

He shuddered. It was a force of will for him to continue. Apparently ready to gag, his voice was choked, strangled.

"Oh, Mac, there's an incredible, terrible meanness in me," he moaned. "I don't want you—or anyone—to know this. I don't want to recognize it *myself.* I'm so ashamed."

"What, Steve? What horrible secret have you been keeping?"

He put his head in his hands, pressed his fingers into his forehead, and groaned.

"C'mon, Steve," I said softly. "What's so bad in there?"

He raised his head slightly but did not look at me. Barely above a whisper, he said, "I hated Dad and Mom. Really hated them, for as long as I can remember. When I was a kid, I hated them so much I used to imagine them dead. Lots of times. And then all of a sudden they actually *were* dead. Bam." A huge sigh.

"See, before I was miserable because they were around and making me miserable. Now, I'm miserable because they're gone, and I feel like I caused their deaths. Like I *murdered* them with my own hands . . . really, my thoughts. And even worse than that—" It was getting harder and harder for him to speak. At last he whispered,

"Brad's gone, too, and it's ***my fault he's dead!"*** He couldn't meet my eyes.

"You feel responsible for Brad's death, too?"

He nodded miserably. "I wished my folks dead, but I never wanted Brad to die, too. That was never s'posed to happen. I mean, he was my brother. We were never all that close—we fought and stuff—but he was a neat guy. I thought he was ashamed of me, but he really went out of his way, trying to keep Dad from riding me so much."

His voice was hushed. "I know now we could've been real close . . . I wish so much that he was still alive, that I could be a real brother to him, redeem myself for how I treated him. And I never even had a chance to thank . . ."

He choked and hid his face with his hands. His shoulders shook with sobs. "His death is punishment for my terrible thoughts—"

"That's a lot to take on, Steve," I said softly.

"But it's ***true!"*** he shouted, slamming his fist into his other palm. "I feel so horribly guilty. I killed them by thinking, visualizing that they were dead. First I wished I had the power to wipe them off the face of the earth. And then that power actually came from somewhere. I didn't know it could really happen, but it did. Because of my powers. *If I hadn't had those thoughts, they'd all still be alive!*" Tears were running down his cheeks.

"Tell me the rest, Steve."

He shuddered and angrily brushed the tears away. For a long time he agonized in painful silence.

"What's going on, Buddy? Don't shut me out."

He shook his head, looked up at the ceiling, and drew several deep breaths.

"Okay," he said, so softly I could barely hear him. "I miss Brad so much I can taste it, but . . . the worst part, Mac—" He gave another deep sigh and then cried in an anguished cadence, with each word punched out:

"I'm . . . GLAD . . . MOM . . . AND . . . DAD . . . ARE . . . DEAD!"

He lowered his head into his hands and his shoulders shook in violent spasms. He rocked back and forth while the convulsive sobs wrenched his body. And all the agonies of his tortured spirit poured out.

At last the sobbing subsided. He lifted his head, blinked rapidly, snatched a tissue, and noisily blew his nose.

"I'm still having horrible, violent thoughts of revenge against the people who hurt me, Mac. That's what was driving me crazy the night I tried to kill myself. These feelings have always been there, but never right in my face before. I think I kept them squeezed off from the rest of me. I deluded myself into thinking they weren't part of me.

"Except, I see now I've been incredibly warped by these thoughts and feelings. And they were taking me over. I couldn't control them anymore. I was convinced they were turning me into even more of a monster."

Steve's breathing quickened as he pressed into this new

area, the words coming in gasps as he tried to purge himself.

"That night I was being taunted and driven by these—entities—who were so powerful. They were in total control. My rage was pure ***evil.*** I felt downright murderous. I had to do something with that power—or be destroyed by it. The rage had an awesome hold on me. I was the incarnation of evil. I was omnipotent. No one, nothing could stop me. So I ran to my room before I hurt someone."

I waited quietly.

"Once I made it to my room, my imagination ran wild. I sat there weighing options: Which nurse to kill, or maybe first I should knock off that new guy they transferred in who's driving everybody crazy.

"And then it came to me. Clearly, without a doubt, I knew what to do: I had to save the world from ***me!*** Here I'd been acting like I was trying to help the world, when all along I was an imposter who really wanted to destroy it! Talk about hypocrites! God, I couldn't stand myself! And if no one else could stop me—I'd have to stop myself.

"But it was like someone else was doing it. In slow motion, I watched myself untie my shoelaces, twist them around my neck, and then—I climbed into the closet."

He let out a low moan and was sobbing again. I moved closer and held him. Then he shook his head and gasped, "I'm a monster."

"No, you aren't, Steve." I squeezed his shoulder. "You fell victim to your dark side—the self-destructive side. The only way you thought you could control those destructive impulses was to kill yourself. You thought suicide was your only option. It turned out to be the wrong one, yes, but at least you're acknowledging that energy. Now you can learn to control it and point it in a constructive direction."

He looked at me, disbelieving. "Well, I suppose I have nowhere to go but up. I hope, anyway. I think I've been down about as far as a person can get and still survive. I don't ever want to sink that low again." He wept some more.

"Steve, listen to me. You've dealt with your deepest, darkest secrets. The core of your dark side. By confronting all of that, you're destroying the power it had over you. By accepting your negative feelings about your parents, your feelings of guilt over their deaths and Brad's will diminish. It will take a while for you to realize that, but now you've reached a point where the real healing can begin."

He was watching me, hanging on every word. His face was wet with tears. He wanted so much to believe that he could get past all this, but he was still doubting it. After a time, he sighed. He looked absolutely wrung out.

I hoped I was right.

"You're ready to start making peace with your polarities, aren't you?" It was the beginning of our next session.

"What?" Steve looked puzzled.

"Human beings are paradoxes," I said. "And so are you. I want you to start pulling some of this stuff together, see what kinds of conclusions you've reached about yourself."

"Okay." He clasped his hands. His next words were tentative, exploring.

"You're right. I am very contradictory. People are, I guess, but it's been real hard for me to accept it in myself. I mean, I like consistency." He paused. "And I did do what you said with Jen. You were right on that, Mac. I did want her to be the mother I never had. For a long time I couldn't admit that, but I realize now I have some very big needs and I can be very demanding about them. I crave things like security and love. And to get them, I've learned to play certain roles, put on a certain front. Because I'm ashamed of wanting them so much."

He let out a big sigh. "It's the hypocrisy that bugs me. I mean, why couldn't I just be honest about it? I've used people, done a lot of manipulating to get what I wanted. And

I've let myself be used, figuring it was a tradeoff for getting what I needed. So I became someone I'm not. But hey, I guess being like a jellyfish was a small price to pay for being loved, right?''

''Sounds plausible, Steve.''

''Yeah, well, here's where it gets crazy. All those conflicting messages really tore me apart, messed up my mind. I had a zillion questions about life. And I kept trying to fit my own measly little existence into these huge cosmic concerns.'' He gave a kind of sardonic laugh. ''There's so much cruelty in the world. People doing terrible things to other people. And now I understand the potential is there in me, too. I have to keep it in check, and I also have to try my hardest to avoid people who are manipulative or cruel. I don't want people like that in my life. I'll be civil to them if I have to, but that's it.''

An expression of amazement crossed his face. Then he smiled, a smile of real pleasure. ''Interesting, very interesting.'' He looked directly at me and there was elation in his voice. ''I *am* changing, Mac, I really am.''

''Oh? In what way?''

''Well, the other night the rec therapists took some of us bowling. When we got to town, we were all standing by the van ready to go into the bowling alley, and I noticed a bunch of guys watching us from across the street. Next thing I know they're calling out things like, 'Hey, loonies, how're things on the funny farm?' And worse. Much worse. They were laughing, having a great time at our expense.

''My first reaction was, 'Who're they yelling at?' and I looked around before it hit me they were yelling at us. *Me!* My next thought was to yell over there and say, 'Hey, you got the wrong guy, I'm not a crazy, I'm like you, I'm just—' and then I caught myself. One of the guys I really like—Bobby, he's autistic—started to cry. He was scared these dirtballs were gonna hurt him. It really made me mad. I told him it was okay, no one was going to bother him, so he stayed right beside me. Those scumbags taunted us all the way into the bowling alley. Lousy, insensitive jerks. I could tell how upset the other patients were, too, but they just stared straight ahead. Maybe they're used to being laughed at. Then it hit me how I pitied all the patients. Including myself. See, we're different, cut off from everyone else in the world. I hate it. And for a few minutes I wished I were The Karate Kid instead of The Confetti Kid!

"And then suddenly I remembered something Kayla said. About not fighting so hard, stepping back, learning to be loving and generous of spirit. Using positive energy instead of letting a few jerks fuel my anger. And right about then I happened to glance up, and there's Bobby, smiling at me, and all of a sudden I felt a deep caring for him, you know, just one human being to another. A warmth, a closeness I've never felt before. He came over and touched my arm. You know how hard he is to understand, but he said something like, 'You my friend.'

"It was incredible, Mac. All of a sudden I saw just how destructive all the anger has been, how it's undermined everything I've ever done. And a big part of the puzzle filled in."

"How so?"

"You're the one who's been telling me to take responsibility, Mac. Make decisions. But I didn't know how. And that experience helped me see what's really important, how I have to think and act for myself, be true to myself."

"Oh? And how's that, Steve?"

"With personal integrity, with decency and honesty. I've always read about acting in moral and ethical ways, but I never understood exactly what it meant. The other night, first I denied—they couldn't be yelling at me. I wanted to tell them not to lump me in with the other crazies. That's how I've always reacted, the hypocrite part of me."

"And then?"

"It was great. Somehow I was in control, just standing

off observing myself. When I saw Bobby crying I was angry. But then the anger was replaced by deep compassion for him and his pain, for everyone like him. Even, believe it or not, for the dirtballs yelling at us. I *understood* as I never have before. I could actually feel the hurt Bobby and the other people were feeling. The world doesn't need any more of that kind of pain.

"But you know, those guys who were sniping at us are full of fears, too. They were probably more afraid of us than anything. Maybe afraid of their own dark sides. So what do they do? They take it out on people who can't defend themselves, or who remind them too much of that thin line."

"I think you're right about that, Steve."

"I'm sure I am. Anyway, it taught me a lesson. From now on when I see something that isn't right, I'm going to say something about it, no matter what happens. That's the responsible thing to do."

He glanced up at me and I nodded. It was so good to see him feeling better about himself.

Abruptly he stood. "Thanks for the hour, Mac. I got some thinking to do. I need to take a walk in the woods."

27

OVER THE NEXT MONTH I CONTINUED TO BE IMPRESSED with how rapidly Steve improved. He seemed transformed—more focused, more mature, and quietly determined about the direction he wanted his life to take.

"I'm ready to get out of this bughouse," he told me at the start of a session in early April. He'd told me that a hundred times before, at least once a session. Always before I had brushed him off, but this time I said,

"I agree. You're ready."

He had his mouth open to argue when the impact of my words hit. He stared in astonishment.

"What?"

"I said I agree. The staff agrees. Let's start planning."

"But—"

"But what?"

"I just attempted suicide a couple months ago. How could you think of letting me go so soon?"

"You learned from it, didn't you? I'd say it shocked you back on track."

"Yeah, but—"

"Remember your buddy Nietzsche? He said something to the effect that it's only after a person has considered suicide that he begins to take life seriously. The team feels you've turned a big corner and you're ready to leave. It'll take a while to organize the transition, though. We're not going to cut you loose in twenty-four hours."

Steve shook his head in disbelief. Now that I was agreeing with him, he was having second thoughts.

"You really think I'm ready?"

"Uh-huh."

"But—"

I put up my hand. "Do you see what's happening? For months you've fought tooth and nail to get out of here, but at the same time you've developed a dependency on this place, on me, the team, your fellow patients. It's been a safe haven. Now it's tough to think about dealing with the real world again. But we'll start you out slowly—weekends away from the hospital, continuing therapy, outpatient support. When you actually leave, we'll have a big safety net under you. You've come too far for us to simply throw you out on your own devices."

"The main problem is, I don't know how I'm gonna do what I want to do."

"You'd better do some planning, then, hadn't you?"

A couple days later I returned to my office to find an envelope from Steve shoved under my door. Inside was a note saying he was spending a lot of time in the woods, thinking, and getting closer to knowing what he wanted to do. It was attached to a poem and a sketch.

In radiant morning glow
The Bleeding Heart's petals bend toward the ground
Burdened by some unknown person's naming
Who perhaps distraught with plight and pain
Saw in the red-dropped blossom
Some symbol of human struggle

The tiny hummingbird
Making erratic darting rounds
Comes suddenly upon that crimson bonanza

Aghast at such good fortune
Flitting from blossom to blossom
Gently pushing each cup upright
Drinking long and deep
Savoring early morning nectar

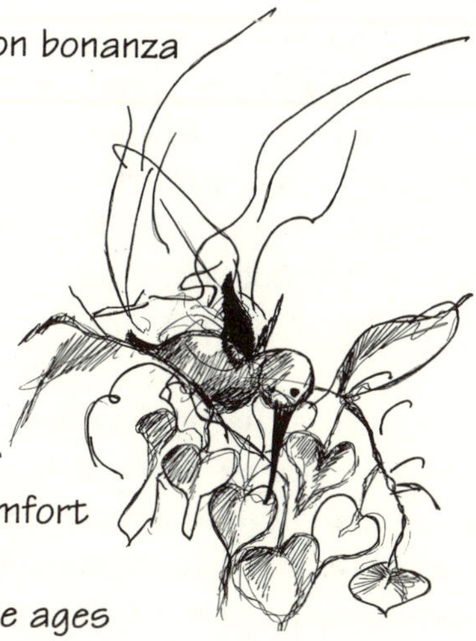

Each filling the needs of the other
One in succulence, the other in comfort
I watch, in awe and reverence
Silently observing the lesson of the ages

At our next session he plunked down in the recliner and opened his journal. "Okay," he said, "here we go."

I sat back, wondering what he'd cooked up.

"Here's my lifeplan." He looked at me quizzically. "Wanna hear it?"

I smiled. "Go ahead."

"What's important to me now is direction. I want to work with other people in some way, maybe children. Maybe people who are mentally ill. I've really enjoyed helping some of the patients, teaching them stuff, doing art with them. They're so appreciative it makes me feel happy to do it. Plus, I want to give something back."

"Sounds good."

"And I keep coming back to Gene. The way he lived, teaching, helping students find their way in life. It was so much more than just showing people how to draw and paint. He taught me the power of teaching—that a good teacher can change how students see themselves, build their confidence, help them decide what's important to them. He made me see how you could really touch people's lives by being a teacher."

"That's very true, Steve."

"Well, that's what I want," he said. "And then I could even have my summers off to draw, read, just think about things. That's important to me now." He looked to me for affirmation and I nodded. He sighed. "The only doubt I have is that I'm not sure I have the intellectual firepower to be as good a teacher as Gene was. And I don't want to be a mediocre one."

"That's the perfectionist speaking again, Steve," I countered. "You're absolutely intelligent enough to be a very good teacher. And the other qualities you'd bring to a classroom are even more important—your sensitivity, your compassion, and the idealism we've talked about. Young people will really connect with all that."

He nodded. "I hope so. I also want to get my life more balanced, more spiritual. For me, success is going to come from being with people I love."

"So getting married and having children are in the picture, too, then."

"Yeah, I hope so." Steve's voice softened. He was looking out the window. "I feel I have so much to give. If only I can find someone who will accept me. Do you think there'll ever be anyone who can put up with a loopy guy like me, Mac?"

"I doubt it. Nah, no chance."

For a second his head jerked back, and then he broke into a sheepish grin.

"That McGarry sense of humor is totally ghoulish. They should revoke your license to practice, you know."

"You're right. That was bad. So what do you think? Is there someone out there for you?"

His gaze was as steady as his voice.

"Yes, I truly believe there is. And next time I'll have a much better sense of what it takes to make a relationship work. The trust you and I talked about, the stuff about mutual respect, being able to laugh, share the world together."

"That's important, Steve. It helps to have similar ideas and values."

"A shared view."

"Yes. But trust is the key. It allows you to feel safe enough to be vulnerable. Reasonable expectations are going to be very important, too."

"Oh?"

"Yes. Many people bring certain expectations to a relationship that their partner can't possibly meet," I said. "Especially in a marriage. It's a variation on the unrealistic expectations your parents had for you and you had for your parents. But unless a person makes a conscious effort to understand how he's superimposing his expectations on a spouse, very soon reality begins to collide with expectation. And no one can possibly fulfill all the fantasies of another person."

"I know that from bitter experience, Mac. If you don't hash out what's realistic and what isn't, you'll probably have big problems, right?"

"Uh-huh. Otherwise people start thinking, 'He doesn't spend enough time with me any more,' or 'She takes me for granted.' And that sets the stage for them to take the next step: 'Maybe I'd be happier with someone else,' or 'So-and-so at work really appreciates me.' That's the kind of sequential reasoning that leads people to drift apart."

"Is that what happened to you?" Steve asked.

I returned his gaze for a moment. "Yes, to some extent. There was an element of that, anyway." After a moment, I added, "I think your expectations will probably be much more realistic in the future."

"Definitely. I won't be such an insecure, flakey jerk next time around. And you know what? I'm going to be ready when she comes along."

"I'm sure you will be, Steve."

"But there's still a practical problem."

"What's that?"

"Money. I've got zilch now. And no job, of course. Between art supplies, tuition and living expenses, I'm going to need some cash. And I'm not sure what my chances are for student loan money now."

"Okay, let's call Andis and rattle his cage, shall we?"

"Sure."

We called Andis's office on the spot and were told that he was not available. He would be in court every day until four.

In my office a few days later, Steve tried again with more success. Good old Andis was true to form. I could hear the high voice and his throat-clearing bark even from where I sat, and the carping barrage that followed.

"That's still not a business major, Steve," he said. "What kind of living are you going to make as a teacher? It's another deadend. A little better than being an artist, maybe, but not much. To begin with, the pay is terrible."

Steve handled it beautifully.

"I know making money means a lot to you, Mr. Andis. That's your choice. But why do you keep pushing what's important to you onto me? What if I wanted to be a minister, or work for a charitable organization? Would you still disapprove? Some people feel good about helping others, even if they don't make big money doing it. Being a teacher is my choice. I think you should respect that." His tone was reasonable, almost friendly.

Andis harumphed some more, barked repeatedly, and raised numerous objections. But Steve was not to be deterred, and even winked at me when Andis began to relent. At last he asked Steve how much he needed. What was the absolute bottom line?

Steve told him his budget: He would need at least $2,500 to get settled—for an apartment, furnishings, a beater car.

Andis, now in retreat, caved in. He seemed to be finding the new Steve difficult to tame. Eventually they completed arrangements for transferring the money. Steve thanked him, hung up, and gave me a big grin. Then we exchanged high fives.

"Well, it's good to have that over with." He sat back thoughtfully. "Now there's just one more loose end—"

"Oh?"

"It's something that's really been bothering me, and I keep putting off bringing it up. But I need to."

"Okay."

"Remember I told you about wishing my parents dead?"

"Yes."

"And then they were killed, and I said I was glad? It was what I wanted?" He looked at me tentatively.

I nodded.

"Those were terrible things to say . . . and think."

I waited.

"It keeps coming back to me, over and over."

He stared down into his cupped hands for a long time. When he finally spoke, his voice was husky and I could barely hear him.

"What I told you wasn't really true. Yeah, there were times I wished I had other parents. But when they were killed, mostly I was just horribly mad at them for abandoning me again. Death is the ultimate desertion." He brushed a tear from the corner of his eye. "The truth is," he gulped, "I miss all of them very, very much. There's never a day that I don't think of them and miss them."

He blinked back the tears.

"I did love them, Mac. Maybe they weren't the kind of parents I needed or would have chosen, but they were mine. They were decent people who did their best. Seeing that has been an incredible revelation to me. The ironic thing is that, for the first time in my life, I think we could all get along. And now we'll never have the chance."

He covered his face in his hands and gave in to the tears.

"It's good that you're finally allowing yourself to grieve, Steve. You've got a bit to catch up on."

He nodded. After he'd wept for a while, he said, "God, how I *miss* them! I feel so bad. There's so much I want to tell them—and now there's no way I can. I didn't even have a chance to say goodbye." He blotted another surge of tears.

"You need to make your peace with them, Steve. Somehow." I wondered if he could find the solution by himself.

We talked a little longer. Then, ten minutes early, he slapped the arms of the chair, pushed himself to his feet, and declared,

"I gotta go, Mac." He headed for the door. "I know what needs to be done."

Just before I was about to leave that day, my phone rang. Great, I thought. Somebody's going to want something and I'm going to have to stay and take care of it. All I wanted to do was go home, build a fire, and put my feet up. I was curt when I answered the phone.

"McGarry."

"Dr. McGarry, this is Brenda Warren, Psychiatric Social Worker at Peace River Mental Health Institute."

"Yes, Ms. Warren, why all the formality?" I was relieved that it was Brenda, but why was she acting so weird?

"I was wondering if I could make an appointment with you. It's a rather urgent matter."

"I see. Well, inasmuch as your office is only three doors away, I'll clear my calendar while you walk down."

"Very well."

Click.

A minute or so later there was a knock at the door.

"Come in, come in," I said gruffly. "What's all this goofiness about?"

Brenda looked very serious as she composed herself in the chair next to my desk. She also looked remarkably fresh after a long day. She was wearing a red silk blouse and a neat navy skirt that revealed the beautiful legs I'd always admired. I tried to keep my eyes on her face and the soft dark curls that framed it. My mood improved perceptibly as she leveled her spirited green eyes on me.

"This 'goofiness,' as you put it, has to do with you and me. It's beginning to look like you're never going to ask me out, Patrick McGarry. So—"

I started to say something, but she held up her hand and silenced me.

"I told you I'd turned over a new leaf, and I guess it's time for me to be a thoroughly modern woman here." She crossed her arms and tilted her head. "Would you like to go out with me for fish Friday night? At Tod's Tavern? A real high-class low-life place: Great batter-fried perch and crispy french fries served on paper plates, a beautiful view of the Mississippi, and the best brandy alexanders on the river. My treat."

Can you imagine turning down an offer like that?

"Sounds great, Bren. What time would you like to pick me up?"

Again I was impaled by those limpid green eyes.

"Don't push it, Pat. I'll expect you around six o'clock. Okay?"

"Sure, that's fine."

"Okay, see you then." She bounced up.

When she reached the door, I said, "Bren . . ."

She turned.

"Thank you for the invitation. I'm really looking forward to Friday."

"So am I. I have been for a long time." She smiled impishly, winked, and was gone.

28

OVER THE NEXT FEW WEEKS BRENDA HELPED STEVE find an apartment in La Crosse. He enrolled at a small college nearby for summer school and came up with a part-time job in a supermarket. True to his grudging word, Andis arranged for the monthly checks to be dispensed. When Steve's start-up check arrived, he went to an estate sale and bought a well-cared-for car and a few furnishings. Then he moved out of his room at Peace River and set up housekeeping. And began re-entry into the real world. He would be coming out to see me once a week and he knew he could call if something came up in between.

His first trip was to Madison to visit Kayla. As soon as he got back, he came looking for me.

"When I called her she laughed and said her powers must be slipping—she'd just written me a postcard. She gave it to me when I got there." He pulled the card out and handed it to me, then slid into the recliner.

The note said:

> Dear Bright Soul Stephen,
>
> You are about to take another step in your quest—your sacred journey of self-exploration, discovery, and enlightenment. Trust the little voice of your soul. It will never let you down.
>
> Your friend, Kayla

''She's a great person,'' he told me. ''I'm going to stay in touch with her. I think she has a lot to teach me.''

''That's true, Steve. I've learned a bit from her myself.''

''You've been a teacher for me, too.''

I nodded. "Our lives are filled with teachers, Steve. Along with opportunities to learn and grow.''

''I guess I'm surprised,'' he said pensively, ''at how much I've changed. I'm starting to put my parents' and Brad's deaths in perspective, dealing with that whole situation better. I even wrote Mom and Dad a letter. Want to hear it?''

''Sure.''

He pulled it out of his pocket and read it slowly and with feeling.

> Dear Mom and Dad,
>
> I've been pretty busy since you've been gone. I wish I could tell you about it in person, but this will have to do. Somehow I have the feeling that you'll hear it and take some comfort in the fact that things are slowly being resolved for me.
>
> I want you to know I'm fine now, or getting there. It turned out that a lot happened to me in childhood that I couldn't understand. That's how I came to be hospitalized. But it's been a good experience for me, a calming experience. I've learned a lot about myself, how I came to be the way I was, and I've gotten rid of some of the stuff that wasn't good for me. I've replaced it with stuff that is.

I just didn't know what you expected of me, or what to expect from you or anyone else. Now I'm more realistic and know a lot more about all that. I think I'm an adult now. Finally. You'd be relieved, I'm sure.

My therapist, Mac, says I've come a long way in healing myself. And he's right. I see now that a lot of the anger and resentment I had toward you was an outgrowth of my own fear of responsibility and growing up. But as I prepare to take my place in the world, I think—I hope—you'd be proud to call me your son. I want to thank you both for being the best parents you knew how to be. It will always be one of my regrets that I never had a chance to tell you that.

I admire both of you for what you were able to accomplish in your lives. Although I plan to follow a different route, I can now respect you for the choices you made and for the successes you achieved. If you'd lived, I think we'd be friends now.

I hope sometime we'll be able to compare notes. My friend Kayla says it's entirely possible. Until then, I want you to know how very much I love and miss all of you. I hope you're at peace.

Your loving son,
Steve

''That's beautiful, Steve,'' was all I could get out. It was tough keeping my own emotions in check.

''I wrote a letter to Brad, too. Telling him I wish we'd had time to get to know each other better, and how I'll always feel cheated because he was taken away from me. He was a neat kid—he didn't deserve to die.''

He paused a few moments. ''Sometime soon,'' he said, ''I'm going back to the cemetery in Milwaukee where they're all buried and read my letters by their graves. I need to do that. I think it'll help. And then I'll be in pretty good shape.''

We talked a while longer and then Steve said, ''There's

something else I want to ask you about." He flipped through his journal, then leaned forward. "I still feel the anger—the resentment—deep down inside, but it's not nearly as overpowering as it was. Even so, the potential for going out of control again scares the heck out of me. Will those feelings ever go away? I mean, completely away?"

"I don't know, Steve. It's probably more likely that the anger and pain you've had will always be with you. It's part of your identity, after all. But it's not necessarily a negative thing. You can use it. You've used it already."

He was watching me intently. "How?"

"When you went bowling that time. Remember, when you told me about it, you realized that you've become more sensitive to pain in others. That's because you're now more sensitive to the pain in yourself. And that pain has deepened your compassion for others, your love for humankind, and for nature. Compassion and love go hand-in-hand."

"Okay, so what I have to do is draw upon that energy and use it to help make the world a better place, which is what I want to do anyway. Is that what you mean?"

"Sure. Redirect the pain and anger into your poems, your art, your writing, your activism."

"Yeah, tap into it, then. Just be sure it's constructive and I control the direction." We sat in silence for several minutes before he glanced up again.

"Let me try something else, then."

"Okay."

"The insecurities I have, the fear that I don't quite measure up? What do I do with that?"

"Same thing, Steve. Everyone has those fears. I do. Even famous or very successful people have deep insecurities of one kind or another. But again, instead of letting them undermine your self-confidence, use your awareness to overcome them. Take some risks, decide the things you want to accomplish—short term and long term—and then use your determination to go after them. So you're turning the doubts into growth and fulfillment. That part does get better. And it gets easier."

"Good. I'm ready for the easier part, Mac." He smiled. "It's amazing how everything's coming together now. You said it would, but I had a hard time believing you."

"I know," I said. "I've been giving you little nudges here and there, but you've built your own momentum. No doubt about it—you're in charge now."

Eventually we were meeting only once a month, but Steve continued to devote a lot of energy to his therapy. He always arrived with his journal tucked under his arm, and checked it periodically during the session to see what other issues he wanted to bring up.

He completed summer school with a "B" average, and midway through the fall semester we decided he was ready to return to Madison for the spring term. He still had his "sources," too. One day as he was on his way out he said,

"My friends tell me you and Brenda have something going. Would you care to confirm that, Dr. McGarry?"

I smiled. "Consider it confirmed, Steve." Everyone probably knew by now. Brenda and I had tried to keep a low profile, but covert relationships were nearly impossible to maintain around here and we'd finally given up.

"Good," said Steve. "Glad you finally came to your senses. If anyone can deal with that streak of Irish melancholy, it'll probably be Brenda."

On the day of our final meeting, Steve showed up with a large plastic shopping bag. He set it on the edge of my desk and then, with great ceremony, he withdrew the confetti suit. This was the first time I'd ever had a chance to experience it in tranquillity, without a crisis looming, and as Steve placed it reverently on my desk a kind of thrill ran through me. It was beautiful.

Steve sat down in his usual place. "I have mixed feelings

about keeping this, Mac. It was so much a part of me for a while, being the Rescuer of the People." His voice dropped and his cheeks colored. "It's kind of embarrassing now. It all seems so far away, and yet—"

"It *will* always be a part of you, Steve."

"Yeah, I suppose it will." He sighed. "For sure, my ideals are still there. To make the world a better place. But I'll try to be a little more low-key about that in the future." He smiled ruefully, then eyed me self-consciously. "I don't quite know how to ask this."

"Just ask."

"Okay. Would you like the confetti suit, Mac? Sort of a souvenir? I feel uncomfortable having it around. It's a reminder of the past and I'm more interested in the future. If I keep it, maybe I'd be tempted to fall back on it again. I don't think that'd ever happen, but anyway, I don't need it or want it anymore.

"The thing is, I don't want to throw it away either. It's too neat. So if you want it, fine. It's yours. Or you could give it to Dr. Farrell for the hospital museum. If he wants it."

"Thank you, Steve. Unfortunately for Dr. Farrell, I would like to have it. I'd be honored. It's an original, like The Confetti Kid was."

Steve laughed. "You can say you knew me when. Anyway, if I ever need it, I'll know where it is."

"I don't think you'll be needing it, Steve. But sometime, perhaps when you're older, you may want it back. Then it's yours. I'll keep it for you 'til then, okay?"

"Okay. Thanks, Mac."

We lapsed into silence. Then Steve cleared his throat awkwardly.

"How do I say thank you?"

"You just did. You're welcome."

"That's not enough. I need to say thank you with the deep sense of gratitude I feel for everything you've helped me get through, everything you've helped me become."

"Just seeing how well you're doing is enough thanks for me, Steve. You're the one who's done the hard work."

"Yeah, but you were my guide. You got me through the rocky parts, never lost faith in me." He placed his fingers and thumbs together and rested his chin on his fingers. "Can I tell you some things? Things that made a big difference to me?"

"Please do."

He sat back, reflectively. "The first is when I was so out of it. 'Catatonic,' you guys called it."

"Yes, you were in a catatonic state."

"Yeah, well, the farther away from it I get, the more I can remember. At least parts of it. It was so weird. It was like I collapsed into myself. Completely. I miniaturized down to where all I could do was watch the world through a tiny little peephole. None of me worked. Sometimes I'd see people through the peephole, but sounds were so muffled I couldn't make them out. It was like they were far, far away. But being vegged out like that was a place of safety for me. I have this strong feeling that that's where I needed to be at the time. In that safe place, the voices in my head were silenced, too.

"I do have some memories of you, though, Mac. Coming in, looking concerned, saying things, even though I usually couldn't understand them. But that meant a lot to me. That you'd come like that and just sit with me."

"It's good to know you were aware of that, Steve. I never knew if you were or not. Being catatonic must have been an incredible experience for you."

"Believe me, it was. And I can't say I'm sorry it happened. It was, well, it was fascinating. But once was enough."

"I'm sure."

"The second thing that made a difference was the journal you started me on."

"Well, you've done exceptionally well with that. I'm very glad it's worked for you."

"Yeah, I really didn't think it would. For a while it was hard. And the first time you asked if you could read it, my immediate reaction was, Oh-oh! Now I'm gonna get it. I expected you to chew me out, cut me down, tell me what a stupe I was. Like my dad did, I guess. I kept waiting for you to echo all the bad things I believed about myself. In fact, at first I censored what I wrote, really watered stuff down.

"But the amazing thing was, you didn't blast me. You took the time to read it and make thoughtful comments back to me. I couldn't believe it. It took a while, but I finally realized that I could actually trust you, open up. And what a wonderful feeling that was! A little seed of happiness began to sprout. And some sadness, too, for what I'd been missing for so long."

"I had no idea, Steve."

He laughed. "I thought you didn't. But that's not all. When you'd give the journal back to me on Mondays, did you notice how quickly I'd disappear? I'd beat it back to my room and just devour what you'd written to me. It was like I had someone I trusted to tell things to, but I didn't have to sit face to face and try to figure out what I wanted to say or how to say it. I could use the journal to be honest with myself—and know that when you gave it back, the honesty would be returned."

"Great. I hope you realize, though, that you may turn into a real journal junkie."

"I already am. I'll probably keep one the rest of my life, especially when I need to get things in perspective. Something would be missing now without it. Probably what I'll regret the most is not having you around to give me feedback on it."

"Anytime you want, send me stuff, and I'll be happy to comment back to you."

"I'll take you up on that. I'm really going to use the journal as a way of stepping back from myself. I'll be able to see how my life is going and whether I'm making any headway. I think the journal will help me make those—what did you call them?''

''Course corrections?''

''Yeah. I've just made the biggest 'course correction' of my life, haven't I? This has been quite an education. Between my family's accident and what I've been through here—the patients I've met and all, and the time I've spent out in the woods—I realize just how fragile life is, how important it is to use every moment life gives me. It's too short, and I've squandered a bit of it. I've got some making up to do.''

''You're lucky, Steve. A lot of people don't learn those things until much later in life. And some never do.''

''Yeah. I've been thinking about all the things that have happened to me here. I really believe there's a Greater Being that watches over us. Someone was taking care of me, making sure I got to Peace River. And the night I tried to kill myself, there was a definite presence. Boy, was that a close call, Mac.'' He shuddered.

I nodded and we sat in silence for a while. Kayla would say Steve's guides had been protecting him. It certainly appeared as though someone had, and, I hoped, would continue to.

''So Mac. How do I thank you? I mean, *really* thank you?''

''There's only one way, Steve.''

''What? Name it, it's done.''

''Be the best person and the best teacher you can be. Help others to learn, grow, gain confidence in themselves. That's the way it works, Steve. And helping others goes both ways: You've taught me a lot at the same time I was teaching you. That's what leads to the just and decent world we've talked about so often, the world we'd both like to live in.''

''Yeah, that's the point of it all, isn't it?'' He glanced down at his watch. ''Uh-oh! My fifty-minute hour's run over. You'll have to charge me time and a half.''

I stood and extended my hand. He grasped it warmly and we looked into one another's eyes.

It was an awkward moment. I thought back to the terror and pathos of those early months, my own as well as his. Now, eighteen months later, Steve was profoundly stronger for all the adversity. He had prevailed.

I gave him a pat on the back and then we hugged each other goodbye.

"Thanks, Mac," he whispered.

I smiled. "Keep in touch, okay?"

"I will. Guess I'd better get going. I got a lot of people to see around here. And then for sure before I take off, I have to walk down to our spot on the river. I couldn't leave without doing that. Which reminds me—" He opened his journal, tore out a page, and handed it to me. "Here, Mac. It's a poem. About the river. I want you to have it."

"Thank you, Steve."

He shrugged. "So . . . see you around."

"Right. Good luck to you."

"Thanks, Mac."

I watched as he set off briskly down the hall, but when he got to Brenda's door, he stopped and knocked lightly. She must have said to come in, because he grinned at me, gave me a thumbs-up, and opened the door.

I put the confetti suit back in its bag and spent the next forty-five minutes dictating a psychological report Stacey needed on a new admission. The patient was a twenty-four year old restaurant manager, quite paranoid, who was convinced that his three-year-old daughter was possessed by a "Nuclear Satan," which compelled him to perform elaborate and dangerous rituals of exorcism. His Rorschach was full of fragmented responses, indicating severe pathology. I sighed. Our work was cut out for us.

Sometime later, I glanced at the clock and wondered where the afternoon had gone. The other reports could wait. I was never entirely caught up, anyway. After scribbling a few notes, I filed charts and straightened the clutter on my desk.

Then I caught sight of the bag Steve had left. I took the suit out and held it, amazed all over again by how much the sequin confetti shapes sparkled. I stood up, switched off the overhead light, and sat down at my desk again, laying the suit across my lap. As I stared at it, I had a strong twinge of regret. I had taken part in gutting a glorious vision, stripping Steve of his wonderfully idealistic convictions. Youth invites the belief that a single individual can be the agent of change, forging a more peaceful, lovingly cooperative venture than the real world can ever be. Such an idealized world order would vanquish the darker side of unbridled human ambition and obliterate power, greed, and maliciousness. Who was I to thwart that vision?

Steve had matured into reality, into scaled-down dreams. Though he was far healthier now, he had also lost something intangible along the way.

A tap at the door interrupted my reverie.

''Come in,'' I called out. The door opened a little way and Brenda peeked in. ''I wasn't sure you'd still be here,'' she said.

''Yeah. Just finished up.''

I saw her take in the fact that I was sitting in the halflight, the confetti suit draped across my lap.

''Steve came by a little while ago. He looks good. Said he'd left the suit in good hands.'' She moved closer. ''I'm not so sure about that. You look a million miles away.''

I glanced down at the suit, and was surprised to see my fingers gently tracing the patterns.

''You doing anything for dinner?'' I looked up to see her reaction.

"Nothing very exciting. Leftovers."

"Hmmm. Well, I was thinking of dinner at the Boathouse. How does that sound to you?"

"Better than tuna casserole. A lot better."

Brenda half turned toward the door, but stopped when I didn't move.

"You coming?"

"Yeah. I was just wondering," I said, only half playfully. "How do you think I'd look in this thing?" I held the suit in front of me.

Brenda groaned and rolled her eyes toward the ceiling.

"C'mon, Pat. I gotta get you away from this place. It's either that or a commitment hearing in the morning."

"No really, I think it might be just what the doctor ordered—to turn the wards into kinder, gentler places. I bet even Mr. Grunske would be impressed."

The lovely green eyes settled on me.

"You are a dreamer, Pat." She shook her head. "C'mon, let's go. Time for dinner."

With some reluctance, I placed the confetti suit back in the bag and shoved it into the bottom drawer of my file cabinet.

The confetti suit still resides in that drawer, behind accumulating folders of therapy notes. Every now and then, usually at the end of a rough week, I like to take it out and spread it on my desk. Strangely enough, the splash of colors seems to have a calming effect. Maybe it does have magical powers, just not the ones Steve thought.

I meant it when I told him it was an original—not only in execution, but in spirit as well. There would never be another Confetti Kid.

Robert Lane

Steve's Farewell

As children we are the stream at its source
A trickle . . . wandering, exploring, questioning,
    delighting
Only vaguely aware that we are slowly growing
    gathering momentum
        beginning to flow

Soon, too soon, we enter the river of life
The exhilaration is fleeting
    with fear at its base
        the struggle constant
As strong currents
    sweep us to our destiny

An occasional respite
    offered in the mirrored pool
        reflects a growing awareness
That may bring depth and meaning
    to our life
        if we can but grasp it.

The struggle is our own

Soon, soon enough,
The churning ceases
And we can
    once again
        taste the sea

29

AFTER SPENDING SOME TIME IN MADISON, STEVE DECIDED he preferred a smaller campus and he settled in La Crosse to finish school. I continued to see him from time to time, and it was reassuring to see the confidence he was building in himself.

Within a couple of years, he had completed his requirements and received his bachelor's degree along with a secondary teaching certificate. Brenda and I attended the graduation ceremony and, like proud parents, cheered and clapped as he strode across the stage to accept his degree. We were thrilled.

During his months of practice teaching Steve had begun sending resumes all over the Midwest, but teaching positions were extremely tight that year. He had several interviews but no job offers. I could tell he was getting pretty discouraged, but he managed to remain optimistic.

Then in late August, just as the school year was beginning, a high school in northern Minnesota called him in a panic. They'd had a sudden resignation; was he still available? Could he teach social studies in addition to art? Could he be there in a week?

"Why not?" he'd replied.

On his last day, he stopped by on his way up the Great River Road to his new position. He was as excited as I'd ever seen him, going to live in an area he described as "the true Northwoods," thick with pine-circled lakes—exactly what he'd dreamed of. We were all touched by his enthusiasm and determination—it wasn't often we saw such success. And then he was off, scheduled to teach his first classes the following Monday. I would have been intimidated by the lack of preparation time; for Steve it was a challenge and he couldn't wait. Eagerness to prove himself was all over his face.

He's not a letter writer, so I didn't hear much from him after that. The cards he sent the next two Christmases bore essentially the same brief phrase: "All going well." The following summer a wedding announcement arrived. And then nothing.

It was another three years before I received a thick envelope one morning with vaguely familiar handwriting. I didn't attach any particular importance to it until I saw the return address: Stephen and Michelle Parker. I smiled and set it aside, saving it to share with Brenda. She was on maternity leave, at home these days taking care of our two-and-a-half-year-old son and month-old daughter. That evening we opened Steve's letter and read it together:

> Dear Mac & Brenda,
>
> I feel bad about not keeping in closer touch with you. As I've gained more perspective on my experiences at Peace River, I've come to realize what a turning point my hospitalization was in learning about myself and what I wanted out of life—what was important. Now that my life has settled in, I've had a chance to reflect on those times and what they meant. So I feel very grateful to both of you. And everyone else there who helped me.

Robert Lane

My teaching job is everything I ever hoped for. The students are great. Always a little skeptical about art at first—when I came here, it was known as a "sissy" course. But that's all changed now. I'm known as a "cool dude," and my classes fill fast.

The major event in my life was meeting Michelle. She's wonderful, you'd love her. She works for the University of Minnesota Extension office. We met at a workshop, dated awhile, and found out we had a lot in common—and a few things not in common. Mainly, that she comes from a very large and caring family. And they've accepted me and made me a part of it. They're terrific—the close family I always wanted but never had.

Michelle and I have been married almost three years now and it just keeps getting better and better. I told her almost from the beginning about my psychiatric problems and, eventually, all about the therapy we did together, Mac. About my discovery that a low-pressure life is a better choice for me. Michelle feels the same way, especially about large cities. She hated her college years in Minneapolis, and was thrilled when she found a job here. We certainly have that in common.

She and I seem to share the same wavelength, too. We agree on nearly everything. We held off on having kids the first couple of years we were married, and now we've pretty much decided not to. We both have so much contact with young people through our jobs that it's all we need. Actually, I consider my students my kids. And Michelle helped raise seven younger brothers and sisters, so she feels like she's had that experience. She's ready for a respite, and thinks she deserves it. Me too. We already have quite a few nieces and nephews, with more to come, plus what seems like hundreds of other relatives.

You'd love our place. We live out of town on about forty acres, surrounded by woods, mostly pine. It's our little piece of heaven. The house is old and needs work, but the trade-off is a large pond, complete with ducks. I spend a lot of time sitting out there, watching the wildlife, enjoying the peacefulness. Deer come out of the woods to drink. They don't pay much attention to me any more. Michelle and I have discovered wonderful trails in the woods around here. They remind me of my walks at Peace River. As you can tell I still love nature, and nearly all my artwork has a naturalistic theme.

I used to think recognition, and maybe fame were prerequisites for happiness. Remember how all my daydreams revolved around being a national hero? But now I find that things like having a solid marriage, helping others by being the best teacher I can be, developing as an artist—all that counts much more than fame or wealth. I'm happy just blending in, quietly doing my thing. Too many people end up fighting the world, the way I did.

I've learned to control the amount of pressure in my life, too, keeping the stress in check. I monitor myself pretty carefully, take some medication if things build up too much, and then cut back accordingly. I've even gone so far as to put rheostat switches on all the lights in the house so I can control the brightness and cut down the stimulation. (Remember how I used to say the lights at the hospital were too bright? I was the one who always turned them off in the dayroom!) And you know what? It makes a difference. Sounds strange, I know, but it helps. Michelle understands.

I still keep my journal, though I don't write in it nearly as often as I should. I use it mostly when there's a problem of some kind, maybe a crisis at school to deal with. Or when I just want to see how my life is going. It helps me sort stuff out. But I still write poems. I hope to publish a book of them with illustrations some day.

Destiny. I remember how Kayla talked about it—the importance of seeking one's path and then not deviating from it. At least not far. I try and pass that idea along to my students: Look for open doorways and worthwhile opportunities. And be willing to take a chance. Sounds familiar, huh, Mac?

I do still grapple with my "demons" at times.

Suddenly the old doubts pop back—especially when I'm under more stress than usual—and the old fears bubble up again: Have I bitten off more than I can chew? Will I fail? Will I make a fool of myself? Taking risks is still scary, and I have to work to keep my imagination in check or sometimes it gets away from me.

On the other hand, now I recognize the mechanisms, the kind of automatic responses that undermine me, so I can avoid them and control the fear. I try to remember that the doubts are temporary, that they'll pass, and that it's mostly a weak part in my personality that I just have to adjust to.

I love teaching! And the kids seem to appreciate my efforts. I've had some super students these last few years who have given me a terrific sense of satisfaction. And when I get kids who are having a rough time, I almost always can connect and help them. So far. It's amazing how kids respond to acceptance, love, and understanding. Come to think of it, that's pretty much what you and everyone at Peace River gave me. You'll be glad to know I'm passing it on.

So now I'm into a wonderful life—a beautiful wife, two dogs and three cats (all strays—what else?—some things never change). I have a great home in the woods and the security of a good job that makes me feel what I do has a positive impact on the world. What more could I want?

Again, my thanks and love to you both. Please share this letter with anyone else there who may still remember me. I think of you guys often. Anyway, Mac, Brenda, we'll call if we ever get down that way.

Take care, guys.

Steve

P.S. Do you still have the confetti suit, Mac? I don't want it back or anything, just curious as to whether it's still around.

Of course I still had it. Over the years it had gained even more meaning for me, coming to symbolize one young man's struggle to save himself, but more than that—to make a difference, to banish the evils of the world, to find a way to harness the idealism and compassion of youth and become a catalyst for change. In Steve's own way, The Confetti Kid lived on.

For readers interested in exploring further:

Journaling

Life's Companion, by Christina Baldwin

Near Death Experiences

The Light Beyond, by Raymond Moody

Psychotherapy

Existential Psychotherapy, by Irvin Yalom

Self Awareness

A Gradual Awakening, by Stephen Levine

Zen And The Art Of Motorcycle Maintenance, by Robert Pirsig

Spirituality

The Tibetan Book of Living and Dying, by Sogyal Rinpoche

Journey of Souls, by Michael Newton

Through Time Into Healing, by Brian L. Weiss

Angels: The Mysterious Messengers, Ed Hauck, editor

a note about this book

THE TEXT OF THIS BOOK IS SET IN ITC GARAMOND, designed by Tony Stan in 1976, and based on the sixteenth-century Garamond typeface. Claude Garamond, whose birthdate is unknown but who died in 1561, was probably the first punch-cutter and typefounder in history. His work resulted in one of the most durable designs in typographic history. Garamond is an elegant typeface, a noble combination of form, function, and grace.

The running heads, poems, and diagram text are set in Tekton, a thoroughly modern typestyle based on the script used for architectural drawings. Noted for its readability, Tekton also conveys a crisp blend of lightness and interest.

This book was written, designed, and typeset in Wisconsin's Fox River Valley. Mary Lane coordinated the book design. Tom and Carole Stinski of the Composing Room in Appleton set the text film and prepared the camera-ready copy. Marcia Tuchscherer created the artwork for the jacket. Production then shifted to Michigan, where the able workforce of Thomson-Shore, Dexter, printed and bound the book.